All the Flowers
of the
Mountain

All the Flowers of the Mountain

A Novel

Christina Holbrook

Sunroom
Studios

Published by SUNROOM STUDIOS
Dillon CO

Manufactured in the United States of America

ISBN
Hardcover   979-8-9861488-0-9
Paperback   979-8-9861488-1-6
Ebook   979-8-9861488-2-3

Cover and interior design by Ashley Prine
Image Credits: Shutterstock: (cover flowers) © Angry_red_cat; (cover background texture) © KOYPIC; 1, 335 © B.illustrations; 17, 147, 354 © Morphart Creation; 235 © Silvia_Ball

Disclaimer

All the Flowers of the Mountain is a work of fiction. Names, characters, businesses, places, events, locales, and incidents are either the products of the author's imagination or used in a fictitious manner. Any resemblance to actual persons, living or dead, or actual events is purely coincidental.

While the lovely New Hampshire country towns of Franconia, Sugar Hill, Littleton, and Landaff are real places, I have written about them in a fictitious manner. Similarly, though the much-loved Polly's Pancake Parlor and Sugar Hill Sampler and the historic Thayer's Inn Hotel have existed for decades, I have created my own imagined version of these and other businesses. The Profile Lake Club and Winthrop Ironworks are also products of my imagination, though Franconia Notch is home to a similarly elegant country club, as well as a history of enterprises that extracted and processed iron ore.

My dearest hope is that this story will convey to the reader my deep and enduring affection for this beautiful corner of the world.

For Alan

I will twine thee a bower
By a clear silver fountain
And round it will I gather
All the flowers of the mountain
Let us go, lassie, go.

—Traditional Ballad

(Adapted from Robert Tannahill, 1774–1810)

Part I

*"When the rude wintry winds
And the storms rattle o'er us"*

Chapter 1

The gallery is open by appointment only. He's arrived early, and the door is locked. Daylight drains from the sky by four o'clock here in Paris, in midwinter, and lights begin to twinkle in all the small shops and cafés. He peers through the big plate glass window but it is too dark to make out much of what's inside.

Instead, his own reflection confronts him, and for a moment the person looking back at him is the young man he once was. Unsure of his talents and abilities, but certain of what he wanted. Amazing how things have reversed themselves over the years, he thinks, turning away.

"*Entrez! Entrez!*" The gallery owner arrives now, and hurries to open the door for the two of them. "*Je suis en retard? Désolé!* I am sorry to be late, Dr. Pearce!" As he'd expected, Monsieur DeLettre is an older gentleman; he fumbles a little with the keys. In the foyer, spotlights glow above elegant bronze type: Galerie DeLettre.

"Allow me to take your coat. May I offer you something warm to drink? *Un café crème, peut-être?*"

"*Non, merci*—well, *peut-être* . . . maybe . . ." He stumbles with his rusty French.

Here, standing on this threshold to his past, he finds he doesn't know what he wants. *This isn't open-heart surgery, Pearce. Make a decision.* "Yes, I'll take a coffee, thank you. And again, I appreciate your meeting me today, on such short notice. I hope it wasn't inconvenient."

It would probably be more inconvenient if he decided to turn and bolt out the door. Which does, in fact, occur to him. *Get a grip, man.*

"You did not mention, Dr. Pearce, how you knew of the artist . . . ?"

"Katherine and I were friends, when we were young. In America. Before she moved to Paris."

"Ah"—he looks appraisingly at Pearce—"a long time ago, then."

"Yes. I've never had a chance to see her work. And since I was here in Paris, giving a lecture, well . . ."

The coffee with cream is ready and DeLettre hands him the cup. "And what is your medical *spécialité?*"

Pearce wonders if the jeans, black sweater, and beat-up leather jacket—the only casual clothes he'd brought with him for this short trip—are making a suspect first impression. That and his jumpiness. Not what you'd expect from a respected and self-assured American physician.

"I'm a cardiologist, at a hospital in Colorado. I'm just in Paris for a few days, for a conference." His presentation this morning, "Cardiac Arrhythmia Among World Cup Ski Racers at High Altitude," had impressed his colleagues. Not a surprise, but still, gratifying. That seems a long time ago, now. His attention has narrowed to the warm coffee cup in his hand. And the coffee is good—strong, fortifying.

"A doctor of the heart, then," says DeLettre.

How French. He immediately discounts this remark as a poetic flourish. But the irony makes him pause. How is it that he who has become an expert on this muscular pump inside the human body should remain so confounded by the figurative matters of the heart? By love? He's remained single all his life, and emotion—intangible and baffling—is a subject about which he still understands very little.

"*Voilà!* Let us view the sculptures." DeLettre shuffles into the gallery space, flipping on the lights, and the figures are illuminated dramatically, one by one.

The pieces are life-size, cast bronze.

As if from a great distance, Pearce hears the sound of his breath catching—the work is so vivid, the resemblances uncanny. The walls of the studio seem to vanish, and all the color and light, the warmth of summer and the sounds of birds from a distant time fill the room.

He spies two children tumbling in play with a prancing calf. And another sculpture of a young man, guitar slung across his back, cradling a small bird in his hands. And a girl—*it's her*—as wild as a forest daemon, arms thrown above her head, emerging from the fluid arc of a waterfall.

A wave of vertigo hits him, and the coffee cup drops from his hands. It shatters as it hits the concrete floor. DeLettre hurries over with a folding chair, and he collapses into it unsteadily, unable even to apologize.

Minutes go by, or maybe weeks, or an entire lifetime, as he covers his face with his hands. His shoulders heave with gasping, uncontrolled sobs. Dimly, he is aware of the old man standing motionless beside him, unconcerned by his sudden outburst. *I am a scientist! A doctor!* And this is not appropriate, not normal. DeLettre places a hand, meant to comfort, on his shoulder.

When he looks up, finally, at the sculptures, he sees his own life.

It is the summer he found—and lost—Katherine Morgan. The sweep of fields, the vastness and the intimacy of the rolling hills surround him. He hears the rumble of a storm moving across the distant White Mountains. Water thunders over a secret waterfall that belonged only to them.

At the center of the spare, white gallery space, a boy and a girl are holding hands, caught in rhythmic stride as they climb a hillside. In his memory, the field was blooming with flowers: daisies and purple lupine, forget-me-nots blue as the sky in summer. The softly burnished bronze figures glow with warmth and passion. He, walking ahead, looks back at his beloved urging her forward toward some secret destination he must share with her; she, hair tossed in the breeze, her head thrown back in joyous laughter.

They could be any two young lovers, from two thousand years ago—or yesterday. Except that they are people Michael Pearce recognizes: himself and Kit.

There is a small plaque on the stone pedestal beneath the sculpture. It reads: *Toutes les fleurs de la montagne.*

All the flowers of the mountain.

From the distance of years, memories he'd had every intention of confronting and processing with rational, scientific clarity come crashing in on him. Turning him upside down until he lands at the very beginning, as if it were yesterday.

Chapter 2

He remembers the first time he saw her.

It would have been hard not to notice a pretty blond girl in a bikini. And he wasn't the only lifeguard on the beach at the Profile Lake Club that summer who had his eye on the Morgan family's oldest daughter. The Morgans were wealthy summer people from the city. "Sweet Sixteen!" crowed one of the senior lifeguards, with a wink. "Jail bait, unfortunately."

Michael, who'd posed as seventeen to get the job, was still only sixteen himself. "Like you think you had a chance with her anyway, old man?" Michael ribbed the other guard, who was probably not even twenty.

Mr. and Mrs. Morgan spent their time up by the clubhouse, playing golf or tennis. The two younger Morgan kids made castles from overturned pails of sand and argued with one another, while their older sister lay on her towel reading a book or bent over a sketchpad, scribbling. She hardly seemed to notice as an entire morning passed. Instead, she studied the lake with its reflection of mountains and clouds, her hand moving across the large sheets of drawing paper.

Eventually, the sun climbed in the sky, and the day became too hot to ignore. The wind-rippled surface of the water enticed her. Michael watched as she put down her sketchpad, strolled to the shoreline, and moved into the water as though she enjoyed confronting the cold shock of the mountain lake. Then, with a sudden, smooth movement, she dove in and swam with strong, fast strokes in a perfectly straight line away from the shore.

And she didn't stop at the red marker buoys, strung on a rope and designating the area allowed for bathers, like she was supposed to! She ducked her head under the rope and continued swimming, straight for the center of the lake. Which was strictly forbidden and against the Club rules.

The first time this happened, Michael jumped down from the lifeguard chair and looked through his binoculars, frowning, as if assessing the seriousness of the infraction. As if he had a plan. But in reality, he didn't know what to do. Maybe it hadn't occurred to her that swimming beyond the red buoys was not allowed? Or was it just that the girl assumed the rules other people had to follow didn't apply to her? He knew there was an unspoken understanding at the Club that the Morgan family did whatever they pleased.

The next time she swam out beyond the ropes, blatantly violating the Club rules, Michael watched as she returned to the beach, twisting the water out of her long hair and flopping carelessly down on her towel. Then he mustered his resolve and walked over to the three Morgan children. They all looked up at him.

"Excuse me—miss?" He wanted to sound as if he were in charge, but not come across as a jerk. "I have to ask you to stop swimming beyond the red markers."

"Really? Why is that?" she asked. Her voice was soft, but confident—not giggly and uncertain like most teenagers. He hadn't expected that. She hitched herself up on her elbow and put a hand up to shade her eyes from the sun. She looked as if she had absolutely no intention of obeying his request and he took this as a challenge to his authority. The two younger kids watched, smirking.

"It's not allowed. For safety reasons."

"I'm a very strong swimmer," she countered.

"Even so." His response did not sound convincing at all.

"Do you think it's right," she said, sitting up now, flipping her hair back and throwing him off balance by sounding so direct, so adult, "to rope off this tiny bit of water and tell people that's the *only place* they can swim?"

"Well . . . I . . ."

"I could swim right across this lake, if I wanted to. In fact, I have. You don't need to worry about *my* safety. Or tell me what to do."

"What? Well . . . that's my job," he stuttered. "When I'm here, I'm . . . responsible for you."

And then, she laughed at him. "That's so sweet," she said, smiling. Her younger sister covered her mouth and snorted.

No way was he going to allow this girl to have the last word. He stood up tall and replied as sternly as he knew how. "So, I'm going to ask you one more time not to swim beyond the markers on my watch."

He turned and walked stiffly back to the lifeguard station before she could contradict him again. His heart pounded. He had actually spoken to her! He was worked up but strangely excited at the idea of further confrontation.

And so began a contest of wills, with skirmishes launched by each of them. Because of course, she did ignore his request and continue to swim out beyond the red markers. Michael would blow his whistle and used the bullhorn to call out a warning that swimming beyond the markers was not allowed; in her own good time, she'd circle back to shore.

Once, he took the rowboat out and chased her as she swam to the middle of the lake. When he caught up to her, she stopped to tread water. "Do you really have to be so persistent?" she said, pouting.

"Miss, I think you know what I'm going to say."

She rolled her eyes. Then she pressed her feet up against the boat and kicked off powerfully, diving deep into the water. When she resurfaced, some distance from him, she called out, "I *do* know what you're going to say! And I . . . I don't give a damn! This water doesn't belong to you, or to the Club. It belongs to . . . nature! And no one has a right to impose their own, stupid man-made rules here! It's just wrong! And I hate it!"

"I hear what you're saying, and I . . . I understand why you're upset," Michael said reasonably, pulling the boat closer to her. But not understanding at all.

She turned to float on her back. Her pale limbs seemed to ripple mysteriously beneath the water, as if she were a creature of the lake. "Do you?" A hint of wistfulness had crept into her voice. "Do you really?"

"Well . . ." He hesitated. "I can see you're a really strong swimmer. It doesn't seem fair that you can't swim wherever you like . . . but . . . I don't make the rules. And I have to follow them, too, whether I agree or not. The thing is, if you keep swimming out here, you're going to get me into trouble—I could even get fired. I'd really appreciate it if you'd just let me take you back to the beach . . ."

He wanted to be straight with her, let her know he felt the same way she did, and that he wasn't just a mindless rule enforcer. Maybe dropping the policeman approach and admitting to his fear of losing his job changed things. Because she skimmed through the water with a lazy sidestroke looking at him differently now. With curiosity. As if he might be a friend, an ally.

And maybe . . . as if she liked what she saw? As she swam back toward him, her gaze flitted to his dark, unruly curls, to his sunburned shoulders and bare chest. He raised his sunglasses and grinned at her, not a lifeguard now but a sixteen-year-old boy falling under the spell of a beautiful girl.

She smiled at him then, a warm, dazzling smile that shone like sunlight on the lake, he mused, as he lost his grip on the rowboat oars and had to scramble to keep them from sliding into the water. Her eyes—blue as the sky in summer—seemed to offer the key to every secret worth knowing. He sensed the forested slopes of the mountains rising up from the lake pulsing and vibrating with life.

"Well, all right," she conceded, and hiked herself up into his boat. Her white bikini clung to her gleaming wet body and her long hair was slicked back. She looked disarmingly innocent and yet thrillingly dangerous. Dumbstruck, but trying to play it cool, he wondered how he had managed to lure this magical creature into his up-until-now boring, uneventful world.

"By the way," she said to him, like an invitation and a challenge, "I'm Kit."

Chapter 3

"Il est parti, Katherine . . ." He's gone.

Pierre is standing outside, at the entrance to the Galerie DeLettre when she arrives. He looks miserable—his hands clutched together against the December chill and his obvious distress. *"Je suis désolé!"*

She'd stood, paralyzed, after their brief phone call. Then his message had kicked in. Flinging a thick woven shawl around her shoulders, she'd rushed out of the studio into the cold, her long hair still twisted into the messy knot she wears it in when she works. "A gentleman, saying he is an old friend of yours, is here at the *galerie*," Pierre had said. "From America. A Dr. Michael Pearce."

She'd struggled to find a taxi, and then the evening rush hour had clogged the avenues. Frantic, she'd shouted at the driver to stop, leapt out of the vehicle and dodged through the stalled traffic. But by the time she'd arrived at the studio he was gone.

"Est-ce qu'il a dit . . . Did he say . . . Where is he staying? The name of the hotel?" Kit swears she can almost feel his presence, the warmth of his just-vanished breath in the frozen air. *Merde alors!* Her eyes search wildly up and down the streets.

"I'm afraid . . . I am so sorry, Katherine . . . He was on his way to the airport."

For one crazed moment she considers racing to the metro—avoid the brutal traffic!—and taking the train out to Charles de

Gaulle, to intercept him. She checks her watch. "What time do you think his flight will leave?"

"Katherine . . ." Pierre says gently.

She stops. He's right, of course. But it is just so hard for her to face the truth: If he'd wanted to see her, he would have stayed.

She flings open the door and strides into the gallery space, where her boots smack down hard on the polished concrete floor. "*Non!*" she shouts, her voice reverberating beneath the tall ceilings. As if her insistence that he still be here, waiting, will make it so. She can't accept that he was so close—and didn't stay to . . .

To what? After all these years?

"He stood in the gallery, regarding this piece in particular for so long, without moving. But when I returned from calling you, he had departed."

Her vision blurs. She turns toward the sculpture, though she does not need to look at it to know the feel of every inch, to remember how it came alive beneath her hands. Is there anything to say, really? Anything more than this: "I screwed up, Pierre. Years and years ago. This is my fault."

Then she drops down to sit on the floor, her back pressed against the smoky gray wall of the gallery. Palms jammed up against her closed eyes, against the pain and disappointment.

"*Qui est-il?* Who is he?"

"A person I never expected to see again," she says, finally, looking up at her old friend through tears.

Pierre studies her now with curiosity. And then he leaves the gallery space for several minutes. When he returns, he holds a glass of wine in each hand. "*Dis-moi.* Tell me . . ." he says.

Kit accepts the glass and takes a sip, then places it on the floor next to her. Pierre sits beside the sculpture in a folding chair.

"It is a story," she begins, "from a long time ago."

Chapter 4

She remembers that she'd laughed at him when he'd finally gotten up the nerve to talk to her.

But he was persistent, and funny. And interested in all she had to say. In the opinion of her teenage self, he was very cute, too. How easily he won her over.

Sometimes, during that summer when she and Michael were both sixteen, she rode her bike to the lake early, to avoid the noisy quarrelsome car ride with her parents and little brother and sister. She would arrive just in time to find him dressed in his orange guard shorts and ready to take the leaky, lifeguard rescue boat out for a paddle.

On a quiet morning the lake glinted with the first light of day. She climbed in beside him, and he pulled the boat out into the lake, dipping the oars into water as smooth as glass. The jagged stone features of the Old Man of the Mountain, the "profile" that gave the lake its name, jutted out high above, right below the peak of Cannon Mountain. She watched its craggy reflection floating like the face of an ancient god on the still surface of the water.

They listened for the shrill chatter of the slate-backed kingfisher cutting through the morning silence. Caught sight, once or twice, of a solitary fishing boat drifting in the distance. And sometimes, if she got to the Club really early while the mist still hung over the water, they'd hear the loons calling, down at the far shore. That haunting, lonesome back-and-forth cry of each bird to its mate echoed across the lake. She looked at him, and a kind of crazy longing welled up inside, like her heart was going to burst.

That summer began with such innocence and hope! But she cannot avoid the sorrow of remembering how it all ended.

The incident that changed everything occurred following the Labor Day weekend in September, after the last big party of the summer at her family's country house, Cedaredge.

She hadn't returned home that night.

The following morning, her father, out searching for her, found her by the side of the road, near the lake.

"Is she all right?" her mother cried out to her father, as he came up the front stairs to Cedaredge with Kit bundled in a blanket. "Get her upstairs, to her bedroom—quickly, now."

She was mute, unable to speak for herself, and anguished to see the pale, frightened faces of her brother and sister—Elliot and Lucy— as she struggled up the stairs under the arm of their housemaid, Elsie.

"What happened to her?" her cousin Genia whispered.

For a very, very long time, she couldn't remember anything.

Calls were made by her father, then, to various connections who could offer discreet help. A physician—a personal family friend—came up from Boston, to examine her and provide a course of sedatives and antidepressants. Her mother, she found out later, offered members of the household and farm staff an "end-of-season bonus," with the firm understanding that they would keep this story to themselves.

On the day the family finally departed for the city, Kit drove back with her father. Her mother, sister, and brother rode to New York in a separate car with the Morgans' driver, Max. Lucy and Elliot had to get back to the city to start school. Brandon took her cousin, Genia, in his car, home to Greenwich. He was the one who'd found her bike, a clue, abandoned in the parking lot by the lake.

Alone, hunched in the front seat of the Mercedes, with her father at the wheel, she stared down at her hands. Unseeing.

"You will go to school in Switzerland, Katherine. It's all been arranged. You'll finish up your last two years at the Institut Montreux. You have really shocked your mother and me this time." Incredulous, he asked, "How could you do this to us, Kitty? To this family? What kind of impression will this make on your younger sister and brother?

"We've decided it would be best if you spent some time away. And there are professionals at the institute. Who know how to handle . . . this kind of situation."

This kind of situation.

Is that what it's called, she thought numbly, as the outside world blurred past them, when your daughter tries to kill herself?

Somewhere over the Atlantic, during her Swissair flight from New York to Geneva, the numbness receded enough for despair to take its place: She'd never had a chance to see Michael again, to explain. She'd never had a chance to say goodbye.

Part II

*"Now the summertime
has come"*

Chapter 5

Two years had passed. The Morgan family was once again at Cedaredge Farm for the summer. Kit, eighteen now, had recently returned to the States, having completed her final classes in Switzerland. There was no reason, the Institut had informed Kit and her parents, for her not to return home and to resume her former life.

They'd finally finished unpacking after the hot, exhausting, seven-hour drive from New York City to Cedaredge—the family country house and farm on the picturesque back road in Sugar Hill, New Hampshire. Of course, it was their staff—Max and his wife, Elsie—who'd done most of the lifting, carrying, and putting away.

And now her father suggested, in that usual hearty tone of voice he used, "Brandon, why don't you take Genia and Kitty to the Profile Lake Club for cocktails and an early dinner? Let Mrs. Morgan and me settle in. Lucy and Elliot can stay here with us. The Club has a nice buffet this time of year. And Kitty—you remember, there's croquet out on the lawn . . . you always liked croquet," her father encouraged her.

Had she *always liked croquet*? Maybe in another lifetime.

"Do you really think that's a good idea, Uncle Robert?" Genia objected. Which wasn't like Genia. Kit was pretty certain that her cousin had never missed an opportunity to charge drinks to her father's account at the Club.

"I'm not sure I understand what you're getting at, Eugenia," her father said.

"Well, I mean—*Profile Lake?*"

Kit swallowed hard against the bitter taste of shame that rose up inside her. Her father frowned and her mother threw Genia a sharp warning look.

Did her cousin really have to make sure Kit didn't forget what a fuck-up she'd been?

"I don't see any problem at all with the Club," her father said, indicating that the conversation was at an end.

Please please please . . . just leave me alone! Kit looked away. If only she could just climb the staircase, go to her bedroom, and shut the door. Get away from everyone. Crawl into bed and sleep. Being crowded into the caravan of cars with her family for all those hours, as they decamped from the city to their summer place, had worn her thin.

But—disagreeing with her father would only make things worse. Make everyone worry. Just go along with him, with all of them. Withdraw inside of herself.

"Come on, girls, we'll take the Beamer," announced Brandon Chambers, the son of one of her father's clients who'd joined the Morgans at the farm—he and Genia had recently become engaged. Outside, Brandon corralled Genia into the backseat of his BMW and pressed Kit into the front—just to annoy Genia.

The BMW cruised down the dirt road, then curved around the bottom of the long sloping pasture, driving on for another several miles to the intersection with the main local route. Brandon swerved onto the paved road.

"Aren't we going to the Club, Brandon?" Genia leaned forward against his seat. Kit looked up, noticed that Brandon was now driving in the opposite direction of the Club.

"That uptight place? No, thanks. Tonight I'm taking you girls on a tour of the wrong side of the tracks. There's this great dive bar I know, in Littleton."

"Littleton? Isn't Littleton trashy?" Genia complained. "I'd rather go to the Profile Lake Club than any place in Littleton. At least they have good cocktails at the Club."

Now the Club's okay? Kit thought. She turned to watch the scenery fly by, dim and indistinct.

"Stick with me, sweetheart," Brandon barked, taking a sharp corner fast in the sports car and flinging Genia back into her seat.

About half an hour from the farm—twenty minutes at the speed Brandon was driving—Littleton was an old mill town on the Ammonoosuc River. They roared down Main Street, past the gas station, the diner, and the novelty store Crafty Creations, where Kit remembered purchasing art supplies once.

Brandon came to a fast stop in front of the big white pillars of the Thayer Hotel, a historic, slightly worn, local landmark. The red sports car stood out among the pickup trucks and unremarkable secondhand clunkers.

At Oliver's Pub, inside the hotel, Genia scowled when the jovial man tending bar laughed, and informed her: *No,* afraid he didn't have any Tanqueray gin for martinis—in fact, he only served beer, whiskey, and a few kinds of soft drinks. Brandon ordered whiskey for the two of them. Kit asked for a soda.

"A soda?" Brandon said in a teasing voice. "You sure you don't want something a little . . . *harder?*"

She ignored him. But he wouldn't leave her alone. He patted her on the head and roughed up her hair, trying to be funny.

"Can you please cut it out." She jerked away from him.

"You feeling okay, Kitty?"

"I'm fine." She was going to lose it, fast, if he didn't back off.

Thank goodness Genia began to use her charms on Brandon, plying her fiancé with questions about football and sailboats. Brandon's favorite topics. He shifted away from her.

Ignore them, pretend to be invisible. Sitting in a bar with Brandon and Genia couldn't possibly be worse than the New York Cotillion, the debutante ball she'd endured the week before.

Kit had believed that she could handle it. And it would make her parents happy. "Every Morgan daughter has come out by the time she's turned eighteen," her father had pointed out.

But what she hadn't anticipated was the sheer number of people: the crowd that had taken on a life of its own, expanding in the gilded ballroom of the Plaza Hotel like a tulle-wrapped, diamond-encrusted monster. The groups of whispering, white-gowned young women she'd gone to prep school with two years before. They ignored her, or no longer remembered her. Their shiny, puffed-up parents in formal dress, and the smug debs from past seasons, beautiful and venomous.

Lining the ballroom, young men—escorts—sized up all the girls. The escorts would make sure each girl had a ready partner on the dance floor. But already, it seemed to her, they were laying bets on which girls would get drunk and stupid, who they could pull off to the dark corner of an empty room.

"I—I can't *stand this* . . . this . . . ritual of *acquiescence!*" she'd gasped under her breath to her older cousin Genia, as she'd waited to be presented. She'd begun to sweat, and struggled against a growing sense of suffocation and panic.

Her cousin had come out three years earlier; she touched her firmly sprayed hairdo, and waggled her head at Kit. "You're letting your imagination run wild, Kitty. It's just a party. Don't overthink it. Drink some champagne, break a few hearts, have some fun."

"Get you a refill, miss?" the bartender asked, as Kit stared into space.

Brandon's and Genia's laughter seemed to come from far away, as Kit hovered like a ghost, her mind wandering into shadowy places inside her head, a world bereft of light, color.

"Um? Oh, sure. Thank you." She made an effort to bring herself back to the wood-paneled, beer-smelling surroundings of the bar.

Musicians began setting up for the band. More young people walked into the bar, laughing. It was early still. Some of the guys glanced her way; in a parallel universe she might have been one of those kids. She tried to imagine what it would be like, being a part of a group of friends—happy, excited, anticipating . . . something good, maybe . . . on an evening in early summer.

But instead, she sat hunched on her bar stool, detached, watching the other kids—watching herself—from a safe, emotionally remote distance.

"Name's Ollie, by the way." The bartender filled up her glass at the fountain.

"Oh . . . thanks, Ollie."

"You look like you might be from out of town, you and your friends."

Ollie was just trying to be nice. She got it. But Kit couldn't bring herself to feel like talking.

"We're from *Manhattan*!" Her cousin leaned over and practically fell into Kit's lap. She chortled, "I'm Genia. And this is my cousin, Katherine Morgan." She flashed a big charm-school smile at Ollie, who grinned back at her. Then, Ollie winked at Kit. And

Genia went back to using her skills at flirtation on Brandon.

"Ah, New York!" Ollie leaned against the wall behind the bar. For whatever reason, he seemed to want to keep talking to her, despite how drab and boring she must seem. "My family lived in New York—Hell's Kitchen—after we arrived from Dublin! We moved up to Boston, eventually. Can't remember much about New York, just a lot of noise and people. Myself, well, I prefer small-town life to the big city."

Crinkles framed his eyes, like the kind you get from smiling a lot. And now Kit heard the slight lilt in Ollie's voice. She blinked. "So, you're . . . Irish?" she asked. But the braying of loud music as the band launched into its first number, and the shouts and laughter as more people joined the crowd at the bar, drowned out her question.

Kit had survived the debutante ball. She'd done what she'd promised to do. She'd been presented, curtsying before the wall of fierce matrons, the old guard of New York society, like all the other girls in their frothy gowns. She hadn't cracked under the cold, speculative glances or false smiles from the glittering and calculating women whom her mother, Bunny Morgan, called friends.

She'd danced with her father, Robert Morgan, who reminded her not to lead. Had her father ever considered, she'd wondered, how it felt when you realized that what lay ahead of you was a life of dancing backward? Unable to choose for yourself which way to go, as you were steered into the future by the demands and expectations of others.

Suddenly, her body was flung from the bar stool as Brandon grabbed hold of her by the wrist and pulled her onto her feet.

"Let's dance, sweetheart!" he shouted, exuberantly drunk. The music blared, loud and rocking, but no one else was dancing.

"Brandon, *stop it!*" She struggled against the arm now locked around her waist. Brandon's body felt hot, damp with sweat, as he dipped and spun around.

"Come on, baby. Why don't you smile? D'you always have to look so sad? It's such a downer!"

He swung her around, her body helpless, and all the faces of people staring at them blurred before her eyes like she was on some sick merry-go-round. Nausea bubbled up in her chest. She started to panic.

"Let me go!" she said. "I want to go—now!" Then, she lost it: *"I want to get out of here!"*

The spinning stopped, Brandon released her, and Kit stumbled, grabbing on to a bar stool. The band was no longer playing. Two young men who'd been drinking at the bar now stood beside them. "Everything all right here?" they asked.

Brandon held his hands up, surprised. Genia hurried over and hissed, "Kitty—do you really have to make a scene?"

"I'm okay, thanks. Everything's fine." Kit's voice shook as she spoke to the two young men. She couldn't meet their concerned glances. Or Ollie's.

"All right, then, let's all calm down," Ollie said. The two young men went back to their friends, and the people staring returned to their jokes and conversations. Brandon shook his head. "Sorry. Didn't realize everyone was so sensitive."

"For heaven's sake!" Genia huffed, and rolled her eyes. "We're all just trying to have a little fun."

Back at the farm, Kit fled upstairs to her room. Seated on the bed, she clutched her knees tightly to her chest, rocked back and forth, and tried to control the panic. There was just too much here that she couldn't anticipate, couldn't control. *How in the hell am I going to survive a whole summer of this?*

She shut her eyes and something dark flickered in the corners of her mind. For the first time since she'd returned ten days ago, she felt an awareness of the dark thing lurking. Like a presence, a dangerous presence, trying to pry open a door that she was hiding behind, that she desperately wanted to keep shut.

"Oh, *no*," she whispered, pleading.

Chapter 6

Tom banged on the door to the screened-in porch. "Mike-eeee!"

Hunched over his guitar, Michael ignored him. All evening, he'd been out on the front porch, hammering out random, angry chords. Right off Main Street, in Franconia, his family's simple, two-story wood-framed house was nice but small; there wasn't a lot of privacy. The raucous, canned laughter from whatever TV show his dad was watching inside competed loudly with his violent, uninspired strumming.

For no reason he could think of, Michael was on edge.

"What's up, T?" He refused to look up from his jagged guitar solo, resenting Tom's intrusion into his boring world.

Which was wrong of him.

Because Tom was his best friend. They'd known each other for as long as either of them could remember. He and Tom had played in the same mud puddles as little kids. All through high school, they'd raced on the ski team together. And now Tom had a crush on Michael's younger sister, Jennifer, which, so far, he hadn't managed to do anything about.

Things had changed when Michael decided to go to college. They were both eighteen now, just weeks away from high school graduation. And his friendship with Tom had hit a serious bump in the road.

"We live in a place that other people *pay money* to come to, for their stinkin' two weeks' vacation!" Tom had argued. He still looked like a scrawny teenager, and his red face matched his red hair when he got worked up. "What d'you want to *leave* for?"

They'd grown up in Franconia, a small, unpretentious resort town in the White Mountains. Michael would be the first person in his family—in fact, the only person he knew—to go to college. But like most of his friends, Tom had no definite future plans.

They hadn't seen each other much in the past few weeks. "Come on, man!" Tom wouldn't let up, and rapped his hand on the screen door frame again. "Besides, I think you're hurting that thing. Why don't you give it a rest?"

He stopped playing, looked up at Tom. Tom grinned back at him.

"The night is young! We are finally friggin' done with school! The world is our tomato!"

He couldn't help cracking up, and finally gave in. Tom was such a bozo. "I think the saying is 'The world is your oyster,' knucklehead."

"Whatever! There's a band playing over at Ollie's tonight. Come on—let's go have some fun. Besides, after next week you start work, right? And then"—Tom ended in a whiny falsetto—"it's . . . *college boy* . . ."

"All right, all right." Michael got up, put the guitar away. Do him good to get out. "But knock it off with the 'college boy' crap, okay? Hey, Dad," he said, looking into the living room where his father slumped, nodding off in front of *The Price Is Right*. "I'm going with Tom into Littleton, to see some friends. You okay with that?" He grabbed his jean jacket from the back of a chair.

His dad blinked and then sat up on the couch. He looked groggy. Things were starting to get busy again at the family hardware store, with summer people returning, and Michael knew he'd had a long day. "Sure, you boys enjoy yourselves. But not too late, okay? Need your help in the shop tomorrow."

As soon as they got on the road, Tom lit up a joint.

"Man, roll your window down, will you?" Michael complained. "And what's that thing next to you?"

"It's my new pet—a Pet Rock."

"How is this a 'pet'? What makes this any different from a rock you'd find at the creek—or in your driveway?"

"It comes in a box that *says*: Pet Rock."

"Seriously? You need a girlfriend, Tom."

Tom blushed—thinking about Jenny, probably—and spun the radio dial, landing on "Free Bird." The truck roared north along Highway 93, with Tom singing off-key at the top of his lungs, breaking into a hacking cough every time he took a hit off the joint.

The last bit of sunset dropped behind a dark, spiked wall of tall pine trees. Michael kept quiet, his eyes on the road. He was ready to move on, from all of this, from everyone he knew who had no dreams of anything beyond small-town Franconia. But these were his friends. This was the only life he knew.

He had to admit it—the blank slate of the future scared him.

Right off the lobby of Littleton's only hotel, Oliver's Pub drew a big, regular crowd. By nine o'clock, the place had filled up with what looked like every kid graduating from high school within a fifty-mile radius. With proper (fake) ID, Michael and Tom, like most of the locals, had been coming to Ollie's since they'd been sophomores in high school.

The band was in full swing when they walked in and worked their way toward the long bar at the back of the wood-paneled pub. *Cheer up*, he told himself. Tonight, anyway, he was determined to be just good ol' high school Mike, the guy who whipped everyone's ass on the ski slopes, played a mean guitar, and liked to hang out with his pals. Relax. Enjoy himself. He could worry about the rest of his life tomorrow.

Michael looked around to see who was here tonight—who he knew—and immediately spotted Theresa, his girlfriend, with her usual gang of friends. She caught his eye and gave him an unfriendly stare, then turned to say something to the girl next to her. Then all the girls turned to look at him—a mafia squad of big hair, red lips, and accusing eyes. *Now what?*

Theresa wore her long dark hair so that it fell over one eye in a dramatic, seductive way. And she had this amazing body that she packed into tight jeans and clingy, low-necked tops. The guys at the bar, he noticed, were appreciating the view as much as the horny teenagers he'd gone to high school with. Six months ago, he might have had a few friendly words with guys like that, set things straight. But tonight, he just shrugged.

"I'll catch up with you, man." Michael left Tom at the bar, where his friend was attracting jokes and laughter with his ridiculous Pet Rock, and pushed through the groups of partiers, saying "hey" to people he knew. He made his way over to Theresa. He could hardly wait to hear what he'd done wrong this time.

"Hey, babe." He bent to kiss Theresa and she turned her face from him, offering just her cheek. "Hi, Dawn, Sherrie . . . and . . . ?"

"I'm Jackie!" said an awkward and extremely tall girl. Jackie didn't seem to fit in with the other "popular girls" in Theresa's gang. But whether from bigheartedness or a more strategic sense of consolidating her overall influence in high school, Theresa had a way of drawing outsiders under her protective wing.

"Can I get you girls something to drink?"

Tom helped him to bring the beers back to the girls, juggling his rock and three glasses. "You chicks are looking mighty hot!" He sounded like a complete goof.

"You are never going to score if you keep carrying that thing around with you." Michael laughed and shook his head at Tom.

"Don't dis the Rock! It's reliable, nonjudgmental. A good listener . . ." Tom offered the beers to Theresa's friends, then jammed the rock into his jeans pocket.

Dawn, Sherrie, and Jackie sipped their beers, glancing from Michael to Theresa. Their dark, dramatically fringed eyes were filled with girlish secrets. Then they drifted away strategically, pulling Tom with them. "What is that *lump* in your jeans?" he heard Dawn tease Tom. "It's my Rock!" Tom replied, to the gleeful squeals of the three girls.

Silent and awkward, Michael stood beside Theresa. He and Theresa had been dating most of his senior year.

He hadn't wanted a girlfriend. But for reasons he could never figure out, last fall Theresa had started leaning over his desk just in case he hadn't happened to notice her cleavage. Paying attention to him. She'd laugh or ignore him when he put her off.

"See this?" she'd purred, fluttering her hand in front of him, where a big, purple-stoned ring sat conspicuously on her middle finger. "When the stone glows purple, my mood is Passionate. I don't know why, but it's always purple when I'm around you."

Not Interested, on his part, turned out to be just a challenge to Theresa.

She was sexy and popular—practically every guy he knew had fantasized about going out with her. Which was the lame excuse Michael gave himself, finally, for just giving in—interested or not. Before long, and with seemingly little effort on his part, he and Theresa were a couple.

Theresa's long earrings jangled as she jerked her head toward him. "It's time to make a decision, Mike." She slid a cigarette out of a pink case and handed him her lighter. "Time to *fish or cut bait.*"

Theresa was a year younger than him, and wanted the two of them to come to a decision about their future before he left for college in the fall. "We're practically like a married couple, Mikey," she'd insist. On top of that, her mom was putting the pressure on her to give him an ultimatum: Fish or cut bait.

Michael took an uneasy swig of his beer. He realized that no one would have been surprised if they'd gotten engaged that summer. He tried to put her off. "I've got a lot on my mind right now, you know."

In April, Dartmouth College had offered him a scholarship. Getting accepted at a really good school was something he'd wanted more than anything, and a part of Michael couldn't believe it had actually happened. No one else he knew was going on to college. Compared with the life he'd grown up in, it would be like entering a different world.

Already, envisioning himself as a student behind those high, ivy-covered walls required a gargantuan leap of the imagination. He drew a total blank when he tried to picture himself engaged or married to Theresa in that setting. And this knowledge made him feel terrible.

Theresa exhaled, and blew a puff of smoke so that it barely missed his face. "Oh, really? You've got so many other important things to think about?" she said. "Our relationship is pretty fucking important, too, don't you think?"

Her mood ring glowed red—Angry, if he remembered correctly. This line of conversation was going nowhere good. "You know, babe . . . I can't wait to see what you're wearing to the prom." He put his arm around her waist and gave her a squeeze.

Theresa looked at him, her dark eyes sharp with suspicion. Then, she gave in, and flashed him her big megawatt smile. She obviously had something sexy in mind.

She laughed, then shook her hair back. "I'll bet you can't."

Conversation successfully sidelined, for now. Things settled down after that, Theresa leaned into him, and they turned to listen to the band.

Chapter 7

People continued to pack into the bar, ordering drinks, and smoking so much that somebody had to pry open a window. Theresa's girlfriends and Tom had disappeared into the crowd. Once in a while some yahoo would get rowdy, shout out something.

All of them knew that things were changing, that this part of their lives where they could still be considered kids was nearly over. He could smell the emotion in the air—the hot, sweaty excitement and the fear—and it jacked him up, made him feel a little crazy. Michael downed the rest of his beer and ordered another.

The band took a break, about an hour in. In the quiet that followed, it didn't take long for the crowd to get restless. Someone shouted, "Hey, Mike! Give us a tune!"

"You're drunk!" he hollered back.

"Come on, Mike!" Someone else joined in. And then the whole bar began to chant: "Mike! Mike! Mike!"

The chanting and whistling grew louder. "All right! All right!" he shouted, and shook his head, laughing. He handed his beer to Theresa and made his way up to the stage at the front of the bar.

His grandparents on his mom's side were Irish, and their love for the traditional music of the old homeland had rubbed off on him early. He could play by ear dozens of songs on the guitar: the raucous ballads of death, drunks, and disaster; and mournful tunes of shipwrecks and heartbreak. Michael looked like his mom's side of the family, too, with dark curly hair, hazel-green eyes, and a build that was not too tall but strong, sturdy.

He'd given up his daydreams of playing music for a living. Still, his friends knew that, give him a beer or two, and he'd be happy to knock out a tune.

He strode up to the front of the room, picked up the guitar, and slung the strap over his shoulder. He turned toward the crowd, looking out at all the faces of people he knew. Lifting his hands in the air and hamming it up, he called out in his best corny Irish brogue: "Calm yourselves, lads! And I'll give ya a tune!"

He ran through a riff, tuning up the instrument. Then he slammed out a chord: *"This is for us!"* The bar erupted in cheers. Adrenaline pounded through him now and he launched into a raucous drinking song:

"I've been a wild rover for many's the year
And I've spent all my money on whiskey and beer!
Now I've saved up my wages, keep money in store
And I never will play the wild rover no more.

"Wild rover, wild rover!
Wild rover no more!
I won't play the wild rover
No never, no more!

"I went to a pub where I used to resort
And I told the landlady my money was short.
I asked her for credit, she answered me, 'Nay'
Saying, 'Custom like yours, I can have any day!'"

By now, everyone was singing, stomping on the floor, and shouting along:

> "*Wild rover, wild rover!*
> *Wild rover no more!*
> *I won't play the wild rover*
> *No never, no more!*"

Theresa smiled, too, clapping her hands. She blew Michael a big kiss and he went in for one more round:

> "*Put my hand in my pocket so manly and bold,*
> *And down on the table threw a handful of gold.*
> *'Here's beer and here's whiskey,' she said, 'you're a good bloke,*
> *And don't you take notice—I was having a joke!'*

> "*Wild rover, wild rover!*
> *Wild rover no more!*
> *I won't play the wild rover,*
> *No never, no more!*"

He finished the tune amid crazy cheering and hollering, all mostly his buddies and all thoroughly drunk. He took a bow, wiped the sweat from his face, and jumped off the stage to let the professionals take over again.

"You sure you don't want a regular gig, Mike?" Ollie asked, half joking, Michael assumed. "You know, if that college business doesn't work out for you . . ." Ollie slid a beer across the bar to him.

The frosty brew hit the spot. "I'll let you know," he said with a grin.

Theresa wrapped her arms around him, and kissed him

possessively. The bar was wall-to-wall people and as he scanned the room, Michael noticed a lot of unfamiliar faces mixed in with the regular crowd. "Looks like the summer people have discovered you, Ollie," he commented.

"Yeah, and I'll not be complaining. Speaking of summer people, there was a group from New York City, stopped in last night. I think the name was Morgan. Those city girls certainly turn some heads." Ollie made a low wolf whistle.

Morgan. Michael froze. He hadn't heard the name Morgan in almost two years. Now, it caught him off guard. He put his beer down. "Are you talking about *Katherine* Morgan?" *Slow down, Mike,* a voice inside his head warned him. The beers had given him a disorienting buzz.

"That's right. Katherine—Kitty—I think," said Ollie. He looked at Michael with curiosity. "D'you know her?"

Theresa caught something strange in the tone of his voice. "Mikey? Who's he talking about?"

"Just some rich, summer people," Tom joined in. "I've heard of that family. One of the daughters—that one, Kitty?—she's a nut case. They had to lock her up in a mental institution or something."

"That's a stupid-ass thing to say!" Michael shot back at Tom. Now his head was spinning. How would Tom know anything about the Morgans? Was he just being an idiot? "What the hell do you think you even know about her?"

"Hey, take it easy! I'm just saying that's what I heard—the Morgans have some big spread, outside of town. A friend of my brother's worked there last summer. Said he heard the oldest daughter was messed up."

Michael drained the beer Ollie had put in front of him and slammed the mug down hard on the bar. "I'm outta here."

"Mike—what the hell?" Theresa balked. "Everyone's having a good time. What's wrong with you? What do you care about those people?"

"Hey, and what about my ride?" Tom chimed in.

The last beer had kicked in and he looked at Tom like he might hit him. Michael swung around and began pushing his way toward the door. "I'm so *sick* of this crowd. I'm sick of all these small-town rednecks."

"Watch your mouth! Who're you calling a redneck? Who do you think you are, anyway, Michael Pearce?" Theresa snapped. He ignored her and stormed back to the truck while Theresa, fuming, followed him.

They drove back to Franconia in silence. When they pulled up in front of her house, Theresa asked, "Do you want to come inside?"

The house was dark; her parents were probably upstairs, asleep. And even though Theresa's voice sounded hard and unfriendly, from the way she looked at him he could tell she wanted him to stay.

But taking advantage of her offer now just didn't seem right. Which was messed up—and he wondered if there was something wrong with him. "I don't think so, babe, I'm pretty tired."

Theresa looked down at her hands, clenched her jaw. It didn't much matter that he couldn't see the color of her mood ring—her frustration was obvious. She asked, "What time are you picking me up next Saturday?"

His mind went blank.

"Prom night? Remember?"

"Yeah, I know, Theresa." He hated himself for sounding like a sarcastic jerk. And for lying. "When do you want me to come by?"

"Six o'clock. Don't be late."

Michael took off, driving too fast, not paying any attention to where he was going. He knew Katherine Morgan. *Kit.* Two summers earlier he had run into her family while working at the Profile Lake Club.

That summer, it had become his entire mission in life to find a way to talk to Kit.

He continued along the empty main street through town, crossed the river and drove through the quiet night, past newly planted fields and stretches of woodland. A feeling of separateness engulfed him, like he didn't know where he belonged anymore. As he drove on, his mood shifted from barely contained anger to something he couldn't explain—a flat emptiness.

So, Kit was here again. But where had she been since that summer two years ago? And if she was here now—why?

Eventually he pulled up to the small local airfield. Over the years he'd stop sometimes and watch the planes landing and taking off. Like a marooned sailor trapped on the desert island of Franconia, New Hampshire, he'd tried to imagine where those other, luckier, people might be going.

What the hell had happened to Kit? Tom's clueless babbling at Ollie's played over and over in his head. *Was something really wrong with her?*

But seriously—how likely was it that Tom would know anything about it? And after all this time, why did it matter so much to him anyway, for fuck's sake?

He made a U-turn in the middle of the dark road, and drove home.

Chapter 8

Kit's eyes fluttered open as she lay motionless in the antique maple wood bed, her limbs relaxed and heavy. Five a.m. Tuesday morning. Her gaze drifted to the tall, draped windows facing the mountains. A feeling of peace enfolded her, and she allowed herself to drift on the blissful absence of anxiety that the night's sleep in her childhood bedroom at Cedaredge had given her.

The past few days had been better. A pause had settled on the Morgan household, the lull before any grand summer plans were launched. Now, her mother and their housekeeper, Elsie, busied themselves with long shopping lists and getting the house in order to both of their liking. Her father organized meetings with the farm manager, Bud Granger.

For the rest of the family, it was a grace period. A quiet time that Kit navigated cautiously, doing her best to avoid everyone.

She stretched, her fingers sliding along the smooth wood of the curved headboard. She tried out a smile, but her face felt tight and unnatural. Pathetic. The second attempt went better. Then, she tossed off the covers and the fringed white bedspread, and sat up. The wood floorboards were cool beneath her bare feet.

A pale morning light glowed through the thin linen curtains. A chickadee scolded in the cedar trees outside her window and the soft voice of the thrush—the high fluty whistle, then the low trilling ripple of notes—calling from somewhere in the woods drew her up and out of bed. Kit pushed the curtains aside and slid the window fully open.

The colors of the mountains poured over her. The world had regained its rich luminosity, expanding with brilliance, subtlety, and chromatic saturation. She let the many layers of greens in the forest, the blues and purples of the distant mountains, and the wildflowers—like spattered shots of color in the field below—soak into her brain.

And the *air*—it smelled like summer. Like summer going back in time to every summer of her entire life. Like a day filled with hope, with things to look forward to.

But as she pulled on shorts and a T-shirt, the reflection of herself in the mirror above the dresser dismayed her. So pale, and those dark circles still hung under haunted, sad eyes. People had thought her pretty, once; at least, they used to say so. She was tall, with blond hair falling to the middle of her back and the Morgan family's blue eyes and full lips.

She'd been a child, then, that pretty little girl. Flinging her hair over her shoulder, tilting up her chin with self-assurance. Enjoying the admiration of others.

Kit was no longer that child. But she didn't recognize the person she'd become. She sighed and turned away from the mirror's reflection. All she knew for certain was that she no longer sought that attention, and did her best to move under the radar. Avoid the looks, the speculation, the pity.

Elsie and Max might be up already. But the couple's rooms—a bedroom, a sitting room, and a bath—were located in a different part of the house, over the kitchen. Still, she walked carefully on tiptoe, bare footed, down the front stairs. She didn't want to wake anyone—or start the dog, Banjo, barking.

Outside on the long front porch, she paused. The morning air carried all the familiar smells of the farm: the fresh, sweet scent of grass and clover; the sharp, earthy tang of cow manure; and the luscious, heady aroma of the lilac trees coming into bloom across the gravel driveway. The pleasure of return, of her senses reawakening to this familiar and beloved place after such a long absence, made her shiver with delight.

She'd missed everything! The ancient, rounded mountains with their steep, rocky trails that she'd climbed as a child, testing her endurance after a stagnating year of school in the city. The freedom of walking out the back door and setting off on her bike, riding along the quiet country roads where she might come upon deer or discover hidden places to swim.

And the slow, drawn-out days by the lake. With only the easy responsibility of keeping an eye on Elliot and Lucy while her parents golfed or drank cocktails with their summer country-club friends. She'd filled her sketchbook with drawings, and dedicated herself to becoming reacquainted with her body—building her strength and stamina, and swimming in the breathlessly cold water.

Each day by the lake blended into the next, and the water fueled her imagination. Sometimes, Kit as a child had daydreamed that the lake was, in fact, her natural element—that her original home existed beneath the water, illuminated by the green-gold light filtering down through its depths. How was it possible that she existed for three quarters of the year as an exile in the city without this?

Now she walked down the porch stairs, but paused on the grassy front lawn. The beauty of the New Hampshire morning dimmed.

She'd ruined everything, two summers ago. Guilt and apprehension twisted in her gut, and she stiffened. She'd been sixteen, on the verge of taking control of her life. But then, somehow, she'd fucked it up! And now, here she was, living a life of suspended animation.

The gravel drive hurt Kit's soft, uncalloused city feet as, hands shoved in her pockets, she set off down the driveway toward the road. But bare feet were part of summers at the farm, her body making contact with all the sensations of the earth—cold, wet, warm, soft. Soft feet would strengthen, toughen up.

"I know what happened," she'd informed her psychiatrist in Montreux. "Because they told me. 'Attempted suicide by drowning.'" Here her voice had faltered. "But I can't actually remember . . . anything."

"Memory is like a familiar garden, Katherine," her psychiatrist had said, in his dull, monotone voice. "We wander around, following the well-worn paths, and everything looks the same to us. But one day, we notice in a different way. We see the strange flower or the lizard or stone that was there all along. In front of our very eyes, but somehow hidden from our awareness until that moment. We bend to pick it up, look at it. We understand, all at once, its significance . . ."

"Sorry," she'd told the psychiatrist. "I just . . . it's a blank."

So far, her memory had remained locked to her. Week after week, month after month. But Kit needed to remember. Her parents had told her what had happened—everyone in the tight circle of her family knew—but now their insistence that she put this episode behind her somehow made moving forward impossible. She needed to remember, and to understand: *Why?*

The deeply familiar balm of farm smells comforted her. She was going to explore each well-loved place—the pastures, the woods, the backroads, and all her favorite haunts from childhood—as if these places were that "garden" that the psychiatrist had talked about. Walk, observe, be alert for clues. Something would strike her memory; it had to.

Today, she said to herself, *I am ready to think about this.* Here, now, this summer, I am going to find the truth.

She turned up the dirt road, her pace quickening, and hiked toward the barns. She would start with the farm, then.

The soft clank of cow bells, from the pasture behind the two barns, carried across to the road. Kit turned onto the pathway that wound in front of the farm manager's cottage, continued between the two massive barns—the milking barn and the hay barn—and then came out to a wide expanse of fenced-in pasture. A herd of twelve black-and-white Holstein cows grazed in the long grass, their big, flat teeth making a rhythmic, noisy crunching.

She clambered up over the cedar fencing and dropped into the pasture beside the cows. They looked up, one after the next raising long, inquisitive faces. Their ears angled in her direction and their tails swished.

"Hello, ladies!"

The big animals ambled toward her, stepping slowly, snorting and tossing their heads. They still recognized her! She'd known most of these cows for all of their lives. All of their lives except for the past two years, anyway.

She stood quietly, giving the first cow a chance to approach and reach its head forward. The animal sniffed her fingers with its large, damp nose. She rubbed its forehead and moved her hand to scratch the warm furred cheek and neck. A second cow pushed forward for a scratch.

"Where's Freddie?" she said to the big, curious animals. A young bull named Ferdinand—Freddie for short—had been a rowdy member of the otherwise stolid herd. "Did Freddie get too

rambunctious for you girls?" She hoped her father hadn't sold the
yearling bull who'd been her favorite, though a naughty annoyance
at times to the docile older cows.

"So, what do you notice?" she asked herself aloud. Herself,
and the cows, that is, if they happened to be paying attention. She
looked around, doing her best to focus her awareness. Out front
lay mountains, a soft rosy purple in the morning light. Then up on
the barn siding, beneath the roof, a woodpecker banged, paused as
if to observe her, then banged some more. The cow bells clanked
and rang out their simple, pastoral farm music.

Then *crunch* went the collective chewing of the herd. If you
were a cow, the delicious grass caught your attention.

And for her, nothing to notice but peace and contentment.

Down at the main house, the screened front door slammed—
thwack!—a dog barked, and the noise traveled up the road and out
into the field to where she stood. That must be Elsie, letting Banjo
out. Everyone would be getting up now. Before long, Elsie would
be ringing the bell for breakfast.

Sitting at the table for breakfast. *Everybody would be watching her.* The sharp jab of panic made her heart race.

Opposite the barns, the fence line enclosed the pasture from
the bordering woodlands. What if she just slid through the gap
between the poles, disappeared into the trees? The idea of vanishing pulled at her.

The breakfast bell rang now. *Ring-ring-a-ling!* Insistent.

In the dark woods there would be no one directing her every
move or asking "How do you feel today, Kit?" Asking, but not
really wanting to know. Or wanting only to hear: "I feel fine! Better than ever!"

No one wanted to hear: "I am scared. I am confused."

The cow shoved and snuffled at her, and Kit pressed her face into the animal's furred neck, breathed in its solid strength. "Shit shit shit," she whispered. "I don't know what to do."

The cow shook and bellowed out "Mmmmuuuuuuuuoo!"

"Was that comment intended for me? All right, all right," Kit sighed. "Maybe I can do this."

She stood up tall. Grabbing the top fence pole, she climbed up and over the enclosure. She walked back between the barns to the road, then down toward the house.

Chapter 9

Michael's dad pulled up into the driveway right behind him as he returned home from school that afternoon.

"Hoping I'd catch you, Mike," his father said as he climbed out of his pickup. "Dr. Landsman called from the clinic on his way to a dairy farm on Sugar Hill. He ordered some supplies and I don't have time to run them up. Can you help me out and get this delivery to him right away?"

"Absolutely, Pop. No problem." He followed his dad to the back of his truck.

"You'll go all the way through the town of Sugar Hill, then take a left at Easton Road. Keep an eye out for the turnoff—it's not well marked," his dad instructed. "Follow that dirt road for about five miles or so, until you come to a big open pasture. Turn right and head up the hill for another mile. Cedaredge Farm will be on your right."

They transferred the bales of hay, rope, and tools that Dr. Landsman had asked for into Michael's truck.

"Not sure you've ever been back up that way. But Cedaredge's a big place—when you see it, you'll know it. Thanks, Mike. Can't leave the store right now, summer folks are back and it's just too busy." His dad returned to his pickup with a couple of quick, long strides and drove off, back to the hardware store.

That year, the local veterinarian, Dr. John Landsman, had offered Michael a summer job. He'd be starting work soon—right after graduation.

Michael liked animals and he'd done well in biology and chemistry. He'd decided to apply to Dartmouth as a science major. Maybe he'd want to be a veterinarian himself one day. Landsman operated a busy clinic in town for small animals, but the real, interesting veterinary work was taking care of all the livestock in the area. Sometimes the vet had to perform surgery on animals, too. Blood and gore didn't bother Michael, and he enjoyed fixing things.

It also hadn't escaped his notice that people respected Landsman, both locals and summer folks alike. The vet drove a nice car (when he wasn't visiting patients in the clinic van), and got to work outside instead of behind a shop counter indoors, or in some stuffy office. It was a profession that seemed to have a lot of advantages.

His dad's delivery offered Michael the chance to show Landsman he'd made the right choice in hiring him. Michael jumped back into his truck and pulled out onto Main Street. Besides, who wouldn't say yes to a drive out into the countryside on a beautiful late-June afternoon?

Loose boards banged under the truck as he crossed the bridge over the Gale River and left behind the traffic created by the arriving summer people who were shopping and running errands in downtown Franconia. He ground the truck into second gear, and the old Ford pickup rumbled up the hill. A field lined with spears of purple lupine flowers swept out in front, beneath a view of the Presidential Mountain Range.

The broad shoulders of Mt. Lafayette sat square in the middle, with Mt. Washington in the distance. In the foreground, close enough to touch, it seemed, the now-green ski slopes zigzagged across the face of Cannon Mountain. Michael had spent every winter during school on those runs, racing with the ski team. To him, Cannon had always looked so impressive. But this afternoon, with college only a few months away in the fall, the mountain appeared smaller. Like something he'd outgrown.

He rested his arm on the open window frame and leaned on the gas as the road continued to climb. The cool breeze in his face smelled like sunshine and newly mown hay. He passed Hildex Maple Farm, and Polly's Pancake Parlor where Theresa had landed a summer waitressing job.

The road leveled out and then began a long twisting descent toward the Sugar Hill town center. If you blinked, you'd miss the tiny, pretty village that consisted of a post office, a library, a garden center, and Harmon's cheese shop.

Sugar Hill was a wealthy community, at least compared with Franconia. Outside the small town center and farther off along the postcard-perfect country roads, big, expensive houses and farms overlooked rolling pastures, deep forests, and unobstructed views of the White Mountains. Cedaredge Farm must be one of these places.

He didn't know this area well, but he'd get more familiar with these fields and farmlands once his job with Landsman started. He swung a left onto Easton Road, and dust kicked up behind the truck as the road turned from pavement to dirt.

Dr. Landsman was just coming out of one of two large barns as Michael's truck pulled into the gravel lot in front of the farm. He got out of the truck and stood admiring the massive structures. Both barns were painted classic farm red and supported by thick stone foundations.

"Afternoon, Mike," Dr. Landsman grunted. "Glad you could make it out here with the supplies. Thanks! Saved me a trip into town."

John Landsman was a big guy, in his fifties, mostly bald with a fringe of close-cut blond hair. He was strong and solid, and had a calm, steady way about him that made him nice to be around.

Michael understood how he had earned the trust of both his human clients and the big farm animals he worked with.

"No problem, Dr. Landsman. Pretty amazing place up here." He looked around at the multiple barns and sheds, and the extensive and carefully groomed grounds. Were those acres of fields he'd passed on the way up the hill to the barn also part of Cedaredge Farm? Most likely. Which meant this place was probably a couple hundred acres—at least.

A completely different world from Main Street Franconia, that was for sure. What kind of people would actually own a place like this, he wondered?

They began unloading the truck.

"Certainly is beautiful," Landsman agreed. "You passed the main Cedaredge residence coming up the hill—though you might not have seen the big house, behind those tall lilac trees. The family likes their privacy.

"The owner, Robert Morgan, and his family arrived end of last week," Landsman continued, "from New York City. Bob called me yesterday. It looks like Bud, the farm manager, has been sleeping on the job. Morgan nearly blew a gasket when he saw the mess things were in. The heifers have started to knock some of the fence rails free around the field behind the barn. They'll be off into the woods before you know it. Seeing as Bud's nowhere to be found, Bob asked if I wouldn't mind spreading some hay for the bull, and knocking together a few of those fence posts once I finished checking on the heifers—"

Michael interrupted: "The family's name is Morgan?"

"That's right. Bob and his wife, Bunny. They've got three kids. I think one of them—one of the girls—might be about your age.

"This is a beautiful herd of Holsteins." Landsman went back to talking about cows. "They've won some prizes, too. Cedaredge

Farm came in first place last year in the New Hampshire Dairy Competition.

Michael had stopped paying any attention to Landsman's long-winded ramblings. Instead, his heart pounded in his chest and a thousand questions battered his brain. *This was Kit's place? Was she here? Now?* He picked up the pace, heaving the heavy bales out of the truck.

"I'll take those tools, there, Mike, thanks," Landsman said. He walked over to the barn, then came back for the heavy coils of rope, continuing the whole time to go on about the problems with Cedaredge's farm manager. "I just don't know what's wrong with Bud these days, he doesn't seem to be minding the shop the way he should be."

Landsman would be his boss starting next week. So being rude and cutting the vet off was probably not a great idea. At the same time, Michael could not stop the voice inside his head from shouting: Kit is here! *She's here.* He had stopped believing he would ever see her again—almost convinced himself he didn't care. But he did care. And now, she was literally minutes away from him!

What he didn't want to consider, but struggled to push out of his mind, was: What if it turned out that Tom had been right and she'd gone crazy or something? There was no way he could leave Cedaredge Farm without finding out more.

When they'd finished unloading the truck, he said, "I think I'll go say hello to the Morgans, on my way out."

Landsman turned and stared at him. "Oh?"

Was Landsman challenging him?

Michael tried to sound casual, like driving up to the Morgans' house was no big deal, just a stop on his way home. "I know the Morgans' daughter . . . Kit."

Landsman raised his eyebrows. "Well, suit yourself," he said. "But keep in mind the Morgans have just arrived. They may not be in the mood for company."

In other words, he should watch his step—him, a local kid—and not bother Landsman's wealthy New York clients.

But Landsman didn't try to stop him.

The Cedaredge residence was a big, sprawling country estate. And yet despite its size, the rambling structure appeared as natural in the setting of the upward slope of the landscape as the tall, old cedar trees towering behind it and the granite slab on which the house rested.

He'd heard about places like this, hidden at the end of long, private driveways. Dark brown shingles the color of pinecones were set off by the crisp white of deep-set windows and forest-green trim. With panoramic views of the White Mountains, the long white-railed porch that spanned the front of the house and wrapped around its eastern flank impressed Michael most of all.

To say he was nervous would have been an understatement. But there was no turning back now. Michael parked the truck and walked across the gravel drive to the porch. Totally faking a confidence he did not feel, he took the wide front steps two at a time and called out a friendly "Hello!"

Chapter 10

In the shade of the deep, curving porch, two women sat in white wicker deck chairs. Glasses and a pitcher of iced tea were arranged on a table between them. The women were blond, slim, and intimidatingly beautiful, and they stopped in midconversation, turning like two graceful birds to look at Michael. The older woman he recognized from the Profile Lake Club as Mrs. Morgan. She was probably around the same age as his mother—but as different as if she'd come from another planet.

They wore what summer people from the city think of as "country clothes": Mrs. Morgan had on pressed khakis, a white blouse, and pearls around her neck. Her hair looked like a blond helmet. A thick gold bracelet gleamed on the younger woman's wrist, and she wore a short white jean skirt and a pink fitted top with the collar turned up.

From their expressions, it seemed obvious that the two women had determined he must be one of the farm workers, lost and somehow ending up on their porch.

He stood at the top of the stairs, uncertain of what to do next. The women stared at him coolly. As if they assumed he came from such a different world that it was okay to just give him the once-over. Instead of being friendly or polite, or just saying hello.

Shaking off his nervousness, he smiled and crossed the porch toward Mrs. Morgan and tried to sound like a self-assured adult.

"Hello, Mrs. Morgan. I don't know if you remember me? I'm Michael Pearce. A friend of your daughter Katherine's."

"Michael Pearce?"

"I worked at the Profile Lake Club."

Mrs. Morgan's face hardened, like a mask.

"As a lifeguard."

"A lifeguard? I see," she said. "And what brings you all the way out to Cedaredge Farm? It's quite a surprise to see anyone from town all the way out here," she said pointedly.

The younger woman ignored him. She probably wasn't much older than he was, but the bored, superior look on her face made her seem older.

Michael pressed on. "I'm working with the veterinarian, Dr. Landsman, this summer. He said this was your place, so I thought I would come over and see if Kit—if Katherine, that is—was here. Say hello." The two women exchanged glances, but said nothing. Were they trying to hide something? Mrs. Morgan's companion smirked and looked away.

But he refused to give up. What could he say that would break through this wall of aloofness? "I'll be going away to college this fall. To Dartmouth. I wanted to let Katherine know."

"Dartmouth! You mean in Hanover?" the younger woman asked. Like she just wanted to be sure that there wasn't another Dartmouth College that accepted townies like him.

"That's right."

"Well. Congratulations. And it's *Genia*, by the way." She actually smiled at him now.

She turned to Mrs. Morgan, her pretty, catlike face smug and a little mean. She said, "You know the Theobolds from the Yacht Club in Greenwich? Mummy and Daddy's friends? Well, Ted Theobold is a Dartmouth alum, gave them oodles of money for an endowment. Anyway, I just heard that Richie Theobold—their son—did not get in this spring, he's on the wait list! You can only imagine the Theobolds' reaction to that!"

Somehow, this exchange of gossip seemed to shine a positive light on him. Both women relaxed. They turned back to him. Even Kit's mother seemed curious now.

Just at that moment, Robert Morgan walked out onto the porch, calling to his wife—"Bunny!"—as he came out the front door. Morgan was tall, with sandy blond hair and bushy eyebrows. He gave off an impatient intensity, like someone who was busy and used to people paying attention when he came into a room. When he saw Michael, he stopped short.

"Darling, this is Michael Pearce," Mrs. Morgan said. "A . . . local boy working with John Landsman this summer. He says he's a friend of Katherine's."

"Hello, Mike," Morgan said. Kit's father had something else on his mind and wasn't really listening. Like Mrs. Morgan, he obviously did not remember Michael from the Club.

"Michael's just told us he's going to Dartmouth in the fall, too." Genia winked at Michael. Suddenly on his side.

"Dartmouth? Well, now, good for you, my boy." Morgan looked at Michael again as if just seeing him for the first time. "Say, isn't your father Walt Pearce, who runs the hardware store in town?"

"Yes, that's right, sir. That's my family's store."

"I must have seen you in the shop. Nice for a son to be helping out his father. Well, your parents must be very proud. Dartmouth's a damn good school, not easy to get into." Morgan gave him a nod of approval.

From Morgan's point of view, their brief conversation had now come to an end.

Then Michael asked, "Where did *you* go to college, Mr. Morgan?"

Morgan frowned and his eyebrows pulled together. He hadn't expected the kid whose family owned the hardware store to ask where he had gone to college. As if they were equals in any way.

"Princeton '53; Yale Law '57," Morgan grunted. Then, unable to resist a competitive male jab, he added, "We clobbered Dartmouth in football every year!"

"But we probably beat you in skiing," Michael said, surprising himself with his nerve.

Morgan chuckled, and seemed to take the comeback in stride. Appreciated it, even. "Well, that's probably right. You like to ski, Pearce?"

"Yes, sir."

"Good, good." Morgan turned his attention back to his wife. "Brandon was looking for Kitty—do you know where she's gone? Elsie's cleaning up in the kitchen; she didn't seem to know, either. I can't find any of the kids."

"Why is Brandon looking for Kitty?" Genia sounded peeved.

"She and Lucy went into town," Mrs. Morgan said to her husband. "As far as I know, Elliot is off playing with Banjo somewhere. I warned him not to bring that dog back covered in mud."

Genia grumbled. "I don't see why Brandon needs to know where Kitty is."

The Morgans' conversation about their kids seemed boringly normal. A weight of uncertainty lifted from his shoulders. "How is Katherine?" Michael asked. "I stopped by hoping I'd have a chance to see her."

He could tell the Morgans considered the few polite words they'd exchanged sufficient, and now it was time for him to go. He was pushing his luck and he knew it.

"Kitty's doing great. Came out this spring, at the Plaza in New York, had a pack of young men trailing after her," Mr. Morgan said, chuckling. "She certainly had her pick of escorts. She'll be here at the farm all summer. Then it's off to college this fall, near Boston—Wellesley College, following in the footsteps of her grandmother Morgan. She's doing *great*," Morgan emphasized.

Michael had no idea what "came out" meant—came out of what? And what were "escorts?" It seemed kind of ridiculous that, having not seen Kit in two years, it now bugged the hell out of him to hear there was a "pack of young men" following Kit around.

And who was Brandon—her boyfriend?

"We'll let Kitty know that you stopped by, Mike." Mr. Morgan reached out to shake his hand. Their conversation had now definitely come to an end. "Give my regards to your dad, I'm sure we'll be in to see him soon enough."

Holy crap! So, Cedaredge Farm was where Kit's family spent their summers!

He peeled out of the driveway. A sudden sense of possibility, of life opening up in amazing ways he hadn't even known to consider, surged through him like a tidal wave. It was the same incredible high he'd felt that summer two years ago as his unexpected friendship with this girl, who was irresistibly out of his league, began to turn into something more.

On the beach at the Profile Lake Club, Kit had mentioned she was from New York City. She'd been vague about where her family was staying in the area. It hadn't occurred to Michael to ask; all he'd cared about was that she'd be coming back the following summer. And she'd promised him that she would be.

All junior year, he'd anticipated with certainty his friendship with this girl from out of town—from sophisticated, far-off New York City—continuing when summer returned. The following June he'd been seventeen, and he'd gotten his lifeguard job back. But Kit never showed up at the Club—not once—and he'd only rarely caught a glimpse of any of the Morgan family.

Hurt and disappointment had won out, then. Obviously, Kit had forgotten about him. In the fall, school had taken over. Theresa had come along, and Michael had thrown himself into his last season with the ski team. He was a senior now, and despite the huge let-down of losing touch with Kit, he'd followed through with the ambitious decision to apply to college.

And now, he thought, roaring along the dirt road on his way back to Franconia, Kit was here again!

But so much for him had changed. And from Mr. Morgan's description, Kit's life sounded like it might be one big New York party and deciding which slick, prep school guy to go out with.

Two years later, everything was different.

Chapter 11

Safe from the storm beneath the awning of Franconia's ice cream shop—the Dairy Bar—Kit and Lucy slurped at their melting towers of chocolate and vanilla swirl ice cream cones. Passengers from an unloading Trailways bus marked "Boston–Franconia Notch" huddled under rain slickers and umbrellas as thunder boomed and a brief hard shower of rain passed over them. The Dairy Bar doubled as a bus depot. A clever decision, Kit noted, as hungry arriving passengers lined up for ice cream and fried clams.

With her ice-cream-free arm, Lucy clutched to her chest a stack of celebrity magazines she'd just purchased at the General Store. Kit smiled. It had been a good day so far. At the General Store the cashier had winked at Kit and Lucy with cheerful recognition, and the owner of the Dairy Bar had greeted Kit by name.

They hadn't looked at her strangely at all. And she had to admit that it felt nice, actually, to see people who knew her, remembered her as just a normal girl.

Maybe she could do this after all.

Now, on their way back to the farm on Kit's bright blue moped, Lucy—hanging on to her sister—shouted in Kit's ear over the noise of the bike. "Where're we going, Kitty?"

"I'm taking a different way back!" At the crest of the hill, Kit curved onto a side road. It was unpaved, and she drove more slowly now. The sun shone again, after the storm. Shafts of light pierced the green canopy of trees, while the leaves shook drops of rain onto the two girls as they motored on below.

If she took this dirt road, Kit thought, it would run by the pond with the cattails and redwing blackbirds. And then, a little farther up, she'd take another left . . . she was pretty sure she could remember . . . there was a foot track, right where the road made a sharp curve to the left.

She accelerated, and the buzz of the bike's engine filled the quiet dirt road.

"What is this place?" Lucy said.

Following a narrow path, Kit led the way through a thick pine woods while Lucy straggled behind, swatting at rain-drenched branches and holding tight to her magazines. As they came out into the open, a cold, damp mist still hung in the air after the storm. Somewhere above the two girls, hidden from sight by the mist, water roared over the edge of a falls.

They'd come to a rain-slick slope of granite, beside a pool of moving water. From the falls above, water pounded down into the dark pool. Her heart thumping, Kit stood as silent and still as one of the granite boulders. Lucy shivered.

"It's a secret." The noise of the falls swallowed Kit's voice. "I used to come here," she said more forcefully. There was something important about this place—the waterfall, the pool. So hidden. She had hoped it would conjure up some memories.

"When did you come here?" Lucy demanded.

"Before." Kit stared up at the horseshoe-shaped falls.

Lucy wandered over to the pool, peered down into the water and frowned. The mist was lifting and floated in among the arms of the pine trees. She sat down on the edge and dipped a toe in. She grumbled, "It's cold. Too cold for swimming."

Her gaze caught in the falling water, Kit made no reply.

Long ago in a life before this one, in which she hadn't always felt ashamed and full of dread, Kit had found this waterfall and rock pool while exploring on her bike.

How magical it appeared to her on that first summer afternoon! With the sunlight filtering down through the trees, bouncing off the swiftly tumbling water, warming the moss-speckled granite boulders. So hidden and private! A place to elude the increasingly rigid expectations of home.

She'd snuck off to the waterfall on many slow afternoons, peddling down the long dirt road from the farm on her bicycle, in the lazy hours while other family members were napping. It was her secret, a place so hidden from the road that she assumed no one else knew about it. She skinny-dipped, explored the rocky shapes and hidden spaces of the falls, and felt the boundaries soften and dissolve between herself and all of nature.

Then—that's right!—she'd made another discovery. She remembered now. At the shallow end of the rock pool, visible only to the eyes of a young girl who had a talent for observation, she found a submerged bank of blue clay.

She'd known it was a sign! Because Kit had already decided that, one day, she would become an artist—even if she didn't know how or when.

She would arrive full of creative purpose to the waterfall and pool, and experiment with the smooth, cool, malleable clay, mixing it with dirt or sand to make it firm enough for molding figures. She pressed ferns into the wet clay, or flowers. Assured of her solitude and privacy, she never wore a bathing suit. She rubbed the blue earthy material through her long hair and over her entire body and lay in the sun while the clay cracked and dried to the pale gray color of granite.

And so, it came as a shock the day Kit discovered that she wasn't the only person who knew about this hidden waterfall and pool, after all.

That summer, two years ago. She was lying on the warm rocks beside the pool on a late afternoon. It was the summer she'd met . . . Michael. The lifeguard at the Profile Lake Club. To her complete surprise—and horror—Michael had come bursting out through the pine trees, singing loud and clueless at the top of his lungs!

He stepped onto the wide granite slab, a fishing rod resting on his shoulder, and discovered her, buck naked and slathered in blue clay, sprawled out on the rocks. He'd stood there, seemingly glued to the spot while the water poured off the cliff above them. What was he doing *here*?

And what was *she* supposed to do *now*? She lay perfectly still, pretending to be unaware of his presence—pretending to be a rock herself!—almost unable to breathe.

Was he just staring at her?

Her heart raced. She felt completely mortified. Because, not only was this awkward, to say the least, but . . . she really liked him. In fact, once he'd stopped annoying her so much with all the rules and regulations at the Club, they'd become friends. She found she could be exactly the person she wanted to be around him.

But now he'd discovered her secret!

Knowing he stood just a few feet from her was beyond horrifying. But somehow, here, away from all the judgments and restrictions and warnings that were a part of her life in general . . . here in this magical place that was hers . . . a rebellious excitement came over her.

Her body—concealed at all other times by her bathing suit—was now completely revealed to him. She was showing herself to him, wild, smeared with blue clay. A person not confined by rules of propriety, but a part of nature!

He was seeing her as she wanted to be seen.

Just keep your cool. The voice inside her head spoke without fear or embarrassment. With confidence.

She got to her feet, her back toward him, her clay-streaked blond hair falling below her shoulders. She strolled over to the edge of the pool and then dived in. When she swam back up to the surface through a pale blue watery cloud of dissolved clay, she opened her eyes. She looked directly at him.

"Hello, Michael." She raised her voice over the noise of the waterfall. "What are you staring at?" Her only option, she decided, was to go on the offensive, to act completely unfazed. Her boldness seemed to take his breath away. She could have laughed out loud!

"Throw me my dress, will you?" she ordered him, pointing at a pile of blue cloth. The sheer nerve of appearing stark naked in front of him—and observing him so befuddled—made her giddy, fierce even, with a blood-curdling rush of female power.

She hopped up out of the water and onto the ledge where he'd dropped the clothing, and pulled the dress over her head. It fell to just above her knees.

"Jesus, Kit!" Finally, Michael found his voice, "Someone could come back here, and . . . see you!"

"I guess 'someone' did. Sorry if I embarrassed you."

Served him right! He always acted so cocky around her. All that summer, Kit had been trying to maintain her edge of control, as she'd felt her attraction to him pulling her off balance. Now, the effect she was having on him filled her with self-confidence.

"I'm not the one who should be embarrassed . . ." Michael tried, pathetically, to come off as cool, to regain an advantage.

Then, she sauntered over and kissed him, square on the mouth.

Kit stood transfixed by the memory of that afternoon two summers ago. *She'd been so sure of herself!*

There was something that she had meant to tell him. About what she had planned. *Yes*—because on that afternoon she had been pretty sure that life was about to take a big turn in her favor. She was on top of the world—she had just planted a big kiss, right on the lips of this very cute boy, and now couldn't wait to see the astonishment on his face when she told him about her triumph!

But before she'd had a chance to say anything, *he'd* surprised *her.* He'd caught hold of her, awkwardly, but firmly. Pulled her tight into his arms until she felt his hard erection pressed up against her. She wasn't expecting this—she'd gasped *"Michael!"*—as he pulled the flimsy cloth of her dress up her smooth, bare thighs, over her hips . . .

The heat of his body crushed against her. His hands were all over her. Her excitement at being trapped in his arms, at her own desire . . . and then . . . and then—what?

She waited, as the memory faded; braced herself against the return of that shadowy figure in her mind elbowing forward. She readied herself . . .

"Kitty!"

"Hmmm?" Kit responded absently.

But there was no shadowy figure. There was nothing, now, but a dim memory of happiness and laughter. And a kind of glow, a light that—as she came back to the present—slowly faded.

"Let's go home now," Lucy said. Her sister was clutching her magazines to her chest with one hand, and tugging at her arm with the other. "It's getting dark."

Chapter 12

At seven a.m., the Ammonoosuc Hardware and Building Supply Store was the unofficial headquarters of Franconia's working men. When summer came around and things started to get busy, trucks and vans pulled up early in front of the store as workers and the local crew foremen made Ammonoosuc Hardware their first stop of the day.

Year-round, Michael's father, Walt Pearce, kept an industrial-size coffee urn brewing on the counter at the front of the store. A box or two of doughnuts contributed by one of the regulars sat nearby. Men out of work and some of the old-timers came in for their cup of coffee and to swap news.

With summer people returning now, the gossip turned to what kinds of projects these folks would be getting into—fence repair, driveway grading and graveling, roofs that needed reshingling, a garage or new addition.

Michael's grandfather had started Ammonoosuc Hardware, and his dad had grown up working in the family business. Both Michael's mother and father had been born and raised in Franconia. They had dated in high school, been prom king and queen; not long after graduation they'd gotten married. In short order, he had been born.

His mom knew that people had been "counting the months on their fingers," and they didn't exactly add up to nine. But she didn't care. All she'd ever wanted to do was get married and raise a family. His dad already worked after school in the hardware store, and with a new baby, Michael's grandfather had made his dad a partner in the business.

Since Michael had been old enough to see over the counter he'd helped out at the store, putting in an hour or two before school and filling in on weekends if his dad needed him. From nails and screws to doorknobs and duct tape, sheetrock and cement, animal feed, camping supplies, garden plants, and outdoor hoses, Michael knew every inch of the place. When stock ran low on a certain item, he made sure to reorder, and no matter what a customer might be looking for, he could find it.

He knew most of the local men by first name.

"Well, business is picking up again," Bernie said, holding tight to his Styrofoam cup of coffee with old, weathered hands. Like most of the old guys, he wore jeans, a checkered flannel shirt, and a cap with a John Deere tractor logo. "Fredericksons are back at their place over on Chandler Pond now. I'm sure we'll be seeing their man Yves down here soon enough. Yves told me the pipes burst during the winter and he'll likely spend the next month replacing all the maple flooring."

"You all know old Esther Winthrop died this past winter, I guess?" Rick said. "Wonder what that Victorian mansion of hers will go for? I heard some relatives in California are planning to sell the house and auction off the entire estate, beginning of July."

"I heard Bud just got sacked at the Morgan place, Cedaredge Farm," Roland announced. This piece of news put Roland in the spotlight. The other men joined in, asking, "You don't say, Rollie?" and "You sure about that?"

Landsman had mentioned Bud, Michael remembered, so he stopped working to listen, too. "Seems he'd been running around with Sam Wilson's wife, Vera. When Sam found out, he kicked

Vera out of the house. Now Bud's got more trouble on his hands than he bargained for."

All the men took this in, grunted. Michael wondered, were they imagining themselves in Sam's position, or in Bud's? An unwanted picture of some old guy humping another old guy's wife suddenly invaded his imagination and he grimaced. *Ugh.* Did old people really still *do it*? That was hard to believe.

"Bob Morgan's hired Charlie Overbee to take over," said Roland importantly.

They were itching to ask more. But just as his name was mentioned, Charlie himself walked in, making the bell on the front door jingle. All the men got quiet.

"Mornin', Bernie, Rollie, Ricky, Mike." Charlie looked around, taking in the silence. "Somebody just die in here or what?"

"Rollie says you're taking over at the Morgan place," Rick said.

"That's right, and I'll ask you boys to behave yourselves now. My new boss is right behind me."

Michael's father came out of the storeroom just as Mr. Morgan walked through the front door. "Welcome back to town, Mr. Morgan," he said.

Kit's father had said he'd been in the store before. Now Michael could tell that Morgan and his dad seemed to like each other, too. His dad was a hard worker, which he guessed Morgan would approve of. And maybe Morgan scored a few points with locals because, despite being a wealthy out-of-towner, Cedaredge's owner wasn't above showing up at the hardware store, like this morning, pouring a cup of coffee and shooting the breeze with the regular working men. Even if he did look out of place in a pin-striped shirt, khaki pants . . . and loafers!

"How can we help you today?" his father asked. Michael watched the two men. He chewed on the inside of his cheek—had

Mr. Morgan told Kit he'd stopped by to see her? He'd have to speak to him.

"Charlie here is my new manager at the farm and has permission to charge things to my account."

"That's no problem at all."

Morgan continued, "Say, do you still have those cedar fence posts out back? I'd like to take a look." Michael's father led the way and Morgan and Charlie followed, making their way through the aisles toward the back door.

"I think you know Bud, my former manager?" Michael heard Morgan say. "Well, I had to fire him. Sleeping on the job, I'm afraid. And sleeping around, too, as you've probably heard by now. Anyway, the cattle have started busting through the fences. First thing we need to do is replace some of the posts before they take the whole fence down and disappear into the woods."

The men were out back for a long time. When they returned, Morgan and Charlie were discussing the number of posts they'd probably need as they walked back to the front of the store. Michael left off with restocking and came up to the counter where Morgan now reviewed the order with his dad.

He didn't have any kind of a plan about what he was going to say or do. All he knew was that Mr. Morgan was Kit's father, and maybe his best hope of getting to see her again.

"Well, now! Here's the Dartmouth man!" Morgan greeted him, and gave him a firm clap on the back. "Walt," he said, "you and your wife must be very pleased. Shows you what intelligence, hard work, and ambition can do!"

Michael smiled and stood up taller. Mr. Morgan obviously saw him as a person with potential. He doubted Kit's father even remembered him, from two years ago, as the lifeguard at the Profile Lake Club. Which was fine with him. Now he was a "Dartmouth man."

"We're very proud of Michael, Eileen and I. Though, I won't deny we'll miss him this fall." His dad's face took on a long, sorrowful expression that made Michael feel guilty and sad—and resentful, too.

When he'd first been accepted to Dartmouth his mother had actually been angry. She'd accused the guidance counselors of going behind her back, filling her son's head with delusions of "Ivy League" grandeur. Why did he have to leave? What was wrong with the local two-year college if he wanted to take some classes? And didn't he know that his father had always hoped Michael would follow in his footsteps and take over the family business?

Did he think he was better than them?

He loved his parents, but at a certain point Michael knew one thing for damn sure: His future was not going to be running a hardware store in Franconia.

"Dad, it's not like I'm leaving the country." He didn't want to sound disrespectful, but his father's comments ticked him off, and embarrassed him in front of Mr. Morgan.

His dad sighed, and at that moment seemed pathetic to him, selfish, compared with Morgan, who showed so much enthusiasm about his Ivy League college future. He hated when his dad sounded this way.

Charlie walked out to the truck while Morgan remained at the counter, looking over the receipts. Morgan paused, as if making up his mind about something. "Mike," he said, "we're having our usual summer kickoff party this Saturday. There's always a big crowd. I guess you know Katherine. And, of course, you've met Eugenia, my niece. Well, I'm sure the kids would like to see you.

Liven things up a bit so it's not just a bunch of old folks. What do you say—why don't you stop by?"

The conversation around them dried up, as all the men became quiet. The townspeople liked to gossip about the extravagant parties they'd heard summer people threw in their big, fancy houses. None of them had ever been to one, except maybe as help.

Michael felt his face get hot. "Thank you, Mr. Morgan," he replied stiffly. "I'd really enjoy that."

"Good! It's settled. We'll expect you Saturday then! Walt—you'll take care of Charlie now, won't you?"

"You bet."

Avoiding whatever expressions the rest of the guys had on their mugs, Michael put his head down and went back to work, stocking the shelves.

Not long after, his dad tracked him down. "That sure was nice of Bob Morgan to invite you to their party. He and Mrs. Morgan must think very highly of you, son."

He muttered something in response.

"It's just too bad you won't be able to go," his dad continued.

His head jerked up. "What do you mean I *won't be able to go?*"

Suddenly, all the restless ambition Michael felt mixed together with a burning, confused determination to see Kit. He'd been given a chance, and he wasn't going to blow it! Anger erupted in him, toward his father, his mother, the guys at the hardware store—all of them! Happy with just this small, narrow life. How could this be enough for them? It wasn't enough for him.

"I'm going, Dad. You can't stop me! Mr. Morgan invited me as a guest." So what if they were townies, and didn't go to parties with people like the Morgans and their friends? That didn't mean that Kit's father wasn't serious about inviting him.

His father stepped back, caught off-guard by his son's violent reaction. "I'm not trying to stop you, Mike. It's just . . . isn't your senior prom Saturday night?"

Crap. The prom.

He'd totally forgotten about that. Again.

Chapter 13

"This was a lovely idea of yours, Robert."

Kit's mother smiled at her father as they all strolled into the dining room at the Profile Lake Club. Out front, the lake reflected the gleam of the setting sun, and lapped at the shore below the clubhouse's secluded overlook. The smooth slope and undulation of the golf course extended behind the grand lodge.

They'd come for the summer buffet dinner, a particular favorite of her father's. Her father liked to dress up, and wore his navy sports jacket with the New York Yacht Club patch, paired with those goofy, bright plaid summer slacks. He enjoyed showing off Kit's glamorous mother, too, who tonight wore a lemon-yellow skirt and short jacket ensemble from her dressmaker in Italy.

Elliot squirmed in his blazer, while Lucy appeared deceptively sweet in her sporty green-striped sleeveless dress. Her mother had raised an eyebrow—but said nothing—about Kit's thrift shop find: a gypsy dress, long and red, and flowing to a point in the front and back, like a red bandanna.

"Yes, I thought it would be a nice idea, Bun. No reason—no reason at all—to avoid the Club. The dinner selections look excellent, as always."

Seated at the table now, Kit squinted out across the lake. Her stomach clenched. It was there again, the dark flicker of memory.

With a kick under the table, Elliot brought her attention back to the family group. "Sorry!" he said, grinning. "I meant

to kick Lucy!" Genia waved a hand in the air, flagging the cocktail waiter. Her snug white shift with big pink roses showed off
her tan.

"Genia, dear, is that your second martini? I'd slow down if
I were you," remarked Kit's mother. "Your parents will be here
tomorrow, so there will be no sleeping in."

"Shall we see what they've put on for us tonight?" her father
announced. At this signal, they all pushed out their chairs and
walked over to the long white-clothed tables. "I'm surprised Brandon didn't want to join us," he remarked.

"He came home from tennis this afternoon with *a terrible* sun-
burn." Genia responded to the edge in her uncle's voice with an
exaggerated excuse.

Kit wondered if Brandon was on his way back to his favorite
bar in Littleton.

Enormous ice sculptures of leaping trout and geese on the
wing decorated the long tables. Platters of French cheeses, stuffed
mushrooms, cold meats, and shrimp cocktail were followed by
lobster tails, poached salmon, roasts on the carving board, an
array of desserts. Her father presented his plate to the chef who
was sawing off slices from an immense filet mignon. But he had
his eye on Elliot. "Some steak first, chum, before you start in on
cake and ice cream."

Back at the table, while everyone else ate, Kit picked at her
food. An uneasy desire to get away from everyone, an urge to go
down to the lake, kept heckling her. Finally, she looked up. "I'm
sorry, Daddy, Mother. I'm just not that hungry. I think I'll take a
walk outside, until we're ready for dessert . . ."

"Now, Kit—" her father began.

"It's fine, Robert," her mother cut in. "This won't be produc-
tive, arguing at the dinner table."

Her father grumbled. "Well, at least take Lucy and Elliot with you, for a game of croquet! Go along now, kids, join your sister."

As the three Morgan children got up to leave, Kit overheard Genia say to her mother, "Aunt Bunny? I wonder if we could talk about . . . you know . . . !"

The grass croquet playing court lay directly below the clubhouse. Beyond this precisely mowed lawn, and reached by a wooden walkway and flight of stairs, a crescent of sandy beach hugged the shoreline of Profile Lake. The beach, where Kit and her family had spent every summer, appeared empty and quiet this evening.

The lake glowed in the waning light; the shifting movement of its surface made her skin prickle.

Lucy and Elliot banged around in the green chest holding croquet mallets and balls: "Kitty, you can be yellow. I'll be red, and Elliot—you're green."

The crack of the balls echoed as the game started. "Kitty! Come on, pay attention," Elliot complained. "It's your turn."

"Sorry," she said. She grasped the mallet with her two hands, eyed her target, and thwacked the ball through the wicket, earning another shot. Her second hit flew across the court and out of bounds. The sight of the water unnerved her. *Stop looking at it, then*, she told herself, turning from the lake with its secrets, and trying to focus on the croquet field.

She'd had a plan. She remembered how excited she'd been to tell Michael. Almost every day she'd come to the Club, meeting him for an early-morning paddle and looking forward to his breaks when he'd stroll over to her and they'd spar and tease and flirt. He'd be so surprised!

Her scheme had come about as a result of a conversation, at one of the summer parties at Cedaredge, between an old friend of her grandfather's named Esther Winthrop and her parents. She liked Miss Winthrop. And even though Kit had been sixteen at the time, and Esther Winthrop was beyond ancient, Kit could tell that this opinionated old woman in the exotic flowered Chinese jacket had once been a rebel. Maybe still was.

Kit overheard Miss Winthrop mention that she was a trustee of a private school near Franconia.

"It's a kind of 'alternative' school—with high educational standards, but more outdoor activities, and art—and believe me, Bunny, it's just as good as any place in New York City—and less narrow minded!"

The school was here, in New Hampshire. Near *Franconia*!

Kit was suddenly paying attention. "I'd like to see that school," she said, interrupting the conversation. And perhaps because her parents didn't want to appear rude to the elderly and extremely wealthy Miss Winthrop, they looked at each other, smiled politely, and agreed.

Miss Winthrop secured an interview for her, in which Kit, grasping at the chance being offered, blurted out: "I want to study studio art. Three-dimensional art, I think. I . . . I plan to be an artist!"

It was the opposite of everything she knew her parents wanted and expected of her. Supporting "The Arts" was one thing, her father emphasized, as he wrote out his yearly check to The Metropolitan Museum of Art. "Your mother and I are all in favor of 'The Arts,' however . . ."

However, in her parents' view, artists themselves were self-absorbed, drug addicts, antisocial proponents of free love, troublemaking, irresponsible members of society who frequently "died in the gutter." An embarrassment to their families. And on and on.

But with Miss Winthrop at her side, Kit had felt emboldened. And the old lady encouraged her, as if she were Kit's champion. She assured Kit that she would be a "shoo-in!"

Kit had been on the verge of telling Michael. Was just dying to see his face. *Look!* I am designing my future, as an artist. She would stay in New Hampshire; they wouldn't have to wait until the next summer to see each other. She didn't want to wait.

Going to school in Franconia, she'd be able to meet Michael after classes, for hikes in the fall. They would discuss art, of course. She wondered what his opinions were about nature . . . from a . . . metaphysical, creative perspective . . . and not just as a lifeguard. Maybe, she would agree to let him teach her to ski.

The future had unfolded in her mind, in brilliant, breathless color. They would be together.

"Elliot!" Lucy's shouts across the croquet court drew Kit back to the gray and confused present. Her brother had hit the ball out of bounds, on purpose, and stormed off, back toward the clubhouse. "He always does this when he's about to lose," Lucy fumed.

"He probably hasn't been able to stop thinking about the dessert table. I'll go get the ball," Kit offered. Lucy followed her brother.

She could admit to herself, without Elliot and Lucy around to see how crushed she felt, the pain of remembering those aborted plans. In New York, where the kids at school moved around in tight, self-conscious cliques, she hadn't any close friends. She mistook, or was oblivious to, the social clues of her peers, which made others think her odd, someone to avoid. She was a dreamer, and mostly preferred her own company.

She'd wanted to stay here! And go to school where she could focus exclusively on art. She had a talent, she knew she did, for realizing an idea in a drawing, or a three-dimensional piece. But in all of her other classes she struggled or, perversely, dug her heels in and failed. Which only led to all her free time being taken over by tutors. In New York, failure was not a socially acceptable option. If nothing else, she would pass.

At this school in New Hampshire, it would be different, she believed.

And . . . she had wanted to be near him.

It made her feel weak and pathetic to admit this to herself. She was *a loser*—because she had failed. But it didn't matter anymore, did it? Kit walked down the steps to the beach, and went to pick up the green croquet ball from the sand. The water lay out in front of her, iridescent and silent, drawing her to look at it.

As the sun's reflection faded across the lake's surface, another memory flickered.

She was swimming across the lake. She'd been in the habit of sneaking back here in the evenings, after the beach had closed, escaping from the farm on her bike. When it was dark enough to swim unnoticed, she'd pull with long strokes out to the center of the lake.

Floating on her back, her body rising and falling with the movement of the water's surface, she'd watch as the first stars appeared. And then the moon! A deep sense of belonging, of being connected to water and sky, suffused her being. She felt safe, cared for, as if held in the cupped hands of some greater benevolent force in the universe.

She always made it back to the farm without being noticed. The rounds of summer cocktail parties kept her parents busy most nights until late. Everyone drank a lot. And it was easy to disappear in Cedaredge, the house rambled in so many directions. Her absence was never observed, as far as she knew, or remarked upon—not even by Elsie.

The shadow was there again, now, standing right beside her. It chilled her, made her tremble: *Wasn't it strange*, this shadow seemed to be asking, that she could be gone, disappear, for hours, without attracting any attention? *Wasn't it strange* that no one ever noticed where she'd been, even until the next day? So many things could happen . . .

The lake flattened into darkness. Now, she couldn't imagine going back into the water again, she couldn't fathom ever wanting to swim again. Not after what she'd done.

As she walked back up the stairs from the beach and across the croquet field, she felt old—as if, at eighteen, everything good in her life, worth looking forward to, was over. Finished.

Once, she'd been fearless, it seemed—fully at home in her own strong body. She'd taken for granted, as she swam and swam across the cold night water, that the forces of nature were looking out for her. Protecting her. But they hadn't been able to protect her from herself.

"Robert, dear—you did what?" As Kit walked up the path from the lake, she could hear the tension in her mother's voice as it emanated from the clubhouse porch. Her parents were seated, with after-dinner drinks in their hands.

"Yes, I invited him. Why not? He's ambitious and well spoken. I want to see her enjoying herself this summer, Bun! And she doesn't have many friends here."

"He is not the kind of friend we want to encourage, Robert!"

"Mother? Daddy? What are you talking about?" Kit asked. She forced a smile for her parents.

"Go take a look at the dessert table, Kitty, dear. I'm sure you'll find something you'll like," her mother coaxed her. "Your father and I are just enjoying the evening."

Chapter 14

Saturday came, and Michael and Tom met in Littleton to pick up their rental tuxedos. He owed Tom an apology. "Sorry about leaving you stranded the other night at Ollie's."

"Yeah! You seemed pretty ticked off, man. Things all right with you and Theresa?"

"Fine." He sounded unconvincing.

But Tom quickly dropped it. "Good! So let's forget about it because tonight is 'Cruise Night'—or whatever they're calling the prom this year!"

"And lucky for you," Michael needled his friend, "you've got a prettier date than a Pet Rock."

Tom had finally gotten up the nerve to ask Michael's sister, Jennifer, to the prom. She had agreed, and now Tom couldn't resist acting all cocky and basically annoying the heck out of him.

They drove back to Franconia, to Tom's place, to put on their tuxes. Tom's family lived downtown in a small two-story house like his family's. They elbowed each other in front of the tiny living room mirror trying to see just exactly how ridiculous they looked.

Michael had picked out a black tux—low profile, he hoped. Tom had gone for flashy powder blue. In their clip-on bow ties and ruffled white shirts, he realized, miserably, they both looked exactly like—

"Waiters?" Tom joked, reading his mind.

"Damn—yes!"

"Cheer up! It's not what the guys are wearing that counts, right, man?"

Half joking, but half not, he grabbed Tom by the shirtfront: "You better not have that horn-dog expression on your face when I see you with my sister!"

"Hey! Hands to yourself. You're messing up my ruffles!"

Tom took one more fortifying hit off his joint. "See you at the prom!" he crowed, and then took off in his souped-up Camaro to pick up Jennifer.

Michael stood next to the truck in his monkey suit. Completely weighted down with a sense of doom.

In Theresa's mind, he knew, tonight was the deadline to make a decision: Fish or cut bait. For weeks he'd been: *one*, doing his best to avoid thinking about it at all; or: *two*, trying to talk himself into the idea that getting engaged might be the best thing, the most grown-up and realistic.

After all, hadn't he always been attracted to Theresa's fiery, take-no-shit personality? And Theresa always said that it would be hard to find anyone else who would put up with him the way she did. Maybe those were good enough reasons to get married. Maybe that's what it all came down to.

And yet, he was afraid of what his answer would be, if he were really honest and asked himself: Did he love her?

"Congratulations!" announced the principal, who stood at the entrance to the high school gym to welcome all the couples in their fancy dress-up clothes. Theresa wore a strapless pink sequined gown with a neckline that just managed to contain her breasts, while a long slit up the side of the dress revealed most of her thigh. Definitely not the subtle approach. Michael took a deep breath and wished he could feel anything but dread as she tiptoed beside him in high heels, and enveloped them both in an invisible cloud of cherry vanilla perfume.

The principal shook Michael's hand and gave Theresa an awkward pat on her bare shoulder. "You two have a wonderful prom! Remember, this is your night!"

How many proms had the high school principal been to, standing there and repeating those same stale lines? As if high school prom somehow represented the biggest thing that was ever going to happen in any of their lives. Michael tried to ignore that incredibly depressing thought.

This year's prom theme was "Cruise Night," and the Prom Committee had gone all out, decorating the gym with streamers, balloons, and flashy travel posters to places none of them would probably ever get to see—Mexico, Tahiti, the Greek Isles.

As he and Theresa got in line with all the other couples to collect their fake tropical cocktails, some way-too-enthusiastic members of the Senior Yearbook Club handed them each a pair of silly-looking plastic sunglasses and draped Hawaiian-type necklaces over their heads.

Everyone around them was talking and laughing at once. As if they hadn't just seen each other in class the day before. "Oh my God! I love your dress!" Dawn, Sherrie, and Jackie tottered over to them in their wedgie platform heels. Even gawky Jackie had snagged a date—probably with some coaching from Theresa. *Christ*, he thought. They were all wearing mood rings now. And as if to confound the entirety of mankind, each stone glowed a different color on each girl's hand.

He stood there, an accessory, knowing full well that what was called for was a smug expression plastered across his face. The look that said, "Yeah, I'm dressed up like a clown, but so what?

I'm just here for the post-prom action." But the whole thing felt unreal, like an out-of-body experience.

It was beginning to dawn on him what a terrible, hypocritical position he had put himself in. If he hadn't really been sure before, as the night dragged on Michael knew that no way would he be asking Theresa to get married.

Like some kind of crazy, possibly disastrous miracle, Kit had returned. Now the vivid memories of her sudden bright laughter and her fierce opinions, and that feeling he had in her physical presence that every nerve in his body was on fire, had busted through the steel bolts guarding a past he had tried to forget.

Why had he just gone along with the whole prom idea? Why hadn't he thought this through? Was it just that he'd felt too guilty to even consider letting Theresa down? Like, did he seriously think that was going to change how hurt and angry she would be later on?

He snuck a look at his watch again. On top of all the other weak, sneaky-ass deceptions, he had to add this: While he stood stiffly by Theresa's side, giving the impression—to Theresa and everyone else—that he was her soon-to-be fiancé, his mind was obsessing: *Would there still be time to get up to the Morgans' party tonight?*

The music cranked up louder. "Come on!" Theresa shouted. She pushed Michael toward the dance floor, where the rest of their friends were gathering.

As the evening turned to full-blown cruise theme with the Styx ballad "Come Sail Away," all the couples tried to get down with the dance moves in their fancy prom clothes. When "Wastin' Away Again in Margaritaville" came up next, everyone in the room—including Tom and his sister, Jenny—cheered, pumped their fists in the air, and sang along with Jimmy Buffett's Key West crooning.

As Buffett wailed, "some people claim that there's a *woman to blame*!" Theresa spread her arms wide, threw her head back, and shook her body in a belly dancer shimmy, shaking her sequined breasts first at Michael and then at everyone around them—including Tom. Jenny, beside Tom, gave Michael a little wave as if she felt sorry for him.

"You are getting lucky tonight, my friend!" shouted a beefy football jock in his ear, as the big beef and his pals whistled and clapped.

By 9:30, he had to get out of there.

The gym started to empty out as couples slipped away to find some private place to park in the woods by the lake, the traditional location for drinking, smoking pot, and making out. The far side of the lake was the supposed haunt of the mythical axe-wielding "Hermit of the Lake"—the Franconia version of Bigfoot. Michael shook his head as guys teased their dates about leaving them to the mercy of this terrifying madman. Then lots of drunken shrieks and giggles. He dragged Theresa toward the exit.

Normally, she would have argued and wanted to be the last one to leave the party. But she didn't tonight. And he knew why: She assumed that now he would be taking her off to some quiet place to propose.

Instead, he drove her directly home.

"So, is this it then, Mike? This is how our big night's going to end? Are you just going to drop me off and leave?"

What a colossal jerk he'd been! Why had it taken so long to see things clearly, to be honest with himself—and with her? He fumbled for something to say.

"I'm so sorry, Theresa. I'm sorry tonight didn't turn out the way you'd hoped. You look so incredible, you really do. You were absolutely the hottest girl at the prom."

"I don't understand what's wrong with you, Mike." Theresa's voice shook. "This was supposed to be a really important night for us. And it still could be, *in a lot of ways*," she hinted. "Is it something wrong with me?"

"No, Theresa! God, no. It's me. I just—I'm not sure . . . I'm not sure what I want," he lied. And now he felt embarrassed for them both, that the temptation she dangled no longer stirred him. He repeated, lamely, "I'm so sorry."

She twisted in her seat to face him, and her eyes narrowed. "You're sorry? All this time, you made me feel like you *knew* what you wanted, that you wanted me! And now I've wasted all my time on you. *Fuck you*, Michael Pearce!"

Tears rolled down her cheeks, trailing dark mascara. Her hand flashed out and she slapped him, hard.

In his shock, he couldn't tell whether his face burned more from the sharp, unexpected blow—or from the humiliation of knowing that he totally deserved it.

Theresa began to sob, and then she grabbed the door handle. He jumped out of the truck and hurried around to help her, but she was already out and running up the walk to the front door of the house. She slammed the door behind her.

A few seconds later, the outside light over the front door snapped off. He stood in the dark, then turned and walked slowly back to the truck.

He could have just gone home. It was after ten o'clock.

All evening, as couples had posed for their prom pictures, as he and all his friends had slow-danced to the songs that had been the soundtrack to their high school years, Michael's brain had been feverishly trying to work out if he could still make it up to the

Morgans' place that night.

Knowing how hopeful Theresa must have been, that this would be the special night confirming their future together, and meanwhile he was trying to calculate how quickly he could wrap up the dance and take her home, filled him with shame.

He could have just gone home. Contemplated what a complete shit he'd been. But instead, he put the truck in gear, floored the gas pedal, and took off for Sugar Hill.

Chapter 15

In the dark countryside far from town, at the top of the long sweep of pasture, lights shone through the trees from the house at Cedaredge Farm.

Michael turned his truck into the driveway, and drove slowly around to the front of the house. Here, a few cars were still pulled up on the grass below the porch: the usual family station wagons, a jeep, and a pack of gleaming convertible sports cars—two BMWs, an Alfa Romeo, and a Mercedes. He continued past them, and parked his pickup truck beside the stand of tall lilac trees. The night had grown warm and humid, and the sweet smell of lilac blossoms hung in the air.

He walked toward the house, and as he got close to the front steps, he stopped.

A girl with blond hair, with her back toward him, leaned against the railing of the porch. She wore a short, white tennis dress and her feet were bare. Was it Kit? It had been two years, now, since Michael had last seen her, and in the dark he couldn't tell.

She waved a cigarette in her right hand, and said something funny to the rest of the group lounging around her. Michael heard laughter and the clinking of glasses. He saw the girl lean forward toward one of her friends, as if with a private joke. More laughter.

Suddenly, he couldn't imagine himself barging in on that scene. Parents and older people had probably left or gone to bed. And now, here on the porch lounged Kit and her friends from New

York, who obviously partied together, drove expensive cars, and presumably all went to the same exclusive private schools. What the hell had he been thinking?

He didn't belong here. He'd been an idiot to accept Mr. Morgan's invitation in the first place!

The blond girl turned her head to the side, blowing cigarette smoke, and as she did, she noticed Michael. "Hey! The party's up here!" she called out to him. She moved to the staircase, and started down the front steps. Unsteady on her feet, the girl tripped and grabbed the metal railing.

It was Genia. And she'd obviously had a few drinks. "Well, look who's here! It's the lifeguard!" she called to her friends.

He hurried up the stairs, then, not wanting her to fall down the steps in her apparent enthusiasm at seeing him. "Hey, handsome," she said, flirty and tipsy, and linked her arm through his, "come join us." Definitely a friendlier version of Eugenia than the girl he'd met on the porch a week or more ago, who could barely bother to speak to him.

Two other girls and a guy with this face screwed up in a sulky expression had draped themselves across the porch furniture. The girls in big armchairs, the boy sprawled with his feet up on one of the couches. They all looked rumpled, but in a rich, country club way. The low table between them held scattered glasses and an impressive collection of booze: gin, bourbon, vodka, two kinds of scotch. A couple of tennis racquets and a pair of sneakers lay piled up against the porch railing.

Everyone was smoking.

"Hey," he said. "I'm Michael."

"He's Kit's friend, and he's a lifeguard—isn't that *adorable*?" Genia announced to the others. "Come sit down next to me, lifeguard," she ordered him, and plopped onto one of the wicker couches. "Make yourself a drink if you like."

The girls appraised him like smiling tigresses deciding where to take the first bite. Then the dark-haired girl, whose oversized white T-shirt had slipped off one smooth, tanned shoulder, said invitingly, "So you're really a lifeguard, Michael? I'm Emily. You can rescue me *anytime*."

"What a little adventuress you are!" Genia chided Emily. "What about Chad?"

"Chad is a bore. And—Chad chose to stay in the city. To work. Besides, it's a free country, isn't it?" Emily winked at Michael.

"The New Hampshire state motto *is* 'Live Free or Die,'" Michael joked.

She laughed. "That is so cute! The lifeguard has a sense of humor, too!" Then Emily turned to Genia, "Gigi, speaking of your cousin, where *is* our little wounded bird, Kitty, anyway? I haven't seen her all night."

Wounded. What did she mean? he wondered.

"How should I know where she is?" Genia snapped, and chewed on the thick gold chain around her neck. "All this fuss about Kitty. It's so tiresome! *Kit, Kit, Kit.* Get over it, I say! It's just enough already!" She took a sharp drag on her cigarette.

Emily said, "Oh, you'll be the center of attention soon enough, Gigi dear." The sly remark seemed to make Genia happy. "Ha!" she chortled, and the two girls clinked glasses. "Cheers to that!"

The boy took a slug of what looked like scotch. He flashed around a big, stainless-steel watch—one of the new, outrageously expensive kind, with the digital face. He announced: "Lifeguard? He doesn't look like a lifeguard to me—he looks more like . . . a waiter! What's up with that outfit?" The boy burst into a high-pitched cackle, as if he hoped to get the girls to join in with him.

Michael had tossed his tux jacket into the back of the truck on his way to Cedaredge, but otherwise he was still, unfortunately, dressed in his monkey suit. "I was at my senior prom tonight," he said to the group. "I didn't have time to change."

"The prom!" The girls giggled delightedly.

Embarrassed, he unclipped the ridiculous bow tie and jammed it into his pocket. Like that was going to make a big difference.

"Oh my God, a clip-on!" The boy droned. "How tacky!"

What a douche bag. Michael thought about asking the kid if his great big shiny watch compensated for something else that was pathetically small.

"Reggie, shut up and don't be so mean," said the other girl with a short, red-haired bob who'd been silent, sucking on her drink. She tossed an ice cube at Reggie. "Aah! Stop!" He batted it away with a weak flap.

Emily broke in smoothly. "Michael, you have to excuse us— Anne, Gigi, Reggie, me—we're *jealous* of you, that's all. We went to private schools, where there aren't things like 'proms.' We just have these stuffy debutante cotillions, where girls 'come out' and have to curtsy in front of a bunch of old sows. Terribly stiff. Nothing as sexy as a high school prom!"

Reggie frowned, and Genia started to make herself another drink. "Oh—we're out of limes. Damn. I need a lime," she moaned dramatically. She looked around as if expecting one to appear out of thin air.

No one moved. "I haven't seen any of the staff for hours, if that's who you're looking for, Gigi," Anne said. "You might just have to go without, sweetie. Sacrifice."

Michael grabbed the opportunity to make his exit and explore the house. "I guess it's on me, since I'm in the waiter outfit," he joked, and got to his feet.

"See," Genia cooed, "he *is* a lifeguard. He's saving my life! I am going *to die* if I don't get a lime for my gin and tonic."

Genia looked up at him with big eyes and the kind of smile that, obviously, she used to get guys to do what she wanted. He didn't care. "Wish me luck!" he said, grinning back at her, relieved to make his getaway.

The front door with its heavy brass knocker had been left open for the party, and Michael wandered into the house, down the long walnut-paneled front hallway.

A pair of 1950s cross-country skis as well as a couple of sets of wood and rawhide snowshoes decorated the walls, mounted between expensive-looking antique gold sconces that glowed in the dark passageway. The flickering light seemed to add glamour to the vintage black-and-white photographs at the end of the hallway, of familiar resorts he knew like Cannon and Mittersill, and Bretton Woods at Mt. Washington.

At the entrance to the living room, Michael hesitated, intimidated by the grandeur of the space. The large stone fireplace on the far side of the room immediately caught his eye, while to the right, a curved staircase with a carved railing led to the upstairs. A chandelier with amber-colored crystals glowed above the stairs.

The golden-yellow color of the walls, the dark reds and blues of the thick, patterned rugs on the polished wood floors, the silky-looking materials that covered several couches and arrangements of chairs—it all looked so different from the houses of anyone he knew.

Paintings hung from the walls, too, in elaborate gold frames, and they must have been real, not posters or prints like in his house. He realized this when he recognized the large painting over the fireplace as a portrait of Mrs. Morgan wearing a gown and posing with a very young Kit and her brother and sister.

To one side of the fireplace, two older men sat in tall armchairs. Behind them rose a wall of built-in bookcases. The only place Michael had ever seen that many books was in the Franconia library. The standing lamp beside the bookshelves threw a soft light on the men's faces. One of the men was Mr. Morgan.

He took a deep breath and crossed the room toward the fireplace, to say hello, and to thank Mr. Morgan for inviting him to Cedaredge. The men bent toward each other, a chessboard between them, and muttered in conversation.

"I took a real beating on that fund Jeffries recommended. So, Bob, the loan I'm suggesting would just be to tide us over until after the wedding," said Morgan's companion. "You know I hate to upset your sister, Libby, with discussions about money."

"She's not going to be any happier having that conversation with me," Morgan grumbled. "Wes, this might be a good time to reevaluate that suite at the Carlyle and all those club memberships, in addition to the Connecticut house. And the trip to Italy this spring? You and Libby are overextended. Time to cut back."

"So, you'll help us, Bob? It's just a short-term loan."

"I'll call my man over at Merrill Lynch and see what he thinks I can do. But, Wes, something's got to change."

"Absolutely. And it's going to, right after the wedding. You have my word."

"Excuse me," Michael said. He was standing in front of the two men. "Sorry to interrupt. But I wanted to say hello, Mr. Morgan. Thank you for inviting me to the party."

Morgan looked up at him and squinted. It took Kit's father a second to figure out who he was, and the tux probably didn't help. Then Morgan said, "Ah, Mike! Glad you could make it. Did someone get you a drink?" he asked.

"No, sir, but that's fine. Actually, I'm looking for Kit."

"Kit? Well, now—it's late. I know the younger kids have gone upstairs to bed. Kit may have followed them. Or, she may be around here somewhere. Check the billiard room—it's just down those stairs, other side of the fireplace; Brandon should be in there with his college chums. He might know where to find Kit. And he can get you a drink. Stay as long as you like, my boy."

Brandon, again.

Michael crossed the living room and took the short flight of stairs down to a more intimate room with an enormous pool table in the center. A big, square-jawed young man at one end of the table was just setting up for a shot. He was probably in his twenties, Michael figured, with sun-bleached hair and movie-star good looks—like one of those Calvin Klein jeans models. His white shirt rolled up at the sleeves showed off a deep tan; a woven rope bracelet wrapped around his wrist.

"Nice one, Brandon," the kid next to him said, as the big guy took his shot and sunk three balls into the pockets. The two other guys studied the remaining landscape of balls.

So. This was Brandon. Kit's boyfriend? According to Mr. Morgan, he would know Kit's whereabouts.

Brandon raised his head. "Help you?" he asked.

"I'm a friend of Kit's. Her father thought you might know where she is. Name's Michael Pearce."

Brandon looked at Michael curiously, as if appraising him, while the kid beside him snorted, "I didn't know Kit was friends with any waiters." Michael's face burned as chuckles went round the pool table.

Anne, the redhead from the porch, came tottering down the stairs and into the billiard room, interrupting them. She stopped, and reached for Michael's arm to steady herself. "He's not a waiter!" she said, drunk and too loud. "He's a *lifeguard*! Isn't that just sooooo sexy?" She wrapped her arms around Michael and, to his astonishment, slid a hand down inside the front of his shirt.

He almost burst out laughing. Normally—well, not that this was in any way normal—he would have been totally uncomfortable with this girl's drunken antics. But after yet another insulting "waiter" remark, Michael figured he'd make the most of it. Like, this was just the usual, having pretty girls throw themselves at him.

"Happy to see you again, too, honey." He grinned at Anne. Then he gently removed her arm. He caught Brandon watching him.

"Duckie," Anne whined with a babyish voice as she turned her attention to one of Brandon's other friends, "let me have a hit of that magic powder, too, will you?" Michael had never seen cocaine before, but he guessed that must be what Duckie was now snorting off the side of the pool table.

Anne slid over toward Duckie with her hand on the table to steady herself. She stumbled and her hand slipped, accidentally knocking into a couple of the pool balls and scattering them.

"Jesus, Anne!" Brandon flushed purple, and looked like he was going to explode.

Anne cried out, "Oh! I'm so sorry!"

On impulse, Michael moved toward Anne, as if she needed protecting. Then Brandon smirked at him, and he pulled Anne into his arms. Teasingly, he muttered into her ear, "You owe me, sweetheart. At least a fresh drink! For ruining my shot."

"I'm so sorry!" Anne babbled. "Really, I am."

Brandon patted Anne's rump. "Make me another drink!" Then he turned back to Michael.

"Kit's not here," he said, "as you can see. Are you interested in joining us for a game?" His tone wasn't hostile—but not particularly friendly either.

"I'll pass," Michael said. He hadn't given up on finding Kit.

"Suit yourself."

Michael felt Brandon's eyes on him as he left through the door on the far side of the room. Then he passed through a music room with a big grand piano. From here, another doorway led down a short hall with a telephone table, through a pantry, and into the kitchen. In the refrigerator, he found a bowl of limes.

Back on the porch, he put the bowl down in front of Genia, Emily, and Reggie. Anne, apparently, had stayed to mix cocktails or snort coke around the pool table.

"Sorry," Michael said, "I got delayed." All three looked up at him blankly; he no longer held any interest. The limes, too, had been forgotten and the bottle of gin—empty.

Chapter 16

"Oh, Freddie! This is where they've put you? Locked up like this!" Kit peered through the slats of a large, bunker-style pen that had been constructed behind the milking barn. Inside, the bull stood alone. He'd grown to massive proportions, no longer the gangly calf that Kit remembered.

He raised his head at the sound of her voice, and she reached in between the slats with a handful of grass. Freddie turned, snuffled at her hand, and pulled at the fresh, green offering.

"I'll talk to Daddy about getting you out of here," she whispered. "I promise."

Finding poor Freddie barricaded into what seemed like a prison cell somehow made Kit think of her own isolation. Two years ago, they had both been free. Now, look at them! Each, in their own way, had become trapped.

A feeling of gloom at discovering the poor, incarcerated bull dragged her down as she returned toward the main house. The raucous shouts of laughter and competing musical selections on the stereo still blasted in waves across the fields, as they had been all evening: Johnny Mathis crooning "Come Back to Me" to her parents' friends. As the night wore on, Mick Jagger barked, "I can't get no satisfaction!" and Blondie shouted, "Call me!"

The summer rounds of parties had begun.

Guests had arrived hours earlier to Cedaredge, laughing and parading—or stumbling—up the front staircase, some carrying their own cocktails from a previous stop on the party circuit. Kit cringed at the thought of joining the rest of her family, a stiff smile plastered across her face, as she faked being just a normal, happy-kid-on-her-way-to-college for her parents' inebriated friends.

Instead, as soon as the first cars had rumbled up the driveway, she'd blown through the kitchen back door, ducking past Elsie on her way out while the housekeeper gave orders to the staff. She'd cut across the field beyond the house, a handful of hors d'oeuvres pilfered from Elsie's tray stuffed into her sweatshirt pocket.

Then, she'd made her way up to the barn to hang out with the cows.

It was so quiet here, and calm. The placid, accepting demeanor of the animals blotted out the frenzy of humans down at the house.

Kit did her best to avoid these evenings in which the summer residents of Sugar Hill circulated from one party to the next. Almost always, the party-goers seemed to end the evening at the Morgans' farm, the women dangling wineglasses on Cedaredge's expansive porch—and the men entangled with Brandon or her father in the billiards room, brandishing cigars and cue sticks.

But now, hours later, most of the cars had pulled out of the long driveway, disappearing slowly down the hill, headlights flickering, until they were gone. The house had settled into quiet. The stars seemed to brighten as the commotion of people faded, and the big cedar trees stretched up toward the lush, inky-dark sky.

Banjo had come to find her in the garden gazebo; she'd ducked in here to wait, on her way back from the barn, and fallen asleep on the cushioned bench.

She got up, rubbed her face, and walked through the garden. She followed the dog as he trotted toward the back entrance to the porch that was overhung with purple blossoming clematis vines. In the still darkness, her spirits lifted and she breathed in the scents of cedar and lilac. Peepers—tiny frogs—chirped loudly from a marshy pond down by the woods below the field; she noticed the blinking of fireflies in the tall grass bordering the groomed lawns and gardens.

She would move inconspicuously into the house, then up the stairs to her bedroom. Once again, she had pulled off her vanishing act. Her parents' parties made it easy to disappear. She yawned, stepping onto the porch.

Her feet were bare, her hair rumpled, and she had on jeans and a bulky sweatshirt with the hood pulled up. In the dark, Kit might have slipped unnoticed past the figure who emerged now, out of nowhere, startling her.

He'd been leaning against the waist-high stone parapet, staring out at the night sky. But suddenly, as if he'd felt the shift in the atmosphere, as if he'd recognized the charge in the air from the particular protons and electrons that surrounded her, the young man swung around on the porch, and faced her.

"*Kit.*" He stood completely still.

Banjo ambled over to him. Hoping for a pat, the dog looked up, expectant, wagging his tail.

Kit froze. As if she had come upon a stranger standing in front of her. But—he knew her name.

Michael? It couldn't be.

The Michael she remembered from the lake had been . . . a boy. Wiry and young. Standing before her now was some-one else: taller, broader, more substantial. A person standing his ground.

"Hello?" She pushed back against the truth as it became evident before her own eyes. The dark, unruly hair. That particular way he'd had of holding his body: shoulders relaxed, feet slightly apart, alert, facing her head-on and direct. How many daydreams had she lost herself in, these past years, remembering . . . She hadn't honestly believed she would ever see Michael again.

"If you're here for the party, I think it's almost over," Kit rattled off, still posturing that she didn't recognize him. She hunched and shoved her hands into her jeans pockets. How would he have even known where to find her?

He smiled and studied her more closely. Those hazel-green eyes she remembered by heart. She pulled back, trying to hide herself beneath the baggy jeans and oversized sweatshirt. "Kit," he said. "It's Michael. From the Profile Lake Club. Remember?" He took a step toward her.

Blood drummed in her ears.

He had seemed to haunt every place she revisited, a ghost from another life, as she'd moved through these last days alert for clues to her past. And now—he was here. At her house! How was that possible? Not a ghost but a warm, breathing human being. Standing very still, waiting for her to make a decision. Waiting for her . . . to say his name.

"Michael?"

Her voice rose barely above a whisper. "What . . . what are you doing here, at Cedaredge? I mean, out here . . . all alone on the porch?"

She felt a gentle fluttering, like butterflies winging inside of her. "I guess . . . I didn't recognize you. Without the binoculars and the orange shorts. I mean, a tux? Aren't you . . . a little overdressed?" How easy it was, to fall into teasing him again! Like they were back at the lake and no time had passed at all.

"What—this? Just my usual party clothes! And, hey, before you start in on my wardrobe, what about that sweatshirt, Kit? It's, like, gorilla-sized. I doubt they'll let you into this party looking like that," he said, grinning. "This is a high-class establishment."

It was the voice she remembered, playful, poking fun at her. She could feel her face relax, her body, too. She planted her hands on her hips and stuck her chin out at him. "Gorilla!?" Something inside of her moved toward him.

He smiled, and then confessed, "Truth is, I came directly to Cedaredge from my senior prom. I didn't have time to change. Unfortunately, now your friends are under the impression that I'm one of the waiters."

"*My* friends?" She raised her eyebrows. "Oh . . . Genia. Yeah." She rolled her eyes and laughed. "A waiter? Really?" A nervy excitement gripped her, pleasure at seeing him. But . . . he was looking at her so intently. It scared her, a little. She dropped her gaze.

He took a step closer, and spoke in an easy rhythm, as if they were just picking up an old conversation. "Your father stopped by my dad's hardware store this week, when I was working—he told me your family always had a big party to kick off the summer, and, well, he invited me. I was pretty stoked! I wanted to come earlier, to see you, but . . . the prom . . . and then . . ." His voice trailed off.

"Daddy invited you?" Kit looked up, surprised.

"Hey, Kit—what are you doing out there? Who're you talking to?" Kit turned. From where they stood, she could see the large male silhouette at the far end of the porch. Brandon.

"Kitty!" he barked.

But she ignored him. Since when did he think he could shout at her? And Michael . . . he was here! Their eyes locked. And she knew! *Of course*—of course he would have somehow ended up here, standing in front of her! Had she forgotten—or just stopped believing—that the universe worked in strange but intentional ways?

It was her own longing that had summoned him. No, that was crazy. But was it wrong now, to want him here, right in front of her? She felt the electricity running between them, burning and snapping in the air.

He was holding his breath. He felt it, too. And the intensity of his gaze forced her to look away.

"*Oh, Michael . . .*" she said.

And her voice broke as she whispered his name. She couldn't do it.

It was hopeless—dangerous, even—to want what was in the past. She understood that too much time had gone by—too much had happened! She was a different person from the one he'd known.

"It's been such a long time, Michael . . ."

He moved nearer. If he sensed her shutting down, he gave no sign. "It's okay, Kit."

"Kitty!" The voice at the other end of the porch called out again. "Genia needs help getting up to her room, she's wasted. And it's late. Everyone's packing it in for the night." Sweet-talking her, he tried, "Come on, baby."

Her hands were shaking as she swiped at a tear and backed away. "I'm sorry," she whispered, and the spark between them went out.

"Come on, Banjo," she called to the dog, and moved past Michael, turning her face away from him. Arms folded tight across her chest and shoulders hunched, she walked down the porch toward the front door.

Chapter 17

Graduation day came. On the outdoor stage set up in the school ball field, surrounded by their families, Michael and his friends accepted their diplomas. He got caught up in all the excitement, too, cheering and throwing his cap up in the air like the rest of his classmates.

As his parents took snapshots of him, Tom, and their friends horsing around in their lumpy, black graduation gowns, it hit him that all the kids in these photos would probably never leave Franconia—they'd still be here, years from now. All except for him. Maybe someday, one of his friends would pick up a photo and ask, "Hey, anyone know whatever happened to Mike Pearce?"

That vision of the future made him a little sad. But it also made him feel like something inside was being *set free*.

And Kit was here again.

In the days that followed their encounter on the porch, Michael had played out the scene in his head over and over again. Kit was not "crazy." Tom hadn't known what he was talking about.

But she had changed. The girl Michael had known two years earlier—strong, self-confident, a little stuck-up—was gone. A wounded bird, Eugenia's friend had called her that night, as if it were a joke.

And why the tears? Why had she just walked away from him? What had happened in the two years since he'd last seen her? He had questions—a long list of them. But something about the way she'd looked at him, the way she'd said his name, told him that Kit remembered those days at the lake. They had meant something to her, too.

Kit was back, and nothing would stop him now from seeing her again. Whatever was bothering her, he could talk her out of it. They would pick up where they'd left off two years ago.

He would tell her about Dartmouth—his mind leapt ahead—Hanover, New Hampshire, was not that far at all from Boston, where Mr. Morgan had told him Kit was going to college. It would be easy for them to visit each other. And Michael wouldn't be just some townie lifeguard at the beach club. He'd be a freshman in college, just like her.

What was clear now was that during that summer two years ago, being with Kit had changed the way he'd looked at himself—she'd changed who he believed he was, and could be in the future. Because of Kit, he'd started to see himself as someone with more ahead of him than a life stuck in small-town Franconia.

The sparring and the circling in on each other, his slow-motion fall toward her—the irresistible desire to be with Kit had caught fire that day he'd persuaded her to come back to the beach with him, in the lifeguard rescue boat. He'd started to stroll over to see her during his breaks, finding ways to strike up a conversation. To get to know her. To win her over.

One time, he remembered, she'd been looking through a big art book. She raised an eyebrow and asked in a sexy voice what he thought of a line written by an artist named Georgia O'Keeffe: "I feel there is something unexplored about woman that only a woman can explore." She liked him—he could tell!—and he had babbled like an idiot, trying to suggest that he had plenty of experience when it came to women and would be happy to challenge that statement any day.

Kit had just snorted and shook her head dismissively.

Arguing about ideas and challenging each other's opinions had been a turn-on. It was hard—like a game Michael didn't know the rules to at first—and it got him all fired up. But once he had the hang of organizing his sometimes-off-the-wall ideas, these verbal contests gave him the feeling of having something important to say. He'd never felt that way before.

The two younger kids had been impressed with Michael's lifeguard status, even if Kit was not. Eventually he'd coached seven-year-old Elliot on his swimming technique. And he became an expert on celebrity trivia from being quizzed by Lucy, who, at age thirteen, always brought a stack of *Tiger Beat* magazines to study at the beach. They'd gotten used to him stopping by.

Sometimes, during the long days of their sixteenth summer, he and Kit would take walks together. He could see them now, in his memory, following a path in the woods beside the lake. He'd be goofing around, trying to flirt with her, bumping into her by-accident-but-on-purpose. Meanwhile, she would get all serious and insist on knowing what he thought, about almost everything.

She seemed to believe that he was smart, and even funny. And because Kit had seen him as a person with interesting ideas and worthwhile opinions, Michael had begun to see himself that way, too.

"Do you ever feel . . . trapped sometimes? Like you just want to get away? I mean, what do you really want to do with your life, Michael?" Kit asked one day, with unexpected intensity.

How did he know? Besides plotting how he was going to kiss her before the summer ended, he hadn't really put much thought into the future.

In private, he started to ask himself the same questions.

Everything shifted. The world opened up in a way he never could have imagined. He began to think about having actual goals. Why should he be just another guy in Franconia or Littleton with a high school diploma, who skied and was trapped in some dead-end job at his parents' hardware store? Well, he didn't have to be.

Even as that summer came to an end, Kit and Michael spoke about "next summer," as if it were understood that they would pick up where they had left off. That fall, as his junior year in high school began, he got up his nerve and stopped by his science teacher's office after the first day back at class.

He asked his teacher the question that would never have occurred to him before Kit: "What would I have to do, if I wanted to go to college?"

"Hellooo?" A girl, laughing, answered the phone. "Cedaredge Farm. Max! Oh, Max, will you be a dear and freshen up my drink?"

Damn. He'd gotten Genia.

"Hello," he said on the other end of the line. There was no reason not to pick up the phone and just call Kit directly. He'd gone through the phone book and found the number for the Morgans' residence at Cedaredge Farm. "This is Michael, Kit's friend. I wondered if Kit was around?"

"Michael *who*?"

"Michael Pearce. The . . . ah . . . lifeguard. Is this Genia? I talked with you and your friends the other night at the party."

"Oh, yes," she said unenthusiastically. "I have no idea where Kit is. Yes, the Tanqueray gin, Max. I'll tell her you called. 'Bye now."

"Wait! Can I give you my phone number?"

He heard a muffled voice in the background, calling: "Gigi! Get a drink and come join us on the porch! We need a fourth for bridge."

Genia replied irritably to Michael. "Yes. What is it, then?"

He was almost certain Genia was not writing anything down, as he heard her giggle, "Thank you Max, you're my hero!"

"Ta ta!" she said. And hung up the phone.

Chapter 18

Kit was so jumpy now. She could not seem to outrun or shove aside the emotions chasing after her ever since the night of the party. Michael had just appeared! Out of nowhere! And taken her completely by surprise on the porch.

She kept remembering the way he'd cocked his head to listen, trying to figure her out; the wry, puzzled smile. He'd moved toward her as if trying not to frighten her, yet compelling her to look at him and to see him. To remember. The gravitational pull of his attention had made her react physically, drawing her closer and closer to him.

She'd dug her heels in, resisting, even as something inside her wanted to let go, give in.

Two years ago, they had been a couple of kids on the beach, flirting, goofing around.

It all felt different now.

And in complete contradiction to her impulse—that night—to scurry away from him *like a silly panicked mouse*, seeing him again was all she could think about now.

At night, she woke up tangled in the sheets. Too hot! Stripping off her nightgown, she lay on the top of the bed, craving the sensation of the cool air moving across her body. At dawn, bleary-eyed, she scrambled up and out of bed, pulling on jeans, a T-shirt, and flying, silently, down the stairs, out the kitchen door.

She charged up the road, head down, her breath coming fast— and plunged down paths that wound deep into the woods. Bare feet carried her from sun's warmth into the forest's cool shadows, and she paid no notice.

Suddenly, it seemed to her she'd been sleepwalking these past two years. She must have been! Moving in slow motion, weighted down with guilt and uncertainty. Today, it was as if her feet had pulled free of that quicksand—she was moving! Running! She had woken up.

Michael had come out of nowhere, whispering her name. She couldn't stop hearing his voice in her head.

When—how—would she see him again?

The Morgans were eating breakfast out on the porch. Kit, sliding into her seat beside Elliot and opposite Lucy, grabbed a slice of toast from the bread basket Elsie had set on the table. She slathered it with honey.

"Whoa! Shark bite!" Elliot piped up, as she chomped down on the toast, ravenous. The sweet stickiness of the honey smeared her hands and face.

"Mind your own beeswax," she said, and nudged him with her knee. And then, to her father, "Daddy, I was up at the barn this morning. Why is Freddie in that tiny pen? Why isn't he out with the cows?"

"Freddie? And who, may I ask, is Freddie?" her father said, without looking up from his *Wall Street Journal*.

"The bull, Daddy!" Lucy chimed in. "Don't you remember? He was born here. Me, Elliot, and Kitty named him after *Ferdinand the Bull*, from a book. Freddie."

"The bull? Now that's really none of your children's concern."

"It's cruel to keep him in that pen!" Kit protested. "He's lonely!"

"Katherine, you are referring to a three-thousand-pound farm animal, not a puppy."

"Dad!" All three kids protested in unison.

"All right, now! If it will make you kids happy, I'll talk to Mr. Overbee and see what he thinks. I won't promise anything."

Kit sighed, and Lucy and Elliot rolled their eyes. Then Kit announced, "I'm going into Littleton this morning."

Mr. Morgan put down his paper; Mrs. Morgan paused in her conversation with Genia.

"To get some art supplies."

"*Art* supplies?" her mother said, as if Kit had announced she was going to pick up a machine gun.

"Yes. Art supplies. Is there something suspicious about a pad of paper? Pencils?"

"Don't be smart to your mother," said her father.

"I can take you into Littleton," Brandon offered.

Genia cut in, reminding him, "But you're coming to the Club with me, silly."

"Why don't you join Genia and Brandon at the Club today," her mother suggested. "Play some tennis. I'm sure Genia can find a fourth for doubles."

Kit took a deep breath. If she got angry now, her parents would pile on, insist. Instead, she smiled. This morning she felt strong, strong enough to hold her temper to get what she wanted.

She answered sweetly, "I won't be long. And, Mother— weren't you waiting for a price list from the florist? I know you're really busy now. I could pick that up for you in Littleton. Save you some time."

"Well, hmmm. That would be a help. There's an awful lot to do," her mother conceded.

"See? So, call them, tell them I'll be stopping by." Knowing her parents were keen to monitor her movements, she gritted her teeth and added, "I'll be back by lunch. I promise."

Kit tore through the woods on her moped, accelerating as soon as she'd driven, slow and sedate, to the bottom of the hill and was out of sight of the farm. Giddy with freedom! She'd hardly realized how *sick* she was of limping around, feeling her life was over. The dirt road rolled out ahead of her, empty and quiet, and she curved and swooped in big arcs, lifting her face to the sky.

What a massively huge relief to be out from under the weight of parental supervision—and the constant gnawing preoccupation with the past. It felt so good to get away from the farm, to be all on her own, driving through the woods. To just *be*!

Arriving into Sugar Hill, she slowed the moped to a sedate putter; then, turning left onto another back route, she leaned forward and revved up the engine. Her hair flew out behind her as she sped past woods and pastures, then across the Gale River; she followed the Old Franconia Road, finally crossing the Ammonoosuc River into downtown Littleton.

It was way past time she got back to her art.

Inspiration had swept her up again, she felt that itchy and impossible-to-ignore feeling of wanting to make things! Crafty Creations, the local novelty store, stocked three sizes of white pads. Kit chose the biggest, plus a box of #2 yellow pencils, and a kid-style pencil sharpener. Not exactly real artists' supplies, but good enough.

She paid for the supplies, then slid them into her bag and slung the thick strap across her chest. Next on the list, Rita's Nursery. She puttered along Main Street, toward the far end of town, enjoying the cheerful bustle of people: women with their shopping bags, men talking importantly to each other on the sidewalk outside the bank or real estate office, couples drinking coffee at outdoor tables in front of the diner.

"Here's our proposal for your mother," Rita said as she folded two crisp pages into a pink envelope and handed it to Kit. "Please let her know that many of these flowers will have to be a special order. But I know this is a *special* day! Are these flowers . . . for you, young lady?" Rita inquired.

"Me?" Kit's eyes widened. She blushed. "Ah, no."

"Well, I'm sure it won't be long." Rita offered Kit an encouraging smile.

Kit shoved the envelope into her bag. Before, her standard reaction might have been to say nothing. Of course, Rita assumed a girl like Katherine Morgan would want to be next. Maybe most girls would. But instead, Kit laughed, and grinned like a wise-ass. "Thanks, but I sure hope not!" Poor Rita looked confused. Outside, Kit climbed onto her bike and took off with a roar of the accelerator.

Her life had hardly gotten started! She sped out of town, then across the river and up into the hills and farm country again. In these past few days, the idea that she had her whole life ahead of her no longer seemed like an immense, untenable burden—but instead, a gift. There was so much she wanted to do!

As a child, Kit had been fascinated by the strange and beautiful illustrations in books of fairy tales. Her interest in stories led to the discovery of the illustrator Arthur Rackham, and the painter of Nordic myths Akseli Gallen-Kallela. Rackham imagined elves and mermaids, while in the paintings of Gallen-Kallela goddesses rode through the star-filled sky on horseback. And at the Metropolitan

Museum she'd stood transfixed in front of the mythical landscapes of Japanese artists of the Edo period, where dragons wrestled with heroes and magicians.

She'd immersed herself in how these artists saw the world—romantic, fantastical, sensual, bold. Infused with a love of nature.

Art wasn't just pretty pictures. Nor was it some last resort, taught in a class to students because they were failing math or English or after-school sports, the way it had been at her private school in New York. Art was a way of looking at the world. Not just an escape valve for expressing a flood of anger or frustration, art required effort, and an ability to focus attention. To learn what it meant to really see.

During the past two years, Kit had discovered that art mattered enough to her to make that effort.

Her counselors had encouraged her, and a kind teacher who took art seriously had taken a special interest in her. And she'd learned how to draw forth her own creativity—at first it felt like hauling a heavy bucket filled with nothing out of a well. Little by little, the daily work she applied to sitting still and concentrating began to pay off. Her heart and mind calmed. She experienced the strange, miraculous sense of clarity, of what it meant *to see*. And once able to focus, she started to reimagine—with a pencil or paintbrush, and then with clay—how she wanted to interpret and express her vision of the world.

The bucket started to come up from the well fast and easy and full.

In the privacy of the garden gazebo at Cedaredge, Kit returned to one of the first exercises she'd been given—drawing her thumb without lifting the pencil from the paper, paying attention to the curve of nail, the folds of skin around her knuckle. The act was like a meditation. Next, she drew her hand, her foot.

In her bedroom, she sat in front of the mirror above her dresser, studying her eyes, her mouth. On impulse, she rested her elbow on the dresser, put one hand up as if to cover her face, and stared through her spread fingers. Barely looking down, she allowed the hand grasping the pencil to transcribe what her eyes saw. Putting the pencil aside at last, she studied the image of a face, all but hidden except for one eye burning through tensed and claw-like fingers.

Am I hiding from something—from myself? Kit asked herself. *Or is there something that I am trying to see—and I can't?*

Chapter 19

Late spring turned to early summer, and he began his job as veterinary assistant to Dr. Landsman. For now, at least, Michael would have to focus on learning the ropes, and try his best not to be distracted by obsessing over Kit.

She'd not returned his phone call.

Michael's days now started at the clinic, which operated out of Landsman's home just outside of downtown Franconia. The Landsmans' farmhouse overlooked a couple of pretty acres along the Gale River, with a flower garden in front and a big yellow barn out back. Between the house and the barn, Dr. Landsman's wife, Frances—who was also his secretary—grew a vegetable garden.

The clinic offices were located in a modern addition, with its own separate entrance, that Landsman had built onto the house himself. Work started at eight o'clock sharp. First thing in the morning, if no emergencies came up on one of the farms, their appointments began at the clinic for house pets and other small animals.

"Morning, Mike," Landsman greeted him. "We just had a call about a porcupine encounter. Not the most exciting work for a vet, pulling out those quills. But it's something you'll see a lot of. Dogs, horses, goats—they're all curious when they see a porcupine and sometimes end up getting too close. If you don't get those quills out right away, they just keep digging in deeper and can even kill an animal."

"Got it!" Maybe the case seemed boring to Landsman, but it sounded like a challenge to him. He wanted to jump in, start proving himself.

Not long after, a car pulled up in front of the clinic. An old man got out, stiff and moving slowly. He lifted an equally old dog out of the back and placed him gently on the ground. The black mutt had a grizzled snout, and a face and neck pierced with dozens of barbed quills.

"Hello, Ed." Landsman shook hands with the old man, and then bent down to give the unhappy dog a talking-to. "Blue, I thought we'd come to an understanding about porcupines the last time you were here. I thought you'd learned your lesson."

Blue whined, laid down, and tried to place his head gingerly on his master's foot.

"Mike," Landsman said, and opened the door to an exam room just behind the front desk, "lift Blue up onto that exam table. And be careful of those quills. I'd like to see if we can pull them out without having to put the old guy under anesthesia."

Porcupine quills, the vet explained, have barbs that point in one direction—*in*. Having them pulled out hurts like a son-of-a-bitch for the victim. As Landsman extracted the first quill, the pain transformed Blue into a howling maniac.

Michael had a solid hold on the dog, luckily, because Blue lunged snarling and snapping at Landsman, barely missing him. But then he squirmed and twisted, and wrenched himself free. The dog slid off the table and backed himself into a corner of the exam room. Blue curled his lip and snarled.

"Damnation," muttered Landsman.

"Blue!" his owner shouted with dismay. "Bad dog."

"It's okay, Ed," Landsman reassured the old man. He slowly approached the dog from one side—"Grab that leash," he ordered—and Michael came in from the other side with a soft ribbon leash.

You couldn't help but feel sorry for old Blue; his legs quivered and his cloudy eyes were wild and scared. "Come on, Blue," Michael encouraged the frightened animal, "you're a good dog, Blue. *Had a dog and his name was Blue,*" he began to sing a soft tune to the panicked dog, "*betcha five dollars he's a good dog, too.*" Blue quieted, the growling turned to a low mutter.

"Come on, Blue," he sang softly. "Good dog." The dog whimpered and tried to lie down.

"Whatever you're doing there, Mike, keep doing it." Landsman sounded amused. "And see if you can slip the leash over his head without bumping into any of those quills."

"Good dog, Blue . . ." The leash slid over his head; Michael pulled it snug, avoiding the porcupine quills.

Eventually they got Blue to lie still and Landsman administered a dose of anesthesia. In the next hour they pulled 107 quills out of the dog's face and neck. When they were finished, Ed thanked them, paid his bill, and carried the sleeping dog back to the car.

"Well, I guess we've got a new technique to add to our tool kit," Landsman remarked, "'Singing to Soothe the Savage Beast.'" Michael wasn't sure if his boss was ribbing him, but then Landsman smiled and said, "You had a good manner with that dog, Mike. And you thought fast, on your feet. Other first-timers might not have had that presence of mind. Animals can surprise you, even the oldest and most domesticated. Never underestimate what fear and pain can do, to man or beast."

The praise made him feel pretty good about himself.

Next was a pet crow named Squeaky, whose leg was injured from being stuck in a wire fence. Their morning appointments concluded with rabies and distemper shots for two tiny kittens, rescued from a dumpster by a local teenage girl. When it came time to pay, the vet refused her money and Michael got a lesson in doing the right thing. "This one's on the house, young lady," Landsman said, as he quieted the mewing kittens with gentle strokes from his big, farm-weathered hands.

He was learning quickly. As the days went by, his satisfaction grew as he became more and more confident in his ability to help his boss with patients at the clinic. Still, there was no denying that what he really loved were the afternoons when, work completed in the office, he and Landsman set off into the hills of Sugar Hill, Landaff, or Lisbon to make a call at a local farm.

Landsman would dictate his morning notes to Frances, then give her a kiss on the cheek. Then he and Michael would zip on their canvas coveralls, gather the medicines and gear they might need. As they set off on those warm summer afternoons to work out in the fields with the bigger farm animals, Michael swore he could hear his boss breathe a sigh of contentment.

And every time they packed up the van, Michael felt himself get edgy with stupid, irrepressible hope.

Landsman would take the main route out of town, eventually turning off onto one smaller, less-traveled road after the next. More than once they'd headed in the same direction as the turnoff for Cedaredge.

"Are we . . . going to the Morgans' place today?" Michael asked, unable to hide his eagerness. How was he going to get Kit to see him again? That night on the porch she'd pushed him away. And the phone call to Cedaredge—the direct approach—had failed. Had Kit not wanted to return his call? More likely Genia had not passed on his message. But there was no way to know for sure.

The next-best plan might be a strategic coincidence. "I thought . . . well . . . you mentioned that Mr. Morgan has an award-winning herd. Don't we need to check on . . . their vital statistics?"

Landsman chuckled. "You seem awfully interested in the Morgans' cows. Don't you worry. I'll make sure to bring you with me if we get a call from Cedaredge. It's early in the season yet. I've no doubt I'll be hearing from Charlie Overbee soon. He's new on the job." Michael sighed and sat back in his seat as Landsman passed the turnoff for the Morgans' farm and drove on.

On a warm day with the windows down, they'd drive along in easygoing silence just enjoying the afternoon and the earthy smells of the pastures and hay fields. In the woods, the pungent scent of pine trees, or a breeze coming off a woodland lake, would wash over them with a refreshing coolness. More than once, the van had to come to a sudden stop as a moose ambled right in front of them with loose, long-legged strides.

Keeping his new assistant's mind on the job, Landsman put Michael right to work. Most of his clients were farmers with herds of cattle—the milk-producing Holsteins, and several herds of Black Angus beef cattle. Michael learned how to administer routine vaccinations with cows harnessed in their stalls. And he became expert at dodging a sharp hoof and avoiding being kicked in the head when treating common problems, like an infected udder. He got experience examining pregnant cows, and—just a few weeks into the job—eagerly assisted his boss with the delivery of twin calves.

One afternoon he was driving his own truck back to the clinic after a visit to a farm in Landaff. Landsman had to go on to Wells River, so the two had driven out from Franconia separately. Michael came around a bend and then stopped to take in the view of Pearl Lake from the highest point beside a wide slope of pasture.

Big bunches of daisies and black-eyed Susans grew along the side of the road in the ditch. And down at the farthest edge of the pasture a small herd of cows grazed. The bells around their necks clanked softly as the animals moved, unhurried, through the tall grass.

A breeze rippled across the grass and a pair of swallows flew overhead. The birds called to each other, and swooped and dived like acrobats as they performed their courtship flight. Michael remembered his guitar in the truck, and just for the hell of it, he pulled the case out of the back of the cab where he'd stowed it.

He leaned back against the warm side of the truck, tuned up the guitar, and began to play. The music rang out across the tranquil hillside. In a rush of unselfconscious happiness, he offered up a song to the swallow and its mate, to the beauty of the afternoon, and to the quiet stillness of the lake below. The summer had hardly even begun. He had plenty of time to figure out how to see Kit again.

Sometimes when he played, the weight of all that was confusing and uncertain in life would lift. He'd experience a moment of understanding, a bigger, wider perspective that was usually hidden from him, where everything in life flowed together and made some kind of sense, even if he couldn't see it most of the time, or even comprehend how.

Then something strange happened.

One of the cows broke off from the others and started to make her way up toward the road. Toward him. The others looked up, ears twitching, and then two more split off from the herd. He kept singing, and before long, the entire group was headed across the pasture toward him.

Michael started to laugh—it was such a ridiculous sight. He switched to a cowboy tune—*I'm just a poor cowhand! Yippie yi yo kay ay, Yippie yi yo kay ay!*—and one by one the cows arrived at the fence. They pushed and shoved each other for the best position, stretching their necks toward him and ogling the guitar with curiosity.

It was time to get back to work, but he kept up with one more song anyway. How often did he have such a genuinely appreciative audience?

As he drove back into Franconia, a newly strung banner hanging from the town hall proclaimed, "Happy Independence Day!" And now he noticed that neighbors had begun decorating their houses with red-white-and-blue bunting. The Fourth of July holiday was coming up this weekend!

The days were passing by while he remained frustratingly stuck, still no closer to finding a way to see Kit again.

Chapter 20

With relief she'd watched as the Cedaredge family station wagon pulled out of the driveway—without her in it! She'd have the morning to herself while everyone else went to the Club.

Early that morning, she'd remembered a tub of blue clay from the waterfall, stashed two years earlier in the barn refrigerator. She'd wrapped it in plastic, stuffed it into a cardboard box, and shoved it to the back of the extra refrigerator where Elsie stored emergency provisions.

Now Kit slid open the heavy barn door. Tractors rumbled in the field behind the barn as Mr. Overbee and his men tried to get the mowing done before the heat of the day bore down. Inside the barn, the dark, cavernous space felt cool, and shafts of light filtered in from the high-set windows.

She crossed the hay-strewn plank floor to where the refrigerator hummed in the near corner. Elsie insisted on additional freezer and refrigerator space, to stock extra food for cocktail parties and unexpected guests. Those appliances had ended up here, in the hay barn.

The box sat lumpy and nearly shapeless in the bottom of the refrigerator. No one had moved it, or thrown it out! And inside— the plastic bag containing a cold, hard lump of clay.

On a rough worktable, Kit peeled back the damp cardboard and unsealed the plastic bag. The clay felt cool under her warm hands. Earth, with a capital E—organic and smooth. It aroused all her senses.

She focused her attention on the solid lump of matter. She pounded on the clay, and threw it hard against the tabletop. What could she do with it? Last winter, before coming home to New York, she'd taken a course in modeling with clay—learning about the tools and beginner techniques, and experimenting with simple projects.

The heat from her hands infused the hard mass, allowing her fingers to begin shaping it. All her life, it seemed to her now, she'd walked around in a kind of fog. Like one of the walking dead! She'd get to a certain point and then give up, lose track of who she was.

She smacked the clay hard on the table.

Ironically, it was only being far away—from New York, from her family—that had allowed her to see some things more clearly, about herself as a person. Who she was, and who she wanted to become. She wanted to be doing this—she dug her hands into the clay—*this*!

The contours of a face began to take shape under her fingers. She pressed, and smoothed. There was the broad forehead, yes, and the strong jawline. In her mind she could see the warm tan of his skin. She wanted to see him, his face, come to life beneath her hands, she thought dreamily. So, her fingers worked to form two coils of clay that would become his lips . . .

"Hey."

Kit nearly jumped straight up in the air. "Brandon! I didn't hear you come into the barn. I thought everyone had gone to the Club."

"Everyone but me and you. I needed some time to myself, too." He crossed his arms in front of his chest and his smile was friendly, curious even. "I didn't want to disturb you. You seemed pretty into . . . whatever it is you're doing. What is that?"

"Nothing." She pulled the plastic over the clay relief.

He stood back from her, in a way that seemed unusually cautious, solicitous. Why had he come looking for her, she wondered?

He leaned his tall, muscled form against the worktable. "I'm glad I found you. I've been meaning to apologize."

"Apologize? For what?"

"Oh, you know. That first night when we all got up to Cedaredge. At the bar. I was wired that night, after the drive. And then you looked so pretty—and kind of lonely, sad—sitting on that bar stool. I don't know if you noticed that other guys were checking you out, too."

"No, I did not." She eyed him suspiciously.

"Suddenly, I just wanted to dance with you. I don't know . . . cheer you up. Make you happy. It was dumb of me. I realize now I was out of line. And I just want you to know—after all you've been through—that it was wrong of me to act that way. And I'm sorry."

"You were kind of a jerk." Was it within the realm of possibility that Brandon actually felt bad about that night? That he was capable of considering how anyone else felt, besides himself?

"Can you forgive me?" If it was possible for a six-foot-tall jock to look like a puppy dog, Brandon was doing a pretty good job.

"Maybe." She gave him a reluctant smile. He was okay, really, probably just used to girls fawning all over him. She wasn't completely unaware of how flattering his interest in her felt.

She remembered the night, recently, when her family had gone out to dinner at the Club—Brandon hadn't joined them. She'd made the unkind assumption that he'd just snuck off to the Littleton bar, to drink. That wasn't really fair. He probably just needed a break from her family, too, the way she did.

"I'm sure it's been hard, being home again." His brows came together in a sympathetic expression.

"Yeah," she sighed. "It has been."

"I guess that's why I was a little concerned the other night."

"About what?"

"That guy. At the party."

Kit stiffened. "What guy?"

"You know who I mean, I saw you talking to him—that local guy. Is he really a friend of yours? Believe me, I'm not trying to hassle you, Kitty. I'm just"—Brandon's brow furrowed—"worried, that's all."

"Worried?"

"I guess that might surprise you, but, yeah, actually, I am. Worried."

She waited.

"Genia said the guy was a lifeguard? Just seems like a strange kind of friend."

She narrowed her eyes. "I can't have a friend who doesn't come from the city, or some prep school? His name is Michael, for your information. We hung out, before . . . two years ago at the Club."

"At the Club?"

"Yes! What is this, Brandon? The Spanish Inquisition?"

Brandon's face took on a hurt, misunderstood expression. "Kitty, the reason I'm asking . . . you probably haven't heard this—I know you've been preoccupied, and Genia's trying to keep it quiet—but one of her friends, Anne, I think, well, she had a bad experience the night of the party."

She became aware of her chest tightening. "What kind of bad experience?"

"I guess someone, some guy . . . took advantage of her. When she was drunk."

"What? What are you talking about?"

"We were all partying, shooting some pool, and no one noticed that Anne had disappeared. Anyway, the next day she was pretty messed up."

"You think Michael hurt her, Brandon? Is that what you're getting at? There were a lot of people at the party that night. A lot of *your* friends. What does Anne say?"

"She was too wasted, she blacked out. The next day she just wanted to go home before people started talking. Genia got Max to take her back to the city. Then Genia swore me to secrecy."

"Kitty, all I'm saying is . . . I worry about you. You've got a lot to deal with. And then this guy shows up at the party—at your parents' house—out of nowhere. And now you tell me he was hanging around you at the lake, two years ago, too? You still don't remember anything . . . do you? Like—what happened?"

"I tried to off myself. As you know." She looked away from him, absently noticing her own hands, clenching each other, covered in wet clay. There were so many holes in her memory. Blank spots. The shame spawned by that uncertainty came piling back on. "But, no . . . no, I don't remember the specifics. But I am damn sure it had nothing to do with Michael. And that Michael didn't hurt Anne, either."

Was she sure?

"Okay, okay. I'm sorry to bring it up." Brandon let it go. He sounded relieved almost. "I'm sorry."

He eased toward her. "It's so cool that you're an artist."

"Oh. What?" He'd thrown her off guard again.

"I like to think of myself as a creative person, too. That is, I enjoy reading. Literature." He smiled at her. "Don't look so surprised."

She glanced away, embarrassed that she had perhaps misjudged him, considered him just a "dumb jock."

"As part of his campaign to get me into Princeton, Dad made sure I read 'the greats.' He's a hard-ass—not a fellow to disagree with, if you're a kid—and definitely not one to 'spare the rod,' as they say." Brandon pulled up his shirt and turned to show Kit a scar across his lower back.

"Oh my God, Brandon! I'm sorry." She reached out to touch his back.

"Hey, it's nothing." He dropped his shirt. "I was probably about ten, screwing around with the docking line on the boat, not paying attention. He smacked me over the back with that rope, teach me not to fuck around out on the water. A good lesson. But it hurt like hell. I was a stubborn little bugger. Refused to give my old man the satisfaction of seeing me cry. Later that night, Dad made me drink a shot of rum with him—my first drink—he was proud of me for being such a tough little shit."

Kit stared at him and felt an unexpected wave of compassion.

"'Great literature builds character,' Dad always taught me. My favorites are authors who write about the sea: Melville, Hemingway, Conrad, Jack London."

The only book she could think of by any of these writers was Herman Melville's *Moby Dick*, assigned reading when she was in prep school in New York. She'd never finished it. This unexpected side to Brandon surprised—impressed—her.

"The fact that you're an artist, well, I think it's . . . so attractive—sexy, really. Promise me, Kitty, you won't be offended. It's just that, I've always been drawn to how creative you are. Really. We're like two kindred spirits. Sometimes I wish that you and I . . ."

Brandon's presence was unsettling her.

"I want to give you this." He undid the woven rope bracelet from his wrist and offered it to her.

"Brandon, I don't know. This doesn't seem like a good idea." He was so confident—so sure of himself, and of what he wanted. All of the qualities she wished she possessed herself. He slid the bracelet into the back pocket of her shorts. Then his hands slid up her back and he bent to kiss her.

"'We live in the flicker'—I think Conrad wrote that," Brandon murmured. "In other words, live for today, Kitty, because tomorrow the candle may go out."

"Brandon." She tried to pull away from him. "Stop it, okay? Please." This was definitely not cool. Brandon was Genia's fiancé!

"If this guy, this lifeguard dude, if he hurt you somehow . . ." He kissed her more insistently. "If that's why . . . I'm just saying, I'll kill him."

"I said stop, okay? Cut it out!" Her hands pushed against his chest, hard.

"What? Hey, what the—?" He released her abruptly, and looked down at his shirt front.

Kit squeezed out from between Brandon's bulk and the worktable.

She left him standing, frowning at the two blue hand marks made with cold, wet clay, pressed into the front of his white polo shirt.

Chapter 21

Two weeks had passed, with the rigors of his new job occupying Michael's days. But he thought about Kit constantly. He had to see her! Had to make a move. Turning various strategies over in his mind kept him up at night. In the morning, he was so preoccupied that his sister, Jenny, nudged him at the breakfast table: "*Hello? Earth-to-Michael-Pearce? Anyone there?*"

Finally, Landsman received a call at the clinic from Charlie Overbee, manager at the Morgans' farm. He and Landsman were going to Cedaredge! A pregnant cow had gone into labor and was having difficulty. She'd been at it for more than twenty-four hours, Charlie estimated, with no birth. Something was wrong.

Michael and his boss packed the gear into the van and took off from the clinic in a hurry. They were racing to his first real emergency on the job. That, combined with the possibility of seeing Kit, had his heart thumping with adrenaline.

Charlie was waiting for them as they pulled in to park near the barns at Cedaredge. The last time he'd seen Charlie Overbee had been at the hardware store; the farm manager had come across as pretty cocky and sure of himself that day. Now Charlie looked pale and anxious, and pulled his cap off to wipe the sweat from his forehead. "She's up in the northwest pasture, Doc. It's a bit of a hike."

Landsman, calm and steady as always, turned to him. "Go through the checklist, Mike, make sure we have everything we need. It's about twenty minutes to get up there, if I'm not mistaken. So, we don't want to forget anything."

They crossed the road, carrying all the gear, and Charlie unhitched the heavy wooden gate to the fenced-in pasture. These acres of grazing pasture opposite the barns connected, one to the next, by way of a steep, rocky trail through the tightly spaced maple and birch trees. There was no room to take a vehicle and the men had to pick their way carefully, and slowly, on foot.

About halfway up, a shower of pebbles from the trail above rained down on them. A few seconds later, Kit ran scrambling down toward them, then skidded to a stop when she saw Charlie, with Landsman and Michael. She wore cutoff jeans, and her legs and white peasant blouse were streaked with dirt. Her hair flew around her face in a wild tangle.

She was animated now—fired up in the face of the emergency—in a way she hadn't been the night Michael had tried to speak with her on the porch.

"Hurry!" she shouted. She took off back up the trail.

"Come on, boys," Landsman urged them on, "let's move!"

The three pushed even faster, and in a few minutes came out of the trees into a remote, steeply sloping pasture. The cow must have broken away from the rest of the herd to have her calf, and wandered off on her own. With bears sometimes prowling the bordering forests, it wasn't a safe place for one vulnerable pregnant cow. She lay on her side in the tall grass, about thirty feet in front of them. Kit was kneeling beside her, stroking her neck.

Landsman hurried over to where the cow lay, with Charlie and Michael close behind. Things looked bad. The cow's tongue extended and foam bubbled from her mouth. She rolled her eyes in pain as Landsman bent to examine her. "It's a uterine torsion.

She's got a calf in there, all right, but she can't push it out because the uterus is twisted."

"Can you help her, Doc?" Charlie asked. His voice sounded tight with fear. No farmer likes to lose an animal, particularly when it is one of Cedaredge Farm's two-thousand-dollar, award-winning milking cows.

Landsman stood up. "We're going to try. But we need to get that calf out now, or it's going to die. And we may lose the mother, too." Landsman turned to Kit. "Miss Morgan, I think you should be going back to the farm now. We're going to take good care of your cow."

"I'm not leaving her." Kit stood her ground.

"It was Katherine who found her, way out here this morning," Charlie spoke up. "Might not have gotten to you in time if Katherine hadn't let us know."

"All right, then," Landsman said sternly to Kit. "But, Katherine, it's going to get messy. And, I'm afraid, the outcome is uncertain. Be ready to help if we need you."

Landsman started giving orders. "Strip down, Mike. You're going to reach inside, examine the cow, and tell us which way we need to move her. Then Charlie, you and I are going to roll the cow over, nice and easy, and untwist the uterine canal."

By now Michael had been up to the shoulder inside a cow a few times to inspect the animals for signs of pregnancy, and he'd helped with two other calvings. But he'd never been in a situation where his part might affect the life or death of the animal.

"You can do this, I trust you," Landsman said, as he and Charlie positioned themselves on either side of the cow. Michael unzipped his coveralls to the waist and pulled off his shirt.

He lathered up, peeled on a plastic examination sleeve, and gently slid his arm into the cow. He needed to find the calf's

hoof, to have something to grab on to. But, reaching and prod-
ding, his fingers found nothing. The birth canal was twisted
shut, with the calf trapped inside. "I think, if we roll her over,
I'll be able to reach the calf," he yelled, and prayed his judgment
was correct. He wiped the sweat from his eyes with the back of
his free arm.

With a huge effort, Landsman and Charlie gently began to roll
the 1,500-pound pregnant cow to her opposite side, legs flailing.

"I think I can feel something now!" he shouted, as the men
maneuvered the big animal. Charlie and Landsman continued to
push, landing the cow on her opposite side.

"Yes! I can feel a hoof now!" Michael extended his hand as
far in as he could. And then he felt another tiny, slippery horned
foot. Charlie held the cow in place while Kit spoke soothing
words to her. Landsman rushed over to Michael and handed him
a loop of rope.

"You've got this, son. Now go ahead and slide this rope in and
try to get it around both legs."

Slowly, slowly he worked the rope in. It seemed to take hours—
the legs were slippery, hard to grasp—before he got it around first
one and then the other leg. And every minute counted. He pulled,
tightening the loop. "I've got it!"

"Okay—Charlie, you stay where you are and hold her still;
Katherine, can you keep the mother calm?"

"I'm trying!" she answered, as the cow struggled. Michael
heard exhaustion and panic in her voice. He clamped his jaw, grit-
ting his teeth. He had to save these two animals!

"Mike, you and I are going to pull like crazy and get this calf
born!"

At first nothing happened at all. They dug their heels into the
ground and pulled hard on the rope, straining with the effort.

Michael felt desperation building, knowing that the calf was going to suffocate if they couldn't pull it out—*now*.

"Michael," Kit screamed, "you've got to pull harder!" She held on to the cow as it kicked and gasped in pain.

And then, Michael felt movement. "Pull!" Landsman shouted. And, with more strength than he ever believed he possessed, Michael pulled on the rope with Landsman. The calf inched forward toward them. First two legs, then the head. And then all at once the whole slithering, wet newborn calf slid out onto the grass.

But something was wrong. "The calf's not breathing!" he shouted. Landsman dropped down beside the calf and they both began smacking the small, motionless animal hard, trying to stimulate it to take a breath. *No!* Michael's brain hollered. He hadn't been quick enough, and now he'd lost the calf.

But then, the calf coughed and sputtered and gave Landsman a sharp kick in the groin. "Holy shit!" Landsman groaned, and then began to laugh with relief. The newly born calf stretched from head to hooves, and tried to roll itself over.

"Good job, everyone! We did it," Landsman congratulated them all. They'd been at it for almost two hours. Now the men let out a shout of celebration. Kit was laughing and crying at the same time, and tears were running down her cheeks.

Michael dropped down, resting on his heels in the grass and mud, and tried to catch his breath. The vet picked up the newborn and gently placed it down in front of its mother; instinctively, the exhausted cow began to lick her baby clean.

"Well, that was a close one there, I sure wouldn't have liked to lose her," said Charlie. He'd been white as a sheet when they'd first arrived, and now was back to being his red-faced and overconfident self. "I thank you, Doctor. And you, too, Mike—you're going to be a fine doctor one day, I can see that."

Kit got up and walked over to Michael. With her arm, she wiped the tears and sweat from her face. He could see she wasn't sure what to say to him—maybe because of their last, strange, encounter on the porch, or because of the crisis they had all just come through.

He reached up and took her hand. "She's okay," he reassured her. "They're both okay." They looked over at the cow and her calf; the baby was now boldly attempting to stand on wobbly legs.

Michael hadn't had a chance to clean up, and his chest was smeared with blood and gore. Suddenly, Kit sat down beside him and wrapped her arms around him anyway. "*You saved them*, Michael," she said, her voice intense and emotional.

The heat of her body, the warm fragrance of her hair falling against his chest, overwhelmed him, made his brain dizzy and hyperfocused all at the same time. He was speechless and afraid to hug her back, with his arms all covered in disgusting muck.

"Mike"—Landsman cleared his throat to get his assistant's attention—"why don't you clean up and take Katherine back home now, while Charlie and I discuss follow-up treatment with this cow."

Of course, he should have stayed. He knew it, and his boss knew it, too. But he'd done well, and maybe Landsman felt like giving him a gift that day—letting him walk Kit back to the farm. Michael took it.

"We'll meet back down at the farm in forty-five minutes," Landsman said. And just so Michael wouldn't think his boss was going soft, Landsman added, "*Sharp*."

They crossed the high pasture, neither one saying a word to the other. He felt nervous now—he could tell Kit did, too—both were concentrating much too seriously on their feet. What was she thinking? Was she going to say anything, he wondered desperately, or just act all moody and withdrawn like she had that night on the porch? Still . . . she had just hugged him. Maybe there was hope.

When they reached the tree line, they began the scrambling hike down through the trees. Somewhere deeper in the forest, a hermit thrush began to sing, as if weaving a circle of enchantment around them with its magical, flutelike call.

"I didn't know you were such a fan of cows," he said to Kit, finally breaking the silence with that inane remark. *Ugh, Mike!* he groaned to himself. *That's seriously the best you can do?*

Her bright, silly laughter surprised him, and he snorted with laughter, too, despite himself. The awkwardness that seemed to have had them both tied in knots began to loosen. The two started to giggle uncontrollably.

"What?" he asked, still laughing, trying to act offended that she was making fun of him.

"That's quite a conversation starter." She swung around behind him on a steep part of the trail, using a small tree as a handhold.

"All right—so what *were* you doing up in this middle-of-nowhere pasture, Miss Morgan?"

"Sketching the cows." Her hand went to her jeans pocket, as if to check, where corners of a folded sheet of paper stuck out. "Avoiding my family. What about you? Are you working for the vet now? *I didn't know you were such a fan of cows,*" she teased him and they both cracked up all over again.

All at once, time dropped away, and his uncertainty vanished. He and Kit were close again. Just like they had been once before. Nothing had changed. "*Very funny.* And actually, as it turns out, I do like cows, and farm animals in general."

He walked ahead of her, where the trail turned into a jumble of boulders, and then he began jumping from rock to rock. Half an hour earlier, he had been teetering on the edge in a desperate life-or-death struggle; now happiness exploded inside of him. He felt superhuman!

He launched himself off a particularly large boulder and landed with a thump, feet spread, on the soft dirt below. "I'm working for Dr. Landsman this summer, and then this fall, I—" But before Michael could finish his sentence, Kit slipped on the loose rocks and he turned around just as she tumbled on top of him. "Whoa!" he said, catching her in his arms.

Maybe, if she had pulled herself away once she'd gotten her balance back, Michael would have let her go. But she didn't pull away. And he didn't let go.

Instead, Kit looked at him with the same mischievous smile she'd had the day he'd discovered her skinny-dipping at the waterfall. *Daring him to make the next move*—wanting him to. How had he forgotten that her eyes were this amazing sky blue? And that when she smiled, her teeth showed a little behind soft lips; that they were ever so slightly crooked?

Whatever Michael had been intending to say next vanished from his mind. He locked her in his arms, and pressed her body against his. The smell of their sweat and the scent of the cool dark earth filled his nostrils. "Oh!" Kit's breath caught, and she curved into him as he brought his mouth down hard on hers.

Chapter 22

"Katherine—*what on earth*?" Her mother's voice, sharp with surprise and indignation, greeted them as Kit and Michael walked up to the house.

They had stumbled down the rest of the trail through the woods. Michael was kissing her face, her mouth, and running his hands all over her mud-stained blouse, as if he meant to *devour* her. And she—laughing and crazy and not wanting him to stop!

It was only knowing that Mr. Overbee and Dr. Landsman were not far behind on the trail that pulled her apart from him, and kept the two of them moving forward, giggling and tripping over each other.

Coming upon her mother, and the chaos of activity that seemed to have taken over Cedaredge, Kit let go of Michael's hand.

Trucks from the 5-Star Painting Company and Rita's Nursery blocked the driveway, and workers tromped all over the grounds around the house. Her mother was at the center of it all, in full director's mode: dictating instructions to the men, with poor Rita, the florist, trailing after her with a clipboard. Shouts came from up on the porch as the painters relayed where the floorboards, railings, and trim would need a fresh coat of paint.

The flush of excitement still burned Kit's cheeks, and she could feel red marks on her face and neck where Michael had kissed her. Michael's expression, as they came toward her mother, could not have broadcast more clearly: *I just made out with your daughter in the woods.*

"Katherine—where in the world have you been? And what is that on your blouse? Is that blood?" Then, her mother turned on Michael. "May I ask what you are doing here, young man?"

Now the red of her cheeks rose from anger and embarrassment: Why did her mother have to be so rude? "Michael's working with Dr. Landsman, the vet! One of Daddy's cows was in trouble; she was trying to give birth but her calf got stuck. Mr. Overbee called them out to the farm. Michael and his boss saved the cow and her calf—he saved their lives! In fact, Mother, we should be very grateful to Michael."

"I see," her mother said coolly. "And how did your blouse get that way, Katherine?"

"I helped them," she said, and folded her arms across her chest in defiance.

"Katherine was actually a huge help, Mrs. Morgan." Michael jumped to her defense. "Thanks to Katherine, we were able to keep the cow under control while we delivered the calf." He shouldn't have bothered. He was no match, Kit knew, for Bunny Morgan's condescension when she was not pleased.

Her mother ignored Michael. "Your father has Charlie Overbee and his men to take care of the animals," she reminded Kit. "That's something for the help—not you—to be involved in. And we agreed you would not disappear anymore without telling someone where you were going! I've got enough on my mind right now without worrying about you. What is this?" she said, snatching the piece of drawing paper from Kit's pocket.

Her mother unfolded the sheet of paper. It contained a pencil sketch Kit had been working on in the early morning: cows grazing among the trees in the north pasture.

"Mother, give it back!" Her mother had no right to rip her drawing away from her like that. Her mother thrust it back at her, as though the drawing were something repugnant. A piece of garbage! Kit clenched her jaw to keep from bursting into tears.

"Katherine, I don't think you understand what thin ice you're skating on. You are not a child anymore, daydreaming and scribbling with crayons. You know what your father and I think about this fantasy of yours, of being artist—it is misguided at the very least! Something you need to grow out of. It is high time you took responsibility for your future.

"Genia was looking for you earlier this morning to play tennis. She's making a special effort to include you. What a pity you missed the opportunity to spend time with your cousin and her friends—your peers. Come inside and change out of those filthy clothes."

Michael moved closer to her, as if in solidarity, and Kit's expression hardened. She didn't budge.

Her mother put her hand on Kit's arm, and her tone softened. "Let's go inside, now, dear . . ."

"Mother, I'm coming, okay?"

She was trapped. Trapped by her own upbringing, which dictated against "making a scene." And, worse, trapped by her own fear of appearing crazy, emotionally unbalanced. She looked at Michael with apology. Then followed her mother up the front stairs.

"Your father and I both expect you to make more of an effort," said her mother, like a broken record. "You need to spend more time with *nice* people now that you're back and things are so much better. Are you listening to me, Katherine? Because that expression you're making is very unattractive—that is where your future lies. It is certainly not out in the mud, wrestling with cows."

"*Nice* people?" Kit said.

"Don't play ignorant with me, Katherine Morgan. You know what I'm talking about."

Inside the house, Kit shook off her mother's arm. Her mother had succeeded in ruining the morning. How could she be so rude to Michael? And so dismissive toward something that Kit really cared about—her art? But Kit refused to burst into tears in front of her, and certainly not in front of Michael!

From her upstairs window, she caught sight of Dr. Landsman's van pulling over, onto the grass. The vet, Mr. Overbee, and her father got out of the truck. Her father spoke excitedly.

"Bunny!" her father called up to the house. "We've got something to celebrate today! A healthy new calf—dividends!"

Kit peeled off her muddy clothes and dashed into the bathroom to scrub her face, arms, legs. She would go back outside, at least to say goodbye to Michael, no matter what her mother might think. He was her friend! She would make that crystal clear. Then, in front of her closet, she hesitated. Suddenly, it mattered what she put on—she wanted to look pretty to say goodbye to him.

"I heard the good news," Kit heard her mother say pleasantly. "Hello, John, how very nice to see you." It struck her then, what a flirt her mother was with Dr. Landsman. Wasn't that a little hypocritical, after her diatribe to Kit about "the help"?

Dr. Landsman's reply was formal and stiff. "Good day to you, Mrs. Morgan."

Then her father interjected, "Well, well—and here's the other member of the team! Good to see you again, Mike. I hear you did great work out there. Charlie was very impressed."

"Thank you, Mr. Morgan," Michael said to her father. He sounded so grown up! She chose her favorite green dress and pulled it over her head. It was longish and slim, and had a white batik design of leaves and flowers. She hoped she looked nice. Michael had saved two of Cedaredge Farm's cows—and that gave her a rush of pride.

"I'm just glad everything worked out fine," she heard Michael say.

"You and me both, son!"

Kit hurried down the curved staircase to the main floor. Moments later, with Banjo panting excitedly at her heels, she pushed the screened door open, and burst out onto the porch.

Chapter 23

The men were still gathered down on the lawn. Michael saw her come out onto the porch and his attention locked in on her. Kit couldn't help blushing and returning his stare with a huge smile. Ignoring her mother's pointed look of disapproval.

"Overbee! You're still looking a little pale. Like you could use a stiff drink. Would anyone else like one?" her father suggested to all the men. "Is it too early for a drink?"

"That's very kind of you, Bob," Dr. Landsman said. "Mike and I'd be grateful for a couple of glasses of water, and then we'd best head back into town, see what other emergencies might be waiting for us."

"Suit yourselves. At least come up on the porch for a few minutes—enjoy the view. I'm sure you've all had quite a morning." The painters had moved to another part of the house. All of the men tromped up the front stairs and sat down on one of the various scattered pieces of wicker furniture.

"You can put that tray right here, Elsie, on the table." Her mother directed the housekeeper, who arrived now on the porch balancing a tray with glasses and a pitcher of water. Her mother began to fill the glasses, and seemed to be purposefully avoiding eye contact with her.

She perched on the cushioned chair opposite from Michael and the curve of her lips acknowledged their secret kisses in the woods. Michael responded with a wolfish grin. She could still feel the firm warmth of his hands all over her body!

Then, he got serious, making a big effort to rearrange his expression. With all the adults around, Michael clearly wanted to come off as the veterinarian's no-nonsense assistant who had just played a major role in saving the day. As if to show his support, Banjo ambled over and slid down to a comfortable position lying on Michael's feet.

"Planning some kind of special event, Bob? Or is this just the usual preparation for one of your weekend parties?" Dr. Landsman nodded toward the trucks in the driveway.

"Hell, no! I'll be damned if I went to this kind of expense every time we had a cocktail party! No, my niece Eugenia—Libby and Wes's daughter—is getting married at the farm this summer. Apparently, we need to get the place up to my sister Libby's standards. Everything needs repainting! Flowers, champagne, musicians, and tents are going to cost another small fortune. And Libby's insisting on enough staff to compete with the Waldorf-Astoria. My sister's idea of a simple country wedding." He gave a short bark of laughter that communicated his pleasure, despite his grumbling, at the elaborate and expensive plans.

The porch door swung open again. Brandon stepped out. "Good morning, everyone," he said smoothly, scanning the group as he leaned against the door frame with his hands casually in the pockets of his plaid shorts. He offered her parents a relaxed, congenial smile, and acted as comfortable, she noticed, as if he were already a member of the family.

Michael stiffened. She saw him narrow his eyes, looking at Brandon. Unwelcome and unbidden, Brandon's insinuation about Michael repeated itself in Kit's head. *One of Genia's friends, Anne, had a bad experience the night of the party. Some guy . . . took advantage of her. When she was drunk.*

"Good morning, Brandon!" said her mother, obviously pleased

to see him. "There's coffee in the kitchen, shall I ask Elsie to bring you some?"

"No, thank you, Bunny," he said. "I've already had two cups! You make coffee just the way I like it—*nice and strong.*"

Kit barely noticed the silly, flirtatious exchange between her mother and Brandon. Why had Michael become so tense, the moment Brandon appeared on the porch?

"Well, if it isn't the groom-to-be! This is my niece's fiancé, Brandon Chambers," her father said, introducing Brandon to the other men.

Michael's eyebrows shot up. He looked just like he'd been handed the unexpected answer to a baffling pop quiz. He sat back in his chair and practically grinned from ear to ear.

What was that all about? Kit wondered.

"Brandon, son, this is Dr. Landsman, our esteemed local veterinarian. And his assistant, Michael Pearce. Michael's a Dartmouth man—or will be. Brandon's an alum of my alma mater, Princeton," her father said proudly. "Another Princeton Tiger!"

Kit would have rolled her eyes at her father's corny collegiate remark—if she hadn't been so surprised by Michael's news. "Michael! You didn't tell me you'd gotten into college." She leaned toward him. "And *Dartmouth?* That's . . . that's so great!"

"I meant to." He stammered, and blushed. "I haven't had the chance."

"You two know each other, I guess." Brandon's eyes slid to her and to Michael. His hands were hanging at his sides; Kit noticed him clench and unclench his fists.

Brandon's behavior annoyed her. Was he "worrying about her," as he had insisted? Trying to be protective? Because the way he stared at her now looked more like a judgment. Or a challenge.

"We do know each other," Kit responded. She was not going to be rude to Michael, though that would likely have pleased her mother. "We're old friends, actually." She had to stop herself from letting out a ridiculous giggle.

Just to make her point, she shifted in her chair, leaning closer to Michael. "So . . . Brandon," she said, "how's the wedding planning going, by the way?" After his behavior in the barn, it wouldn't hurt at all to remind this guy that he was Genia's fiancé.

"Fortunately, Bunny is handling most of the details," Brandon said evenly. He turned and flashed a big movie-star smile at her mother. "Eugenia and I are so grateful. No one has better taste than Bunny!"

"Oh, Brandon!" her mother said, waving off the compliment. "Don't be ridiculous. Eugenia is a bit scattered when it comes to planning, that's all. And I'm afraid her mother intimidates her, which doesn't help."

Brandon continued smoothly, "I think we've all just accepted that no one throws a better party than Bunny Morgan. In fact—Kitty—I've heard that it was your mother's help on the Cotillion Committee that made the event so successful this year." He added, as if it had just occurred to him, "Say, wasn't Barkley one of your escorts at the cotillion? Let's invite him as your date to the wedding. Genia may already have him on the guest list, and Bark and I go way back. You two are perfect together."

"Don't worry about setting me up, okay?" she snapped back. How humiliating—and wrong—for him to be suggesting a date for her with Michael sitting right beside her!

"There's an enormous amount to do really, with the wedding in August," said her mother, standing and smoothing her slacks. "So . . . if you'll excuse me? John, thank you for saving Bob's cow. We can always count on you."

Kit noticed with resentment that she ignored Michael, yet again.

"We'd better be going ourselves," said Landsman. "Charlie—call me and let me know how mom and baby are doing, or if you have any trouble. And thank you for your help, too, Katherine. Congratulations, Brandon. Bob, good to see you as always. Best of luck with the wedding plans."

"Let's check to make sure Barkley is on our guest list," said Brandon as he held the door for her mother, then followed her inside.

Her dad smiled as the screen door shut behind Brandon, and then he turned to Dr. Landsman. "A nice young man," he said. It almost sounded as if her father were looking for the other man's approval.

"Seems to be. My congratulations to your family," said the vet.

Kit joined Michael and Dr. Landsman as they walked down the porch steps and made their way over to the van. Something made her glance back over her shoulder—where her father, still on the porch, stared at her, his brow slightly furrowed. She turned back, ignoring him.

As she came close beside Michael, the thin fabric of her dress grazed his leg. His hand came up—warm, firm—and slid around her waist. Behind them, her father cleared his throat and muttered "Hmpf." Then, presumably, he went in search of the workmen.

The excitement of the morning was slipping away. In its place, an uneasy feeling began to rattle around inside Kit. Michael had surprised and impressed her. Not only had she discovered this morning that he had a serious job in which, it seemed to her, he held all the responsibility of a real veterinarian. But he was leaving Franconia to go to a prestigious Ivy League college in the fall.

In the time she had been gone, Michael had grown up, become focused and serious. All of which, now, just reminded her of the things he did not know *about her life*—none of which were good secrets, or anything to be proud of.

"See you." She hesitated. Their closeness, the easy laughter they had shared, seemed to have faded like a distant memory. Or like something she had only imagined.

"Yeah, definitely!" he replied. He stopped and faced her, as if he were about to kiss her again.

Landsman turned to Michael, and she saw him raise an eyebrow. Then he went around to the driver's side of the van and got in.

"Sorry about . . . them," she said, "my parents. And that whole thing about Barkley! I hardly even know that guy." Her hands fluttered in a helpless, uncertain gesture, and fell to her sides.

"Don't worry about it!" he said. "Please. I feel bad that we got your mom so upset. Brandon . . . he's just trying to get a rise out of me. I wasn't sure, until today, if you two were, you know, a couple."

"Me and Brandon? Not at all! My cousin would have a fit if she thought he was giving that impression." She shook her head and stared down at her feet. She knew he had to get going.

"Hey! Have you ever been to an auction?" he asked suddenly. "There's one going on in town this weekend, at this big old mansion."

"Auction? Umm . . . no. I don't think so."

"Well, if you've never been to a country auction, it's absolutely something not to be missed!"

Her face brightened at his corny sales pitch. She cocked her head and her long hair tumbled forward over her shoulder. "Oh, really? Tell me more."

"Well. It's a big local event. Everyone in town will be there. The auctioneer is pretty famous around here. There'll be food—doughnuts in the morning and great Sloppy Joes for lunch. And lots of interesting old stuff to look at. We could meet there. It would be fun . . ." He stopped, and looked hopeful.

She wrinkled her nose. "Old stuff?" she teased.

"Not 'stuff' exactly—antiques. Anyway, I can virtually guarantee that you will have a good time!"

Kit laughed. "Okay, okay . . . it's a deal. It's right in town?"

"Yes—on Main Street, near the Dow Theatre. I'm sure there'll be a lot of people there, tons of cars parked out on the street. It'll be easy for you to find."

"Okay then!"

"So, I'll see you there? Saturday morning, around ten?" He took her hands.

Inside the van, Landsman turned the key in the ignition and the vehicle rumbled to a start.

She held her breath, her hands in his, for the space of one eager, hopeful heartbeat. "Yes. I'll see you Saturday," she said, letting go.

He was her friend. Maybe more. Did that mean she would have to tell him the truth?

Part III

"All the flowers of the mountain"

Chapter 24

Michael woke up early on Saturday, bursting with excitement and unable to stop his brain from shouting, "I have a date! With Kit Morgan!"

Could meeting at a country auction be considered a real date? Like taking a girl to the movies? Probably not, and Michael fought against letting his hopes soar too high. But even as he stood in front of the bathroom mirror brushing his teeth, he couldn't help grinning at himself like a happy idiot.

"I wasn't expecting you today," his dad said when he showed up at the hardware store at 6:59 a.m.

"Maybe you could use a little help?"

His father looked skeptical. Michael usually slept in on Saturday mornings, but he'd been up since the crack of dawn. He was way too jumpy to hang around the house until it was time to walk over to the auction.

After the longest two and a half hours ever, he slipped out of the store and walked the few blocks over to the Winthrop Mansion.

Not many fortunes were ever made in Franconia, New Hampshire, as far as he knew. But Nathaniel Winthrop, who discovered high-grade iron ore in Sugar Hill in the late 1700s, was among the few who did strike it rich. Over the next twenty-five years, Winthrop built ironworks in Franconia, they'd learned in high school. The business, which his son took over and then passed to his grandson, eventually employed most of the able-bodied male population of Franconia. Winthrop Ironworks would supply cookware, tools, and iron bars to towns as far away as Boston until after the Civil War.

And now the last direct descendant of Nathaniel Winthrop had died. According to local gossip—which Michael got an earful of at the hardware store—distant family members had inherited the old mansion and had instructed that the house be sold and its contents be put up for auction.

Cars and trucks were already taking up most of the parking in the shade of tall elm trees along both Dow and Main. A crowd had gathered, with people squeezing and pushing in order to examine the big Victorian mansion's contents spread out across the lawn. Everyone liked to get a good look at things before the auction began.

A flash of blue caught Michael's eye—it was Kit, blond hair flying, riding a sky-blue moped. The sporty bike impressed him as foreign, glamorous. She curved into the Winthrop Mansion's driveway and then came to a stop, looking around for a place to park.

He watched her and thought again about what Tom had blurted out that night at the bar a few weeks ago, some story about Kit being "crazy" and "institutionalized." And then he remembered something he'd overheard Kit's mother say to her as they went up the stairs of the Cedaredge house together: "Now that you're back." *Back from where?*

But it was just impossible to believe there was anything wrong with Kit. How could there be? She'd seemed so steady and determined jumping in to help deliver the calf. And later, he thought, feeling desire flood through him, as eager as he was when the two of them had started making out in the woods.

Still, as she locked the moped to a tall iron lamppost, she seemed to be looking inward as much as outward. And what was she thinking, now, as she stared up at the Winthrop Mansion?

Kit turned around and saw him. Her face lit up with simple, happy anticipation. Maybe he was just giving himself a head trip. He put his worries aside.

"Cool ride!" Michael called out as he walked over to her.

They stood facing each other.

"You look really pretty," he whispered, admiring the cute stylish shorts that showed off her strong, tanned legs, and flowered T-shirt lightly skimming her curves. But—did that sound as if he thought she hadn't looked pretty before? "I mean, nice, dressed up," he fumbled.

The girl in front of him suddenly came into sharp focus while everything boringly familiar about his life up until now faded into the background. What in the world was she doing with an ordinary, dime-a-dozen guy like him? He was so clearly out of her league. He detected the sheen of lip gloss, too. Had he really kissed those lips just a few days before?

"I guess we both clean up pretty well." Kit made a silly, smiley face. He got up his courage and gave her a kiss.

"I'm glad you came," he said.

"Me too!" They laughed, both letting go of bottled-up nervousness.

"I wasn't sure you'd come," Michael confessed. "You know, after your mom got so mad at us."

"Everyone is preoccupied with Genia and Brandon's wedding now. I doubt they'll notice I'm gone. And I'm so glad to be out of the house! And here . . . with you!" He wondered if Kit had mentioned to her mother that she was meeting him. Doubtful. Which was probably a good move.

The gut punch of his attraction to her overwhelmed him, and he found himself infuriatingly tongue-tied. He had questions he wanted to ask Kit; so many things he wanted to tell her, too. But where to begin? Finally, instead of standing there like a doofus, he took her hand, interlacing his fingers with hers, and said, "Come on—let me show you around!"

They walked past folding tables piled with lamps and books, small household items and knickknacks, and then through what seemed like a forest of dark, old wood furniture. He marveled at the strange-looking stone sculptures and carved art pieces, too, that stood in the grass by their feet as they walked around. Things you wouldn't normally see in a house, Michael thought, but maybe in a museum instead.

Kit stopped. "I realized when I pulled up to the house, I've been here before, Michael. I knew Miss Winthrop, the woman who lived here."

"No kidding."

"Yeah. I didn't know—that is, nobody told me that she'd died."

"Oh. I'm sorry about that," he said. He had to admit, he found it hard to imagine Miss Winthrop of the Winthrop Mansion as a real person.

"She came to our summer parties. I only remember her as being old, but even so, she was cool, really original. And she wore interesting clothes: long, flowing dresses, embroidered jackets. Sometimes a scarf wrapped around her head like a turban! But what I remember most is that she always said exactly what was on her mind. Miss Winthrop tried to help me, too . . ."

"Help you? With—"

"Oh, look at these!" Kit interrupted. She stopped to pick up a carved African mask and ran her fingers along its contours. "My father visited Miss Winthrop a few times, to give her some legal advice. I came, too. I remember she had an entire collection of masks from different countries. And there were all sorts of other strange objects in her house, from trips she'd taken all over the world. I thought that was so amazing. The way I grew up, we were never allowed to touch things. Everything was 'fragile,' 'an heirloom,' 'off-limits.' So I was always getting into trouble because I couldn't resist picking stuff up. Feeling it. Miss Winthrop let me touch anything I wanted in her house. I loved that about her."

She brought the African mask up to her face. "Rrraaah!" she growled at him. Without thinking, he grabbed her by the waist and pulled her close, whispering into her ear, "Hmmmm . . . Terrifying." Her laughter sounded so light and happy. It instantly turned him on. But she squirmed away and, with care, placed the mask back on the pile where she had found it.

She was an irresistible mystery.

"This is her, I think—Miss Winthrop when she was younger." Kit lifted up a silver-framed photo that lay flat on its back on a bookshelf. "She lived such an adventurous life." The photo was a black-and-white portrait of a young woman in a robe—like Lawrence of Arabia—standing next to a camel. "She used to horrify my mother, telling dirty jokes at our parties—and she must have been eighty years old, at least!"

He chuckled. "You're kidding!"

"No—Mother would get so embarrassed and call her 'that crazy old spinster.' I think Miss Winthrop was actually too wild for my mom! Daddy said she was a 'free spirit.'"

Michael was pretty sure he would have gotten along with Miss Winthrop. "Is this really weird for you," he asked, "seeing all Miss Winthrop's stuff out on the lawn, for sale?"

People were now beginning to swarm onto the front steps of the mansion, some of them trying to see if they could get inside. Curious locals pushed and shoved as they picked through boxes, dropped things, argued over lamps, kitchen gadgets, a sparkly necklace. He suddenly sensed an uncomfortable parallel between Mrs. Morgan's dismissive reference to the "help" and his own equally thoughtless lumping together of "rich people." Like everyone else pawing through the items up for auction, he hadn't really thought to connect the house or its contents with an actual person, an actual life.

"I guess, a little," Kit admitted. "But, you know, Miss Winthrop might even have gotten a kick out of the idea that, now, other people would end up with artifacts from her life, just like she had collected artifacts from other places, other lives."

He squeezed Kit's hand, and drew her away from this scene.

Which is how they walked smack into his mother.

Chapter 25

It shouldn't have surprised Michael, he instantly realized, to see his mother at the Winthrop auction. He and his dad made fun of how his mom loved digging through other people's old, second-hand junk at every local tag sale or flea market. She was holding up a large, gold-framed mirror that definitely wouldn't look right anywhere in their house. His eyes met hers, and she lowered the mirror, resting it on the lawn.

"Hi, Mom." Suddenly, he felt on guard. After things ended with Theresa, Michael hadn't mentioned anything about his personal life to either of his parents. Well, there hadn't really been anything to mention. He realized he wasn't sure how either of his parents would feel about Kit. If he found it difficult not to see Kit as some beautiful alien girl from a parallel universe, how would she come across to his mother?

"I'm surprised to find you here, Michael," she said, while looking directly at Kit, whose hand he was holding.

"This is my friend, Kit."

"Hello, Mrs. Pearce. It's very nice to meet you." Kit greeted his mother politely, as if she knew instinctively how to speak to adults and to look them directly in the eye, which automatically made her different from any of his squirmy, immature Franconia high school friends.

"And where are you from, Kit?" his mother asked, carefully taking in Kit's spotless white shorts, pressed T-shirt, and expensive-looking leather sandals. The way his mother said her name—*Kit*—sounded rude and unfriendly to Michael. Like what she meant to say was, *What kind of a name is "Kit"?*

"We have a house on Sugar Hill," Kit replied.

Calling Cedaredge Farm "a house" was an understatement. But she smiled at his mother and seemed to ignore the once-over.

His mother kept prying. "I see. And how do you know my son, Kit?"

Time to shut down the interrogation, Michael decided, and jumped in. "Dr. Landsman and I were up at Cedaredge, her family's farm on Sugar Hill, last week, delivering a calf."

The appraising look his mother now directed at Kit made Michael realize his mistake. Did he think his mother would be fooled into thinking that she was some local farmer's daughter? If it hadn't been obvious already, it was now perfectly clear to his mother that Cedaredge Farm was some big spread—and that Kit was an outsider. Someone to be suspicious of.

"Anyway," he said, "we're going to walk around a little. See you later, Mom."

"I'll expect you home for dinner, Michael."

"I hope you enjoy the auction, Mrs. Pearce!" Kit gave a little wave. His mother smiled, a fake smile, and made no reply.

"Your mother seems nice . . ." They continued to wander around the random tables and chairs, tools, and farm equipment. He heard the question in her voice.

It was embarrassing to admit, but his mother's reaction to Kit was not so very different from Mrs. Morgan's reaction to him. "Yeah, I think she really liked you," he lied. Michael now concentrated on putting as much distance and as many large pieces of furniture between his mother and the two of them as possible.

"Now here," he announced, changing the subject, "we have a veritable treasure trove!" The two of them stopped in front of a display of stacked kitchenware, all sorts of dishes and other things for the table, each one looking like a chicken: plates and cups decorated with chickens, china salt-and-pepper chickens, pitchers in the shape of chickens, chicken candlesticks. He guessed the weird collection included at least fifty odds and ends all shaped like or decorated with chickens.

Kit picked up a painted oval platter that looked like a flattened chicken, its head and feet the handles. "I knew Miss Winthrop was eccentric, but who knew she had a chicken fetish!" she said, and they both laughed.

"Oh!" She put down the chicken dish and reached for a small lined box that lay open but nearly obscured by all the chickenware. A sculpture of a bird rested on the dusty velvet interior of the box, with wings outstretched.

"It's the Bluebird of Happiness!" she whispered. She held it up for Michael to see. "I made this for Miss Winthrop. I can't believe she saved it."

"You *made* this?"

"She knew I liked to draw and to . . . make things. So, I made this for her in art class. I must have been about thirteen, I guess. It's not bad, really," she said, turning the little sculpture around in her hands.

"Wow! This is really good."

He wasn't much of a judge, but to him it looked very professional, with a blue enamel glaze and lifelike feathers. Like something you would buy in a gift store, not like some Play-Doh blob he would have made at thirteen.

"I gave it to Miss Winthrop one time when we were over for tea. She seemed so pleased and called it her 'Bluebird of Happiness'!

I'd completely forgotten about that. How weird to see it here with all of these chickens."

She placed it gently and a little reluctantly back in the box on the table.

It was nearly noon. "Something smells good!" he said. He wanted to pull Kit back to him, and away from memories that seemed to make her pensive, and sad. And, he was hungry.

"I'm starving, too!" she announced. "Let's get something to eat and find some shade. It's hot!"

They got in line for steaming Sloppy Joes. Then, balancing the big, messy sandwiches on paper plates, they went to find seats for the auction under the giant white tent. By midday in July, it was a relief to get out of the sun.

He glanced around, keeping an eye out for his mom, but there must have been more than three hundred people under the tent—the place was jammed. There seemed little chance of bumping into her and getting grilled with more uncomfortable questions. But then Michael recognized a few of his neighbors up front staring at them. Obviously checking out Kit.

He could guess what they were thinking: *Who is that? She's not from around here. And what is she doing with Walt and Eileen's son?* On the one hand, he was proud to be walking around with Kit as his date. But on the other, he didn't feel like being the object of local speculation for the rest of the day. "Let's sit in the back," he said, pointing with his paper plate to some seats toward the far end of the tent.

"Yeah," she said, nodding in agreement. She'd noticed the nosy looks, too.

The first piece hoisted up onto the auction block was an

armoire the size of a small elephant. The auctioneer opened the bidding, and Kit's face lit up with amazement as he began the classic rapid-fire, nearly incomprehensible chanting.

The auctioneer was an old guy, very dapper, and wearing a jaunty yellow bowtie. He began to work up the crowd, calling for bids, playing one bid off another. He talked faster than you would think humanly possible.

"How much for the armoire-armoire-armoire? How much for the antique armoire? I see you, sir, offering one hundred for the armoire! One fifty? Do I have another bid? Yes, another bid! Two hundred? Two hundred from the lady! And back to you, sir, that's two-fifty from the gentleman now. Do I have another bid? Three hundred? No? Last call, then—going once, going twice, SOLD!"

Piece by piece and lot by lot, furniture, tools, rugs, jewelry, and other goods were sold to different bidders. One by one, the buyers left their seats to claim their prizes at the cashier's table.

"What do we have here?" The auctioneer continued his chanting. "A box of chickens!" he said, holding up a set of chicken candlesticks for the crowd to see.

"The chicken collection! Are you going to bid on them?" Kit nudged him.

"What'll you give for a box of chickens box of chickens box of chickens? Give me ten dollars for a box of chickens." The crowd seemed less than enthusiastic. The auctioneer dug around in the box and with a theatrical flourish, he lifted up the small bluebird sculpture.

"What can I get for a box of chickens *and* one bluebird? Chickens and bluebird, chickens and bluebird, fine porcelain bluebird? Give me ten dollars for the chickens and bluebird."

Michael's hand shot up.

"Ten dollars here from the young man at the back, ten, ten, ten from the young man for his lady friend," the auctioneer said slyly.

The guy was slick. "Who'll give me fifteen can I get fifteen?"

And just to piss Michael off, someone else raised a hand. *Fifteen!*

"Back to you, young man," shouted the auctioneer, "will you give me twenty, twenty, twenty, for the chickens and the bluebird, for the young lady?"

"Thirty!" he shouted.

"Michael!" Kit cried. Thirty dollars was a lot of money for a box of chickens. "You're crazy!" she said, kissing him.

His competition shook his head no. At least that guy had some sense.

"Sold! One bluebird and a box of chickens to the young man and his lady friend!"

Kit and Michael slid out of the row and went to pay for their loot. If someone had told Michael that he'd feel so exhilarated paying thirty bucks for a box of chicken-shaped crap he would probably have said that person was crazy. Or that he was.

"Whatcha gonna do with all them chickens, young man?" the cashier asked.

"Christmas presents? I mean, who wouldn't want chicken salad forks? Or a chicken gravy dish? I'm predicting chickens are going to be a hot item this holiday season!" Michael said, and Kit giggled. "I'm getting in early, before the rush."

"Your bluebird, miss." He presented her with the box that held her bird sculpture.

"This was one of the first things I ever made, that I felt sort of proud of," she said softly, turning the little bird in her hands. "And Miss Winthrop thanked me for it, as if she considered the sculpture a real piece of art—and me, a real artist!"

He hadn't expected the gift to make her so emotional.

"I'm really sad she's gone, that I didn't know. She was a great

person, Michael. Having this to remind me of her means a lot."
She looked at him as though she were going to burst into tears. But
to his relief, she smiled. "Thank you!"

He gave her a hug. "I think Miss Winthrop would approve of
the fact that you ended up with this particular 'artifact,'" he said.
All in all, he was pretty pleased with himself.

The late-afternoon sun began to lower over the mountains. Carrying the box of chickens, Michael walked Kit back toward her
moped. A hedge ran along the circular gravel drive close to where
she'd locked up the bike, and there was an opening into the thick
shrubbery, leading to an inner garden. "Let's take a look in here,"
she said, ducking into the cool passageway.

Two curved benches, with honeysuckle growing beside them,
faced each other across a shaded circular flower garden. A hum-
mingbird buzzed in and out of the trumpet-shaped flowers. In the
center of the private garden was an old-fashioned wishing well
with a copper roof.

He put the box of chickens down on the grass and Kit took
a seat on one of the benches, placing her Bluebird of Happiness beside her. He hesitated. This could be the right moment
to bring up some of the questions that had been on his mind.
Where *had* she been? And how was it that she'd returned now,
like a miracle, into his life? He couldn't shake the uneasiness of
not knowing.

Kit reached into her pocket and pulled out a few coins.

"Want to make a wish?" she said, handing him a penny.

Michael thought for a minute, then tossed the penny into the
well, listening for the distant "plunk."

"Your turn." This time, he offered her a penny.

She dropped it into the well, closed her eyes, and her mouth curved into a dreamy smile. He thought about the softness of her lips beneath his, remembered kissing her. Maybe his questions weren't so important, at least right now.

He sat down beside her on the bench. "I bet I know what you wished for," he said.

"Oh, really? So, you're a mind reader?"

"Was it this?" Riding high on the confidence of his "bluebird" success, he leaned in and kissed her, sliding his tongue between her lips. When she didn't object, he pressed his mouth against the warm golden skin where the scooped neckline of her T-shirt skimmed her cleavage. Her skin tasted salty, and she smelled like cinnamon and flowers.

"Pretty good," she whispered. Her fingers were tangled in his hair as he moved his lips across the smoothness of her skin. "Of course, I can't reveal my wish," she said, leading him along in the guessing game, "but I can give you a hint. It's more like . . . this."

Then she pulled him toward her and kissed him back. He slid his hands up to caress the fullness of her breasts, and she seemed to melt into him.

Later, after they had more thoroughly explored each other's unspoken wishes, Kit leaned back against him, her head resting on his chest. Holding her in his arms was like being drugged with happiness, Michael mused, in a hazy delirium.

She pulled away finally, and picked up the little bluebird sculpture. As she turned it around in her hands, her thoughts seemed to slip far away.

"It looks like it's sailing home," he suggested, seeing in the outstretched wings a bird that was coming home to rest exactly where it belonged.

"I don't think so," she replied, as if to herself. "I think it was always just about to fly away, to soar up into the sky where it can be *free*."

That afternoon, if Michael had been paying attention, he might have noticed the difference between his version of the Bluebird of Happiness and Kit's and added that to his list of questions for her. But instead, he brushed his cheek against the top of her blond head, breathing in the warm perfume of her skin, and allowed himself to fall, flat out and completely, in love with her.

Chapter 26

Gasping, Kit started up from another nightmare. Had she been shouting, too?

In the dark, heavy silence of the sleeping house, she lay rigid in bed. Her heart battered against her ribs. The minutes clicked by—*tick-tick-tick*—on the clock beside her bed and she waited for the anxious, urgent taps of some worried family member to drum on her door. But none came.

In the dream, she had been standing at the lake's edge. Darkness shrouded the sky, as if it were early morning. Or evening. Her toes curled and flexed in the chill, wet sand. She shivered—from the cold? From fear?

Her feet took one step into the lake. And then another.

Water rose up around her, up to her waist now. In a sudden, forceful movement she plunged in, then pushed back up to the surface. Her body felt the shock from the cold but alive, too—exhilarated.

Arms stroking, pulling forward and kicking hard, she swam and swam until the world surrounding her became only water: rising and falling, dark and shifting. She rolled onto her back, kicked her feet high so that the light of the now-visible full moon caught in the splashes that seemed to explode in slow motion. The sparkling droplets hung in the air, floating, like diamonds.

The dream shifted.

Some kind of force slammed against her, pulling her legs down, her body down. Down. She tried to cry out as her limbs refused to work and panic overtook her. She was going under! Icy blackness closed over her head and she sank beneath the surface. And terrifying because without explanation, in this cold, silent world she heard a slow, metallic, zipping, tearing sound . . .

Tick-tick-tick went the clock on the bedside table.

She sat up straight in bed now, and pounded her fists down on the covers. What was happening to her?

Could this fear and confusion—this memory of drowning—have anything to do with seeing Michael? Allowing herself to get so close to him? Is that what was driving these terrible dreams?

But how could that be? With him, she was conscious only of an abiding happiness, as the world stood still—her sense of time vanishing entirely. The past . . . the future. So that all she wanted to do was to be in that joyful moment, deep diving into the hours they had together. Leaving every other hope or fear, plan or intention behind.

And yet, the nightmares were back. Had they returned as a reminder that she was still no closer to understanding *what had led her to try to kill herself* two years ago? That she had to keep searching, questioning, or there would be no peace?

Brandon had to be wrong about Michael—to him, Michael was some "local guy" he didn't know or trust, an outsider. But she couldn't get his insinuations about Michael out of her head. Was it possible that Michael had pushed himself on Genia's friend Anne that night at the party? Is that something he could have done, after Kit had seemed to rebuff him?

Could Michael have had anything to do with what had happened to *her*, what she had done, two years ago?

None of this made any sense to her!

Cold and sweaty, Kit crawled out of bed. The red slash of early dawn cut a line over the mountains in the dark sky, and moths battered against the window screen like desperate souls. With a blanket wrapped round her, she began to pace back and forth across her room. And as she did, another kind of dread surfaced, one she hadn't wanted to acknowledge.

Not only was the past closing in on her. For too long she had put off confronting the question of her future.

Her parents spoke with blithe confidence about her attending college in Boston in the fall. But the truth, which she'd avoided acknowledging, was that the idea of college was just a story, a place holder. For her, at least. A thing to say to put off any confrontation, to allow her to keep her doubts to herself.

Michael hadn't asked her anything about the past at all during their day at the auction. Thank God! But then, with the discovery of the bluebird sculpture, something from inside her had spoken anyway, revealing her own longings, and—perhaps—her true intentions about her future: *It was always just about to fly away, to soar up into the sky where it can be free.*

She put her hands to her face to muffle her sobs. The days were accelerating. Time was running out, and she didn't know what to do.

"Kitty! Come see!" Genia called from Kit's parents' downstairs master bedroom suite, which had a corner view across the porch toward the mountains. It was late morning now, and a light rain fell outside, tapping on the porch roof. Kit stopped beside the open door on her way from the kitchen.

Her cousin, Aunt Libby, and her mother were all struggling with a tall box. Max had brought up the immense package with the mail and other deliveries from the city the night before.

The scene was so comical that, despite her dark state of mind, Kit couldn't help but pause to watch. "What's going on here?" she asked. The three women were straining to be polite with each other while at the same time aggressively tugging at an expanse of fluffy white fabric that seemed to explode from the garment bag hanging inside the enormous box.

Genia's wedding dress.

"Let me!" Genia elbowed between her mother and her aunt, and succeeded in pulling the gown into her arms. She hugged the dress close to her, and gazed at her own reflection in the full-length mirror with wonder. As if she were falling in love with the vision of herself as a glamorous and queenly bride.

Aunt Libby studied her daughter while adjusting the Hermès scarf she always wore tied into an elaborate draping bow in her hair; with the addition of the scarf, Libby's upswept hairdo—which had gone out of style decades ago—gave her a slight height advantage over Kit's mother. In her goosey voice, she pointed out, "The gown will need to be fitted and hemmed, of course. Bunny, dear, who have you lined up for that?" Libby gave her mother a particularly challenging stare.

"I've arranged for a dressmaker to come Saturday, to fit all of our dresses," her mother said.

Libby sniffed, partially mollified. "I hope this person knows what they're doing. It's Dior, after all."

"She is quite sought after, Libby, by our friends from the city."

The two women had an ongoing competition, it seemed to Kit, to show off who was the bigger snob. And in a sleek floral tunic over white slacks, her mother appeared smugly confident this morning that she came out ahead of her sister-in-law, at least in the style department.

"We'll see, I suppose," said Aunt Libby. Then she lobbed another put-down at her mother. "On another topic, Bunny, I'm anxious to hear if you located those missing diamond earrings? The pair Robert gave you as an engagement present. Careless of you to misplace them—those earrings were my mother's, you know . . ." Her aunt pointed out. "It might be nice for you to lend those to Genia to wear the day of the wedding. 'Something borrowed' . . ."

"I'm sure they'll turn up." Her mother looked defensive and made a frosty reply. "I should never have mentioned it."

"With all the parties, there's a lot of help we don't know, coming and going," Genia said, jumping in, her face flushed. "It wouldn't surprise me in the least if one of those local girls slipped the earrings in a pocket!

"But, Mummy, Aunt Bunny, can we talk about the earrings later? And all just admire my dress right now? It really is so spectacular, isn't it?" Genia twirled with the dress as if it were a partner in a dance, and tangled her feet in the long train.

The arrival of the dress had transformed her cousin; Genia's sharp edges softened, and she was all girly wiggles and giggles. Her genuine happiness made Kit happy, too. "It's so pretty," Kit said warmly. "You look just like a princess!"

"Don't fret, Katherine," Aunt Libby remarked. "Your turn will come." Kit looked away, but caught Genia staring at her in the mirror. What expression, she wondered, had revealed itself on her face? Wanting to be tactful, Kit hoped her reaction to her aunt's comment had not betrayed alarm or distaste.

"Yes, let's hope so," said Kit's mother. "But Katherine needs to *circulate.* Which is why we're going to make sure she's connected to all the right people in Boston this fall."

"Bunny, darling, can we discuss what the plans are for outdoor decorations on the porch?" Libby said, very businesslike now that the dress had been deemed satisfactory. "Let's leave the girls, shall we? And go out and take a look. Frankly, I'm worried that we haven't ordered sufficient flowers . . ."

The mothers, both talking at once, bustled out of the bedroom and out of earshot.

Genia swayed dreamily in front of the mirror. Kit tried to imagine what she might be thinking, about the upcoming wedding, about marrying Brandon. She looked softer, sweeter. And she certainly seemed over the moon with happiness.

Catching Kit's eye, Genia said, "You look down on me, don't you, cousin?"

"What?" Kit stared at her in surprise.

Genia continued to smile at herself in the mirror, her expression angelic as she turned this way and that with the long gown. "You think I'm . . . caving in, somehow, don't you? Succumbing to . . . oh, I don't know, 'societal pressure' or however you think of it."

"No, Genia, I—"

Her cousin continued. "Sometimes, I have the feeling you think you're just above it all, Kitty. So much better than me—and everyone else. Even now, your expression says it all: Look at me, everyone! Aren't I the unconventional one? I'm in love with a *lifeguard.*"

Kit had no idea Genia thought of her this way. When she spoke at last, her voice shook with defensiveness. "He's not a lifeguard anymore! And besides, I am not in love, if that's what you think. We're friends!"

"Oh, really? When do you plan to tell the poor boy? He calls the house leaving his pathetic little messages. And according to Brandon, you made quite a spectacle the other day, in front of your parents. Brandon said that boy hangs on your every word, that he stares at you as if he were . . . a stray dog, and you a piece of meat!"

"When did he call here?"

"Ages ago. I'm sure I told you. What is this all about, Kitty, a power trip for you? Do you think that's fair, to dangle hope in front of a boy like that?"

"A power trip? You don't know anything at all about . . . about how I feel! And a boy like what, exactly?"

"Really? Do I have to say it? He's . . . *common*—he just happens to live where your family has their country home. I don't suppose you've told him your sad little secret, either, have you?"

The color drained from Kit's face.

"I didn't think so." Genia's voice was so warm and sisterly, while her words cut to the heart of Kit's self-doubt. "You see, the difference between you and me, Kitty, is that you are like some . . . some lost sailor, staring out to sea toward a destination that doesn't exist. Because you don't know what you want. I suppose all you really know is that it's not here. With your *own family*!

"But I do know what I want. Brandon may not be perfect— don't think I'm not aware that he . . . flirts. It means nothing. And, sometimes, drinks too much. But I'm a realist. I love him and we're a good match. I'll be able to lead the life I want and be comfortable. Enjoy the society and the friends—the privileges—that I . . . *that we* . . . grew up with. We'll have a place by the shore, too. Bigger than Cedaredge—oh, I *adore* the farm, but we have so many friends and love entertaining."

She turned and faced Kit with a chilly smile. "It's so funny! You used to make me mad, with your superior attitude. So silly. Because I know what my priorities are, and now I just feel sorry for you."

Kit was speechless, and hurt, at the unexpected attack. How dare her cousin judge her like this! "I don't have to listen to you," she said, finally finding her voice. "I'm sorry that looking forward to your wedding hasn't made you a nicer person." But just as she spun around to leave, her father walked into the bedroom, interrupting the two girls.

"Has anyone seen Max? I've got a check for John Landsman and I'd like Max to run it down to him at the veterinary clinic."

Genia turned to hide the dress. "Uncle Robert! Men aren't supposed to see the bridal gown!"

"Oh. Well. Excuse me, ladies . . . my eyes are closed." He backed awkwardly out of the room.

"You can give it to me, Daddy. It's stopped raining. I'll go into town on the moped." Kit followed her father out the door. Her terrible dreams, and now this attack from Genia, all pointed to one thing: She needed to see Michael. She could hardly bear to consider the possibility, but would it be better—for him? For her?—if they decided that it was best . . . to go no further?

"Kitty! Are you going into Franconia?" Kit heard Elliot pounding down the front hallway. He careened around the corner and into the living room with his hand held out in front of him. "Look what I found!"

From inside the bedroom, Genia shrieked, "Snake! Oh my God! Don't get anywhere near me with that thing!" She dropped the gown and threw herself at the bedroom door, slamming it with a bang.

"Where did you find this little guy?" Kit asked. Elliot was so annoying, but she had to admit, his timing was good. She'd seen enough of Genia. The small black-and-brown-striped garter snake, lulled by the warmth of his hand, looped lazily through Elliot's fingers.

"Under a flat rock in the flower garden. Look how tame it is!"

"Hmmm. Very interesting," her father remarked, looking over his reading glasses at Elliot's outstretched hand. "I think he'd be more comfortable outdoors, chum. And for goodness' sake, don't let your mother or your aunt see it. Or I'll be spending even more money, on pest control!"

Her father wrote out a check to Dr. Landsman and handed it to Kit, tucked into a Cedaredge Farm envelope.

"Come on, then, Elliot," Kit said. "We can go together. We'll stop up at the barn on our way out. I want to bring the Landsmans some fresh milk, too, from the farm. And we can drop your friend off where he lives, okay?"

As she and Elliot went toward the front hallway to go out, they passed their parents' bedroom, where the door was open again. Genia once more smiled her dreamy smile, no doubt imagining her brilliant future with Brandon as she admired herself with satisfaction in the mirror.

Chapter 27

As Kit handed the long envelope to Mrs. Landsman in the veterinary clinic reception room, Elliot piped up, "Do you think we could get a tour, Mrs. Landsman? Please? We know Dr. Landsman's assistant, Michael," he said importantly. "Maybe he could show us around!"

Kit blushed. "Elliot!"

"Well, of course, dears," the vet's wife responded, studying Elliot and Kit with interest. "You two just take a seat right here."

A five-alarm-level shriek from an outraged parrot broadcasted from behind the closed door of one of the examination rooms. Mrs. Landsman pushed the door open cautiously. Kit heard her say, "You've got visitors!"

A few minutes later Michael emerged, swatting bits of feathers from his scrubs. "Difficult patient," he said, smiling with embarrassment. "Not happy about the wing trim and toenail clip."

Kit slid off her chair. Images rose in her mind, of her and Michael kissing beside the fountain at the Winthrop estate. She'd been so reckless! Giving in to her attraction to him, without thinking of the consequences. Now she crossed her arms in front of her chest, embarrassed at the memory, feeling her heart pounding.

Michael, she noticed, seemed to have forgotten how to breathe.

Presumably wondering *why* the two of them were just staring at each other, Elliot poked her.

"Oh . . . um . . . my father had a check to deliver to Dr. Landsman. So . . . I offered to drop it off," she said. "I hope we're not disturbing you? You remember my brother, Elliot, right?" Elliot stood up tall. "He wanted to see where the 'animal doctor' works."

Michael looked so grown-up, dressed for work in his scrubs. The way he stood, here in the vet's office, like an actual doctor—or at least like an adult with a real job. Again, she couldn't help seeing how much he had changed, matured, in these past two years. While she . . .

"Of course I remember you, Elliot!" Michael said. "How you doin', man?"

Elliot, very formal, reached out to shake Michael's hand. "Fine, thank you," he said.

"I'm glad you two came by." Michael smiled at Kit and she blushed bright red. "Let me find out if I can show you one of the exam rooms," he said finally.

Mrs. Landsman, eavesdropping on the whole conversation, said, "Exam Room Two is free. And when you're finished," she added, as if she were speaking to an important doctor with a packed schedule of patients, "I'll be happy to go over your list of appointments for the day."

"Oh, ah—good!" Michael stuttered.

Kit and Elliot followed Michael into the exam room. It smelled of anxious dog and chemical disinfectant. Posters of cats, dogs, horses, and cows of different breeds decorated the four walls. A glass cookie jar filled with dog treats meant to reward well-behaved patients sat in dog's-eye view on the counter near the exam table.

"Here's where we weigh the animals, and up here on the table is where we put them for exams and if they need any shots," he said to Elliot.

"Do you bring cows and horses here, too?" asked her brother, carefully inspecting everything that Michael pointed out.

"No, no!" Michael laughed. "For the bigger animals, we make house calls—that is, we go out to the farms, where they live. Like Cedaredge, your farm."

"We have a bull at the farm, too. Not only cows. Do you know anything about bulls?" asked Elliot.

"Umm. A little. Why? What's your question?"

"He used to be allowed to go out with the cows. He's locked in a pen now. Why can't he go out? Kitty and I just saw him this morning. He's so lonely."

"Elliot's right," she added. "We feel terrible about it."

"Well, I guess farmers have different opinions about letting a grown bull mix with the rest of the cattle. But I'll ask my boss, Dr. Landsman, about that. Promise."

"Elliot heard all about how you delivered the calf the other day. He was very impressed. Right, Elliot?" She nudged her brother.

Her brother nodded.

"Well, I'm glad we don't have cases like that every day! But it all worked out in the end. In fact"—Michael grinned and looked directly at Kit—"I was really pleased with how things worked out."

She pretended to ignore him. "I didn't realize you were so busy here." Something in his hair had caught her attention. Something . . . green.

"It's been pretty crazy," he agreed. "And Dr. Landsman's great. He's given me a lot of responsibility. Though mostly I take on the easier cases—if you call being chased around the exam room by an angry parrot easy!"

After the tour of the office, Michael walked them out to the parking lot where Kit's blue moped was parked at an angle in the shade. "We brought you something," she said, and unstrapped a cooler attached to the back of the bike.

As he came up beside her, she lifted the lid. "Milk?" he asked. He looked at the six bottles wedged inside the rectangular Styrofoam box.

"Fresh from the cow this morning!" she said. "And the milk has a layer of real cream on the top. Dad wanted you and Dr. Landsman to have this as a thank-you for saving the calf." She handed him the cooler. "Actually, it was my idea," she admitted, and blushed all over again.

"Wow, that's great, I *love* milk—and cream, too!" They both cracked up at how goofy that sounded. Then Michael said, "Ummm, Elliot? How about carrying the cooler inside? I don't want the milk to go bad."

"Sure!"

"Ask Mrs. Landsman if she'll give you some ice cream, too."

Elliot practically sprinted back toward the clinic lugging the cooler.

Once her brother had disappeared inside, Kit found herself in Michael's arms. He pulled her close and a dizzy rush of longing swept through her. So much for self-control.

"Elliot's a huge fan of yours, you know," she whispered. Why did it have to feel this good, to be pressed up against him?

"Awww. He's a cute kid. I like your brother."

"And," she said suddenly, "and I am, too! A fan, I mean."

Michael leaned back and looked her straight in the eye, as if he wanted to make sure she wasn't pulling his leg. "What do you mean?"

"I mean," she stumbled, flustered. "I mean, you're so grown-up, Michael! You have real responsibilities. You're . . . you're taking your life into your own hands, *doing something* with it. You have no idea what most kids are like, in New York, where I grew up. The guys, for example—"

"Oh, like Reggie . . . and Brandon?"

"Yes! Exactly. Most of the time, they're just thinking about themselves, drinking, trying to look good and one-upping each other. Can you imagine Reggie or Brandon as a lifeguard, actually having to save someone's life? Can you imagine either of them delivering a calf?"

"Ah—no. Definitely not delivering the calf. Too messy," he quipped, kissing her hair.

"I can't think of any boy from that group who is really serious about anything."

Instead of acknowledging her praise, he brought his hands up to her face. "*I* am serious, about you," he said, and kissed her mouth.

"I mean it," she whispered.

"Hmmm me, too. What else do you like about me? How about how good-looking I am?"

"Michael!" She shook him. "I just wanted you to know, that's all! That I . . . I think you're a really *good person.*"

He cocked his head, as though he didn't understand where all this was coming from. "'Good person' sounds kind of dull." Then he put her on the spot: "So, when can I see you again?"

Kit tensed up. She heard Genia's voice in her head: *What is this all about, Kitty, a power trip for you? Do you think that's fair, to dangle hope in front of a boy like that?* Was it wrong to see him— *was* it unfair—when so much of her life was tangled in confusion, and the future so uncertain? *I don't suppose you've told him your sad little secret?* Kit shuddered.

"I'm not sure, to be honest," Kit answered, evaded his question. She looked away and didn't meet his eyes.

"Kit?"

"There's a lot going on right now at the farm, with the wedding coming up and all. Lots of people at the house, so . . . I'm . . . just not sure." She began to list all the roadblocks.

"But—you're not the one getting married, so . . . ?"

"I know. But . . . I promised my cousin I'd be around to help and, you know, be there for moral support." As if Genia really cared about her support. What a hollow excuse that was.

Michael didn't look convinced. In fact, he frowned as if he suspected her of being untruthful, playing some kind of a stupid girly game. Leading him on. No—that *wasn't* her.

"What if," he proposed, "we go for a hike this weekend? Just a few hours out of your busy schedule?" He added, "And that way I could bring the cooler back."

She wanted so much to be with him, but . . . was it unfair? To him? To her? And how much was she willing to open up, to tell him?

Of one thing she was certain: The truth would ruin everything. She looked past him, toward the river, the woods. It was an impossible dilemma.

Gently, he forced her to look at him. Now his tone was serious. "Where did you go, just now?"

"I don't know . . ." She shook her head.

Why did everything have to be so mixed up? So layered with doubt! If only she could talk to him . . .

She gave in. "That would be great, actually, a hike." She nodded, swallowing her fear and ambivalence. "Yes, I'd like that, I would. Saturday I have to stick around when the seamstress comes to hem all our dresses for Genia and Brandon's wedding. But Sunday would work. There's church with everyone in the morning, but I'll say I'm going to the Littleton bookstore after. So no one will be quizzing me about what I'm doing Sunday afternoon. I could meet you up at the Sugar Hill Sampler instead."

She hated having to confess that her life was practically like being under twenty-four-hour parental surveillance. It was so humiliating. The thought of having to tell him why made her sick.

"The Sampler it is!" he said, and kissed her.

She envied him his carefree smile! But then his lips pressed against hers, and how could she not let herself be happy, too? One afternoon, that's all, one afternoon all to themselves. She'd push everything else out of her mind. For that one afternoon.

Elliot walked back across the parking area toward them. His face had chocolate ice cream smeared all over it, and a grocery bag bulged in his arms. An entire vegetable garden seemed to be jammed into the brown paper sack: lettuce, zucchini, beans, and tomatoes.

"You scored, Elliot!" Michael said. He let Kit go.

She stowed the paper bag in the basket that hung off the handlebars, then came up to Michael and kissed him on his warm, sunburned cheek.

Then she noticed that green thing in his hair again! She reached up to pluck it out of the dark tangle of curls. "By the way, what is this?" she said, holding a green parrot feather between her fingers.

"Ummm . . . hazards of the job? Was this in my hair the whole time? While you were telling me how great I am?"

"Uh-huh."

"Now I know you were just messing with me!"

She shook her head and laughed at him. "Featherhead!"

"Hey!" He grabbed and tickled her until she wriggled free.

She stuck her tongue out at him, and let happiness have its way. Elliot rolled his eyes, as if he were above the silly shenanigans of his sister and her boyfriend.

"See you soon!" Kit shouted brightly, and tooted the horn as they drove off down the driveway.

Back at Cedaredge, Kit and Elliot ran into Max in the front hallway.

"Elliot, could you take the veggies to Elsie?" Kit nudged him toward the kitchen. "She's going to lose her mind over those tomatoes! You're going to be her hero!"

Max did an every-other-week, round-trip drive to the city during the summer to pick up mail or other deliveries for the Morgans. The mail was usually for her parents. And then, there had been Genia's wedding dress.

Now Max stopped her. "There's something here for you, too, Katherine." His eyes lingered on her as he handed her the blue airmail envelope. The envelope was postmarked "FRANCE."

Chapter 28

His mother was straightening up the kitchen after a late Sunday morning breakfast when Michael thumped down the stairs, humming to himself and carrying his guitar.

She stopped what she was doing—drying dishes. "Good morning, sleepy. Do you want anything to eat?"

Damn. He had hoped to make it out of the house unnoticed this morning, but obviously that wasn't going to happen now.

"No, thanks, Mom, I'm just heading out."

"You look nice," she said. "Where are you off to in such a hurry?"

"To see a friend. Kit, actually. I'll be back later in the afternoon."

His mother stood in a way that intentionally blocked him from passing her and going out the door. Her expression got serious. "I saw Theresa at the grocery store yesterday," she said. "She made a point of coming up to talk to me. She asked how you were, what you were doing this summer. She said she's dating someone who manages an electronics store in Littleton."

Already his relationship with Theresa seemed like a million years ago. "That's great. Good for her." Relief must have shown on his face. Apparently, it wasn't the reaction his mother was expecting.

She looked at him with her sharp blue eyes. Like she was trying to drill into his head for answers. "It's funny—for a while there you and Theresa were pretty serious."

"Yeah, I guess so. I guess we just . . . wanted different things . . ."

"*Michael*," she said, confronting him.

"*Mom*," he came back at his mother like a wise-ass, mimicking her tone. He could tell that she wanted to get into it with him. And he was already running late. "Since when are you such a big cheerleader for Theresa?" he threw back at her.

"That's not what I'm saying, and don't you get smart with me, Michael," his mother warned, "just because you're going to college this fall. I'm still your mother, and I've seen a lot more of life than you have. You be careful about getting too involved with that flashy girlfriend of yours, *Kitten*, or whatever her name is. Do you hear me, Michael Pearce? I know that kind of girl—she'll give you the runaround. Just to make her summer more interesting."

He ignored his mother—blew her off, actually. Like, it was just a case of his mom never approving of any girl he dated, so why argue? He gave her a big hug, and in the process, he squeezed by her. "I've got to go, Ma. See you later."

Michael swung his guitar into the back seat of the truck, checked to see that he had the Morgans' cooler to return to Kit, then drove to the deli in town to pick up a couple of sandwiches and some sodas for later. A tune played in his head. "*Oh, the summer time has come*," he sang, and smiled to himself.

The Sugar Hill Sampler was a gift store inside a big red barn, and just up the road from the Episcopal Church in Sugar Hill. His truck rumbled up the hill and at the crest, turned off into the parking lot of the well-known tourist landmark. Kit's blue moped was leaning against a tree beside the front door to the Sampler.

A sweet, spicy blast that smelled exactly like someone's grandmother's house practically knocked him over as he opened the door to the shop. Here, tightly packed shelves held every sort of odd-ball knickknack and gift: scented candles and small red and blue glass vases; novelty postcards with illustrations of cats dressed up as people; unidentifiable things made with lace that seemed to have no particular use but were somehow irresistible to women.

Kit stood by a display counter. She was studying the different kinds of fudge behind the curved glass and discussing the choices with the old man who'd made the sweets for as long as Michael could remember. "Hey!" He came up beside her.

"We used to come here when I was little, for fudge. Let's get some!" Kit said. The sweets were not the first thing on his mind—he wanted to kiss her. She seemed to shy away from him.

"Sure." Take it easy, he told himself. They had the whole day together, after all.

Michael added a huge chunk of chocolate ripple to Kit's selection of raspberry swirl. "You know, just in case we get lost and have to live on fudge for a week," he teased, and saw her cheeks dimple. Then they went outside and loaded her moped into the back of his truck.

With her back to him, Kit pulled a pair of shorts from a big cloth shoulder bag and hiked them on under the skirt she had worn to church. She slipped the skirt off, over the shorts, and jammed it into her bag. Her dressy sandals she replaced with a pair of sneakers.

"Impressive!" he blurted out, at the quick change.

Oh, man, he was in deep trouble now. Because everything Kit did amazed him. He loved that she wore no makeup, and was dazzled by the fact that she could casually change outfits in the middle of a parking lot. She made the girls he had gone to high school with—and known all his life—seem so artificial. Here was Kit, going from dressed up for church to ready for a hike in under ten seconds! All the girls Michael had ever known took hours to get ready, for even the simplest outing.

She was incredible.

As they drove past the church, he asked, conversationally, "How'd it go this morning?"

"You mean church? Awful. As usual. It's all these people my parents know, from New York City and Connecticut. They dress in fancy clothes and smile at each other like they're *best* friends—meanwhile they're throwing poison darts at each other's backs. Like, 'Is that Ginny Thompson? She's so thin and she used to be as big as a house. I wonder if it's that new Scarsdale Diet? Or maybe she has cancer?' You'd think they could give it a rest, in church at least!"

"Ouch! Doesn't sound like a lot of fun. But you go?"

"I have to play the game, Michael. For now, anyway."

The comment puzzled him. "What do you mean? What's the game?"

"Pretending to be someone you're not!" She turned to look out the window. "Besides, as far as religion goes, I consider myself a pagan."

"A pagan?" Michael raised his eyebrows. "Doesn't that involve, like, human sacrifice?"

She turned and gave him a withering look. "Duh . . . no."

"Just checking. Before I head off—alone with you—into the woods for the rest of the day."

"Very funny!"

He knew she was trying not to smile.

"No, it doesn't involve human sacrifice, smarty. For me, anyway, it's . . . experiencing the spirituality of nature. It's the trees, the animals, streams, even rocks—they're all animated, have their own energy! And we're part of that, too. I guess being in nature is where I've always felt . . . not alone. Like I belong. Maybe that's how other people feel in church."

Michael had never had much to do with religion himself, besides being roped into going to church with his family at Christmas. "Hmm. I can't imagine that you being a pagan goes over too well at Cedaredge."

"Yeah, that and a lot of other things," she sighed. Then, "Where are we going, anyway?"

"Someplace nice. You'll see."

He turned off the main road. He planned to drive out to a farm in Landaff that he'd recently visited. The owners of the place were never there, so the rundown farmhouse sat empty, with the fields rented out to a local farmer for grazing cattle. Michael and Dr. Landsman had been up to the farm once to dehorn some of the new calves. As soon as he'd seen the view from the top of the hill, he knew he wanted to share this place with Kit.

They pulled into the gravel driveway and drove up past the farmhouse and the barn.

"This is it? Are we hiding?" Kit said in a conspiratorial whisper now, as Michael parked the truck behind the big dilapidated barn. Here the truck would be concealed from the road.

"Keeping out of view of any nosy neighbors. It's not just people from New York and Connecticut who like to gossip!" He hoped he sounded mysterious.

The sandwiches, sodas, and fudge he packed into his knapsack, and then he slung his guitar strap over his chest. "Let's go!" he said, hefting the knapsack over his shoulder.

"Where? Up this way?" Kit stood taking in the long slope of field that rose to meet a forest border high up on the hill. Wildflowers grew everywhere.

"Wowwwwww! All this color! It's like a dream. I feel like I'm hallucinating!" she exclaimed as they started up the cow path.

"Daisies, black-eyed Susans, Indian paintbrush. Pink mallow and bluebells . . . and by the woods, over there, those big orange trumpets are daylilies. And look at this whole bank of purple irises! It's so beautiful!" She took off, half running, half skipping, following the cow path up the hill.

"Hey, wait up!" he said, the tall field grass brushing his calves as he ran to catch up with her. He took Kit's hand and they slipped into the intimacy that had grown deeper and more natural, he believed, each time they were together now. On impulse, Michael stopped, dropped his bag, took Kit in his arms, and kissed her.

No longer was she distant, or holding back. Now, standing beside him in the tall grass, among all the flowers, she seemed as eager as he was. He slid both arms around her waist and pulled her hips closer, kissing her more deeply. The beauty of the afternoon and his desire for her made him dizzy. He couldn't keep his hands off her.

Finally, untangling herself from him, she said, "Let's keep walking!"

He picked up the knapsack and followed. His heart was soaring. He began to softly sing words from the old traditional tune that had been playing in his head all morning:

"Now the summer time has come . . .
Let us go, lassie, go . . ."

"You can serenade me when we get there—wherever that is! Come on, slowpoke," she said, pulling him along. "No more dillydallying!"

When they arrived at the top of the hill, near the bordering forest, he took her by the shoulders and spun her around to look back at the way they'd come.

"The view!" she exclaimed.

"I wanted you to see it." They stood high up with a nearly 180-degree perspective of the fields and farmlands below. The farm buildings and houses looked like toys set beside the tiny, curving country roads that dipped and climbed in and out of view. In the far distance the mountains rippled like a dark blue ribbon beneath a few puffy white clouds and a turquoise sky.

He loved this landscape, the way it made him feel as if he could reach out and touch the rolling pastures, the gleaming river that ran in and out of sight, through Lisbon and Littleton, and the soft rounded peaks of the ancient mountains. Michael realized, as he and Kit gazed out from their high perch on the top of the hill, that he loved this place because here—beneath these mountains, this sky—some elemental and unchanging part of himself would always be at home.

Though he might not have been able to put it into words for her, he knew that sharing this place with Kit was his way of sharing himself with her. He wanted her to know . . . him.

"I think that's our farm there." Kit pointed excitedly to a tiny cluster of buildings in the distance, with a few small dots to one side that might have been cows.

"I bet you're right. When I came up here with Landsman, and saw this view, I thought that must be Cedaredge, too. I even wondered if I could see you." He wrapped his arm tight around her shoulders and pulled her close. "But there's more I want to show you!" he said. "Let's keep going."

He took her hand and they followed the trail as it sloped down slightly and came to a fence. Three poles slotted into gateposts on either side. Kit yanked at the middle pole, sliding it out from the gate. She squeezed through the gap in the fence, and then he followed.

Michael replaced the fence pole, not because he thought that anyone might be out here in the middle of nowhere and notice, but more from a desire to close them off—at least in his mind—from the world outside. For these few hours, he wanted Kit all to himself.

From the gate, the path continued through a shady tunnel of trees. Then it climbed up a short, steep, grassy incline and came out into the open.

Kit sprinted to the top of the rise, and then she stopped short.

Chapter 29

He came up beside her and they stood looking down at the pond. On this brilliant afternoon, the water reflected back the intense blue of the sky like a giant mirror. Clouds seemed to float across its surface, and a hawk, drifting high above, appeared to also be emerging from the water's depths. With the exception of the rocky outcropping of a cliff on the far side, a dense forest surrounded the pond and made it completely private.

Kit was so quiet. As he took her hand, he could feel that she was trembling. "You okay?" He looked over at her.

"Yes," she said. And then, more forcefully, "*Yes*. Oh, Michael. This pond is so beautiful."

"I thought you would like it! And I thought this would be a great place for our picnic."

"Right. A picnic." Her voice was strange and on edge. "But first—I want . . . to *swim*."

"Swim? Ah," he groaned, "of course. That was so stupid of me! I should have thought about swimming, and bringing bathing suits." His voice trailed off in apology. "I remember how much you loved to swim."

They looked at each other, and then Kit confessed, "I haven't been swimming—haven't even been anywhere near the water—for two years." Her voice sounded tight.

"Really? But you were a *fanatic* about the water!"

"Not since that summer . . . I . . . ."

Suddenly, she closed her eyes and her face began to crumple.

What was wrong? What should he do now? He took her into his arms. "Well, that's okay." He tried to sound reassuring. Maybe she just needed a pep talk. "I'm sure you haven't forgotten how to swim."

She'd buried her face against his chest, and he held her until her breath stopped coming in gasps. Then, in another lightning mood change that made his head spin, she looked up at him and, to his surprise, the smile that lit her face was one of pure mischief.

"Now what are you thinking?"

"We don't have bathing suits."

Okay, that was obvious.

"But I'll go in if you will."

"Really? Now?"

Kit blushed. "If you're not too embarrassed, that is."

Michael grinned.

Then all of a sudden, she was taking charge. "Okay, turn around. Close your eyes while I get undressed. I'll let you know when I'm in the water and then you can open them."

Following orders, he turned around. The blood was pounding in his head. His senses on high alert, he heard every small rustle of her clothing, and felt himself getting hard. With his eyes closed he followed the sound of Kit's feet running through the grass, the splash as she entered the water.

"Oh my God, Michael!" she cried out. "The water—it's fantastic!" He turned around to see that she had swum out to the deep center of the pond. She was laughing and splashing—actually, she was screeching like a crazy woman. She dove under and then seconds later erupted back up through the surface.

"It feels so good to be in the water!" She flipped on her back, kicking up a shooting geyser of water. At last, she lay motionless, and the surface of the pond settled and became a smooth mirror. From where he stood, she seemed to be floating among the clouds.

"Okay," Michael shouted, pulling his T-shirt over his head. The excited naked girl thrashing around in the water had given him a huge boner. He held his shirt in front of his crotch. "Now you have to keep your eyes closed!"

"Says who?" She flipped over to look at him.

"Hey! No looking!" he said with mock outrage.

"Scaredy-cat!" she yelled, and turned her back to him.

Michael tossed his shirt in the grass and stripped off his shorts and underwear. When he looked up, he saw that she was facing him again, staring at his erection.

"You are cheating!" Now she was making him crazy! Totally turning him on. He pretended to be outraged. "You're going to be sorry!" He walked down to the pond, feeling her eyes on him. "I closed my eyes for you! You are not playing fair!" Fueled with lust, he dove in and swam after her. Kit took off across the pond, shrieking with laughter.

Kit may not have been in the water for two years, but she was still a damn strong swimmer—and fast. But he was faster. He caught up with her and grabbed her by the foot. She flipped around, splashing him. They were both breathless, laughing, and trying not to drown as they wrestled with each other in the deep water.

Michael caught her up in his arms. "I've got you now," he growled, as Kit protested, "Michael!" and thrashed her arms at him. "You don't fool me," he said, "you wanted me to catch you." But then he exhaled sharply as her hands, searching in the dark water, found his cock. An excruciating ache of pleasure wrenched through him.

He recovered and grabbed hold of her, spinning her body away from his. Now as she tried to escape, he came from behind and slid his hands over her breasts. *She was the one gasping now.* He held his breath and dropped under the water, raking his fingers along the length of her body. His hands slid up between her thighs.

Kit floated in the pond nearly motionless, as his fingers found their way. Then suddenly, her body snapped, as if jolted with electricity. She writhed, pulling out of his arms, kicking hard and swimming away from him, fast.

He let her go.

His breath came in ragged gasps. *Slow down,* he told himself, or he might do something he'd regret, push her too far, too fast. Still, a lusty grin split his face as he watched Kit swim to a safe distance from his cock, like she was fleeing from the Loch Ness monster.

Kit regained her composure. Ignoring him—or, provoking him—she floated on her back, arms and legs spread wide. The sight of her rose-colored nipples breaking the surface of the water was more than he could take, and he dove down, down, down, touching the murky bottom of the pond.

Far above, her pale body shimmered like a star in a watery sky. He held his breath until his lungs howled for air, then rocketed back up, exploding through the surface right beside her—splashing her and making her scream.

He didn't try to touch her again. Instead, they raced each other to the far side of the pond and back again. Kit plunged backward in ecstatic, seal-like flips in the deep water, while Michael dived down beneath her. He watched the twist of her body, her hair streaming out in all directions.

By the time they swam to shore, they were both shivering from the cold of the pond. Kit snuck a glance at Michael. She must have noticed that, at least for the moment, his ardor was under control.

"You're checking me out, aren't you?" he said.

"Oh right, you wish!" she tossed back, to put him in his place. "I'm freezing! Let's lie in the sun and dry off." Kit pointed to the wooden float at the near side of the pond, anchored to shore by a long plank walkway.

He gave her his shirt to use as a towel, and watched her brisk strokes as she rubbed it up and down her legs, down her arms, across her breasts. "Well, I guess you still know how to swim." He lay back on the sun-scorched wood planks of the float and pulled her on top of him. "Come here. Let me warm you up, now." She came into his arms and didn't resist, despite the fact that as soon as she slid on top of him, he was hard as rock again.

Her wet hair fell across his neck and chest, and he ran his hands down the length of her soft body. In that moment, it seemed to Michael that they became one creature, one life, with the fierce energy of the sun, the softness of the afternoon, and the brilliant colors of the trees, the sky, the wildflowers, all breathing through them. Maybe he was turning pagan, too.

Kit planted her hands on either side of his shoulders and pressed herself up, smiling down at him. Far above, clouds drifted in the blue, blue sky. So, this is it, Michael thought, this is heaven.

"You are so beautiful," he whispered. A flush of pleasure rose in her face and warmed her whole body. All of Michael's previous sexual encounters had been furtive scrambles: in the back seats of cars, on a couch in a living room with parents sleeping upstairs. To have this outrageously gorgeous naked girl on top of him, in broad daylight—no one else around for miles—was beyond anything he had ever dreamed of.

His fingers slid up to her breasts where he gently teased the pink circles of her nipples. He watched her face, and she closed her eyes as if she couldn't bear to have him see how he was making her feel. Melting, she lowered down to kiss him.

The elegant sweep of her back, the dip of waist and swelling of hips, the curve of her buttocks—her body felt so smooth beneath his touch. An animal possessiveness gripped him, and he pulled her upward, and spread her legs wide with his hands so that she straddled him.

Her body trembled. He was overwhelming her with his hands, his mouth, his desire. His tongue tasting her tongue. And for one exquisite moment, he pressed the head of his cock between her spread thighs and pushed deeper. It would be his first time, and probably hers, too. All he had to do was thrust into her, slip inside all the way. All she had to do was say *yes*.

Kit sat up abruptly. As if she were coming out of a dream. She must have realized, suddenly, how far they were going. "Ummm. I think you better do something with *that*." She slid off him and looked down at his hard cock.

"I have some ideas," he tried. His heart pounded and his hands still reached for her.

"I know you do." She pulled away.

"What if I offered myself as a human sacrifice? Ravish my body, oh sacred water nymph!"

"Michael, that's really not funny." She was trying not to laugh.

But he was crushed. He lay back, closed his eyes, and groaned pathetically, hoping she would have mercy on him.

She turned away. In the quiet, she sat beside him, looking out across the pond. He sighed, noisily and dramatically—as if this rejection was the worst thing that had ever happened to him in his life—but she paid no attention. It was just too soon. Not for him, obviously. But for her.

Finally, the warmth of the wooden float lulled him, and he dozed off.

When he opened his eyes, sometime later, she had a big sketchpad lying across her lap. She was drawing—and she was drawing him. Naked!

Michael sat up. "Hey, what're you doing? Let me see that."

She handed him the pad.

At first, he didn't know what to say. He hadn't fully appreciated it before, but Kit was an artist. A really good one. The drawing was of him, and as realistic as any photograph he had ever seen. Except for one thing—his dick was *huge*!

"Kit—first of all, I don't think this is exactly accurate, I mean—"

"That's what's called 'artistic license.' And actually, I think it's pretty close . . ."

"Give me that thing!" he said, grabbing at the sketchpad, while she yanked it out of reach. They laughed and wrestled on the dock for the big fluttering pad of paper, and finally Michael relented as she pulled it away and flipped it closed.

"Let's put some clothes on! And have our picnic!" Kit broke up the tussle before things got out of hand again. They were both laughing so hard they were practically choking. "Come on!" she said, trying to untangle herself from his arms.

Never in his life had pure joy just bulldozed him so completely. And by now, he knew that this was just the beginning. He and Kit were getting more serious about each other. That was obvious.

They had the rest of the summer ahead of them. But more than that, they'd both soon be moving on to college, launching their adult lives, with the future wide open for the two of them. They hadn't even begun to talk about all that lay ahead! His heart expanded with hope and desire. He knew that afternoon that he wanted his future to be with Kit.

They ate the sandwiches he had brought and drank their sodas. Kit took a bite of sweet, creamy raspberry fudge, then fed him the remaining half. "What was that song you were singing as we were hiking up the hill?" she asked in a dreamy voice, leaning against him.

"*Now the summertime has come*," he sang, whispering the words into her ear. He pulled over his guitar, tuned it up, and began to play:

"*And the trees are sweetly blooming
And the wild mountain thyme
All the hillsides is perfuming
Let us go, lassie, go.*

"*I will twine thee a bower
By a clear silver fountain
And round it will I gather
All the flowers of the mountain
Let us go, lassie, go.*

"*I will range through the wild
And the deep glens so dreary
And return with the spoils
To the bower of my dearie
Let us go, lassie, go.*

"*When the rude wintry winds
And the storms rattle o'er us
So merrily we'll sing
With a light and happy chorus
Let us go, lassie, go.*

"If my true love she'll not come
No, I'll never find another
To pick wild mountain thyme
All around the bonnie heather
Will you go, lassie, go?"

The song finished, with the last chord fading into the quiet of the afternoon and Kit staring at him with an expression in her deep blue eyes that he could not read. Love, Michael hoped, but also something else.

"What's the matter? My voice isn't that bad, is it?" He tried to sound light, as if he were joking.

"That song . . . it was just so beautiful. Michael, I will never forget this day. Ever." She closed her eyes, as if pushing away all other thoughts. Then she came into his arms, kissing him with an intensity that surprised—and thrilled—him.

The wooden slats of the float were warm, and they lay back, the knapsack as a pillow, resting in each other's embrace.

Chapter 30

A long shadow reached from the cliff and spread across the pond, and the afternoon had grown cool by the time she woke up.

Beside her, Michael stretched, already on his feet, exuding optimism and purpose. He seemed to her infinitely far away, in a place where everything was straightforward and good, and anything damaged or broken was so easy to set right—no more than patching a tire on his trusty pickup. He offered Kit his hand and pulled her up beside him.

"We should be going," he said, and kissed her. "I don't want to get you in trouble with your parents."

How unutterably sweet it would have been to go on sleeping! The afternoon had swept her off her feet, held her like a dream that she had never wanted to wake from. Why couldn't time have just stopped?

But dread had reeled her back in. She was chilled to the bone, as if she were sick. The words thudded in her head: *It's over now.* It's over, and it's time to tell him *Goodbye.* She stumbled as she looked for her sneakers, as if tripping over the sticky threads of despair. She gathered her things, her drawing pad, and stuffed them into her bag.

They climbed through the barred gate once more, and began to walk back down the hill toward the farmhouse. It was late in the afternoon. Now the sun had dropped behind the trees that bordered the pasture, and the warmth of the day receded as they returned along the shaded path.

He walked slightly ahead of her and so did not notice as she struggled to keep from crying.

She loved him.

But she could not trust her feelings.

Her mother was wrong: Kit vehemently rejected Bunny Morgan's high-handed snobbism, she cringed remembering the dismissive remarks about "the help." And Genia, too! Wrong! Kit's relationship with Michael was not some kind of ego trip. *They were both wrong!*

But did Kit really know that *she was right* about how she felt? How could she be certain, after what she'd done? She, who was capable of such willful self-destruction?

Her mind zigzagged back to the letter from France. Paris. She'd read it, unable to fully absorb the significance—not because of the language, she was fluent now in French. But because of the offer it held. She'd hidden it in her dresser drawer, refusing to think about it, but the words floated in front of her now, forming a pathway to escape. A way to put an ocean between herself and everything else. Her family, her own confused feelings, what she had done and her inability to understand why. She could have a clean start. She could become the person she wanted to be.

Except . . . *she loved Michael.*

Lying with him beside the pond that afternoon, she'd seen herself as a shining star in his eyes. For those few brief hours, she'd felt like a different person—a better person—because of how he saw her. Beautiful, good, happy. Truthful. But all that would change. She knew he would never look at her in that way again.

Even so, she owed Michael the truth.

It was time. "So, you're going to Dartmouth . . ." She had to say something. But as they continued down the hill, Michael seemed to have caught her mood, to have withdrawn, too. "Dartmouth's a really good school," she tried again. "I bet your parents are very proud of you, Michael."

"Actually, Kit, the whole thing kind of blew up in my face." He glanced at her and sounded angry. The abrupt harshness of his words felt like a reproach.

"If you really want to know"—his gait became faster, and she had to hurry to keep up with him—"Mom and Dad felt betrayed that I was leaving town, leaving my father to run the store alone. Like I thought I was so much better than them, rejecting the life they'd brought me up in. Just to go to school 'with a bunch of spoiled, rich kids,' as they put it."

The conversation was taking a turn she hadn't expected, and she couldn't think of how to respond. He kept talking. "Most of my friends are getting jobs around here. Some are even getting married."

"Married?"

"Yeah, Kit. The people I grew up with, in 'small-town Franconia,' get married, have babies. They don't go to college like kids from New York. When my best friend Tom found out I was going away to college, he wouldn't even talk to me!" His voice rose.

"But . . . you're going anyway." How had she ended up making him so upset?

"I wanted something different . . . something more." He stopped right in front of her, turned to face her, and said, "Because of you, Kit! If you really want the truth."

"*Me?*" She tried to catch her breath.

"Yes! The only reason I ever got it into my head to think about college was because of you! Because of that summer, and everything we talked about. Because you had faith in me. That was the first time I'd ever really imagined a life outside the place I grew up in! I'd never considered having goals beyond high school. Or planning for the future. You motivated me, gave me confidence in myself.

"And then, Kit, you just disappeared. I thought we'd see each other again. You said you'd be back. Don't you remember? But then—nothing. You vanished. Until now. I mean, what happened? Where did you go? Because the truth is . . . I changed my life because of you."

Kit's face flushed red. It had never occurred to her that she might have had this influence on Michael.

He stood blocking her. The hard set of his jaw and his unblinking stare told her: He wanted answers. But it wasn't as simple as he assumed! He knew nothing about how she had tried to transfer to a school in New Hampshire. Couldn't he imagine that she had had hopes and plans, too? He didn't understand!

She panicked, became defensive. "Well," she said, shoving down all her feelings, "that's too bad."

"What are you talking about, Kit? What do you mean 'that's too bad'?"

Her voice shook. "I mean, I'm sorry if I somehow encouraged you to go down a path you didn't really want to go down." What was wrong with her? *She sounded exactly like—Genia! Or her own mother!* Cold. Hiding her true feelings, because she didn't know what to say, how to make sense of what was happening.

Her opaque remark only frustrated him. "I *do* want to go to college! Being with you that summer just made me realize it. Don't you see?"

Suddenly, he was almost pleading with her. "Kit, what matters is that you're here! We're together. And, well, it seems to me that we could start planning for the future, when we both get to college. Do you realize we'll only be two hours away from each other? And no more parents—we'll be *free*."

Her heart pounded with fear, knowing what she had to say.

"We could be a couple, Kit." Standing in front of her, he held both of her hands. "We could get serious. Don't you want that? I do."

"Except . . ." Kit caught her breath. "I'm not going."

"What do you mean?"

"I mean," she confessed, "I'm not going to college at all."

"What do you mean?"

"My plans . . . have changed."

Confusion sucked all the happy enthusiasm about their college future from Michael's face. Suddenly, he turned away and took off, walking ahead, fast.

Everything was spinning out of control! She ran after him and he stopped short and turned to face her. "I don't know what to think, Kit," he said harshly. "I mean, your dad told me flat out that you were going to college this fall. He made a huge deal out of the fact that you'd gotten into Wellesley. 'Following in her grandmother Morgan's footsteps' is what he said."

"It doesn't matter what he said." She spoke through clenched teeth. "Or what he thinks."

"What is that supposed to mean?"

She stared back at him, unable to speak. He was frightening her now, backing her into a corner. And provoking her, too. Who did he think he was, demanding so much of her? He looked at her, shook his head, then strode down the path, as if he no longer gave a damn about her, if she followed or not.

Michael threw the knapsack, the remains of their picnic, and his guitar into the back of the truck and slammed the door shut. Kit climbed into the passenger side without a word. She'd never said anything to him about college! He had no right to be so angry at her.

She was hugging herself and shaking on the drive back to Sugar Hill, refusing to look at him. Finally, Michael said simply, "I don't understand, Kit." He waited as she tried to find the words.

"Mother and Daddy don't know, not yet anyway, that I've decided not to go to college," she said, and turned to face him. "Michael . . ." It was no use trying to hold it together, or to choke back her tears. She broke down.

Michael pulled the truck over to the side of the road and turned off the engine. He reached for her hands and took them in his. She felt so small and pathetic beside him! "What's going on here?" he asked.

"There's so much you don't know, don't understand, Michael!"

"Tell me, then. Help me understand."

"When I saw you at the beginning of the summer, that night on the porch . . . now I wish I hadn't! I wish you hadn't come!" she sobbed.

"*What?* But *why?* How can you say that, after today?"

"Oh . . . I don't mean that . . . not really. It's just that, I can't go back to the way things were two years ago, even if I wanted to. You think you know me, but you don't. I'm not the same person, Michael! Things happened."

"What things, Kit? Please . . . talk to me."

Chapter 31

The truck was parked beneath the trees, beside old wire fencing that marked the property line of another farm. They sat in tense silence, paying no notice to the faded, weather-beaten yellow sign posted on one of the trees: NO TRESPASSING PRIVATE PROPERTY.

Finally, Kit took a ragged breath. "That summer, two years ago. Michael, you said your life changed—right? Well, mine did, too.

"I hated New York. I don't belong there! So, at the end of that summer I got into this huge argument with my parents. Screaming at them, just freaking out at the thought of going back to school in the city. And they were just like . . . stone. Nothing I said seemed to touch them." She hesitated, then blurted out, "It just infuriated me. I got so angry I told them, 'If you try to force me to go back to New York, *I'll kill myself*!'"

"*Kill* yourself?"

She didn't reply to him, but went on. "You see, I'd found out about this prep school, not far from Franconia. From Esther Winthrop, actually—the lady with the mansion. I begged my parents to let me transfer there. And with Miss Winthrop's help, the school accepted my application. '*This is no different from Brearley!*' I argued. When they said they'd consider it, I was sure they would agree. Why wouldn't they?"

"You were planning to go to school *here*?"

"Yes! I . . . never got to tell you. It was going to be a surprise. And then, we could have . . ."

He looked at her as if this discovery hurt him physically. "We could have been together," he said simply.

"Yes. That's what I wanted."

Neither said a word. Finally, Kit went on in a quavering voice: "But then, a few days later they said no.

"Mother gave me this big speech about 'what would people think?' and how it would *affect me* socially, not to graduate from Brearley with the girls I'd grown up with. Daughters of all their friends. And God forbid I wouldn't 'come out' in New York like every other Morgan daughter—I know that's all Daddy cared about! What they really meant was how it would affect *them* socially. Daddy, as usual, let Mother be the heavy. But I'm sure they both felt the same way."

"I'm so sorry, Kit," he said at last, and moved to take her into his arms.

She pulled back. "There's something else you need to know. Right before we left Cedaredge to go home to New York, something happened. Something bad."

He waited.

"I—I almost drowned. In the lake. Profile Lake."

"What? But Kit, you're like *a fish*. How—?"

"I tried to kill myself, Michael," she said in a hoarse whisper.

"You *what*?" And then, gently, "Are you serious?"

She didn't answer, but kept talking in a flat, monotone voice. "They decided I should go away, then, to a boarding school in Europe. They'd changed their minds about New York. They told me this school in Switzerland would be the best place for me. All they really cared about was that under *no circumstances* could the word get out that I'd tried to . . . *off* myself. It would just be our little family secret. 'No point in having your whole future ruined over one foolish mistake,' said practical Dad. By November I was in Montreux. There was nothing I could do. That's where I've been for the past two years, finishing high school."

After a long silence, Michael said, "Jesus. Kit, if only I'd known. Why didn't you try to get in touch with me?"

"What could you have done?" Her voice shook. "How would that have made a difference, anyway? We were sixteen, Michael. Just kids." She remembered the speed with which her bags had been packed for her, how she'd been hustled onto a plane to a foreign country.

She crossed her arms defensively. She'd done it. She'd told him. And now, she knew she was completely alone in the world.

But Michael leaned over and pulled her stiff, wooden body into his arms, pressing his forehead against hers. "Oh, Kit."

"Michael, don't you see? There is something really wrong with me! Really screwed up."

Why wasn't he shocked, repulsed even? His compassion confused her. It was just pity! He felt sorry for her. Inside, she cringed with shame.

They drove on at last, and he said, "Why come back here, to Cedaredge?"

She took a deep breath. "I'd finished up school and my parents wanted me to come home. There's Genia and Brandon's wedding, for one thing, which is a big deal for the family."

He asked, "So, you're here because your parents wanted you to be around for Genia's wedding?"

"That's one reason, yes. For the family. But I wanted to come back, too, to Cedaredge. I . . . I needed to understand—*why*? Why would I go so far . . . ?"

"You mean, why would you want to commit suicide?"

She was unable to speak for a moment, then, instead of answering him, she blurted out, "I never stopped thinking about . . . *us*!

About that summer." Kit turned to face him, the truth of her feelings exposed in her eyes, in the intensity of her voice. "Those two years I was away, I thought about you . . ."

They'd arrived back at Cedaredge now. Michael stopped at the entrance to the residence driveway, in front of the big archway of lilac bows. He brought his hand up to stroke her cheek. "It's so hard for me to believe you tried to—kill yourself. What happened?"

Something flickered deep inside of her, in the hidden past. "I don't know. Maybe I wanted to punish my parents. To show them that I would not allow them to control me. I was so angry. I wanted to stay here! And I just kind of lost it. I guess . . . in that insane moment . . . I decided that nothing could possibly be worse than going back to my miserable existence in New York. There's just no other explanation."

Michael seemed to brood, in silence. He asked, "That was a pretty drastic solution, don't you think? I mean, not to sound selfish, but did you ever consider how I would feel? To lose you?"

"No," she whispered, ashamed that she could not remember having had those thoughts. "No." Like she'd told him. She was fucked-up. Broken.

There was nothing else for her to say. She'd done what she'd done. And her mind spiraled back along the well-worn path that had no exit: Even if she could get to the bottom of her motivation to try to end her own life, what future could there really be for her, as long as she stayed here? None.

He still didn't understand that.

Suddenly, she hugged him quickly, then sat back, faking a smile and a phony cheerfulness. "I'm so glad we got together again, Michael. Today was a perfect day. And I'm really proud of you! Dartmouth's such a great school. You're going to do so well."

He picked up instantly on the false brightness—and the finality of her words.

"Okay, so you've decided not to go to college. Fine. But Kit, that doesn't mean . . . that is, we can still see each other, right? We have the rest of the summer and then . . . What are you doing after this summer and the wedding? Where're you going? Do you have any plans?"

"It's probably best if we don't see each other again." Her artificial smile crumbled. She bit her trembling lower lip and looked away.

Michael turned to her, his face flushed and angry. "Kit! I am pretty damn sure I didn't imagine the afternoon we just spent together. And now, out of the blue, we can't see each other? What are you talking about? *Why?*"

"Because then we'll always have this beautiful afternoon as a perfect memory." The words exited her mouth like a string of mindless soldiers.

"*What?* I don't want a perfect memory of you!" He began to shout. "Kit! I want to spend time with you *now*, tomorrow . . . after the summer is over. Why can't we do that?"

"I have to go now, Michael. It's late."

He pulled into the driveway and around to the front of the house. She carried the cooler left at the clinic as he helped her unload the moped from the truck and push it up onto the grass.

"Hey. You forgot this. It was on your seat." He held up a braided rope bracelet.

Brandon's bracelet. She must be wearing the same shorts as the day she'd been working on her sculpture in the barn and Brandon had shoved his bracelet on her. The bracelet had fallen out of her pocket and onto the truck seat.

"It's nothing," she said, flustered.

Michael's voice came out flat and angry. "Nothing? This belongs to Brandon, doesn't it? Your cousin's fiancé. I've seen it—he was wearing this the night of the party at Cedaredge. Is that what's going on here? You and Brandon?"

"No! He . . . he pushed that on me. I didn't want it!"

"Kit!" he said between clenched teeth. "None of this makes sense!" He took hold of her arm and the cooler dropped to the grass. The pain of his grip made her freeze.

"Let go of me," she said, her voice shaking. He needed to stop! Get away from her . . . it was too . . . *much*!

"I'm sorry," he said, immediately releasing her, "I didn't mean to . . ."

She held herself as still as a statue, while all her emotions withdrew from her heart, fleeing to some cold, lonely hideout. She might have been a block of stone. And then, she kissed him, a very different kind of kiss from the last one they'd shared. A kiss that said *goodbye*.

"I'm fine," she said. She squared her shoulders and walked up the steps to the house without a backward glance. Because she could not trust her feelings, she would no longer allow herself to feel.

Chapter 32

It was all Michael could do not to slam the truck into a tree on the way home, put himself out of his misery.

By the time he got back to Franconia, to his house, it was right in the middle of dinnertime. His mother, father, and Jennifer all took one look at him and said nothing. He stormed through the kitchen, pounded up the stairs to his room, and slammed the door shut.

Kit loves me! He repeated it over and over to himself as he paced around his bedroom. In her eyes, he'd seen the same longing he felt for her, returned just as deeply; in the way her body had melted into his, he knew her desire was every bit as strong. She wanted to be with him! As much as he wanted her. *That was the truth.*

But why had she been carrying around Brandon's bracelet? Was the whole "perfect memories" speech she'd given him just a cover for the fact that she and Brandon were involved in some way? He leaned against his closet door, hit it with his fist. He couldn't accept that! Wouldn't!

A few days later, he was out with Dr. Landsman on a farm call. In a rare moment of silliness his boss had gotten into a boxing match with one of the friskier bucks at the small goat farm. The goat had reared up on its hind legs to butt and play with the big human being. Landsman chuckled as he brushed mud off his shirt; maybe he was expecting that his assistant would find the ornery goat's antics amusing, too. But Michael stared into space, lost in his own dark, hopeless thoughts.

"You've been awfully quiet lately, Mike. What's going on?" Landsman asked gruffly.

"Nothing."

"Doesn't seem like 'nothing' to me. You've hardly said a word in three days. If I were to guess, I'd say this glum mood has got something to do with that Morgan girl."

It must've been obvious, after that day they'd delivered the calf, that Michael had fallen for Kit. Frances had probably mentioned that Kit and Elliot had stopped by for a visit to the clinic, too.

He didn't respond, didn't know what to say. The last thing he felt like listening to was a lecture on his personal life from his boss.

They walked up from the goat pen toward the van. "I've known the Morgans a long time, Mike. In fact, Bob Morgan and I have known each other since we were young men, about your age."

Michael looked at his boss with surprise, and Landsman whacked him across the top of the head.

"Yeah, I was your age once, too, smart guy. Bob and I met on the ski lift at Cannon, took a run together, and then another—really hit it off.

"It's funny. These kinds of families are often snobbish and unfriendly toward outsiders. But somehow, Bob and I became good friends. The Morgans lived in New York City, but spent summers and winter vacations at Cedaredge. Bob and his sister, Libby, have been coming to Sugar Hill since he was a kid, when his old man decided he wanted to have a farm for the family.

"Not long after Bob got out of law school and had joined his father's New York City law firm, both his parents died in a car accident. A terrible tragedy, and it put a lot of responsibility on Bob's shoulders—he took over the law firm, Cedaredge Farm, and managing the family's money. I guess Libby got her parents' place in Connecticut.

"I remember Bob confiding in me back then that he wasn't sure he could handle it all. Wondered if he should just sell the farm and the dairy business, buy a house on the shore in Connecticut or Long Island, like most of his set."

How did this have anything to do with him and Kit?

"And then along came Barbara Karlsen. Bob fell in love, got his confidence back, and he married Barbara within a few months. Despite Libby's objections that Barbara was 'a gold digger,' that she didn't come from the right kind of background, or any background that the Morgan family knew of.

"And Barbara Karlsen became Fifth Avenue Bunny Morgan." Through his indifference, Michael picked up on something in Landsman's voice. Bitterness? He looked over at his boss.

"Barbara didn't come from money and privilege," Landsman continued. "Her relatives landed in New York more or less just off the boat from Norway. But she's beautiful and clever, and she learned how to make her way in the Morgans' world. Bob's easygoing, sees the good in everyone. But he's never been poor, never had a reason to be envious of anyone else. Bunny's different. Money matters a lot to her, and social position even more. She fought to have that for herself, and she's going to make damn sure her children have it, too, and don't take it for granted."

They stripped off their coveralls and loaded the dirty clothes and the gear into the van. Once inside, Landsman turned the ignition on, but they didn't move. Apparently, his boss wasn't finished.

"All of which I'm telling you, Mike," he explained, "because girls like Katherine Morgan are only going to break a country boy's heart. In the end, they'll stick with their own kind and carry on the family business of being rich. Katherine is destined to marry a young man like herself—wealthy, who went to private school, belongs to country clubs, attended debutante balls. Her parents will see to that, I guarantee you."

"Like that phony Brandon Chambers, for example?" Michael said angrily, pulling away from Landsman's fatherly sympathy. "I don't buy it. Kit's not like that, not at all."

"Maybe, maybe not. But my strong advice to you, son—man-to-man—is that you forget about that young woman and move on."

When Tom called that night and suggested meeting at Ollie's Pub for a beer, Michael agreed immediately.

"Long time no see! What've you been up to, buddy?" Tom punched him in the shoulder as he sat down at the bar.

"Working mostly, how about you?"

Ollie wasn't around and someone else was tending bar. "I'll take whatever you've got on draft," Michael called out, and flashed his ID from his wallet. The bartender nodded, unconcerned, and poured a lager. He slid it across the bar.

"Studying, actually," Tom announced cheerily. "I just enrolled in a business course at the two-year college in Franconia." He smiled at his friend's surprised expression. "The course starts this fall and I want to be prepared, maybe do well for a change."

"Business?" Michael stared at him over his beer. "Really? I thought you were going into the business of beer drinking and ski-bumming."

Tom's face got red. "That was kind of the plan. But then your sister got to me."

"Jennifer?"

"Yeah, we've been going out since the prom. She didn't tell you? I've even given up weed!" He said it as though a miracle had occurred.

"I guess the Pet Rock worked—she felt sorry for you," Michael ribbed him.

Tom took a gulp of beer.

Michael thought of morning breakfasts when he'd rushed out of the house and barely said good morning to anyone; evenings when, if he did eat dinner with the family, he'd stare at his plate completely preoccupied. Even if Jennifer had wanted to confide in him about Tom, he had probably seemed miles away and unapproachable.

He suddenly felt bad. "I've been pretty busy with work, it's a long day and sometimes I get home and just crash." What a weak excuse. He wanted to be straight with Tom, but . . .

"Some girlfriend action keeping you busy, too? Jenny mentioned you might be seeing someone. From the word on the street, I guess it's not Theresa anymore?"

The misery and confusion jammed up inside of him sorely tempted Michael to unload the whole impossible predicament on Tom. He'd fallen head over heels for Kit, but didn't dare allow himself to speak about her. About how incredible and beautiful she was, and complicated, impossible to understand. And how crazy he was about her and scared of losing her. If he got started, where would it end?

"D'you remember that Morgan family . . . that one Ollie mentioned, early in the summer?" he said.

Suddenly, he could hear Landsman's voice telling him to "move on," warning that girls like Kit were out of reach for a local guy like him. Tom might say it differently: roll his eyes, laugh, shake his head at his friend's bad luck. But the message would be the same.

"She's out of your league, buddy." And Michael didn't want to hear it.

"Morgan? Yeah. I think so. Why?" Tom asked.

Interrupting their conversation, some loudmouth trying to get to the bar elbowed his way between Tom and Michael. "Yo! Bartender—another scotch, and make it a double this time."

Then Brandon Chambers looked over at Michael as he leaned on the bar waiting for his drink. "Hey—don't I know you?" he said.

Chapter 33

"We met at the Morgans' farm, a couple weeks ago." Michael glanced in Brandon's direction, then turned away. Why was it that just looking at this guy made Michael feel like punching him in the face? He could think of a few reasons . . .

"Oh, right, I remember now. You work with the veterinarian." The bartender slid the drink over to Brandon. "Put it on my tab, pal, will you?"

Uninvited, Brandon took a seat next to Michael. "You're the dude who stuck his arm up a cow's pussy. What's that got to be like?" He grinned at Michael and made a lewd expression. Then he knocked back half of his scotch.

Michael stared at him, only partly surprised at Brandon's crudeness. He got it now: This guy only took out the shiny, polished version of himself for people like Bob and Bunny Morgan. People he wanted to impress.

Michael said tersely, "It was like this, pal: 'I've got about thirty seconds to save my client's really expensive animal.' That's what it was like." His temper began to simmer. No need for either of them to pretend they liked the other.

"Oh, right, the big hero. My apologies. Hey, let me buy you two another round. Bartender—three more here. And speaking of heifers . . ." He winked. "Any tips for how a guy can score around here?"

Tom raised his eyebrows at Michael, like, *You know this guy?*

Why the hell Brandon continued to hang around him and Tom,

Michael had no idea. He must be drunk. Or maybe he needed a break from his phony nice-guy act. It had to take a lot of effort to make sure that no one in Kit's family ever wised up to the sleaze-bag side of his personality that now muscled its way forward at the bar.

"Tom, this is Brandon; Brandon, Tom," he said, introducing them. "Brandon is getting married next month to Robert Morgan's niece, Eugenia—unless she's wised up and changed her mind?"

"Very amusing," said Brandon, leaning back on his bar stool. "Yep. We're about to tie the knot. The deal is almost done."

"The deal?"

Brandon smirked and shook his head at Michael condescendingly. "I know this isn't your world, farm boy. So let me clue you in. My dad didn't inherit some family fortune—he made his money himself. A lot of it. In certain circles that's considered 'dirty.' And then there's this little problem that my mom split, left town when I was fifteen. Not cool with the Social Register crowd.

"Dad wants 'in'—to the clubs, the parties, and the connections that come with old families and old money. Genia's family has got those connections, *and* they also have a little cash-flow problem. Genia and I agree to tie the knot and, bingo—we've got a deal!"

"Why would you do that?" The idea disgusted Michael.

"Why not? You've seen the girls in that family. Fucking high-class. For starters, any wife of mine has got to be top of the line in the looks department." He stopped blabbering for a second to give it more thought. "But honestly"—Brandon took another swig of his drink—"honestly, the real reason I'm marrying Genia is just to piss people off."

"What do you mean?"

"I mean, I'm pretty damn tired of being treated like an outsider by all these high-and-mighty Upper East Side families!" A jagged edge of resentment cut through Brandon's loud monologue. "This is going to change all of that. Can't wait to see their faces when me and my new wife—Eugenia Livingston of Fifth Avenue and Greenwich, Connecticut—sail the yacht into the Coral Reef Club in the Bahamas. Yeah. That is going to be rich." He savored his fantasy. "Anyway, you have to marry somebody."

Tom cleared his throat and spoke up. "What about, um, love?" he asked awkwardly.

"*Love*," Brandon sneered. "Hormones, my friend, nothing more. It's all just a financial transaction. There's nothing sweeter than revenge."

"And Genia . . . knows all this?" Michael asked. "She's going along with it?"

"Hey, I'm a catch, man!" Brandon laughed. And didn't answer the question. "Genia's father wants this deal," he said. "My dad's money has helped everyone get over their fine sensibilities. And when it comes down to it, Genia knows who pays for the designer clothes, her horse, the trips to Aspen and the Virgin Islands: Mommy and Daddy. She'll do what her parents tell her. And if I get sick of her," Brandon shrugged, "as Hemingway once said, you can always 'trade in one woman for another'—or get a girl on the side."

"Sounds pretty heartless," Michael said.

Brandon turned on him with a cynicism that left Michael speechless. "Let me tell you something," Brandon said, his breath smelling of alcohol and bitterness, "those girls are nothing but bargaining chips. And ambitious men have been using their pretty daughters to make deals since time began. Nothing new there. Read your history books.

"Anyway," Brandon said, "just joking about 'scoring.' Those days are over. For now, anyway. Just had my last screw as a free man with a nice piece of country-club ass. A hot redhead—hey"— his eyes gleamed at Michael—"I think you know her, too."

"I seriously doubt that."

"Yeah, you do: Anne thought you were pretty hot, *Mr. Life-guard*, that night around the pool table. But you know what? I showed her 'hot' later on that night."

Brandon did remember him from the Morgans' party, at the beginning of the summer. And it was the lifeguard bit that had stuck with him, pissed him off. Had Brandon actually had sex with one of his fiancée's girlfriends? Genia's friend Anne had been pretty wasted, too.

This guy was even more repulsive than he had imagined.

"Never forget a face," Brandon said, as if warning Michael. "And I got you on my radar."

"Really? Why's that?" Michael stared at him. That simmer was heating up to a boil.

"You know why. This obsession you've got for Kitty Morgan. Don't tell me you haven't tried to make it with her—I saw you two whispering to each other. You better give it up, man. And anyway, I've been down that road already, and she's nothing but a cock tease."

Brandon's bracelet in Kit's pocket. In front of Michael's eyes appeared the image of Kit, naked, laughing and doing back flips in the pond. The thought of Brandon hitting on her sent him into a rage. "You fucking dick!" he growled, standing up from his bar stool.

Tom tried to hold him back as Michael shoved the stool aside and got into Brandon's face.

"Hey," the bartender shouted, "settle down over there or you're out!"

"Let's have a toast!" Tom joked, elbowing his way in between Michael and Brandon. "To the soon-to-be Mrs. Brandon and the man of her dreams! Or, at least, the man of her parents' dreams!"

Instead of taking a swing at one of them, Brandon leaned back, raked the hair off his forehead, and chuckled. "Yeah, right. Cheers to my darling bride!" He raised his glass of scotch, then drained it. "It may take a couple of Quaaludes to get that ice queen Genia to loosen up so I can fuck her on our wedding night. But guess what, boys? Sometimes unconscious is preferable. I'm not always in the mood for negotiation."

Brandon pushed back his bar stool and got up, swaying on his feet. He guffawed, "That's hilarious!" and lurched down to the other end of the bar, laughing to himself all the way. He was plastered.

Tom shook his head. "Pretty messed up."

Michael stared after Brandon. What was it about this guy that made him both disgusting and hard to look away from? Like road kill. "Messed up doesn't begin to describe it," he said grimly.

Michael sat down again, trying to cool off. He steered the conversation to Tom's new school ambitions as they finished up their beers. As they passed by the kitchen on the way out, they ran into Ollie. "That one down there, at the end of the bar?" Michael jabbed a thumb in Brandon's direction. "He's loaded. I'd keep an eye on him."

"Will do. Not sure I like the looks of him myself. Hope he didn't spoil the evening for you boys."

"You know, Ollie," said Tom, "there is nothing that makes me happier about being just a simple guy from Franconia than meeting a whack job like that from the big city!" Tom and Ollie laughed, but Michael shot one last, fierce glance in Brandon's direction. And then Tom asked, "What the hell are Quaaludes?"

Ollie turned dead serious. "Where did you hear anything about Quaaludes, Tom?"

"That guy at the bar, Brandon, was joking about giving some girl Quaaludes, to make her . . . relax."

"It's a tranquilizer and it's illegal. Not something I want being passed around in *my* bar. If you'll excuse me, boys, I think it's time I cut young Brandon off and send him on his way."

They reached their cars and Tom gave Michael a rough hug, then asked, "What were you saying earlier about the Morgan family? Was it something about that guy?"

"It doesn't matter," Michael lied.

"Okay, man," Tom said. "Hey, don't be a stranger, okay?"

"I'll try not to be. Good luck with your classes! Glad to hear Jenny's crackin' the whip." He tried to let himself feel happy for his friend and his sister. Tom was a good guy.

But as he drove home, Michael couldn't stop hearing Brandon's ugly voice in his head: the story about Anne, and the way he'd referred to Kit—like he had some proprietary right to tell Michael to stay away from her!

Ambitious men have been using their pretty daughters to make deals since time began. Nothing new there. Those words made him sick. Would Kit's family try to use her like that one day, too—the way her cousin Genia was being used? That thought enraged him.

Kit was independent, had a mind of her own. But how long, Michael obsessed now, *how long* until she finally got tired, gave in, and just accepted the way things had to be for girls like her?

Chapter 34

Kit looked up, her eyes red and swollen and her face pale. The door to the barn slid open.

The preparations for the wedding had spun the main house into a whirlwind of phones ringing, gifts arriving, cakes to be tasted, and seating charts to be deliberated over—and her mother, Aunt Libby, and Genia all arguing from breakfast until bedtime. Her father, busy with work and overseeing farm activities, had charged Max and Elsie with keeping the kids out of her mother's way. Who knew what Brandon was up to, prowling around the edges of all the high-pitched female drama.

Kit spent her waking hours here, now, alone in the barn, her absence unnoticed in the excited chaos of wedding preparations. She'd withdrawn from life at Cedaredge like a sick and wounded animal.

Squinting in the doorway, Elsie paused at the big, open space. Sun poured into the barn's interior, where a warm, comforting smell of many summers of dried alfalfa grass rose from weathered floorboards. Her lips pursed when she noticed Kit at the worktable. "Now here's where you've been hiding!" she exclaimed.

Elsie bustled toward the big double refrigerator and the immense freezer in the corner. Kit saw she was on a mission. "I've had a mind to see just what old relics are buried here in the freezer—I wouldn't be surprised at all to find shrimp cocktail or meatloaf from thirty years ago!"

She lifted the freezer lid and began to rummage around inside.

"What do we have here? Chicken potpie—four of them! I think we could save those. And a nice beef fillet. I wonder if this ice cream is still good? Oh! All these trays of pigs in a blanket—from the children's charity picnic three years ago? No—these definitely have to go!" As Elsie dug deeper, heaving the frozen items inside left and right with an energetic *clunk*, Kit feared she might even pitch herself headlong into the cavernous appliance.

"A thorough cleaning of this freezer is what's needed!" came her muffled voice, "and with the wedding just a few weeks away! We'll need every inch of space for the caterers."

"Can I help?" Kit asked, wiping clay from her hands on a cloth.

"No, no, dear. I'll get Max up here later today." Elsie stood back up, and gave the contents of the freezer one more assessing scowl. Then she pulled the heavy lid shut.

Her reconnaissance mission accomplished, she now turned to Kit.

Her keen eyes took in the large mass of clay, and the big sheet of plastic that had covered it, rolled back on the worktable in front of Kit. "Have you been keeping that in my refrigerator, then?" Elsie inquired, approaching the worktable and peering with interest at the clay.

The river clay did not possess the solidity of a block of commercial, store-bought clay. So Kit had fashioned a large frame from tin scraps in the barn. Inside of this she was experimenting, trying to create a kind of relief sculptural panel from the soft blue, earthy material.

She thought about covering up her work; she had lost a sense of whether or not what she was trying to create was any good. In these past days, inspiration had deserted her.

But it was too late now to hide what she was doing.

"Oh, my. That's very lifelike." Kit stood back as Elsie studied the panel of clay. The features of a young man and a young woman were taking form; the girl's long hair swirling in a kind of wave around the two. Elsie's eyebrows raised in surprise. "You've got quite a talent."

Kit said nothing.

"I can see you're serious about this. I had no idea. And here I thought I knew everything about you, dear!" Elsie sighed. "But you're all grown up . . . leaving your poor old Elsie behind . . ."

Elsie's half-teasing, forlorn complaint made Kit smile. "You know I've always been interested in drawing and painting, Elsie."

"I suppose," Elsie conceded.

"Well, after . . ." Kit hesitated, then continued. "After I went to Switzerland . . . these past two years, while I was away at school, I started to get serious—like you're saying—about art. Sculpture especially."

At Kit's oblique references to her suicide attempt, Elsie placed a sympathetic hand on her arm. "Oh, dear girl!" Elsie said. Then, "We're all given our own special gifts and talents. I can see yours is art. Do your parents know?"

"Oh—please don't mention anything to them. They don't 'approve.' Mother in particular."

"Hmm." The housekeeper muttered and seemed to study the sculptural panel.

"Elsie—" Kit spoke vehemently, needing her to see. "This is what I want to do with my life. I don't understand why Mother and Daddy are so against it! It didn't used to be such a big deal with them—and now suddenly all they care about is debutante parties and 'meeting the right people'!"

Elsie sat down on an old wooden bench beside the worktable. She gazed off into the distance. "Max and I have worked for the Morgan family from the time of your grandparents. Did you know that?"

"I didn't realize . . ." Kit said.

"We were just newlyweds when your grandmother offered us both positions," she said. "That was a happy day for Max and me, and we've had many happy years with the family. Oh, how your grandmother enjoyed entertaining! She was such an exuberant and glamorous hostess. An invitation to a party at the Morgan home in New York was very sought after." Elsie smiled, reminiscing. "And she kept busy visiting family, and traveling back and forth to Cedaredge once your grandfather bought the farm. Now your mother," Elsie continued, "she learned to entertain, too, and seems to enjoy the particulars of guest lists and menus, flower arrangements. She's very competitive on the tennis court, and an excellent skier, too, I understand."

Elsie looked at Kit with kindness, as Kit's eyes glazed over.

How could anyone find this kind of a life meaningful? Finally, Kit raised her voice, in protest. "I just can't imagine myself doing any of that stuff! Living that way, Elsie! It seems like such a waste—missing out on *life*."

"To some people, Katherine, what seems to you like 'missing out on life' might be considered a great privilege . . ."

The truth of Elsie's words deflated her. "I must sound like a spoiled brat to you. But . . . I don't want to live the way my father and mother live. And they don't understand!"

"Would it surprise you to know that your mother had creative interests, too, when she and your father first met?"

"Mother? What do you mean?"

"She had a talent for sewing, and made beautiful dresses. I think she could have been a designer, even. Under different circumstances."

"She likes nice clothes, I know that," Kit said. She had a strange thought: Her mother must have been drawn to form and texture and movement, just as she was, and been observant of the human body. At least, once upon a time.

"When your mother was just a young bride, she and your father and your aunt and uncle were at a benefit, at the Frick Museum, I think. Your Aunt Libby admired the dress your mother wore and badgered her until she had to confess that she, herself, had made it. Libby was shocked, and put an end to your mother's dressmaking that very day." Elsie shook her head. "Libby criticized your mother for embarrassing the Morgan family. The very idea of someone in the family making their own clothes simply would not do for your Aunt Libby!"

Kit was silent. She knew Elsie meant her story to be instructive.

"I'm sure that was hard for your mother, but she listened to your aunt, and decided family comes first."

Kit burst out, "But . . . that was her choice!" She looked away and jabbed one of her modeling tools into the wood table. Elsie had always "seen" her: perceived and appreciated who Kit really was. She thought of her as an ally. Couldn't the woman understand now that Kit's dreams had some merit?

"Did you know Esther Winthrop?" Kit asked, almost as a challenge. "My parents' friend, who lived down in Franconia?"

"Well, of course I knew Miss Winthrop!" Elsie beamed, perhaps happy to change the subject. "A very impressive lady. A real character, I might add."

"Miss Winthrop traveled! *She* had adventures! She didn't just hang around, organizing tea parties. She collected art, too. She didn't care what other people thought about her, she wasn't tied down by stupid family rules and regulations!"

"Yes, that's true, my dear. But Miss Winthrop was *very* rich, which certainly helped. And she had no husband and no children. What we will never know is if Miss Winthrop found herself lonely at times, wishing she'd followed a more traditional path. You have to be very strong minded indeed to be that independent."

Elsie's words subdued her. She thought about the fierce, self-assured old woman who had so impressed her as a child; Kit was not at all certain that she had any of the strong-mindedness of *that* indomitable Esther Winthrop.

Then, she confessed, "I received a letter, Elsie. Just a few days ago. From a man who knew Miss Winthrop. The son of a friend of hers, in Paris."

"Is *that so?*"

She bet that Max had told Elsie about the airmail letter, and that she was probably curious about its contents. "This man runs an art gallery, with his wife. His father was a collector and a good friend of Miss Winthrop's. When he heard that Miss Winthrop had passed away, he decided to write to *me*. About . . . well . . . visiting them in Paris."

"You don't say now?" Elsie's eyes widened. Kit detected worry rather than enthusiasm in her voice. "I wonder what made him think to write to *you?*"

Inside the barn, the loud clanging of the kitchen bell reached them. "Who is ringing that bell?" Elsie huffed, and stood up. Then, "Oh, dear! It's nearly eleven thirty. I have to run, dear, and get lunch started."

"Elsie—I'd rather Mother and Daddy don't know about this . . . letter. They've got so much to think about right now with the wedding, don't you think?"

Elsie stood in front of her, rested her hands on Kit's shoulders, and looked at her with affection and concern. "All this talk of art and adventure! Of course I understand how important that is to you.

You're a creative person and a free spirit. But dear Katherine . . . isn't there someone . . . *someone special* . . . who might keep you closer to home?"

Her eyes moved to the clay portrait Kit was working on. A portrait of a young man with a laughing smile and wild curling hair, and a girl with eyes only for her beloved. Sculpted wildflowers bordered the piece. Elsie was so clever, so observant. Kit brought her clay-smeared hands up to her face and began to cry, as all the pain she was trying so hard not to feel overwhelmed her. "Oh, Elsie!" she sobbed, as the older woman put her arms around Kit.

"It's more complicated, isn't it, my dear?"

As if in response, from outside came the mournful bellow of Freddie, still trapped in his bunker.

Chapter 35

The Bluebird of Happiness perched on her dresser. Kit couldn't even look at it without bursting into tears. She slumped in her bed, surrounded by a jumble of books and her drawing pad and pencils. With little energy or inspiration, she turned through the pages of an old fairy tale illustrated by one of her favorite artists, Arthur Rackham. The story of a girl from the water so out of place on the dry land of regular people.

She reached for her pad and tried to make a sketch following Rackham's expressive and beguiling style. But the story just made her sad and she gave up, curling into herself under the covers of the bed.

A light, sharp tapping sounded at her door.

She struggled to sit up as her mother looked in. Her mother smiled—not noticing, or perhaps ignoring, her daughter's dejected posture and unhappy expression.

"Am I interrupting anything?" Her mother walked into her room, seemingly intent on a friendly mother-daughter chat. The drink in her hand, a gin and tonic, Kit assumed, clinked brightly with ice cubes.

Kit mumbled, "I'm just reading." She slid her pad under her pillow.

The perfume on her mother's light cashmere sweater seemed to take over the room. "Have you tried on your bridesmaid's dress since the seamstress made her alterations?"

"I'm sure it's fine."

Placing her drink on the dresser, her mother turned to Kit with clasped hands and a cheerful, determined expression, "Why don't we take a look now? Just us two?"

Her mother unzipped the garment bag hanging in the closet. Kit stood, then slid off her sweatshirt and jeans.

Together they lifted the gown over her head and pulled and tugged it down into place. Then her mother assessed Kit's appearance. "You look very lovely," she announced.

If Kit had been a store mannequin, she could not have felt stiffer or more lifeless. And somehow being encased in the voluminous bridesmaid's dress—contemplating the upcoming wedding—sharpened her grief and heartbreak at the certain loss of the person she loved.

"I'm not sure it's terribly flattering," Kit said, looking down at the mass of fabric. She resembled a small figure being swallowed up by an immense lavender cream puff.

"Well, you'll have your hair up, of course," her mother remarked.

"Do you think that will really make much of a difference?"

"The important thing is your attitude, Katherine. That is what makes *all* the difference."

An anxious sweat began to prickle her skin.

Her mother moved to her bed and sat down, seeming to forget about the bridesmaid's dress. There was something else on her mind. She reached for her drink. "When I was just a little older than you are now, Katherine, there were two young men I liked very much."

Kit stood where she was, the sheer volume of material making it impossible to sit down. Couldn't her mother just leave? She'd tried on the dress.

"One was your father, and one was . . . another young man. This other boy was very nice, too, and handsome." Her mother sipped her drink. "But I knew in my heart it would never work with him, he didn't have money and his prospects were too limited. Well, it's just as easy to fall in love with a man who is rich as it is to fall in love with one who is poor. So why not love the rich man? I thought about the life I wanted, and I thank my lucky stars I had the self-discipline to make the right choice." She looked at Kit as if she wanted to make sure her daughter understood.

"I . . . guess I am, too," Kit said. "I mean, glad you chose Daddy. Since I wouldn't be here otherwise." Was her mother implying that she had not always loved her father, not loved him the most? Kit didn't want to think about this "other young man."

"That's not the point, Katherine. The point is, in life we all are called upon to make difficult choices. To . . . give up certain things."

Kit thought about her mother's talent, as Elsie had described it, for making beautiful clothes. How hard had it been to give up the satisfaction of making something with her own hands? Did it explain why even the most beautiful dresses from her dressmaker in Italy always dissatisfied her in some way? Or—why her mother often seemed dissatisfied in general?

Her mother stood, regarded her own reflection in the mirror, and patted her hair. She turned back to Kit. "There will be some nice young men at the wedding. You'd do well to keep an open mind. And I've already been in touch with Missy van der Kamp—her nephew Andrew is at Harvard. I think you'll like him very much; we'll set up a luncheon together this fall. Katherine—"

"Yes, Mother." Though she stood right beside her mother, Kit felt herself moving away, far away. Perhaps her mother felt it, too.

"*Katherine!* You must put this young man, this . . . Michael Pearce . . . out of your mind. I know that seems difficult right now.

You've allowed your emotions to make decisions for you. Perhaps your father and I have been too permissive, at times . . ."

"What?" Now, anger began to smolder inside of her. "What are you talking about?"

"What I am talking about, Katherine, is how surprised you'll be—once you move to Boston, start making new friends and going to parties again—at how quickly you forget all about him."

How dare her mother presume to know how she felt! She had no idea—*none*! Rage shot through her veins until she imagined herself rocketing through the room like a dragon from a Japanese illustration, flames shooting from her mouth.

She turned to her mother, shaking so hard she felt her teeth chatter. "Don't you tell me to forget him, Mother!" Her voice rose in fury. "I will not forget him!" she shouted. "*Ever!* No matter what you say!"

Her mother flushed. And then, her face grew pale and tight. She smoothed her skirt and checked her reflection again in the mirror. She smiled at her reflected self, a beautiful, hard smile. As if she knew she held all the power in their relationship. "I'd advise you to adjust your attitude, Katherine." The words were uttered like a threat.

Her mother spun around, fast, to face her. "You are eighteen years old—old enough for me to remind you that if you don't like what I have to say, you can *pack your bags and leave*! That's right—you live under our roof; your father pays your bills. But we are under no obligation. And all these privileges you take for granted can disappear"—her mother snapped her fingers—"like *that*."

She and her mother locked eyes, like two combatants. Her voice strangling with emotion, Kit demanded: "Did you forget him, Mother?"

Her mother hesitated, uncertain for a moment. "Forget who?"

"That other boy. The one you didn't marry."

Confusion flashed across her mother's face. It vanished in an instant. "What a foolish question," her mother replied. "Of course I did." She turned and walked out the door.

Kit struggled out of the bridesmaid's gown, leaving it to deflate in a heap on the floor. She pulled her jeans and sweatshirt back on. Wiping tears of anger from her face, she stomped down the hall, cut through Lucy's and Elliot's rooms, and crossed the passageway that led to Max and Elsie's quarters—and a back stairway.

The kitchen was dark, it was long past dinner, and Kit exited through the back door. Then she hurried through the garden, under the deeper shadows of cedar trees, and strode up toward the barns. An awareness that she was trapped pursued her, taunting and belittling her—she had to escape it!

The light in Charlie Overbee's cottage was off, and no one seemed to be around the milking barn or the hay barn—or the yard. But then she heard the restless, agitated sound of Freddie, stomping in his pen behind the milking barn.

Freddie! Her parents didn't give a damn about the poor animal, no matter how many times her father had promised to "look into things." And now, suddenly, the idea of this big, physical animal that by all rights should be free to move around in the grassy pasture but was instead caged like a prisoner enraged her.

She had to do something, since no one else would. She heard the animal snort and bellow again. "Freddie!" She called out.

As she walked quickly down the pathway and past the cottage, a shape appeared, briefly, moving away from the direction of the bull's pen in a hurry. Was someone else worried about him, too? But it was just a shadow, cast by the barn security light.

No one was back by the pen when she came around and found Freddie, huffing and stomping, his large bulk crushed into the corner of the small space. His tight, cramped quarters made her feel like bursting into tears again—if she had not, instead, been too angry.

"I'm getting you out of here!" she cried.

The pen door was not locked because the catch was heavy and complicated to work. Kit struggled with the metal pieces of the latch, gasping, until she finally got it right. She dragged the door to the pen open.

Kit stood back, fully expecting Freddie to come bursting out of his enclosure. Out in the field, the dark shapes of cows lying in the grass began to move. The animals rose awkwardly to their feet. Freddie turned and reached his head forward through the open door. He sniffed, blew hard through flared nostrils, and sniffed again, savoring the night air, and the anticipation of the open pasture. Out in the field one of the cows made a soft, long, guttural call.

Freddie shook his great bulk and trotted out of the pen to join the other cattle. Kit watched him move away to enjoy his freedom and his tribe. Her breath slowly came back to normal.

Mission accomplished.

Elation lightened her step as she strolled through the dark, back around to the front of the barn. Then she noticed light glowing in the hay barn. She veered toward the barn entrance and slid the door open. "Hello?" she called, peering inside.

Her worktable lay overturned and on its side in the middle of the barn. Her tools had been thrown everywhere. "Oh, no!" she cried, running to the table and dropping to her knees. On the

ground, the sculptural relief of the boy and girl—the two lovers—
had been smashed to pieces, beyond repair.

There was only one person who both knew about the piece she'd
been working on and had the brute strength to fling the massive
work table across the room.

Part IV

*"I will roam through the wild
And the deep glens so dreary"*

Chapter 36

Sunday, end of July. The days seemed quieter now, and sometimes, first thing in the morning, the air was cold and the ground sparkled with frost that melted as soon as the sun came up over the mountains. Several weeks of summer still remained, all the sweltering-hot days of August. But these crisp mornings reminded Michael that summer, after all, was finite. Not too far around the corner, fall inevitably waited. For him, a time of change and uncertainty.

He'd gotten out of bed just as the first light began to filter through the treetops outside his bedroom window. Now he sat downstairs on the porch, in jeans, a flannel shirt, and bare feet, strumming a soft tune so as not to wake the rest of the family.

The stairs creaked, one after the next, followed by the sound of footsteps in the living room. His dad, still in his slippers and plaid bathrobe, padded out onto the porch to join him.

"You're up early on your day off, Pop."

"I could say the same of you."

"Yeah, couldn't sleep."

"Well, I expect you've got a lot to think about, with college starting in a few weeks." His dad sat down beside him on the beat-up old couch.

He stopped playing and rested the guitar against his knee. For the first time a question occurred to him that he'd never asked his father. "Did you ever want to go to college, Dad, when you were my age? I mean, do you feel like you missed anything by not going?"

"Well, it wasn't something my friends or I thought about that much back then. Back when I was in high school, I assumed I'd just help Grandpa run the hardware store, which didn't take a college degree," his dad said.

Michael stared out through the porch screen at the quiet neighborhood he'd grown up in. "When I got into Dartmouth, it felt like such a big deal, it felt like the most important thing I'd ever done. Life changing. Now—I don't know—I wonder: Does it really matter that much? Am I really even cut out for college? I mean—you and Mom seem pretty happy and neither of you went to college."

"When your mother and I found out that she was pregnant, that you were on the way"—his dad smiled at him—"a lot of decisions were made for us. We were happy to be having a baby, but it also meant that there were other choices we couldn't make. And that was fine for your mother and me. But I don't think it would be fine for you, Mike."

"Why not?" he said bitterly. "Why shouldn't I just get a job in town, like everyone else? Settle down. Forget about the whole college thing." *Forget about college, and forget about Kit.*

To allow that argument space in his head hurt too much.

As the days had gone by, Michael began to realize that even if Kit did care about him—even if she loved him—she had made her intentions clear. As far as she was concerned, it was over between them. He needed to move on from her. Say goodbye to all the dreams he'd imagined because of her—pointless now—in which the two of them embarked hand in hand into a shared future. Why even attempt to struggle through four years at Dartmouth, a place where he probably didn't even belong?

His dad didn't seem surprised at all at his complete reversal about going to college. And—he wasn't buying it. He looked Michael in the eye.

"You're smart, Mike, and ambitious. You've always pushed yourself. And you're restless, too, in a way your mother and I never were. You need to get out there, see new things, meet new people. Challenge yourself. Otherwise, I don't think you'll be happy.

"Mom and I are extremely proud of you. It may not always seem like it—I know Mom can be tough on you—but we really do want you to take advantage of this opportunity. A day will come when you meet the right girl . . ." His father paused, for emphasis. Michael guessed that his parents had had a discussion about Kit, about her being the "wrong girl" for him. "And then it will be time to settle down, have a family even. There's no need to rush that. Go out now and see the world, son."

But if he and Kit were wrong for each other, how could anything else matter?

"Morning, Mikey," Jennifer said as she came down the stairs. He was sitting at the breakfast table, while his parents drank their coffee and looked through the weekly *Pennysaver*. He was still at loose ends, feet restlessly tapping the floor, not sure what to do with the day.

Jenny looked nice. She had on what he knew was her favorite dress—a sunny yellow, with puffy sleeves—and her purse hung over her shoulder as if she planned to go somewhere. "I heard you and Tom went out the other night," she said. She kissed their parents on the cheek.

"We did."

"Did he tell you about his Bongo Board?"

"He did not."

"Sounds like some new gimmick," said his dad.

"Supposedly it's to improve his balance, for skiing. It's like a surfboard on a rolling pin. Anyway, he fell off of it last night, cut his chin and scraped up his arms."

Michael couldn't help laughing. "Tom's a sucker for stuff like that. You're going to have to keep an eye on him. Have you seen his Pet Rock?"

"Yes!" She rolled her eyes. "Hey, we're meeting for breakfast this morning at Polly's. Why don't you come with us? It might be nice to talk to my big brother *at least once* before he leaves town and goes to college."

"Oh, you just love to bust my chops, don't you?" Michael had cheered up. It made him feel good, he realized, that his sister had taken the initiative and invited him out with her and Tom. "Well, okay. Twist my arm. Are you heading out now?"

"Yeah—but can we take two cars? I need to do some errands afterward."

Polly's Pancake Parlor was a local breakfast place inside an expanded version of what had once been a maple sap process- ing shack, or sugarhouse. In the old days, tapping maple trees for sap and boiling the liquid down to a sweet syrup had been a big industry in the area, and had given the town of Sugar Hill its name.

At least two generations of the same family had run Polly's, which attracted just as many locals with its famous homemade pancakes as summer tourists. The matriarch of the family usually stood by the front door, saying hello to people. With the exception of a few neighborhood girls, the waitresses were mostly daughters and granddaughters of the family. They served breakfast and lunch dressed in short red dresses adorned with a maple leaf pattern, and covered with frilly white aprons.

He would have been looking forward to a breakfast at Polly's more if he hadn't remembered that Theresa was working at the restaurant this summer. Would she have gotten over being angry at him? According to his mother, Theresa had a new boyfriend, so chances were she had moved on and couldn't care less about seeing him. At least that's what he hoped.

As usual, a long line had formed in front of the restaurant. Jenny and Tom had arrived first and already snagged a place not too far from the head of the line. As Jenny had mentioned, Tom had a big cut on his chin and both forearms were scraped up, too.

"Bongo Board?" Michael eyed his friend's war wounds.

Tom blushed. "Yup, Bongo Board."

When their turn came up, their waitress gathered menus and led them to their table.

Theresa was working that day, flipping pancakes at the open grill. He took a deep breath and walked ahead, determined to give her a friendly wave if she saw him. But then he looked across the cozy dining room and practically tripped over his own feet. Seated around a big family-style table were the Morgans: Kit and her family, as well as Genia and Brandon and two other adults he assumed were Genia's parents—Kit's aunt and uncle.

Theresa noticed Michael right away. She scowled—like, *you should've known better than to set foot on my turf!*—unfortunately, not as if she were prepared to let bygones be bygones. At more or less the same time, Kit's sister, Lucy, recognized him, waved, and gave Kit a nudge.

Kit wore her hair pulled back into a severe braid, and the blank expression on her face made it clear that, while her body might be seated with the rest of the Morgan family, she herself was far away. "Kitty!" Lucy jabbed her again, and she blinked and looked up with surprise, and saw him. Unguarded longing filled her eyes, and he exhaled as sharply as if he'd been punched.

Brandon twisted around in his chair. "Well, if it isn't our local James Herriot," he announced. His voice was loud and sarcastic and boomed across the small restaurant. Theresa no longer paid attention to her batch of pancakes; she looked from Brandon to Kit, and then to Michael.

"Do you have to be *such* an asshole?" he heard Kit burst out fiercely at Brandon, as he took his seat at the table. Meanwhile, Tom and Jenny had already started scanning the breakfast options; the sweet smell of pancakes off the grill and warm maple syrup filled the restaurant.

"*Kitty!* What's the matter with you?" Genia snapped.

Mrs. Morgan added, "Katherine! Apologize to Brandon right this instant. And let's not have a scene." She flashed a warning look toward the table where Michael, Tom, and Jenny were seated.

Jenny smiled over the top of her menu. "Seems like you know a few people here, Mike." Tom stared at Kit—and the Morgan family—and then back at Michael; he hit his forehead with an exaggerated smack, and mouthed a silent "Oooooooh," as if he finally understood something.

The tension at the Morgans' table drew looks from other people in the restaurant. Then, like an explosion, Kit leapt to her feet, shoving her chair out of the way so that it screeched against the hardwood floor. She was shaking, Michael saw. She threw down her napkin then walked, fast, toward the front door.

"Let me go see if I can calm her down," Brandon drawled. He got up. "I don't want this to ruin everyone's breakfast." His voice sounded so reasonable, Michael noticed. *What a smooth motherfucker.*

Brandon crossed the dining room in a few quick strides, faster than he would have thought someone that big could move. The door to the restaurant slammed behind him.

"Jenny, Tom—sorry . . ." Michael stood, aware of the twittering of apologies and tut-tuts over at the Morgans' table. "I'll be right back," he said. He felt his sister's and Tom's stares follow him as he walked to the door of the restaurant.

Outside, he came upon Brandon towering over Kit, with his back to the restaurant door.

Kit was shouting at him. "It was you who destroyed my sculpture, wasn't it!"

The polite manners Brandon oozed around her family were gone. Now his voice was low and angry. "You're wasting your time on that shit—and on that guy, too! I don't get it, Kitty. You never gave me a chance. And I could have given you so much more than farm boy. Made your family happy, too." And then he laughed, like suddenly none of that really mattered. "But hey, now I'm marrying your spoiled cousin Genia instead."

"What do you mean? You don't love Genia?"

"Did I say that? You're crazy, you know? Making up all kinds of lies."

"How can you be marrying her," Kit persisted, "if you don't love her?"

Brandon said scornfully, "Marriage doesn't work that way, sweetheart."

"Well, Genia thinks it does. You can't do this to her—marry her if you don't love her. And . . . I intend to tell her what you said!"

"Tell her? She'll never believe you. You are just a crazy bitch who tried to *off* herself. No one takes you seriously. *No one.*" He grabbed her arm and threatened, "You keep away from Genia. Do you understand me? You better play nice or things are going to get ugly."

Then she cried out in pain. "Aaaah! Let go of me!"

Michael saw, then, that Brandon held Kit's arm in a tight grip. "Hey! Let go of her arm," Michael said moving in toward them.

Brandon swung around to face him. "What do *you* want now?"

"I said, let go of her."

"Oh, so you're threatening me? What're you going to do to me if I don't, farm boy?" He was breathing hard, and instead of releasing Kit, Brandon twisted her arm backward, so that she cried out again and dropped to the ground on one knee.

Brandon was taller than he was, by more than a couple of inches, Michael figured. But drinking and partying—or however he wasted his time—had made Brandon soft underneath his clubby polo shirts and Bermuda shorts. And Michael had just spent the summer busting his ass doing farm labor.

His whole body expanded with a rush of anger. He hauled off and smashed his fist into Brandon's face, hitting him square on the jaw. Brandon went down, landing in Polly's flower garden.

"Jesus, Michael!" Kit stared at Brandon, now sprawled out on the ground.

Out of the corner of his eye, Michael noticed a movement. He caught a glimpse of Mr. Morgan standing inside of the front window of the restaurant. Morgan must have taken in the whole scene of Brandon mistreating Kit, because he was glaring at Brandon and his expression registered surprise and outrage. Michael met his stare, but couldn't tell what Kit's father was thinking, or intending to do.

The owner of Polly's appeared at the door, blocking the way with hands planted on her hips and eyebrows raised. A gaggle of waitresses piled up behind her to see what all the fuss was about, Theresa among them. She looked at Kit, and then at Michael. "*Slut*," she said, loud enough for Michael to hear.

Meanwhile, Brandon sat groaning in a patch of petunias. The sight nearly made Michael laugh out loud—if not for all the trouble he was pretty sure he'd just gotten Kit and himself into.

"Let's just go," Kit said. She looked wild, like a cornered animal. "Let's just get out of here!"

He took her hand. "The truck's this way."

Chapter 37

Kit braced herself as the truck skidded out of the restaurant parking lot. Her arm throbbed where Brandon had twisted it back and forced her to the ground. She was breathing hard, and her eyes were wide, unfocused.

The truck tires squealed as Michael took the steep curving road too fast. "Michael!" she said, coming back to herself. She tried to form a coherent thought.

He eased off the accelerator, allowed the truck to slow down the hill. "You okay?" He looked over at her. "That bastard."

"Michael—can we drive to the lake?" She sat up straight now; she was no longer thinking about Brandon.

"You mean Profile Lake?"

"Yes!" The lake. She needed to go back to the lake. Now.

The truck lurched forward as Michael jammed the stick shift into high gear. Taking the back roads from Sugar Hill, they reached the entrance to the Profile Lake Club in twenty minutes flat, half the time it normally took to get there. Michael swerved into the Club entrance.

But this wasn't right! Didn't match the picture in her head. "No. Don't go in here. It's . . . not here. Let's keep driving, down the road a little farther." He swung the truck back onto the road and continued.

Kit scanned the shoreline as they drove slowly, following the curved length of the lake. At last, the water disappeared behind a leafy screen of birch trees. Then, she saw what she was looking for. "Here it is! This is it—turn off here," she pointed toward a dirt track.

Kit turned to see Michael shoot a cautionary look in the rearview mirror. She hadn't even thought that someone might be following them! But the road behind them was empty. He exited the main highway, tires skidding, and floored it down what seemed to be a seasonal access road until the truck was safely out of view. The track became rutted, and then petered out.

"Stop here!"

She scrambled out fast and came around to the driver's side. Michael leapt out of the truck and stood beside her. Weeds had reclaimed the last traces of the man-made dirt road, and sunlight just barely filtered through branches of tall pine and scrubby oak trees. Her eyes searched in all directions. *She knew this place.* But . . . why did she know it? Why?

"What are we looking for?" Michael asked. "Kit?"

She turned slowly in a half circle, staring into the woods. Green leaves fluttered with traces of sunlight. And shadow. Something pulled at her. This place, these woods, looked so familiar. Why?

"I'm trying to remember something."

They had pulled off the road close to the southern, undeveloped tip of Profile Lake. "Does this have anything to do with the time you . . . almost drowned?"

"Maybe. I don't know. But there's something important about this place. This way," she whispered. "I'm pretty sure it's this way." She took off into the woods.

They followed the slope up through the trees. And there it was—like she had known—the impression of a trail, of someone moving through the woods and leaving just the smallest clues: the low-hanging branch of a tree bent backward, crushed stems of creeping forest undergrowth. A scattering of pebbles.

The trail climbed farther uphill, moving over soft mossy ground and through birch trees and evergreens. Then the woods changed. Dense forest opened to a kind of glade. She slowed, stopping for breath, in an overgrown apple orchard. The moss-covered ground of the forest gave way to tufts of long grass.

"Have you been here before?" Michael asked as the two picked their way forward through the tangle of vegetation. Kit sensed his care for her, and his presence gave her courage. Some kind of darkness inside her head was calling and she couldn't have done this alone. He held the gnarled branch of an apple tree out of the way for her, and she ducked under. The voice frightened her—but she had to pursue it now.

The landscape shifted again. They crunched over what might have been a gravel drive. Finally, she and Michael came to a wide walkway made of slate, partly hidden beneath grass and weeds. To their left, what looked like decorative stones placed intentionally to create some kind of formal garden jutted out and formed a ragged border.

She stopped short. "Whoa!" Michael said, as he bumped right into her.

Not more than fifty feet in front of them, but almost completely obscured beneath tall spruce trees, loomed a hulking abandoned building.

"This is it," she whispered. Kit stared up at the dilapidated structure in the shadow of the trees. In the quiet afternoon, the humming of cicadas sounded anxious and uneasy.

"What the . . . ? It's an old hotel!" Michael whispered.

"A hotel?"

A deep covered porch extended the length of the building in both directions, and in the center, a grand entryway arched over the landing at the top of a wide staircase. Paint peeled away from the siding, but Kit could see, now, that the building must have looked very pretty once upon a time, a gracious mountain-white with deep, evergreen trim.

"A hundred years ago, maybe more," Michael began, "there were lots of big hotels like this around Franconia Notch, up on hilltops or near lakes. Rich people stayed in them, to get away from the summer heat of the cities. Sometimes people were sick and hoped the mountain air would cure them. There's a hotel like this, still in operation, near the Sugar Hill Sampler.

"But I guess, as time went on, wealthy people started to go to other places. And by now, almost all of these old hotels have been shut down. This one must have been abandoned, left for the woods to take it over.

"I can't believe I worked at the Club for two years and never knew this was back here. Is this hotel what you were looking for? How did you know about it?"

"I'm not sure." Kit chewed on her lip, shook her head. "Can we . . . can we go around to the other side?" She started toward the building without waiting for his response.

Overgrown honeysuckle and azalea bushes pulled at her clothing as she bushwhacked around to the rear of the hotel. Here, nothing grew but tough grass and weeds.

A narrow flight of stairs leading up to a simple, unadorned doorway. A staff entrance at the back of the hotel? This was it. Kit grabbed the railing and climbed the stairs.

The unlocked door swung open easily. She stepped inside. Her eyes darted to the banks of counters and rows of cupboards along one side of the room. To the stove squatting beside several large sinks along the opposite wall. A strange old-fashioned contraption for wringing the water out of clothes—she remembered that! A large butcher-block table took up most of the center of the room.

"The hotel kitchen," Michael said, coming up behind her.

At the far end of the kitchen, a brick chimney rose above a fireplace. A wooden drying rack stood unfolded on the hearth. A table with two chairs. And the bed, a simple cot.

It was all almost exactly as she remembered it.

Even the smell of the freshly split wood beside the fireplace. And the clothes, wrung out but still damp, hanging on the drying rack.

"Kit." She heard Michael's voice beside her. He'd taken her hand, as if to pull her back from danger. "Someone's living here. Kit," he said more urgently, "this may sound nuts but . . . there's this story in town of a crazy guy—some kind of hermit—living in the woods behind the lake. Right around here, to be exact."

"What?" She turned to look at him, and saw him staring at the axe beside the fireplace.

"We should get out of here."

Kit hesitated, then pulled away from him. "No. No, that can't be right. I woke up in this room." She walked over toward the fireplace and the cot. "And there was a man here, too." She looked down at the cot, ran her hand across the rough wool blanket. Turning back toward Michael, she searched his face, hoping he might help her untangle this riddle. Offer a clue.

"You woke up in this old hotel kitchen? When?" Michael asked. His voice was on edge. Did he not believe her? "Do you remember why—how you got here?" She heard apprehension in his voice . . . *fear for her.* Nausea bubbled up into her throat.

She shook her head, pushed her hair back. Something . . . something had happened . . . in this room. But whatever it was, it wasn't the thing that scared her. Taking slow, deliberate steps, she moved around the butcher-block table, then circled around to the open door and stared into the distance. Just visible through the branches of the trees, the lake glimmered. The lake.

She sat down on the top step.

When she spoke, her voice rose to a bare whisper: "This is what I can remember: It was September, evening, and I was riding my bike from the farm to Profile Lake. I used to sneak into the Club after hours—remember?—to swim anywhere I wanted."

Uneasily, he came to sit beside her. "You nearly got me fired half a dozen times with that maneuver."

"Summer was over. We were all going back to New York, maybe the next day even. Yeah, because I remember being angry. Furious. That's right: My parents had just decided they wouldn't let me transfer to the school in Franconia, that I'd have to go back to school in the city."

"I wish that had been different, Kit," he whispered.

She continued, as if she hadn't heard him. "Brandon was with us, at the farm, that summer—"

"*What?*" Michael interrupted. "How long has that shithead been hanging around your family?"

"I don't know." Kit blinked, shook her head. "I don't know. Four or five years, maybe? Mr. Chambers—Brandon's father—is a client of Daddy's law firm. He owns a company that makes racing boats. He's a businessman, really successful.

"After Brandon got into Princeton, his father made a big donation to the university. Daddy was on a committee, in charge of fund-raising. He immediately forgot that he and Mother had considered the Chamberses 'social climbers.' Daddy sponsored Mr. Chambers to become a member of the University Club in New York, the yacht club in Connecticut. Close to where my Aunt Libby and Uncle Wes live. He introduced them to people.

"And then . . . Brandon and Genia were seeing each other."

Kit looked down at her hands. An image flashed in her mind: blue clay hand marks on Brandon's shirt, as she tried to push him away. Her smashed sculpture.

"Brandon's handsome. And smart, I guess. My parents and my aunt and uncle think he's great. But he's a first-class a-hole, as far as I'm concerned!" She saw the broken pieces of her sculpture scattered across the barn floor.

"He flirts behind Genia's back, too. And not only with me—like with that stupid bracelet." She glanced at him. "It's not right."

He believed her now, about the bracelet. "Brandon said he . . . hooked up . . . with your cousin's friend Anne," Michael said. "After that party at your house."

"What do you mean?"

"My friend Tom and I ran into him, in a bar. He was bragging about it."

"*Brandon* and Anne? What . . . ? Oh, God." Suddenly, Kit jumped to her feet. She crossed her arms over her chest and paced, agitated, back and forth inside the room. Her voice changed, as the words tumbled out:

"After the fight with Mother and Daddy, I took off, late in the afternoon, to ride to the lake for a swim. My pathetic protest. I didn't want to leave here, Michael. I didn't want to leave! Just one last swim, I thought . . ."

As the story worked its way out of her, she could see it all over again, like watching a slow-moving, clicking, clattering black-and-white movie reel unspooling. Like something distant. That happened a long time ago. To someone else.

"The Club was closed for the season. But there was Brandon's BMW parked in the empty lot. As I rode in on my bike, he got out of the car. He smiled, and started talking to me in a way that seemed . . . nice . . . like he was really happy to see me.

"Genia had told him about the fight with my parents, and he figured he'd find me at the lake, he said. He was really sympathetic.

Like an understanding older brother."

"Yeah, I'll bet," Michael said under his breath.

"We were joking around as we walked down to the beach. I remember him saying 'You're really going swimming?' Like he was impressed—as if he really liked me. It was early evening—kind of chilly, I remember.

"Brandon had a bottle of wine. I went to change into my bathing suit and when I came back, he'd poured us both some, into these big red plastic cups. The kind you use for picnics. I had on my Speedo, and he made a comment like, 'Hey, where's the bikini? I like you in a bikini!'

"'I'm not dressing for you, Brandon Chambers! I'm here to do laps!'"

"I think he laughed. He said, 'Okay, okay, but have some wine with me first, little mermaid.' I was only sixteen and not really used to drinking, but he egged me on, 'What do you say we break some rules tonight, little mermaid?'

"He really understood where my head was at, and I thought *yeah, why not?*"

She was back on the beach by the lake, now—that angry, rebellious sixteen-year-old: Brandon was so nice!—handsome, older, and his attention flattered her. He'd brought wine for the two of them! Like she was an adult, not some kid controlled by her parents.

She'd held up her cup for a refill. "Atta girl!" Brandon laughed. And it was after her next big gulp of the sweet red wine that she'd started to feel sick . . .

"I . . . I must have had too much to drink. I started to feel bad, like I couldn't really focus . . ."

Kit stood by the open back door, very still, gripping the door frame and facing the lake. But what she saw now was a figure moving out of the shadows of her memory, taking form, becoming real. She said in a hoarse whisper, "And then Brandon started . . . he started—"

"He started what?" Michael asked softly.

"I can smell his breath, it smells like liquor and . . . then, he's trying to kiss me." Her voice rose, "What's wrong with him? Is he joking? We're sitting at a picnic table and I give him a shove to push him away. I don't feel good. Suddenly he pins me back against the table. *'I like you in a bikini, I said!'* and his face is right in my face, so close I can see the spit stuck to his lips. *'I want to see more of this,'* and he grabs me, really hard . . . between my legs.

"I'm scared," she said, panting. "'Get off of me!' and I try to squeeze out from under him, get away from the smell of his breath in my face. But he's so big. *'Why don't you like me?'* Is he crazy? He yanks the straps of my suit down off my shoulders and throws me onto the ground. I can't breathe! My head is spinning. I hear him. I hear a metallic sound . . . it's, it's his pants zipper . . .

"I'm struggling and kicking like mad. I'm scrambling to get up, to get away from him. I scream. But we're the only people at the lake, and he's right there standing over me, and his face is all twisted . . . and he says . . . he says . . ."

Kit stopped. She stood, frozen. Or maybe she had turned to stone. "He says, *'You better play nice or things are going to get ugly.'*"

Chapter 38

The afternoon seemed to shatter, exploding in silence around her. Dazed, she swung around to look at Michael, searching his face. The answer was so close, why couldn't she grab hold of it?

"Today, outside of the restaurant, he said the same thing to me! He used those very same words: '*You better play nice or things are going to get ugly.*'"

Her breath came hard, and her face crumpled up. "And all this started to come back to me! That night at the beach. He was just waiting for me, Michael. And then he attacked me, he was trying to rape me!"

Kit covered her face with her hands and began to cry, and the crying grew to sobs of shame and humiliation. Michael sprung to his feet and came beside her. He took her into his arms, as the tears and pain poured out of her.

"I will never let anyone hurt you, do you hear me?" Michael choked out. "You don't have to love me. I don't care. But you're safe, Kit. You're safe."

For a long time after, into the quiet of the late afternoon, she sat with Michael at the top of the sagging flight of stairs. Finally, she took a deep, ragged breath. "And then, I woke up here."

She looked straight at him, her face pale and drained, but her voice strong. "Remember you asked me why I hadn't thought about you, about how it would affect you, if I killed myself?"

He nodded.

"Well, I didn't think about it because I never intended to kill myself! I did not come to this lake to commit suicide, Michael!"

"No," Michael said, "I don't think you did."

"For two years I've been convinced I had . . . some kind of breakdown, and deliberately tried to off myself. I was sent out of the country because of this!" The realization stunned Kit. "But . . . why can't I remember more, what happened next? Where did Brandon go? All I remember is waking up in this hotel kitchen, on the opposite side of the lake. And . . . it had to be the next day."

Still weak from crying, she got up. She rubbed her eyes, and turned to look back inside, at the fireplace, the little cot. Exhaling hard, she forced herself to return to that day in September, two years ago.

"I can remember being here, in this room, vomiting into a bucket. And this nice old man was saying reassuring things to me. He was kind—not some axe-wielding crazy, like that rumor you were talking about. When I'd finished puking, he gave me something warm to drink. What are you thinking, Michael?" She noticed now the hard set of his expression.

"You were angry, feeling trapped. And no wonder! So, you came to this lake . . . this lake that you and I both loved, where we'd met . . . for one last swim. And Brandon, *that fucking animal*, was lying in wait for you."

The cold look in Michael's eyes told her what he would not say: *He intended to make Brandon pay*. But she wanted to climb back onto solid ground, needed to feel in control, and to fill in the missing pieces of what had happened that day.

She pulled the back door to the hotel kitchen closed, and walked ahead of him, down the stairs. How had she come to this place? There had to be some other clues. But her memory would take her no further . . .

"There's an opening in the trees—see?" Michael said. "It could be a way down to the lake." They crossed through the overgrown back lawn and found a trail leading down through the woods. Before long, the lake came fully into view.

"Look, over there." He pointed. The path had leveled out and a pile of boulders lay just to the side, with small trees and brush growing up around them. Something big leaned up against the rocks, hidden behind the bushes.

"It's a boat!" Michael said, pulling back the branches. "You know, I remember when I was lifeguarding, sometimes there'd be somebody out fishing in the morning, way at the other end of the lake. Could that be the 'crazy hermit of the lake' my friends and I always talked about? Just a guy who lives back here and has a boat?"

Kit thought back. "I came to the lake a couple of times in the evening. And . . . I remember noticing a small fishing boat puttering in the distance, too. But I never thought anything of it."

She sat down beside the water. Gusts of wind stirred up whitecaps, and waves slapped up against the shoreline. The black-and-white movie reel of her memory shifted, changed. Now, the water was a dark, lurid green under a sky streaked with the reds and oranges of the setting sun. She tugged at a long stem of tiny blue flowers—forget-me-nots growing in bunches along the shore—and then another two. The simple action of weaving them together comforted her.

"What difference does it make, though?" She felt muddled, hopeless.

"For one thing," Michael began, "it could mean that if the old guy you remembered, who helped you, is the same guy with this boat, he may have seen what happened between you and Brandon. He might be a witness. And he must know how you got here. How did you make it home—do you remember?"

They'd started hiking through the woods again, heading back to the truck. She thought about his question.

"Daddy picked me up. I was sitting beside the lake, down the road, closer to the Club," she said at last. "He and Mother were so upset. When we got home, they made me go straight up to my bedroom. I could hear everyone asking 'What happened? Is she okay?' But I couldn't remember anything. Not being at the lake and . . . nothing having to do with Brandon. At the time, I had no idea how I ended up sitting by the side of the road."

"All this time you thought you tried to kill yourself. Why? Why did you believe that?"

"Because that's what they said . . . everyone believed it . . . because Brandon said so." She could hear his voice now. "I was up in my room, listening to them talk downstairs. Brandon told my parents that I'd been acting like I might hurt myself, and so he went out to try to find me before it was too late. Said he'd come across my bike at the beach. Daddy demanded to know why he hadn't mentioned this earlier. But Brandon weaseled out of it, said something like, he'd been afraid I might have drowned. *Committed suicide.* And he didn't know what to do. 'I'm just so relieved you found her—alive!' I heard him say. What a lie that was! But I couldn't remember anything . . . and I felt so tired. So beaten. Like they had all, finally, beaten me.

"My parents hustled me off to a private school in Switzerland, a place for problem rich kids. The perfect solution. Socially acceptable and far away from their New York friends. And nobody talked about it after that. That's the way we are. The decision was made to put the whole thing behind us."

"Nobody talked about it," she said softly, as if to herself. They had reached the dirt road where the truck was parked.

"What is it?" Michael asked. "Is there something else?"

With a sickening wrench to her stomach, Kit remembered how Brandon had described Anne, being driven discreetly back to New York so *nobody would talk about it*. An arrangement apparently taken care of by her friend Genia. Had Anne willingly had sex with Brandon, and been discovered by Genia? Had Brandon raped her? Was the whole story made up, a lie?

"I have a confession to make," she said, turning to him. "Earlier this summer, after that party where you and I met on the porch, Brandon cornered me. He implied that *you* had slept with Anne. And that you'd hurt her."

"Are you kidding me?" Michael stared at her.

"No. I should have told you right away."

"You didn't . . . believe him, did you?"

She thought about how she'd gone back to the waterfall with Lucy, searching for clues. About the blank spots in her memory, the uncertainty, that Brandon had taken advantage of. Now, finally, the rest of that memory of the waterfall came back to her . . .

. . . *She'd laughed and wriggled free of him. "Kit, you're killing me!" Michael had sighed as he had let her go. She'd skipped through the woods, picked up her bike, and peddled home.*

Of course Michael had never hurt her—or Anne. She'd wrestled with the story in her mind, but she'd never really believed Brandon. She shook her head. "I didn't."

"I think you need to tell someone about Brandon, don't you?" Michael pushed her now. "Your parents, the police? And Genia?"

As they sat together, she said, "Who would believe me, Michael? The Club was completely deserted, closed for the season; it would be my word against his. You heard him today—I'm afraid he's got everyone believing I'm '*a crazy bitch who tried to off herself.*' He'd convince them I was making things up to spoil the wedding. My aunt and uncle, my family, they've got too much riding on Brandon and his family.

"It would only make things worse for me—and maybe Anne, too."

Her eyes narrowed as she stared straight ahead, and her jaw clenched. She might not be able to convince her family of the truth, but *she knew*, now. One way or another, she was not going to let Brandon get away with what he'd done.

An uneasy quiet surrounded Cedaredge Farm as Michael slowed the truck round to the front porch of the big house. He cut the engine, and they sat in silence. "Are you going to be okay?" he asked her.

"I think so," she said, looking up at the house.

"I'm worried about you, Kit. Do me a favor? When you get to your room, if everything is all right, will you turn your bedroom light on-off-on, once? And lock your door."

She nodded.

"And . . . if it's not all right, Kit, get the hell out of the house. I'll wait here for a few minutes. If for any reason anything happens, later, tonight, or tomorrow—if Brandon gets in your face again, or your parents try to talk you into something you don't want to do—call me no matter what time it is. Get out of the house and I'll come find you."

"I will. Michael"—Kit turned to him now—"I'm going to New York, tomorrow, with Daddy. Max is taking us."

"Max?"

"Our driver."

Michael stared at her, then sighed and looked away. She felt embarrassed, realizing how pretentious that must sound to him: *our driver*.

It seemed to her that he was willing himself to pull as far away from her as possible. To withdraw his heart and soul—as she had tried to do, before—to walk away. Without saying a word, he was the one, now, telling her: *Goodbye*.

He stared out the side window. "Go on now. I'll wait here until I know you're okay."

But she didn't move. "I'll be back in about a week, right before the wedding. Michael—"

"Um?"

"Michael—*please*. Don't turn away. I want to see you again. Let's not make this goodbye." She took his hands in both of hers. "I know that's not what I said before. I . . . I'm sorry. I've just been so confused about my life, and I don't want to ruin everything between us. I, I just wish . . . if only . . . "

She had no way of telling him, with words, how she felt. And so, she hugged him with a strange intensity, and stayed with her cheek pressed against his heart.

And in that moment, she felt the tide turn back. He came to her again, had never abandoned her. "Oh, Kit." He stroked her hair and whispered her name. She tilted her head and looked at him, her eyes pleading, until at last his mouth found hers.

Sometime later, she sat back and stared at him. He held her gaze and looked at her in a way she could not read.

Then she climbed out of the truck and went up to the house.

Chapter 39

That night, he hardly slept. Sometime around three a.m. he yanked the covers back and got out of bed. He threw on jeans, sneakers, and a dark sweatshirt, and then crept silently down the front stairs.

He drove back to the lake.

Brandon had planted the idea that Kit had tried to kill herself. And Michael understood, now, that it had almost certainly been Brandon who had spread the lies about the "crazy" Morgan daughter being "institutionalized." He'd dropped the rumor among Morgan's employees at the farm, once Kit had more or less been made to disappear. The locals had picked up this juicy piece of gossip and whispered it to other people in town, like Tom.

And Michael could guess why: For starters, if the truth came out, Brandon could be charged with assault. Even if the Morgans rejected legal action in favor of hushing up the incident, chances were Brandon would still be ejected from the family, and become a social pariah. He had worked too hard to ingratiate himself with the Morgans to let that happen. So, just in case Kit ever regained her memory and threatened to tell people what Brandon had done to her that day, he had to be certain that no one believed her.

Nice try, dickhead.

Michael knew what he had to do. He had to track down the one person who might have seen what happened, who could confirm Kit's memory of Brandon's attack. Michael turned the truck onto the utility road, dimming the lights, and came at last to a slow stop among the shadowy forms of rocks and trees. He'd brought a flashlight but kept the beam on low as he hiked up through the woods.

A single purpose hammered down on him, and he barely noticed the rustle of night creatures—a startled deer, a rabbit scurrying to its den. When the trail opened up to the old orchard, he knew the hotel loomed somewhere just ahead. He didn't want to make his presence known, at least not yet, and flipped the flashlight off, letting his eyes adjust to the gloom of the early morning.

The hotel appeared like an enormous shadow, difficult to make out in the dark. Only the soft, mournful chirp of a solitary cricket disturbed the quiet. Tangled grass and long thorny weeds caught at his jeans as Michael walked toward the hulking shape. He made his way to the back of the building where he and Kit had stood only hours before.

Someone moved inside. A light glowed through the downstairs window, and a faint smell of wood smoke from a fire drifted in the air. He was pumped up, beyond fear or caution. He thought about just walking up to the door and banging on it—but realized the stupidity of that plan. What if the guy behind that door was crazy after all, and had a gun?

So, he held back. The one person who might know more about that night two years ago, when Brandon had attacked Kit, could just as easily bolt into the maze of dark, abandoned rooms inside the hotel and disappear. Instead of barging in, he turned and took the path down to the lake. And he waited.

The far end of the lake looked nothing like the more developed side, where the Profile Lake Club owners had tamed the landscape into a smooth, wide swath of sandy beach, tennis courts, and manicured golf course. Here no beach for swimmers and sunbathers softened the shoreline, and the dark water lapped up against rough stones. In places, trees grew right up to the water's edge, making the cove feel hidden and wild.

Just as daylight touched the rounded peaks of the mountains across the lake, he heard the shuffle of footsteps coming down the trail. The grating of the boat being pulled from its hiding place cut through the quiet stillness. A softer dragging noise followed, as the boat was hauled along the path toward the water.

A figure maneuvering the fishing boat took shape. A man—thin and tall, and a little stooped. The light of a pipe glowed near his face. He stopped. Took a puff.

Then he said, "Good morning."

Michael nearly jumped out of his skin. He stood to face the man, but didn't reply.

"So . . . you came back, did you?"

"What? What do you mean?" Michael asked.

The man leaned toward him. The expression on his face revealed neither friendliness nor hostility. "You were here yesterday, with the girl."

"How did you know?"

"I was picking some raspberries for supper," he replied. His voice was mild. "There's a kitchen garden and a very nice stand of raspberry bushes not far from the back door. Everything's overgrown . . . probably why you two didn't notice me."

Michael stared at the man, not sure, now, where to begin.

"I'm Alfred. And you are . . . ?"

"Michael."

"Should we sit down then, Michael?"

Alfred dragged an old stump closer toward him for a seat and settled on it. Wary, Michael sat down on the fallen trunk of a tree that lay beside the shore, watching the man.

"Mind if I smoke?" Alfred asked. The smoke from his pipe smelled sweet and woodsy. Michael shook his head, still trying to get a take on Alfred.

Although his first impression had been that Alfred was an elderly man, Michael realized that in fact he was probably somewhere in his forties. His gray hair grew long and wavy, and he had a quality about him of a person who had seen and lived through a lot, maybe more than anyone should. Sadness weighed down his features. But in the man's eyes, Michael saw kindness, too.

"You live here?" Michael tried to stop himself from sounding so aggressive and challenging. "In this hotel?"

"Yes, I do. Have for some time now. I've been living in these parts since I got back from Nam."

In his father's hardware store, Michael had met a few guys who'd been to Vietnam. Even having a few words with them always made him feel like a punk, like a kid who didn't know anything. He was too young to have any understanding of what these men had been through. So, he settled down, wanting to show some respect to this man he didn't know. Those schoolboy stories of "the crazy hermit of the lake" seemed silly now.

"I grew up not far from here, in North Conway," Alfred went on. "I taught high school, before the draft. When I came home, I found I couldn't work anymore. Tried to, but just couldn't. I wandered around and found this place, which suits me fine. There's magic in these woods, healing, you might say—the bad dreams didn't follow me here. And the hotel, well, it's old and forgotten, just like me."

"Are you the one out fishing in the morning?" Michael asked. He looked at Alfred's boat.

"Doubt it's anybody else."

"Alfred, you saw us here yesterday. Did you hear what we were talking about? Do you know why we came here?"

"To be honest, I didn't think I'd seen the last of that young lady. I'm just surprised it took her all this time to come back here."

So, he remembered. "Can you tell me . . . what happened that night, two years ago?"

Alfred looked out at the lake. He rested the hand that held his pipe on his knee and sighed.

Michael held his breath, waiting. Finally, he burst out, louder than he meant to, "For Chrissakes, Alfred! Tell me what you know about this! That girl you saw—her family's convinced her that she tried to kill herself. She's been living with that burden, and it's ruining her life!"

"And you don't think it's true."

"No! No, I don't."

"You care for her, too."

He closed his eyes, and couldn't answer right away. "I love her."

Alfred paused. He nodded as if he understood. Maybe this solitary man, this hermit, had been in love once, too, Michael considered. Alfred took a long pull on his pipe. "All right, then. This is what I remember:

"It was cold that night, and lovely, really, in that bittersweet way of autumn. I'd taken the boat out, as usual, just to enjoy the quiet, when suddenly I heard a girl screaming.

"It shocked me to hear such a terrible sound in this beautiful place. Had the nightmares come back, from the war? I felt frightened, confused. But, no, the screaming and shouting were real, and seemed to be coming from the far side of the lake. Where the country club is.

"I steered the boat toward the beach. I remember keeping to the shoreline where there was more cover. At first, I couldn't make out much. Then, I got closer.

"I saw a struggle on the beach. The moon had risen, and I could see clearly a girl, on the ground, and a man—a big type—standing over her. He fell back suddenly, screaming, she'd kicked a shovel-load of sand into his face. Then, she was running down the beach and into the water. He yelled, cursed. She started swimming hard toward the center of the lake. She was a strong swimmer. The man on the beach paced back and forth at first—shouting—and then he stopped, and he watched her.

"I couldn't imagine what was going on, but when the girl began to slow down, I got worried. She seemed disoriented and her arms started flailing around. The man stood on the beach and watched her struggling. And all of a sudden—I couldn't understand it—he turned around and left the beach."

"What? He left? You mean he saw her in trouble—and just walked away?" Michael asked.

Alfred winced. "She was crying for help. She was thrashing around. That girl wasn't swimming anymore—she was drowning. If I could see this—if I could hear her—from where I'd positioned the boat, I believe he could as well."

"He wanted her to die," Michael burst out, "to cover up what he'd done!"

Alfred paused.

Michael took a deep breath. "I'm sorry. Sorry, Alfred. What happened then?"

"Well, I didn't like the idea of getting involved in any trouble, but the girl was going to drown. I powered up the small motor on my boat and got to her just in time. She'd stopped fighting and had started to go under. I hauled her up into the boat. She vomited all over and then passed out."

"Wait a second. She was swimming—and then seemed disoriented and started to struggle . . . and then she . . . lost consciousness?"

Alfred looked at him, as if regretting having to say what he knew, the ugliness of it. "Someone had drugged that girl. I'm sure of it. I've seen enough of what that looks like to recognize the signs. I'm afraid there's no other explanation."

"*Drugged?* That son-of-a-bitch!"

It came back to him, the night at Ollie's bar. Brandon hadn't just been making a sick joke about Quaaludes. He knew what he was talking about from experience.

He must have spiked the wine he'd pushed on Kit, hoping to make her an easy victim. Then, somehow, she'd struggled free, gotten away from him. She made it to the water and swam as far out as she could—until the drugs caught up with her.

And Brandon just watched her as she started to drown, ignoring her pleas for help. Maybe he'd been angry at first, furious that she had managed to escape him. Until it occurred to him that things were going his way after all. Because now she wouldn't be around to accuse him of attacking her and trying to rape her.

Michael jumped to his feet, pacing back and forth across the sand. "All he had to do, then, was plant this seed—*this lie*—about suicide! I'm sorry," he said, "I'm just so goddamn angry right now."

"I understand," Alfred said, nodding his head.

"What—what happened then?"

"Well, there's not much more to it. I cleaned her up and carried her to the old hotel. I wrapped her in blankets and let her sleep it off. When she finally woke up, the next day, she couldn't remember much, including who she was. After a cup of strong coffee, she was able to tell me her father's name—Robert Morgan.

"I hiked down to one of the empty vacation cottages this side of the lake, sprang the lock and found a phone that was connected. I dialed information for the number, then called the Morgan house. Said I had found Robert Morgan's daughter, and where she could be picked up. I hung up fast, before anyone could ask questions.

"I walked the young lady out to the road. Told her that her family would be by soon to collect her. She thanked me, was quite gracious, given the circumstances.

"Not long after, a car stopped—I kept an eye from the woods— her father got out, bundled her into the back seat. And that was that.

"For a little while I feared somebody might come looking for me, asking questions. But time went by . . . this place became even more overgrown. Finally, I wondered if the incident hadn't just been forgotten. That is, until you two showed up yesterday."

The sun was up over the mountains now, spreading a warm light across the lake. "You work, son?" Alfred asked.

Michael looked at his watch. It was already past eight. "Why didn't you call the police?" He couldn't let Alfred go, not just yet.

"I stay away from the police. From men in uniforms. From people in general, but especially them."

"You saved Kit's life. And that creep on the beach? He hurt her. You saw—he left her to die! And, Alfred, he's still out there. You have to come forward, say something!"

"I'm glad I could tell you this story. It's been weighing on me. But, son, there's no further part for me to play, I can't be involved." The hermit rose to his feet. "Be careful now, and take care of the girl." Without another word, he turned his back on Michael. He had said all he intended to that morning, and now began hauling the boat into the water. He nodded a goodbye and pushed off into the lake.

An earsplitting racket that sounded like a three-ring circus of barking dogs greeted Michael as he hurried into the veterinary clinic at half-past nine. Pets and their owners crowded the small waiting room. Landsman was already busy seeing a patient and Frances, taking a call from another client, scowled at him with a look that said: *Where have you been?*

He changed quickly into scrubs. Frances ordered him into Exam Room Two with a patient she must have deemed suitable punishment for his tardy arrival to work: a dog with a severe case of fleas.

That evening after work, Michael stopped at the grocery store. He bought coffee, a dozen eggs, and a tin of chocolate cookies. An offering to the man who had saved Kit's life. The provisions were also a bribe. He planned to press Alfred to talk to the police. The hermit was the only witness to what had happened two years ago at the lake—Michael had to convince him to speak up about it!

He had thought about Alfred's reluctance all day, and had devised an argument against every possible objection he might have. Now, Michael climbed up into the woods, determined and confident that he'd get the old hermit to see things his way. He went around to the back of the hotel, then stopped. The door at the top of the stairs hung half open.

Taking the back stairs two at a time, he called out, "Alfred!" He threw open the door to the deserted kitchen. No clothes hung beside the fireplace, and the empty drying rack now stood folded up beside the washer. The neatly made-up cot, the cold fireplace, the hearth swept clean—they could only mean one thing. "Shit!" Michael swore, and ran down to the lake. But he already knew.

I stay away from the police . . .

The hermit had vanished.

Chapter 40

Kit held her breath when she stepped inside the front hallway. Then she pulled the heavy door softly shut. An eerie quiet seemed to permeate the house.

She padded down the hall, and came upon her entire family seated in the living room. For a moment, she was taken in by the quiet and calm of this scene. Perhaps this was the opportunity to sit down, to try to talk with her parents—at least about what had happened earlier in the day at Polly's restaurant. It would be a start.

Her father was reading in his armchair, flanked by the tall bookshelves filled with his collections of biographies, histories, and political thrillers, while her mother sat on the couch working on a piece of embroidery. The beautiful antique couch was so uncomfortable that people rarely actually sat on it, and Kit couldn't remember the last time she'd seen her mother with a sewing project.

Lucy and Elliot were hunkered down on the floor, unnaturally silent, with a puzzle between them.

As if Kit were invisible—or didn't exist—no one looked up, or spoke to her, as she'd entered the room. This was not a serene calm that she'd come upon; instead, it was a kind of arctic stillness.

Only Banjo greeted her, standing up, stretching, and puttering over with a wagging tail. She paused to rub his head.

"Well," she said, "good night, everyone."

"Good night, Katherine." Her father was the only one to speak.

She climbed the stairs and went to her room.

Had something terrible happened? Where were her aunt and uncle, and Genia? Where was Brandon?

Returning to Cedaredge, she'd braced herself for confrontation over the scene at the restaurant earlier that day. But as she'd walked past this frightening, domestic still life and climbed the stairs, she understood that the fight with her cousin's fiancé had been evaluated by her parents and determined to be another thing that *Would Not Be Discussed.*

It was another episode that would cast a shadow of shame upon her.

In her bedroom she couldn't bring herself to get undressed. How could she even sleep in the same house as Brandon?

As of that afternoon, Kit no longer floundered in a dark, confusing swamp of memories. As of right now, she faced head-on the clear and terrifying image of Brandon snarling at her, flinging her to the ground. The dark bulk of him looming over her, fully intent on hurting her like she was nothing more than a broken rag doll. The attack was now indelibly and unforgettably seared into her brain. She understood what Brandon had been hiding, what he was capable of.

Sheer exhaustion overwhelmed her. Once in her room with the door shut, she looked out the window and saw Michael's truck, waiting. She flipped the light on-off-on as she'd promised. She watched until he drove away, and then locked her bedroom door.

That night, she slept the sleep of the dead.

It was midmorning, with the sun already risen high in the sky, when Kit awoke to the sound of the doorknob twisting and turning on her locked bedroom door.

She sat up fast, fear from the night before still lingering. But when she got out of bed and opened the door, she found Lucy waiting. At her sister's feet, on the oriental runner rug, sat a tray holding a plate stacked with toast and a glass of fresh-squeezed orange juice.

"I brought you some breakfast," Lucy said, bending to pick up the tray.

"Oh! That was so nice of you, Lucy. Thanks. Gosh, I really overslept."

This was not her sister's style. In its own way her little sister showing up demurely at her door with a breakfast tray was as odd as the family silent treatment she'd received last night.

Lucy marched into her room and slid the tray with the toast and juice onto Kit's dresser. Then she plopped down into the armchair opposite the bed.

"Well!" she said importantly, tucking a lock of hair behind her ear. "You missed the shit-show yesterday afternoon."

Kit's eyes widened. "What shit-show? What happened?"

"Daddy told Brandon to leave."

"You're kidding," Kit whispered.

"No! He really did."

"Wow!" *Maybe*, she thought, with a tingling of relief, Brandon's luck was finally beginning to run out. "What did he say? What happened?"

"He said to Brandon, 'What was the idea of bullying my daughter outside the restaurant?' *and then* he said, 'You better go back to New York, young man, and think things over!'" Lucy imitated her father's deep, patrician voice. "Brandon left last night. And then . . . Genia went ballistic! She was . . . blaming you."

"Oh, really—blaming me? For what?"

Lucy frowned, twisting her mouth, trying to remember. Now she mimicked Genia. "She said, 'Kitty is still very sick! It hurts me to say this, but she just can't bear for Brandon and me to be happy, Uncle Robert! She's just so miserable herself, she wants everyone to suffer.'"

"How could she say that about me?"

"I thought Daddy was going to blow his top! Then Uncle Wes and Aunt Libby started talking—everyone was talking and talking and changing plans—and anyway I think the three of them have all gone to the Cape."

"What about the wedding?" Kit could hardly believe what she was hearing.

Lucy shrugged. "I don't know."

Kit reached for the glass of orange juice and took a long gulp. She sat back in bed.

"Kitty?" Lucy's eyes were round as saucers. The two of them had finished the stack of buttered toast with jam that Lucy had brought to Kit's room. Lucy's mouth was still sticky with crumbs and raspberry jam.

"Hmmm?"

"Are you leaving, too, Kitty?"

Lucy had caught Kit off guard, and now Kit did a poor job of evading the question. "Well, Daddy and I are going to the city for a few days . . ."

"That's not what I mean."

A tightness clenched her chest. Her decisions didn't just affect her and Michael. "Oh, Lucy. I don't know what I'm doing, if you really want to know!"

Lucy's face turned an angry red and she looked like she was going to cry. "I don't believe that you *don't know*! You—you've got all these *secrets*. Just like everyone else around this place. You're just like the rest of them!"

"It's not that simple . . . !"

"Really?" Her sister leapt from the chair and fled Kit's room, slamming the door hard behind her.

Lucy was right, Kit thought, with a heavy heart. Though she wished it were otherwise, Kit did have secrets.

Chapter 41

"We're heading up to Cedaredge Farm," Dr. Landsman barked at Michael. "I just got off the phone with Overbee. Something's not right with the bull and he wants us to take a look." Michael helped to pack up the van and they drove out of town, up toward Sugar Hill, on the hot August afternoon.

As they pulled into the dusty lot in front of the barn, Michael felt the weight of the overcast sky pressing down on everything and everyone. On a day like this, people and animals were apt to behave unpredictably, with tempers short and moods on edge.

Kit was still away in New York with her father, so at least that meant Michael could avoid Mr. Morgan for now. He knew Kit's father had witnessed the way Brandon had manhandled his daughter that day at Polly's. Morgan had to be angry about Brandon's behavior. On the other hand, he probably didn't approve of Michael decking his niece's future husband at a public restaurant. That is, while he still didn't know the truth about Brandon.

"I know bulls can be bad-tempered," Charlie Overbee said as the three of them walked back behind the barn, "but Freddie here has always been fairly mild mannered."

"Freddie?" Michael said.

"The family's had this bull since he was a cuddly little calf. The Morgan kids call him Freddie—Ferdinand—treat him like a pet. Anyway, this fella has always been pretty tame, good-natured. In fact, the kids have been complaining to Bob Morgan that he should be allowed to roam with the cows. But I'm afraid Freddie is going to hurt someone."

"The bull used to be let out to pasture with the rest of the herd, as I recall," Landsman said. He gazed out at the cows in the open pasture and looked thoughtful. "Cattle are social animals; it could be our Freddie's just gotten lonely and pissed off."

"Well, listen to this: We found him out in the field the other day, with all the cows! Just as pleased as punch. Had one hell of a time getting him back into the pen," Charlie replied. "Bob's not comfortable with letting Freddie roam freely—says it's not what the farm management books recommend. Personally, I'd have nothing against Freddie joining the girls. But not in the mood he's in right now."

They reached the bull's pen, back behind the milking barn. From outside of the pen, through the spaces between the thick wooden slats, all they could really make out of Freddie was a big dark shape backed into the corner. The bull held his head low, with fear or suspicion, and his dark eyes gleamed as he watched the men through the wooden boards.

Landsman had spent his whole life around large farm animals and without hesitation, climbed up on one side of the pen to get a closer look. In a flash, the bull took a shot at him, ramming into the side of the bunker. Landsman flew backward off the pen and landed in the grass, stumbling to stay on his feet.

"He certainly is not the sweet-tempered calf I remember from just a year or two ago," he said, brushing the mud off his pants.

Freddie huffed, and pawed the mud in his pen.

Elliot appeared from around the barn. A second later, Lucy joined him. Elliot frowned, standing right in the path while Lucy slouched against the barn like the teenager she was.

"You stay back now, you hear?" warned Charlie. "This is no place for kids."

Michael winked at them, but the children looked serious.

"Why does Freddie have to be locked up in that pen?" said Elliot.

"Yeah," added Lucy, "he never used to be. It's like he's in prison now. And it just makes him mad."

"We're going to have a closer look at Freddie, see what might be bothering him," Michael said.

Elliot and Lucy came a little nearer.

Michael and Dr. Landsman did what they could to examine the bull through the wooden slats, and the animal seemed well, no obvious cuts, scrapes, or infections.

Elliot came up to the pen. "Don't come too close, Elliot," Michael started to say, but then he noticed that the presence of the two Morgan kids calmed the animal. "It's okay, Freddie," Elliot said. The bull seemed less agitated now, and working quickly and carefully, Landsman extracted a blood sample from him.

"It's hard to get a good look at him, but I'd say he's healthy enough. This blood sample may tell us a little more." Landsman sounded reassuring.

As they walked through the pasture back toward the front of the barn, Charlie called out to one of his men who had just pulled a tractor up beside the hay barn: "Billy—meet me down at the big house. Now, please."

Then Charlie turned to Landsman, "Would you two mind coming down to the house for a few minutes, help Billy and me with a little heavy lifting? Bob Morgan is away. When I told Mrs. Morgan you'd be up here checking on the bull, she asked if the four of us could move an oak table stored in the garage. She wants it up on the porch for the wedding. It's heavy, it'll take the four of us."

Charlie and Landsman walked on ahead, with young Billy hurrying to catch up with them. Michael hung back with the Morgan kids.

"That's not really a good doctor," Elliot said.

"What?"

"That doctor didn't see what's really wrong with Freddie," Lucy joined in.

"What do you mean?"

"Tell him what you saw," Lucy said, nudging her brother.

"Brandon hurts him," Elliot said.

"What? Hurts him how?"

"He burns him, with a cigarette taped to one of those long sticks they play pool with. He showed me once. He thought it was funny."

"That *motherfu*—" Michael said under his breath. "Where is Brandon? I've been meaning to have a little talk with him anyway."

"He went to New York. Daddy said he had some work to do before the wedding."

"Okay. Listen up, you two. I'm going to the house to help move that table Charlie was talking about. Then, before we leave, I'll tell my boss I want to take one more look at Freddie. Are you guys okay with that?"

"Yeah," said Lucy.

Elliot suddenly burst out, "I don't like Brandon! I wish he would just stay away from here—and I wish he wasn't marrying Cousin Genia!"

"I hear you." Michael put a hand on Elliot's shoulder. They'd arrived at the driveway leading to the main house. "For now, anyway, if Freddie's skin has been burned, we can definitely put some medicine on those wounds. He'll feel a lot better after that."

He caught up with the men out on the lawn below the porch. The Morgans' house looked beautiful, the porch now smooth and bright with a fresh coat of paint, and baskets of pink and white flowers hanging above the railing between each of the floor-to-ceiling pillars. More standing pots, gushing with blossoms and greenery, lined the front steps.

Everything appeared ready for a perfect country wedding. But the festive decorations seemed a horrible irony now that Michael knew the kind of monster the family might soon be welcoming in. Would he and Kit be able to do something to stop this?

As the men finished carrying the heavy table out of the garage and lugging it up the front stairs, Mrs. Morgan walked out onto the porch. She was dressed up, just like every other time Michael had seen her, like someone who didn't worry about getting her nice clothes messy from cleaning the house, doing chores, or gardening. Which made sense, since the Morgans had other people to do those things.

"Charlie? Could you please make sure that *this* is removed," she said, pointing the stiff toe of her shoe at a propane blowtorch standing on the front steps.

"Of course. My apologies, Mrs. Morgan. The front railing was separating, just here"—he showed her—"and I wanted to weld those two pieces tight so the rail didn't break loose, or look unsightly when your guests arrive. Billy"—he turned to the young man—"you be sure to take this torch back to the shop when we're finished. You understand?"

Billy stuttered, "Yes, sir; yes, ma'am." Michael doubted he was paying any attention to Charlie. He looked completely terrified in the presence of Mrs. Morgan.

Charlie, Billy, and Landsman went back to the garage to get the chairs. Before Michael could join the other men, Mrs. Morgan intercepted him, placing a firm hand on his arm. The thick, jeweled rings on her fingers somehow made her look old, he thought, weighed down with the finery of her position in life. He flinched at the sharp sting of her perfume. And he braced himself for a dressing-down for hauling off and punching Brandon at the restaurant.

Instead, she complimented him.

"You've really made something of yourself, haven't you?" The encouragement in her voice—the interested way she looked at him—disarmed Michael. Bunny Morgan was a very attractive woman, even if she was his mother's age.

"Thank you, Mrs. Morgan, I guess. I'm not sure what you mean, actually."

"Neither of your parents went to college, did they? And yet, here you are, on your way to getting an excellent Ivy League education. I'm sure you'll meet all sorts of important people, and I'm sure you'll go far, Michael. You're ambitious—I recognize that"— she paused—"and I respect it."

The unexpected praise threw him off. Was Mrs. Morgan beginning to like him? He relaxed, and returned her smile.

"I know you care for Katherine, and she for you," she continued in a smooth, reassuring tone. "You might even imagine that you and Katherine could marry one day."

Incredible! She had read his mind. He couldn't believe they were having this conversation . . . that he might, possibly, even be able to confide in Kit's mother.

"But have you considered," she went on pleasantly, "how a girl with Katherine's upbringing would feel with a father-in-law who runs the Franconia hardware store? And where would you and Katherine live? Some tiny flat overlooking Main Street Littleton, or Franconia? Katherine was brought up in the most cosmopolitan city in the world; she comes from a very important, old family. You must admit, you would never be able to make her happy."

Mrs. Morgan narrowed her eyes. Now the cruelty of her words struck him, like knives. "Her family and friends would cut her off, I can promise you that. In the long run you'd both be miserable."

And then, as if they were old friends, she added, "When two people come from such different backgrounds, it never works. No matter how hard you might try. I hope you'll take these words of caution as they are intended, Michael. I like you well enough to tell you the truth."

He was speechless. *How could someone like Kit ever be happy with someone like me?* She acted so matter-of-fact about it—as if she were simply asking the most obvious question in the world. And with only one possible answer.

When he finally found his voice, his words came out raw with anger, and hurt. "You and Mr. Morgan come from different . . . backgrounds. I would have thought you'd understand."

She looked at him as if surprised that he would challenge her. And maybe, too, she wondered how he knew this bit of personal information. "That was very different. Mr. Morgan and I were unique."

"Unique? How?"

"I don't owe you an explanation, young man," she snapped imperiously, and lifted her chin. "I warn you: Leave Katherine alone." Then Mrs. Morgan smoothed her skirt and walked down the porch stairs.

And though he was too hurt to understand it then, too proud, Michael realized later that Bunny Morgan might have recognized that their situations were more similar than she wanted to admit. Perhaps it made her feel better to believe she was "unique," even if it also made her a hypocrite.

He left Charlie and Billy scrambling with more chores for Mrs. Morgan. And Landsman had been pulled aside into some further conversation with Kit's mother.

Michael strode away from the house, down the driveway and up the road toward the van. His conversation with Kit's mother had shaken and angered him—her words had sunk hooks into him like some evil, poisonous spell.

When Landsman finally joined Michael, his face wore a confused scowl.

"Did she light into you, too?" Michael snorted.

Landsman looked up, puzzled. Then he confessed, "It's not professional of me to discuss clients, but sometimes Bunny"—he cleared his throat—"really steps over the line."

"*Bunny?*"

"Mrs. Morgan." Landsman reddened.

Before Michael could question Landsman further, he remembered what Elliot and Lucy had told him about Freddie. He knew Landsman and he had an important detour to make. He said to his boss, "Something's been bothering me about Freddie. Would it be all right if we went back to take another quick look at him?"

The bull stood quietly in his pen. Slowly, so as not to agitate him, Michael moved around the outside of the stall, peering at the animal's underside. Then he spotted what he was looking for—inside Freddie's back leg. "There, see? He's got some kind of irritation—a burn, it looks like—on the inside of his leg."

"Well, I'll be damned," said Landsman. "How in the hell did something like that happen, I wonder? There are several of them, I see. I've got some ointment in the case here. Let's try to get some of this medication on those sores. I'm going to have to talk to Charlie. I don't like this at all."

Freddie seemed more confident of their intentions than he had been at first. The poor animal was standing in a pen full of mud—with no hay or grass—and Michael had no difficulty tempting him with several big fists full of sweet-smelling alfalfa grass from the field. In this way, he maneuvered Freddie over to one side of the pen, while Landsman reached in with calm, skilled hands to apply the ointment.

"That animal is really quite gentle," remarked Landsman as they got into the van. "I'll talk to Bob about seeing if we can't let him spend some time out in the pasture with the cows. Bulls get mighty ornery when they're cooped up all on their own."

As they drove past the entrance to the Cedaredge residence, gardeners were trimming back the hedges and the lilac trees, and more delivery trucks arrived, pulling into the driveway. All the preparations underway for the wedding.

Michael turned to Landsman, but forgot what he was about to say as he noticed, clinging to his boss, the unmistakable scent of Bunny Morgan's perfume.

Chapter 42

In August, the Upper East Side of Manhattan emptied itself of all the wealthy residents who summered out on Long Island, or up north at country homes in New England. Meanwhile, the city sweltered with heat. And the usual frenzy of activity settled into an uncharacteristic pause.

Kit found herself alone, wandering through the American Art collection at the Metropolitan Museum. The museum was just a few blocks from the Morgans' apartment, and thanks to donations from donors including Robert Morgan, the Met would soon have an entire wing dedicated to American art.

In one of the cool, deserted marble galleries, she sat down on a bench and gazed up at the sculptor Augustus Saint-Gaudens's slim, golden huntress: *Diana*. Toward what target, she wondered, did the goddess's arrow point?

Kit pulled the strap of her shoulder bag over her head and set the bag down beside her. From inside, she extracted a slim blue envelope, unfolded the single sheet of airmail stationery. After two years of school in Switzerland, she had no difficulty reading the letter, which was written in French.

Ma femme et moi, serions honorés de répondre à la demande de notre chère et regrettée amie Esther Winthrop. Katherine, veuillez accepter cette invitation à rester chez nous à Paris aussi longtemps que vous le souhaitez, ainsi que mon offre pour un poste d'apprentie dans notre galerie. C'est avec plaisir que nous sommes prêts à vous aider à débuter votre carrière artistique. Pierre et Céline DeLettre

My wife and I are honored to fulfill the request of our dear, late friend Esther Winthrop. Katherine, please accept this invitation to stay with us in Paris for as long as you would like, as well as my offer of the position of apprentice in the gallery. It is with pleasure that we stand ready to help you begin your artistic career. *Pierre and Céline DeLettre*

It was an unbelievable gift, from people she had never met. And from someone now gone—Esther Winthrop. How strange it felt to learn that Miss Winthrop had thought so highly of her, had understood her and guessed who she wanted to be. Had she heard about Kit's supposed suicide attempt, after her efforts to help Kit transfer to the school in New Hampshire had failed? About Kit's two years in Switzerland?

For reasons Kit would never know, Miss Winthrop had wanted to help her.

Seated in the gallery, Kit pondered another discovery she'd made, an uncomfortable one. A disconcerting truth had revealed itself during the two years she'd spent away at school: She far preferred the Katherine Morgan she was becoming in Europe—at ease with herself and possessed of a sense of purpose and ambition—to the one she'd left behind in the States.

Now she held this letter in her hand with an offer that flung the door open to pursuing her dream, to becoming the person she was meant to be. She would have a way to earn her own money and become independent, and a place to live until she could stand on her own.

And the DeLettres lived in Paris, where so many other young American artists had studied and worked: the sculptor Augustus Saint-Gaudens, the stained-glass maker Louis Comfort Tiffany, the painters John Singer Sargent and Mary Cassatt. Safely on the other side of the ocean, she would be released from impossible family expectations and the insistence that she contort herself into a person she knew she could never be.

She folded up the letter and put it in her bag. She looked up again, at the statue of Diana: cold, hard goddess of the moon. The solitary virgin huntress. If Kit chose to accept this offer, she knew that the price she would have to pay for her freedom would be love.

"Mr. Morgan will be home for dinner tonight," said Nancy, the cook and housekeeper who looked after their apartment and took care of her father during his visits to the city.

Kit was paging through her mother's address book on the telephone table in the main hall. She had found a number for the Courtlands—the family of Genia's friend Anne.

"Thanks, Nancy. What time will dinner be?"

"Your father will want to change and have his drink. So, let's say dinner at seven."

She had come back to New York with her father, determined to have time with him alone. When it was just the two of them, she'd be able to speak to him about her future; to have an honest, adult conversation without the distractions of her mother, Lucy, and Elliot, and all the drama surrounding Genia and Brandon. But during the week they'd been back at the apartment, she'd hardly set eyes on her father. He had breakfast at the Yale Club, close to his firm on Park Avenue. Dinners were often taken uptown at the University Club.

Kit spent her solitary time thinking, wandering among the apartment's many rooms, with their thickly draped windows, paintings, and furniture pieces passed down through generations of Morgans. She brooded in the living room under the gaze of family portraits—the sternly rendered Elijah Morgan and his bonneted wife, Tabitha, whose forebears had come over on the *Mayflower*; her grandmother Elizabeth Bell Morgan captured in loose brush-strokes as a glamorous young debutante.

What would they have said to her? Advised her?

But her father had been avoiding her.

"Courtland residence." A voice picked up on the other end of the line. A formal voice, belonging to some member of the house-hold staff.

"This is Katherine Morgan, calling again." It was her second attempt to reach her cousin's friend. "May I speak to Anne, please?"

A few minutes later the speaker returned. "I'm sorry she's not in right now. May I take a message?"

"Could you tell her I called? I'm in the city for a few more days, if she could call me here, ATwater 9-4889." Kit left the apartment phone number. She was frustrated—yet relieved—with her lack of success, as she hung up the phone.

How was it that her parents had so easily believed Brandon, so quickly decided to pack her off to Switzerland? They'd never really talked about what had happened. As if not talking about it would erase what had actually occurred.

She imagined the panic they'd probably felt at the uncertainty, like a pit looming open in front of them threatening to swallow up their comfortable, well-ordered lives. The family reputation.

Brandon's explanation provided something they could react to—
write a check for—quickly and efficiently.

Her mother had perhaps been convinced that banishing her
to a foreign country was somehow instructive, another lesson in
behaving appropriately or risk being "cut off." While her father,
unable to deal with any unpleasantness, had simply removed her
from his thoughts, only allowing her to exist once more when she'd
learned how to smile again and "buck up."

They had believed Brandon, without question. For that, Kit
wasn't sure she could forgive them.

"Getting your packing done then, Kitty? All set for college?" Her
father cut into the homey meatloaf Nancy had prepared for the
two of them, a dish her father loved but her mother refused to eat.

She'd been readying herself for the chance to tell her father
about the letter from Paris, and to break the news she was not
intending to go to college in Boston after all. She anticipated he'd
be disappointed; this conversation wouldn't be easy. Now, shifting
in her seat at the dining room table, she began.

"Daddy, I've been wanting to talk to you about Wellesley, actually. You see, the thing is . . . I'm really not sure about college . . ."

Her father placed his silverware down hard, with a clatter. Suddenly she realized that this is what he had expected, and had been
preparing for, all week. A confrontation.

His face flushed red and his voice boomed uncharacteristically
loud. "Katherine! Your mother and I have spent too much time worrying about you and your future. I've had enough now! You will go
to Wellesley College next month, as planned, and that's the end of
it. You have no idea how many strings I've had to pull to make sure
they reserved a place for you—given your behavior. Thank goodness

your grandmother Morgan's name still holds weight."

"My behavior?"

"Let's not go into all that now, shall we? Water under the bridge."

Kit's voice shook: "Daddy, do you and Mother even care about what happened?"

"All I know," interrupted Kit's father, "and all I *need* to know, is that I just spent a small fortune to have my eldest child rehabilitated in Europe. And she still continues to defy me and disrupt this family! Let me remind you, Katherine, you have a sister and brother who need our attention, too."

Kit stared at her plate. She took a shaky breath.

"Kitty," her father spoke at last, and his voice had softened. "You're young. You need to trust your mother and me on this. I fought my father, too, about going to Princeton, his alma mater. And yet—those were some of the best years of my life! You'll love Wellesley! You'll join some clubs, find a nice Harvard beau. You'll be able to put all this unfortunate past behind you."

"Daddy . . . *I want to be an artist!*"

"Oh, Kit! Still going on about that? So, take a drawing and painting class! I remember so clearly visiting that beautiful campus on the lake for a Princeton-Wellesley formal. All those lovely young women . . ." her father mused.

"I don't want *a class* in drawing and painting . . ."

Her father shifted out of his nostalgic reverie; his thick, bushy eyebrows drew together and he fixed her with a hard stare. "There will be no more discussion about this, Katherine. And that's final. I want you to know, your mother and I are in complete agreement. Now, let's leave it at that, shall we? One day you'll thank me for this decision. Now I've something else to discuss. I'm leaving New York a day early."

"Are we going back tomorrow, then?" Kit asked in a tight, monotone voice.

"Well, no, not exactly. Max will take you back to the farm, as planned."

Kit was confused. "What are you doing?"

Their conversation was finished. She understood that they'd just had the only exchange they were going to have about her future. With a firm smile, her father moved to a topic that clearly gave him more pleasure.

"I happened to run into Brandon at the University Club. We had dinner together and a good, long heart-to-heart."

"Brandon?" Kit asked, incredulous.

"Now, Katherine. He's quite cut up about his behavior toward you. And I understand the boy! He's on edge. He's getting married this coming week!"

So the wedding was still on.

"The long and short of it is that Brandon has invited me up to Newport for two days, with his father, to take a run on the *Nefertiti*—a yacht that raced in the America's Cup! His father is friendly with the owner. It's not the sort of invitation one turns down . . ."

"So, you're leaving tomorrow? *With Brandon?*"

"Brandon knows very well that he behaved badly, Kitty. See here, sometimes young men and young women understand rough behavior a little differently . . . '"

"What?"

"And Brandon's apologized to me. So, let's put it behind us, shall we? And look ahead now! It would give a bad impression for you to be sour on your cousin's wedding day.

"I'll be leaving early in the morning. Max will take you up to the farm day after tomorrow. Give you time to pack, do any last shopping." Her father rose from the table. "Any new clothes you need for this fall, you just put them on your mother's account at Saks or Bergdorf's."

Lying in bed that night, anger toward her family and a sense of betrayal engulfed her, allowing no room in her heart for love, or for regret over her and Michael. No space to acknowledge the heartbreak that was sure to come.

For she would show her family, no matter what the cost, what bridges burned—show them that she could, and would, walk away from them and their hypocritical lives!

When she finally slept, Kit dreamt about water. Not a lake, but the wide, wide ocean.

"Yes, I'd like to close my savings account," she said the next day to the bank officer in the Midtown branch offices.

"May I see some form of identification?"

Kit slapped the document down on the desk. "My passport."

"All right, then, you have a total of eight thousand four hundred and thirty-five dollars, Miss Morgan. How would you like that, as cash or bank check?"

"I'll take six thousand in traveler's checks and the rest in cash."

She had just one day to get everything arranged.

Chapter 43

Kit was busy helping Carlos, who ran the elevator, ferry the various parcels down to the lobby where Max was waiting with the car. Her mother had requested several additional outfit options for herself and Lucy. More jewelry. And Elliot had forgotten to bring any ties. Kit had her shoulder bag and one small suitcase.

Nancy leaned out into the hallway: "Katherine? Telephone for you. It's Miss Courtland."

"Go on, miss," Carlos said. "I'll take these down and help Max finish loading up." He pulled the elevator gate shut and disappeared as the door closed behind him.

"What is it?" Anne's voice came across the line as cold and unfriendly when Kit picked up the phone. "Are you *stalking me* or something?"

"What? No!" Kit answered. She'd remembered Anne as one of the nicer girls in Genia's crowd. She caught her breath, then went on, "I wondered . . . Anne, you left Cedaredge so suddenly, earlier this summer. Was everything okay? Are you okay?"

Anne snorted derisively on the other end of the phone. "This is about those earrings, isn't it?"

"What earrings?"

"Don't play the sleuth with me, Kitty. You can just tell your cousin she's not getting them back. We had a deal. And furthermore," she added with contempt, "I'm surprised she has you doing her dirty work for her."

"I'm not sure what you're talking about."

"Just leave me alone, all right? She gave me these earrings and I promised not to make trouble for her and Brandon. But you can let her know—*from me*—that if you, or she, or anyone else from your family continues to harass me, I can change my mind, too."

Her mother's missing earrings. Like a clarifying flame, a determination to get to the truth, to get some measure of justice, burned in Kit. She made a decision. "Anne," she confessed, "Brandon hurt me, too."

Anne was quiet. Then, with an equal measure of cruelty and pain, said, "*You really are a very naïve little girl.*" Kit heard her crying, and putting a hand over the phone.

"Are you okay? Anne?"

"Stop pestering me!" Anne's voice sounded cracked and broken. "Do you hear me? I've got nothing to say to you. Leave me alone! *Goodbye!*"

She stared out the window of the back seat as Max nosed the car through the quiet streets of uptown Manhattan and pulled out onto the nearly empty West Side Highway. Soon, the suburbs of New York and Connecticut were flying by in a smudge of green leaves. Three hours later they cruised past busy, industrial Hartford, Connecticut.

"You're very quiet, Katherine," Max observed, catching her eye in the rearview mirror.

"Sorry. Not much of a conversationalist these days, I guess."

By the time they'd reached Brattleboro, Vermont, an hour later, farms and small truck stops could be seen from the highway, and the scenery became more rural. She slept until Woodsville, when the car turned off the highway and onto the winding New Hampshire Route 302. She sat up and took a deep breath. They would arrive within the hour, back to Sugar Hill, and Cedaredge Farm.

Max spoke up. "I want you to know, Katherine, that Elsie and I admire you very much."

"Oh, Max. That's so kind." The directness of the compliment surprised her. Still, she knew her voice sounded sad, discouraged. "But I'm not sure what there is to admire."

"I mean it. You're strong inside, Katherine. The Missus and I both agree you've got some of your grandmother Morgan in you: 'The iron fist in the velvet glove.' Don't you believe otherwise. Strong and determined. You'll do all right—more than all right—whatever path you decide to take."

"Thank you, Max . . . because honestly, sometimes I'm really not sure I'm making the right decisions, about anything."

After a pause, and as if reading her thoughts, Max added: "And your young man? If you don't mind me giving you a piece of advice: Love always finds a way. It may not be today, or tomorrow. But in the end, love finds a way."

How could she even hope for that much now?

Small town centers and fields lined with rows and rows of leafy cornstalks passed by her window. A family campground by the Ammonoosuc River, an old cemetery up on a hill, a stately Victorian farm, and roadside vegetable stands loaded with colorful boxes of late summer's bounty. She clung to each small vignette of life in this place she loved, wishing, somehow, she could postpone her arrival with Max to Cedaredge. Postpone whatever would happen next.

But before long, they were turning off the main route. She and Max were silent, each thinking their own separate thoughts, as they drove along the dirt road, and finally turned up the hill to the farm. The car slowed, and gravel crunched beneath the tires as it eased down the long, curved driveway.

She desperately desired to see Michael again, and dreaded what she had to tell him.

With the wedding scheduled to take place in two days, all pretense of routine—regular mealtimes, organized plans to go to the Club for tennis or golf—had gone out the window. Additional staff, mixed with early-arriving guests stopping by to visit with the bride-to-be, filled the house and grounds with constant chatter and activity.

That evening as the sun lowered behind the mountains, Kit pushed her moped from the garage, climbed on, and kicked off down the driveway. The air was warm and muggy. Heat from the long August days lingered now, pulling heavily on the thick, dense foliage of the birch and maple trees beside the road. Out in the fields, the cows stood nearly still, only their tails twisting and swatting. Cicadas buzzed.

She didn't want to see or speak to anyone in her family. But she needed to see Michael.

As she motored slowly down the hill with a plan to drive into Franconia, up from the opposite direction and headed toward the farm rumbled Brandon's BMW. He'd arrived at Cedaredge with her father earlier in the day from Newport, joining Genia and her aunt and uncle. They were all back now, everyone in a frenzy of cocktails and high spirits. The rehearsal and a party for all the guests were scheduled for tomorrow, with the nuptials Saturday at noon.

Brandon had succeeded in overcoming any reservations her family—or Genia's family—might have held.

He slowed the car as she approached. A confident smile stretched across his face, and his arm rested, relaxed, on the open window frame. "Well, hello there, pretty girl!" he called out to her.

How could he even speak to her like that? Kit wanted nothing to do with him, would be happy never to see him again. With her eyes fixed straight ahead, she sped up, passing him without acknowledgment. Snubbing him.

Halfway down the hill, above the whine of the moped, she caught the sound of car tires skidding. The screech of the BMW pulling a fast U-turn.

She heard the engine accelerate, gravel being torn up, crushed, and thrown from the dirt road. He was following her. The car sped up beside her, and he called out, "Kitty! Slow down. Don't be like this!" *As if she had done something wrong.*

She refused to stop, refused to slow down. The fenced-in pasture on one side, woods on the other, nothing but a blur as she sped down the hill. Her hair, loosened from its tie, streamed out behind her.

The main road from the farm wound toward the town of Sugar Hill at the bottom of the pasture. But straight ahead lay the rough track through the woods. She'd head straight, she'd shake him off. He'd give up pursuing her if it meant driving over rocks and ruts with his precious sports car.

Kit held on tight in anticipation of the bumpy track. She plunged into the woods, and the road became dark and narrow, with the trees crowding in closer along the edge. She flipped on her small headlamp.

Behind her, a bright light shone: the car's headlights flashing on. He was coming after her into the woods.

Her chest tightened. She would outrun him! But then he roared up beside her in the sports car, crowding her and forcing her to drive at the edge of the narrow track. "Hey, bitch!" he shouted at her. His true personality was showing itself—it was intolerable to him that she would rebuff him, not play along and pretend he was a great guy. "You're taking up too much of the road." Then, he laughed and swerved the car, nearly hitting her. He meant to run her off the road!

She pushed the moped to accelerate and hung on tight to the handlebars so as not to get thrown from the bike. She was frightened now. The moped bucked and tossed on the rough road, nearly throwing her, and in the dark she could barely see. But if she let her terror of him force her to panic, she'd crash. The moped pulled ahead.

Just a quarter mile more, down through the woods, lay the intersection with a paved road. She glanced over her shoulder, then nearly lost her balance as her hair blew in a tangle in front of her face. As if in response, Brandon floored the sports car so that it roared up close behind her. He was playing cat and mouse with her! He switched his headlights on to bright, framing her. Like a target.

She shook her hair out of her field of vision and cut sharply onto the paved road. Gaining more traction, her terror began to give way to something else. A vengeful determination to beat him at his own game. *Iron fist in the velvet glove.* It was just the two of them once again. She and Brandon. And Brandon meant to hurt her.

No, not hurt her—the vicious side of him had surfaced again, maybe he had guessed that she remembered something now, that she knew what he was about—and now he meant to kill her. Her teeth clenched behind a grim smile.

Just up ahead lay the path at the side of the road that led to the waterfall. Where the road swerved sharply to the left, the path led straight, through a tangle of brambles. Then the path abruptly entered a narrow alleyway that cut through a wall of tall pine trees on its way to the falls.

She'd walked her bike along that path through the trees many times before, but always during daylight, and it was tight. Now, jumping the road and coming at the path full speed, and in the dark, the risk was deadly. But she saw no other choice . . .

At the curve in the road, Kit flew straight off the pavement. She held on as the bike plunged onto the narrow path, then dove in among the safety of the trees. She barely missed hitting the tall trunks of pines on either side of the trail.

In the dark and in blind pursuit, Brandon's car jumped the pavement after her and smashed through the undergrowth. Kit heard the breaks screech as the BMW twisted right but could not avoid colliding with the wall of trees protecting her. The car crashed at an angle, coming to a dead stop.

The deranged light of the headlamps lit up the tree tops. All around in the dark woods came the roar of the waterfall. Kit struggled to calm her breathing. Easing her bike out from the path, she passed the BMW without a glance. Then she climbed, trembling, onto the moped and drove home.

Before anyone would have noticed her absence, she'd be back in her room, reading a book.

Chapter 44

"Michael! Telephone for you!" From upstairs in his room, he heard his mother calling him.

Kit had been gone for over a week—it felt like a lifetime! So much had happened, and he needed to talk to her, now. Every time the phone rang, Michael practically jumped out of his skin, willing that this time it would be her.

Kit had to know once and for all what had really happened—that she had never tried to drown herself. And he swore to himself that Brandon would not get away with what he had done: drugging Kit, attacking her, leaving her to drown as she cried out for help.

His mother handed him the phone in the kitchen. She was frowning.

"Michael? It's Kit."

At the sound of her voice—breathy and a little nervous—relief swept through him, followed by an insane rush of desire.

"I—I hope it was okay to call you . . . at your house?" she asked.

"Of course! I'm so glad it's you. You're back from New York? Finally!"

His mom would not take her eyes off of him. A big frown of disapproval pulled down the corners of her mouth. Michael walked into the dining room, stretching the cord from the kitchen wall phone as far as it would go. Couldn't she get the message that he wanted some privacy?

"I got back yesterday. Can you . . . can you come out to Cedaredge this afternoon?"

"As fast as the ol' truck will take me!" But Kit didn't seem to catch his exuberant mood. He asked, "Everything okay?"

"I just want to see you," she said. "Michael—"

"Yes . . . ?"

"There's a party at the house this afternoon. It's the cocktail reception for Genia and Brandon. Their wedding is tomorrow."

Tomorrow? Shit.

"I just wanted to warn you. There'll be cars parked every-where—I think my parents are expecting over two hundred people. The good thing is, there's so much going on now at the house that no one will miss me—we could go for a walk. Get away from . . . everyone."

When they hung up, he knew he had to get out to Cedaredge—fast.

"So, that rich girl from Sugar Hill is still calling you, then. The Morgans' daughter," his mother said. It was not a question.

"Yeah." He had no time to deal with his mother giving him the third degree; he ignored her and started up the stairs to his room. She took hold of his arm and yanked him to a stop.

"She has nice telephone manners, I'll give her that much: 'Hello, Mrs. Pearce, this is Katherine Morgan.'" His mother made an unkind imitation of the soft, polished voice Kit used for parents and adults. "I guess that's how they teach them to talk in those fancy private schools and country clubs."

"What the hell, Mom? You have an issue with Kit because she's polite on the phone?" He turned around to face his mother.

"Michael, what are you thinking?" Her grip on his arm tight-ened but he shook it off. She continued to light into him. "This high-and-mighty girl from New York City has got you running in circles! She isn't right for you! I'm not saying Theresa was, either—but honey, this is not going to end the way you want it to. I'm only telling you this because I'm your mother!"

"Stop it!" he shouted. "I don't need to hear any more of your opinions! You don't know anything! You don't know Kit—and you don't know me, either. *I love her!*"

He took the stairs up to his room two at a time. Stripping off jeans and T-shirt, he yanked a pressed oxford shirt and a new pair of chinos off hangers in his closet, and found the box of new dock-sider shoes. Dressed in the clothes he'd bought recently for college, he checked himself out in his bedroom mirror. A sharp prepster with a shit-eating grin mugged back at him. At least he'd fit in.

Downstairs, his mother stared at him with a hurt and worried expression on her face. He brushed past her, grabbed the truck keys, and took off.

As Michael gunned through town, it hit him that something hadn't felt right about his conversation with Kit. She'd sounded strange on the phone: not eager or excited, the way he felt, but anxious, like she was holding something back.

What had happened during the trip to New York? Did it have something to do with Brandon? Were her parents trying to manipulate her, the way his were trying to control and manipulate him? It gave him a bad feeling.

All day long the late-August heat and humidity had been building. Dark clouds loomed over Mt. Lafayette and Cannon Mountain off to his left, as he sped up toward Sugar Hill. Thunder growled in the distance.

Cars lined the road beside the driveway to Cedaredge, so he drove up to park by the barns. As he walked back down the road, he joined other guests making their way toward the house. Many of the young men and women seemed to know one another, and they laughed and shouted back and forth in high spirits and in anticipation of the party.

"Friend of the bride or the groom?" asked a clean-cut guy in a dress shirt and chinos that looked almost identical, Michael realized, to what he was wearing. His date, in a bright green and pink sundress with a matching pink headband and purse, smiled at Michael in a friendly, horsey way. A far cry from the first time he'd shown up at Cedaredge last spring—and been mistaken for a farm hand.

"Friend of the bride. Her cousin, Katherine Morgan, is my girlfriend," Michael answered. Kit might or might not have agreed with that statement. But that was how he felt.

"Really? Good for you, man. I didn't know Kitty was going out with anyone. Always found her a little . . . aloof . . . let's say. Maybe just shy."

"Or not interested," Michael replied, fixing the guy with a cool smile.

"Touché!" He glanced at his date, and accepted the comeback. "Hey, I'm Barkley Prescott and this is my girlfriend, Ginny. Brandon and I were both at Princeton, Quadrangle Club."

"Michael Pearce. I'll be heading to Hanover this fall, my first year," he replied, showing that he, too, held membership in the same elite Ivy League club. And by implication, that he belonged to their world. And, more importantly, to Kit's.

"The Big Green! Awesome! Hey," he said, turning to his girlfriend, "I see the Van Horns! They must have driven up from Newport. Ginny, I want to say hello to Chip." Barkley Prescott turned to Michael. "Nice meeting you, Michael. Catch you at the festivities."

Michael cut away from the driveway and walked up the sloping lawn toward the back garden entrance to the porch. In a corner of the garden, a rustic gazebo stood partly hidden beneath a group of cedar trees. He noticed Lucy and Elliot sitting inside with Banjo. The two towheaded Morgan kids were dressed in party clothes, and looked uncomfortably scrubbed and prim.

"Hey, don't you know that smoking is going to give you wrinkles?" he teased Lucy. She scowled at him, took a big defiant puff of the cigarette, and then crushed it out in the grass. Banjo was staring at Elliot, mesmerized, as Elliot tossed a tennis ball unenthusiastically up in the air, over and over again.

"What's up, you two? I thought for sure you'd be sneaking some champagne and caviar." When Lucy and Elliot refused to acknowledge his ribbing, Michael said, "You don't look very happy. What are you doing out here?"

"We're depressed," said Elliot.

"This whole thing sucks," added Lucy.

Michael couldn't agree more. But Genia and Brandon were not married yet. "Guys, do you know where Kit is?" he asked.

"On the porch, probably, with everyone else," Lucy grumbled.

He came through the garden entrance, beneath an archway wrapped in flowering vines. From this end of the porch, Michael could just glimpse the peaked white tents set up in front of the house for the wedding reception the next day.

The high-pitched, excited sound of people laughing and greeting one another mingled with the tinkling of the music-room piano and drifted from the front side of the porch. All the guests must have been gathering there, at the top of the stairs by the main entrance to the house, to be welcomed by the Morgans and the Livingstons, and to admire the view. Here around back, it was quiet.

All alone, Kit sat up on the curved stone parapet of the porch. Her knees were drawn up, her arms linked around them, and she stared out across the field toward the mountains.

Michael stopped. He wished he knew where her gaze was taking her. Sensing his presence, she turned toward him. She wore a soft, flowing, bohemian-style dress, and her pale hair hung loose, drifting around her shoulders. In the gloomy afternoon she seemed to glow, almost, like some otherworldly creature. Beyond his grasp.

He came to her and lifted her down from off of the stone wall, taking her into his arms. She felt so warm. So *real*.

"Oh, Michael! You're here," she said, wrapping her arms around his neck and kissing him.

Having Kit in his arms like this made everything all right. Today, tomorrow . . . he didn't want this feeling to end, ever. Finally, he pulled back, taking in her beautiful, solemn face. Before she could say anything, he blurted out, "I've got so much to tell you!"

A side door to the porch opened and Brandon pushed his way out, tucking his shirttail into his pants. Michael could see through the open door that the room beyond was a downstairs bedroom.

Michael stared at him: Brandon had *two* black eyes. Leave it to that asshole to get himself into some kind of fight right before his wedding. Michael silently high-fived the guy who had given Brandon the two shiners.

"What the *fuck* are you doing here?" Brandon stopped short when he saw Michael.

"He's my guest." Kit stood facing Brandon. Kit was just a girl, and much smaller than Brandon, but her unexpectedly fierce reaction made Brandon back up a step.

"The hell he is!" He glared at her. His voice rose and his face flushed to near purple.

"Brandon? *Sweetheart!* What's wrong?" Now Genia followed Brandon out from the bedroom, her dress rumpled and her hair messed up. She dabbed at her mouth with a tissue, trying to clean up her lipstick. *It looked like she'd been used,* was the ugly thought that struck Michael. And it looked like she'd been crying.

"Barkley! Duckie! Boys, come here and talk to Brandon!" Genia smoothed her hair and clothing and hurried to the railing. In a shrill voice, she called out to his friends as if she were afraid that there was going to be a scene.

Michael moved forward, putting himself between Brandon and Kit, and he faced Brandon down. He clenched his fists—if Brandon wanted to get into it with him, here at his own party, he was more than happy to oblige. Brandon stared at him, eyes burning, and Michael heard his agitated breathing.

"Hey, Brandon, my man, cool down, okay?" Barkley, the guy he'd met in the driveway, came up and put his arm around Brandon. "It's your *party!* Hey—Duckie and I were just saying we think we could beat the crap out of you in a game of pool. Come on, tiger, let's go inside."

Brandon shook off his friend. "You two beat the crap out of me? In your dreams." He struggled to calm down, to shift back to his usual slick, smooth persona. "Fuck pool, let's get another drink," he said.

Brandon had not forgotten, Michael was sure, how he had humiliated him at Polly's restaurant, landing him on his ass in the flower garden.

And Michael was just biding his time.

Two more couples appeared, wandering down to the far end of the porch. They accepted glasses of champagne from one of several self-important waiters gliding among the guests with cocktail trays. Apparently, Genia's parents had succeeded in bringing in their own "help" from New York City for this big event.

"Gigi, *darling*! There you are," one of the women called out. "Everything looks just lovely. What an idyllic setting for your country wedding. You and Brandon must be *so* looking forward to tomorrow—the big day! Brandon, good heavens—*your eyes*!"

"Leave it to the boys to let the bachelor party get out of hand!" Genia laughed and waved a hand indulgently. Then she gushed, "Isn't my family's place dreamy? It's the biggest house on Sugar Hill—and the prettiest!"

Michael's surprise at Genia's usurping of Cedaredge was just slightly less than his amazement at her easy shift into the happy, preening bride-to-be. She linked her arm through Brandon's as if to steer him away, toward her friends. "We're so thrilled!" she cooed.

Before he let Genia drag him away, Brandon turned back, looking over his shoulder. "I'm not done with you," he growled at Michael. His stare was filled with a crazy, black hatred.

"Oh, we're just getting started, big boy," Michael taunted him.

"Michael! Let's go," Kit said, and took his hand.

They crossed the lush, smooth lawn, walking beneath the tall cedar trees, and wandered out past the neatly planted beds of late-summer flowers. Lucy and Elliot were no longer in the gazebo; now two older men occupied the garden retreat. Away from the noise of the party, the men sat in deep conversation. They seemed to be pondering moves on the chessboard set up between them.

"My uncle Wes and Brandon's father," Kit whispered. "I'm so glad to get out of there!" Kit may have been relieved, but she sounded nervous to him, and distracted, as they came to the end of the driveway. "Let's go for a walk, Michael, up the road. Okay?"

They walked up the hill, and he noticed that the cows no longer grazed in the field but were all bedded down in the grass. Cattle like to keep one spot warm and dry before a storm, and their animal instincts were correct: big drops of rain began to fall. The boom of thunder and a big crack of lightning made Michael and Kit both jump.

"We can get in my truck!" he said, taking her hand as the sky suddenly opened up. "Come on! I'm parked just up by the barns."

Once out of the rain, Michael turned to Kit. He'd been both afraid and impatient to share with her the news he had.

"I went back to that place by the lake. I went back to the old hotel."

Chapter 45

"The hotel? Michael, you did? *Why?* What happened?"

"I wanted to see if I could find the guy who lives there—whose clothes and boat we found—talk to him. And I did! His name's Alfred. He's sort of a recluse, a hermit, Kit." He took her hands. "Alfred saw what happened between you and Brandon. And he saved your life, too."

"What?" Kit's eyes opened wide. He barreled on, telling her everything he'd learned about that night. As Michael described what Alfred had witnessed, she looked away and clenched her hands in her lap. He slowed down, and tried to convey the account as clearly as he could.

"So, Brandon drugged me," Kit said when Michael had finished. "That's why I felt so messed up, disoriented. He spiked the wine he gave me, so he could force himself on me."

The story had been hard for Michael to tell. But harder, he knew, for Kit to hear.

"I'm so sorry, Kit," he said. "But you fought back, you got away from him. You ran to the lake and started swimming. But then the drug kicked in and you started to pass out. By the time Alfred got to you, you were . . . nearly unconscious. That's why you couldn't remember anything! Brandon drugged you. Alfred said he was sure of it. And it made me remember something. About two weeks ago, when Tom and I ran into Brandon at Ollie's Pub, he made some stupid remarks about using Quaaludes—a kind of tranquilizer—on girls, so that, so that—"

"So that he could *rape them*?" she said savagely. "I can't believe how stupid I was! I can't believe I thought, 'Oh, Brandon, he's just being nice, bringing wine to the beach, listening to me complain about Mom and Dad.' God. How could I have been that stupid!" She started to cry.

"Stop! It wasn't your fault!" He couldn't bear for Kit to think that *she* should be ashamed. "There's no way you could ever have imagined he'd do something like that!" He pulled her into his arms as she sobbed angrily. "And you fought back! You were brave!"

"And if Alfred hadn't been there?" she said. She looked at him, breathing hard and gulping back tears. "I could have . . . *died*."

Michael wouldn't even allow that possibility to enter into his mind.

The afternoon passed as they sat together in the truck, listening to the rain come down, harder now, and steady. He held Kit and stroked her hair. At last, she seemed to calm down, to find some peace in knowing what had really happened that night two years ago at the lake.

She took a deep breath and sat up straight. "I'm glad I know the truth now." She looked sad, exhausted, but her voice sounded resolute, like she had figured something out. "And I'm not going to let it ruin my life. I will not let *that fucker* win.

"What I mean is, if I'd had to spend the rest of my life believing I had tried to kill myself, that would have been worse." She turned to him. "I would never have known what really happened if you hadn't gone back there. I would have spent the rest of my life haunted by . . . this dread, uncertainty. I know it's not enough, but thank you. Thank you." She smiled, just a glimmer of a smile, and he thought: *Everything's going to be okay.*

He paused, holding his breath. Then he spoke what had been on his mind and in his heart since his conversation by the lake with Alfred. "I can't really imagine what you're going through, I know that," he admitted. "But, Kit, you *didn't* try to kill yourself. And like you said, that would have been so much worse. And maybe, if we were together, Kit, I could help you—you know—let go of the past and move forward. Live your life. Be happy."

Michael put his hands up to Kit's face, searching, hoping to see a sign that she understood, and felt the same way he did. "There's nothing to run away from anymore, Kit, don't you see? So, couldn't you reconsider the idea of college, and just . . . a normal life . . . with me?"

Tears were streaming down Kit's cheeks.

"What? What is it?" he asked.

"I—I'm leaving, Michael. I'm going away."

"*Leaving?* What do you mean?"

"I'm moving to France." Gently, she pulled away from him.

Michael looked at her, stupefied. "What?" He literally thought his body would shatter into a thousand pieces. "*You're doing what!?*"

"Please! Just listen to me . . ."

"What are you talking about?"

Her voice seemed to come from far away as she tried to explain what was unbearable for him to hear. "Those two years I was sent away to school in Switzerland—something happened to me, Michael. It was like this huge weight was lifted from my shoulders. Like I was free, almost as if I were a child again. I learned French easily. I didn't have trouble concentrating or doing well. And my teachers—they didn't put down my dream of being an artist—they took it seriously. They encouraged me. This past year I was enrolled in a sculpture course at the university. I realized it was better—*I was better*—when I didn't come home. Not for vacations, or anything.

"Last Christmas, I went to Paris for the first time with one of my teachers and her daughter. I wish I could describe how beautiful it was, so you'd understand, Michael. I fell in love with the city. We visited the Louvre Museum—I spent two days there and never wanted to leave! At night, we took a boat along the Seine. I saw the Eiffel Tower light up on Christmas Eve! Paris . . . was like a dream." Kit glowed with the memory of it.

"But how are you going to do this?" Michael shouted, feeling as if he might explode. His heart pounded like a fist punching through his chest. *This was crazy!* If only he could reason with her. "Like—practically speaking—how are you just going to *move to France?*"

The rain was coming down hard now, banging on the windshield, and a distant flash of lightning lit up the sky.

"It's because of Miss Winthrop," Kit said.

"What? She's dead. What are you talking about?"

"She knew I wanted to be an artist. I told you, she tried to help me once, to get into the school in Franconia with the art programs. But then I found out that before she died, she left instructions with friends of hers who own a gallery in Paris to help me—with a job and a place to live. I can be around real artists, apply to art school in Paris."

She took his hand. "I took out all the money in my savings account in New York. Bought a plane ticket. I called them, Monsieur and Madame DeLettre, and they really do want me to come to Paris. It's what I want—it's who I am, Michael."

His whole world was falling apart. How could she do this to him? She was realizing her dreams—and crushing all of his.

Michael threw aside what he knew, about everything that Kit had been through. Now he just wanted to hurt her the way she was hurting him.

"You can't just go to another state, I guess . . . ? You have to go to an entirely different country? *Fucking France?* Is that what New York City debutantes do when they can't handle life—run away to France?" he said savagely. "I'm so glad you have Miss Winthrop and her high-class friends to help you live this rich-girl fantasy of yours. And destroy me in the process!"

Kit's face crumpled. His raw fury frightened her. She opened the truck door and got out and stumbled up the road in the rain. Michael jumped out and went after her.

"Why?" he cried, as he caught up with her. His voice tore in his throat. "I thought you loved this place. Being *here*!"

"I do!"

"Then why? *Why do you have to go away?*"

Sobbing and angry, she turned to face him. "The same reason you do! We're not that different, Michael Pearce!

"You want to go to college—to Dartmouth! You're leaving your family and friends, too!"

"I wanted that because of you!"

"No—you wanted it because you're smart and ambitious and curious about the world—like I am! And because it's not enough for you—or for me—to go through our lives playing the game according to the rules we grew up with. We want more! We want a life where we set the terms!

"I want to be an artist, Michael, I want to make sculptures— maybe that's a pointless fantasy. My parents certainly think it is. But I have to find out for *myself*."

"But why do you have to leave . . . *the country*!" he demanded.

"To see the world through my own eyes." She looked at him.

"The way I finally did when I was in Europe. To experience myself in the world as a person with . . . with free will. With no one telling me how to see, how to feel, how to experience *my life.*

"If I don't put an ocean between myself and my family, I will never escape being dominated by their view of the world. I know it!" Her voice rose, impassioned, angry, beyond any argument he could ever hope to make. "I'll fail. It will always come back to me being seen as a bargaining chip. Like Genia! Pushed around like some pathetic chess piece in a game that is ruled by what people like my parents want—what they insist I should want!"

Michael dragged Kit into his arms. The rain had drenched them both, and their clothes were soaked through.

"Why?" His voice broke. "Why didn't you tell me this before? *Why did you let me fall in love with you, Kit?*"

Chapter 46

Over and over Kit had rehearsed the speech she'd just made to him. But now, faced with the reality of his pain and anger—*which she was the cause of*—all certainty deserted her.

"I tried to stop!" she said, sobbing. "I tried to push you away. But I couldn't because . . . I love you, Michael!" She wept, as if, at last, her soul had perceived what it truly longed for—and would now lose. "I love you more than I can ever tell you. I'm so sorry. Please . . . please forgive me. *I have to go.*"

"I love you, too." He pulled her into his arms so that she thought he might suffocate her—if only he could just crush her body into his, Kit thought, she would be happy! She wouldn't have a choice. She wouldn't ever have to leave him.

Finally, the cold rain pounding down on them forced a sense of clarity on her. Michael stepped back, staring into her face. He looked pale and beaten, and as miserable as she. But in his eyes, Kit recognized something else, something that she understood at last, too. This moment of deepest loss had brought with it a strange relief, to them both, with its knowledge of undeniable love. There would never be anything, anyone, for either of them again. Not like this.

His body shifted, as if jarred by a need to act.

"What? What is it?" Her voice was barely a whisper.

"Kit"—he braced her shoulders with his hands—"Brandon and Genia. We can't let Genia marry that monster. We have to tell someone the truth about Brandon, what kind of person he is, before it's too late."

She was about to respond when the raw bellow of an animal in pain split the air around them.

"My God, Freddie!" Kit cried. The howling was coming from behind the barn. Freddie's pen.

"And fifty bucks says Brandon's back there, too," Michael said. The bull cried out again, and they took off at a run, back down the road toward the barn.

"Get in the truck," he yelled to her as the rain poured down. "Stay here, I'll deal with this!"

She ran after Michael, never hesitating, through the wet grass and muck to the back of the barn.

Brandon stood by the bull pen, swaying on his feet. Why wasn't he back at the house, at his own stupid party? Where was Genia? His college friends? And now, from the unsteady way Brandon swung around to face them, Kit saw that he was drunk.

Then her eyes went to the canister in his hand. *A blowtorch.* Where the hell had he found that? The sadistic monster was using it to terrorize Freddie! Brandon had a sick grin plastered across his face as the tortured animal stomped and snorted behind the walls of the enclosure, trying to avoid the blast of fire.

"Freddie!" Kit cried, and tried to bolt toward the animal's pen. But Michael grabbed hold of her. "Get away from him—NOW!" she screamed at Brandon. She strained against Michael's arms.

Brandon smiled an ugly smile at her. "Well, well. Things just got a little more interesting."

"I know what you did to me, you sick son-of-a-bitch!" Kit snarled, exploding with rage at the hurt and shame he'd caused her.

"You drugged me that night at the lake! You tried to rape me! You thought I would drown, and no one would ever know, didn't you? Do you think you can stop me from telling Genia, telling her parents? Is that what your pathetic attempt to run me down yesterday was all about?

"Let me go!" She wrenched free of Michael's arms and threw herself at Brandon.

With one swipe Brandon knocked Kit to the ground. "Crazy bitch," he mocked her.

On her hands and knees, she gasped, struggling to catch her breath.

"Get away from Kit, and get away from that animal," Michael said, his voice calm and in control, as he moved in on Brandon.

Brandon took a swing at him with the torch, but missed.

Crouched in the mud where she'd fallen, she looked at Michael and caught his eye—"I'm okay," she nodded. And for a split second she saw Michael hesitate. She wasn't hurt—should they walk away? Should they let her father and Uncle Wes—or the police—deal with Brandon?

Then something moved behind Michael's eyes, a crazy anger surfacing. "She could have died," he growled.

"It wasn't meant to happen that way! How was I supposed to know she'd take off into the water like that? Like some nut job? We were having a good time," Brandon taunted Michael. "She was into it, man."

Michael hurled himself at Brandon, "I'm going to fucking kill you!" he screamed. He slammed the bigger man back against the bull's enclosure.

And then all hell broke loose. Freddie, tormented and enraged, rammed into the wall of his pen. The impact knocked the two men to the side, and they both stumbled to regain footing. The bull threw himself against the boards again, bellowing with fury, and this time the wooden slats burst into splinters. Kit leapt to her feet and out of the way, as the enormous animal came crashing through the broken pen.

Taking off in the direction of the cows, Freddie barreled out into the pasture. The frightened herd scattered, bawling, in all directions. Kit turned to see her father's nice new cedar fence posts split and go flying as the cows panicked and broke through toward the woods.

The bull slowed to a trot, and then stopped.

Kit watched the animal standing still in the field. She could sense his restless energy—freed now. She could feel an intention forming.

"Freddie," she called, in a soft, sweet voice.

The bull tossed his head, snorted. He turned toward her.

"Freddie. Come," she called to him, firmly now.

"*Kit!*" Michael said. "What are you doing?" Michael had steadied himself beside the broken enclosure, while Brandon— breathing heavily—still hung on to the one remaining vertical post. The torch canister lay off to the side in the grass.

The bull headed toward them, his huge bulk moving fast. He slowed as he approached Kit.

She stepped toward the bull. "It's okay, Freddie." The bull hesitated, his flanks heaved, and he puffed and snorted, pawing the ground.

"For God's sake, Kit," Michael urged, "be careful."

But with all her attention focused on the bull, and Michael's attention on her, they had allowed themselves to be distracted from the real danger: Brandon.

Kit felt her neck being yanked back violently—Brandon, grabbing a handful of her hair.

Seeing his opportunity, he'd crossed the distance between them in long fast strides, and lunged at her. She twisted and stumbled. He had her trapped in his grip!

In Brandon's other hand, the blowtorch roared.

"You think you're too good for me, don't you, you stuck-up cunt? And now here you are, slutting around with the *hired help*? Some *nobody* who works for your father?

"Let go of me, you psycho!"

"How much do you think farm boy is going to love you, Kitty dear, if I burn off your pretty face?"

Freddie huffed and stamped, his agitation growing. Kit cried out as Brandon yanked her head back to an excruciating angle, turned up the torch, and laughed.

"Brandon, no! Stop!" Through the chaos and her terror, Kit heard a small voice shouting at Brandon.

Brandon, taken off guard, turned to see who had called his name. His grip on her relaxed, wavered.

Suddenly, she was flung to the side, released, as Michael threw himself at Brandon, knocking the torch out of his hand.

Kit scrambled out of the way and jumped to her feet as the men charged at each other again. Brandon staggered to get his balance, then came at Michael, landing a punch in his side. It knocked the wind out of him, but Michael came back even harder, slamming his fist into Brandon's face as the two went down.

Beside her, Freddie bucked and roared.

Kit screamed, "Michael! Get out of the way! Now!" Michael let go of Brandon and rolled fast to the side.

Low and fierce, she whispered to the bull: *"Go!"*

Freddie roared toward the two men. The bull was a freight train of power and rage, and there was only one person he was aiming for. Brandon screamed and made a last, desperate attempt to reach the blowtorch, as all three thousand pounds of Freddie came smashing into him, pummeling him into the dirt.

Chapter 47

The rain pelted down hard across the sodden pasture.

Brandon's body lay trampled in the mud, a crumpled bloody mass. "Don't look at that, Kit," Michael said as he came to her, trying to shield her in his arms.

Tears ran down Kit's face. She stared grimly at Brandon's broken body.

Elliot stood just twenty feet away. It was he who had called out Brandon's name. "Oh, Elliot—and Lucy!" Kit said, now seeing the two children.

Her brother and sister huddled together beside the barn, wet and bedraggled. They were shaking with the horror of what had occurred in front of them, as they hid their faces and held tightly to each other's hands.

"I'm so sorry, so sorry!" Kit ran to them, and pulled them both into her arms.

"I'm glad he's dead," said Lucy. She stood up straight and pushed Kit away. Elliot was as white as a sheet and his chin trembled uncontrollably. "Me, too," he said, in a small quavering voice.

"You two are so brave!" Kit said to them. "And now, we need to tell Daddy that there's been an accident," said Kit. She looked at them seriously. "But, kids—that's all, just that there's been an accident, okay? Can you do that?"

"Yes," said Lucy. Lucy walked over to where the torch lay on the ground, picked it up with both hands, and held it at arm's length. Kit watched as her sister looked at Michael, sizing him up. This fifteen-year-old was trying to determine if Michael was shrewd enough to do what needed to be done. "We shouldn't leave this lying around, you know," she said.

In the face of this brutal incident, her sister was turning out to be one cool customer. "You're right, Lucy," Michael agreed. "We better do something with that. What do you suggest?"

"Elliot, you take this to the barn"—Lucy turned to their younger brother like a general—"put it up on a shelf where no one will see it. Maybe behind the milk vats. Okay?"

Elliot nodded, trying to look brave.

"Good." She handed him the torch canister. "I'll go back to the house and get Daddy. And Elliot . . ." she said. "No crying."

"I am *not* going to cry!" her little brother responded indignantly.

Sometime later, the ambulance arrived, along with Sheriff Brown.

Charlie Overbee had been trying to keep the dozens of wedding guests crowding the muddy field away from the scene, but now Genia pushed through. Kit cringed when her cousin saw the paramedics loading Brandon's inert, lifeless body into the ambulance. Genia stamped her feet and wailed "*Noooo!*" until Uncle Wes pulled her away.

She knew, now, that Genia had been hiding at least some of Brandon's secrets—that she'd bribed Anne to keep quiet with her mother's earrings. And maybe Genia even suspected that Brandon had attacked her at the lake two years earlier. And yet, she'd said nothing.

It seemed to Kit that her cousin's angry howl had revealed more rage, more disappointment, than love or heartbreak. For the sake of Brandon's money and all it would have brought her, Genia had tried to hide the truth. Kit closed her eyes, and turned away.

With reluctance, the sheriff approached Kit and asked if she could provide him with a statement. Her father shoved forward and called out to the sheriff with his objections.

"Sheriff Brown, please. Can't this wait?" he asked.

"It's okay, Daddy, I'm fine," Kit said. "I can talk to the sheriff."

A transformation came over her, as Kit assumed the cool, haughty confidence of her mother. A dubious gift, perhaps, but useful. She stood tall, and took charge now, of how the story of the accident would be told. She glanced over at Michael and saw him watching her, his expression one of surprise.

"My boyfriend, Michael, and I had come out to look for Brandon," she began. "He was supposed to be at the party with his fiancée, my cousin, at the main house. Rain was pouring down, there was a good deal of thunder and we couldn't imagine where he'd gone. Well, as I'm sure my cousin will tell you, Brandon had a drinking problem. We found him, I'm sorry to say, stumbling around drunk right in the middle of Daddy's herd of cattle.

"We tried to persuade him to come back to the party. Suddenly, there was a huge burst of lightning and all the animals panicked, including the bull that broke through his pen. They charged toward the woods." Kit's face composed itself in a masterful expression of grief. "Brandon got caught in the middle of the stampede. It was just terrible. Tragic."

The sheriff looked out toward the broken fence. All the animals had scattered and disappeared into the woods, with the exception of Freddie, who now grazed placidly out in the middle of the field.

Sheriff Brown seemed thoughtful. "I came across that boy just last night. His car had gone off the road into a ditch. Driving under the influence. Well, I knew from Mr. Morgan that this young man's wedding was coming up. Since we were close to the farm, I called a tow truck and just gave him a warning." The sheriff sighed and gazed out at the pasture. "Your father has a fine herd here, I understand."

"Yes," said Kit, importantly. "This herd has won a number of dairy awards for the State of New Hampshire, including First Prize."

Michael watched her, admiring and astonished. He knew what she was up to: If one rampaging bull were to blame, he might have to be destroyed; but there was little chance that anyone would suggest the Morgans' entire herd should be put down. Especially a herd that had won awards for the State of New Hampshire. The incident would be written up as a tragic, freak accident.

"Well, I guess that's about the size of it, then," said the sheriff. "A real tragedy. Thank you, Miss Morgan. I think that's all I need. I'll just finish up my examination of the scene and get back to the station."

She'd done it. Her story was believable enough to save Freddie.

Michael came to her side. He hugged her, and then wrapped his arm around her shoulders. They turned away from the pasture, walking through the clusters of guests and back toward the front of the barn.

News of the accident must have already reached town, she guessed. That was fast. For as they approached the parking area, she was surprised to see Dr. Landsman getting out of his car.

Then, to Kit's greater astonishment, she saw her mother break away from her guests and hurry over toward the vet. "Oh, John, you came!" she cried, and threw herself, sobbing, into his arms.

Kit and Michael stared, dumbfounded at the sight of her mother in the embrace of Michael's boss. "What?" Michael turned to her. Kit shook her head and said stonily, "I don't even want to know what that's all about."

Coming from behind the barn, the voice of her father could be heard urging his family and distraught guests away from the scene and back to the Cedaredge house, where undoubtedly strong drinks would be served to all.

Chapter 48

Michael took Kit's hand. "Come with me?"

As the guests returned to the house—the men shaken and subdued, the women crying—no one paid attention as he and Kit climbed into his truck. They drove down the dirt road, away from Cedaredge Farm. They held hands but said nothing to each other. Michael knew one place where they would be warm and dry, and where no one would find them.

The climb through the woods took less time. He knew the path by now, and led the way. The rain had stopped, and the sky had brightened a little, offering the last pale watercolor light of day before dusk settled. Somewhere in the woods an owl began to call softly, "*Hooo cooks for yooooooo?*"

When they reached the hotel, they both stopped and looked up at its empty, forgotten grandeur in the twilight. "I wish I had gotten to meet Alfred," Kit said. "I would have thanked him."

Inside the hotel, Michael found an old-fashioned flint starter beside the fireplace, and he lit the oil lamp on the kitchen table. His new oxford shirt and chinos, and Kit's pretty green dress, were caked with mud and damp from the rain. Beside the hearth, dry kindling and split wood were organized in a neat stack where Alfred had left them; Michael arranged the wood in the fireplace and soon a crackling fire burned on the hearth. Warmth began to fill the room.

Kit stood close beside him. When he got up from lighting the fire, he stared at her, this beautiful girl in her rumpled dress whom he had imagined a future with. Now, that would never be. He closed his eyes and she wrapped her arms around his waist.

"I always wanted you to be the first," she whispered. "But I was afraid we'd both make such a big deal out of it, you and me. And then I'd never be able to leave."

"So, if we make love now, you won't leave?" he asked. How could his heart be breaking while his cock was getting hard? That was just so messed up.

Her eyes had been as dark and gray as storm clouds, but now they shone a soft twilight blue. "You'll always be here," she said, her voice choked. She pressed her hand to her heart. "You and me, Michael. We'll always be here."

"Oh, Kit." She was tearing him apart.

He sat down on the cot and pulled her down to sit on his lap.

He cleared his voice, and tried to keep from breaking down. "So, tell me about these people you're going to live with in Paris. I want to know. I do."

From a deep pocket in her dress, she pulled out a crumpled, blue airmail letter. "Well, the man who wrote to me, his father was a contemporary of Miss Winthrop's. He and his wife seem so kind. I can read the letter they sent me. It's in French, but I can translate . . ."

"Read it in French. I want to hear you. You can tell me what it means after."

He watched her as she read, saw the different expressions light up and animate her face, and listened to the strange, incomprehensible words running together in her singsongy voice. She translated the message for him in English. When she was finished, he looked down, away.

How could she not accept this life-changing gift? He recognized the hope in her eyes, the excitement in her voice. For, once, on a summer not so long ago, meeting Kit had opened his eyes in the same way. And he would never regret—or want to take from her—that feeling of life miraculously expanding. The belief that anything was possible.

He stood, placing Kit on her feet, and took the oil lamp from the table. "Come on." He pulled back the curtain that had closed off the kitchen from the rest of the hotel. "Let's take a look at this old place."

Her brows came together in a question. Then, a sad smile touched her lips. Maybe she understood what he didn't have the words to say. He couldn't admit—was not ready to, yet—that the time had almost come to say goodbye.

"When was the last time someone walked down these halls, do you think?" she whispered, as if they were two little kids, exploring.

"Who knows? Ten years? Fifty years? It doesn't look like much has been disturbed."

A thick, patterned rug ran the length of the hallway. The years had worn the rug bare in spots but still it felt soft under their feet. Chandeliers hanging from the ceiling still dangled with most of their crystals, though a layer of dust dimmed the once-sparkling cut glass.

They arrived at the central staircase leading to the upper-floor guest rooms. "Will you come upstairs with me—or is the great world traveler scared?" he teased her.

"Scared?" she huffed, as if offended. "Of course not. Are you?"

"Maybe. After all, who knows what we might find up there. You better go first."

"Fine. Hand me that oil lamp, scaredy-cat," she said with a smirk. "Some lifeguard you are!"

At the top of the staircase the hallway fanned out in both directions, running along the back of the hotel, with the rooms all facing the lake. The doors were closed, but, with any luck, not locked. He followed Kit as she turned right and led the way with the lamp. She chose the third door, and the knob turned easily.

Even in the dark, with all the furniture covered with heavy drop cloths, the large guest room seemed to welcome them in with a dreamy old-fashioned elegance. She put the oil lamp on the mantel, and the glow of the flame illuminated the big blooming flowers printed on the faded wallpaper.

The room had probably been closed up for decades, too. He crossed the carpeted floor to open the windows. The heavy sash creaked but responded, so he lifted it all the way open, then unlocked the two large shutters and pushed them to the sides to let in the fresh night breeze.

"The *moon!*" Kit said. "Look at its reflection on the lake!" She came to stand beside him and interlaced her fingers in his. A melancholy tune stirred in him, and he sang to her:

"A ship there is and she sails the sea
She's loaded deep as deep can be
But not so deep as the love I'm in
I know not if I'll sink or swim.

"Must I go bound while you go free?
Must I love this girl who's leaving me?
Why was I born with so little art
As to love a girl who's breaking my heart?"

He pulled her close, kissed her hair:

"When cockle shells turn silver bells
Then will my love come back to me
When roses bloom in winter's gloom
Then will my love return to me . . ."

"I wish," he said in a low murmur, "I wish I could give you everything you needed, everything you want—including that moon, and all the stars." His voice broke as he sung the words

"and all the flowers of the mountain . . ."

He began to sob. "I would give you the last breath in my body, Kit, the last drop of blood in my heart."

She wept, too, as she pressed her face against his neck. "Oh, Michael!" she said. "Don't you see? You gave me back *my life*. And you gave me my future."

Neither of them could say how long they stood there together, as the moon reclined into a deep blue sky arrayed with stars and cast its silver reflection on the shimmering surface of the lake below. At last, Kit took his hand and led him over to the big, four-poster bed. They pulled back the heavy drape that had covered the bed for so many decades. The silky sheets underneath felt smooth and soft.

He kissed her, as if time would stand still for them. And as he did, his hands grasped her pale green dress and pulled it up over her body. She shook herself free of the garment, arms above her, as he undid her bra and slid his hands over her breasts.

He brought her hands to the top button of his slacks. "Well?" He smiled at her. Her lips turned up in a shy smile and she began to undress him, too, with trembling fingers.

"You're beautiful, you know," she whispered at last, as she gazed at his naked body from head to toe. "Your chest and shoulders, your arms . . . and here . . ." She ran her fingers across his taut belly. And, if you don't mind me saying so, you've got a great ass," she giggled.

"Glad I pass muster." He found her mouth again with his. Then he pushed his cock up against her, as her hands slid down his back.

"I mean it, Michael—one day, one day you'll see. I'm going to make a sculpture of you," she said, kissing him.

"One day"—Michael looked at her gravely—"one day, Kit, make a sculpture of the both of us. Together. For all time."

On the bed, they lay beside each other, Michael resting on his elbow. He took in the pale beauty of her body as if he might memorize every detail. Then they held each other's gaze, as his hand drifted, circling her breasts, traveling down the curve of her waist and hips. His fingers moved ever so slowly, and reached finally to the warm place between her thighs.

"You're so wet . . ." He bent to kiss her belly, to kiss the soft thatch of hair below.

Now he felt as if he were the artist, or a magician even, as he conjured waves of desire across her body, compelling her hips to move, the blood to rise. "Don't stop . . ." she gasped, and at last cried out with pleasure.

He had to have her now. He pushed himself up, and slid on top of her.

"Michael . . . I don't really know . . . exactly how this part works!" Kit admitted in a nervous, breathless voice. "I mean, all I've ever done is study a lot of naked statues."

"I think we'll be all right. I've seen farm animals do it," he teased. He brushed the hair out of her face.

"That is so *gross*!"

They laughed, and she struggled against him in play as he held her arms down. Finally, he pushed his knees between her legs and spread her wide open beneath him.

His voice was soft, urgent. "I want you, so much . . . Kit . . . is it okay?" He slipped one arm beneath her, and pulled her hips toward him. She nodded.

Her body resisted him at first, until she whispered with a desperate desire, "Michael!" And at last, she gave way, as he came into her, plunged inside, kissing her as if to devour her.

A great rush of passion gathered them up, and all the pain and the love crashed together until they were no longer two separate people, but one beating heart, one burning flame. Lost inside of her, he vowed: If this was to be the end, their first and last time, then let every moment roar and crackle. Let him explode with light. So that the memory of this one night might be enough to comfort him in the dark, lonely times to come.

Chapter 49

Kit awoke to the cries of the loons echoing across the lake beneath the mountains. Calling.

"Come with me to the lake," she whispered to him.

"It's still dark," he murmured. "I don't want to let you go yet."

But her eyes were opened now, her heart fluttering. And lying here in bed seemed like just waiting for the end to come.

"Let's swim! Let's go out into the morning, before the sun comes up, and take a swim together."

She wanted to meet the day together with him—in joy and not sorrow.

They walked naked through the woods, down the path to the lakeshore, carrying their clothes. The air still held on to the humid warmth of summer. But the light shone differently now, the sun moving more slowly up over the rocky summits. No birds sang in the trees; they rested now, preparing to fly south soon. From the ground beneath their bare feet rose the sweet, dusty smell of fall.

The wild shoreline opened before them, with its tumbled rocks and fallen trees, and the lake's surface began to glow, capturing the brightening of the sky. She dropped her clothes on a boulder and wrapped her arms around him, breathing in the warmth of his skin—memorizing the smell of him—as he covered her hair in kisses.

They looked out at the lake together, and the deep knowledge of her love for him filled her and overwhelmed her—even as tears streamed down her face—like the beauty and everlastingness of this place.

"It's warm!" she said, testing the water with her toes. She wiped the tears from her cheeks.

"Warm compared to what?" He reached for her again, and pressed his body close to hers.

"Well, it's not too cold, not as cold as it is in the beginning of summer. Come on! Come in with me."

If she did not go into the water right this instant, and feel the cold shock of it, she would really start to cry. To cry and cry and never be able to stop. Awkward and half tripping on the stones, she stumbled and slid in, until the water reached her hips. She shivered once, and dived in.

Kit pulled through the cold water, swimming strong. She swam until she was out of breath, and then rolled over onto her back. The sun was coming up now. Back on the shore, Michael stood still and looked out at her. "Come on!" she called to him.

She dived under, swimming down deep to the quiet depths, to the silent, green-gold place of dreams, of wonder. Where the hard edges of the world loosen and float away. The dark presence that had lurked for so long inside of her mind had vanished, for good. The lake had not forsaken her, as she once had grieved. In the form of a kind hermit, the spirits of this lake had come to her aid. She gazed into the blurred, shifting distance.

What awaited her, out in the world? Tomorrow, and the next day, and the next? Her dreams called out to her.

The surface of the water exploded as she burst back up for air. Michael had moved into the water, but it seemed to her that he had decided not to follow her. Instead, he stood watching. He lifted both his arms toward her.

Now she swam back to him. Legs kicking, arms pulling, as strong and fast as she could move. When she reached him, Kit threw herself into his open arms. He gathered her in, strong and unbearably beautiful. How could two bodies fit as perfectly as theirs?

"Torturing me right up to the end, I see." Michael kissed her, and she felt him, hard, up against her.

His hands moved over her body, and his tongue was in her mouth.

She kissed him through her tears. A fear rose up inside of her. "I want to stay! I can't leave you! I love you, Michael." Each tree in the forest drew strength from the earth, the lake owed its existence to the protection of the ancient mountains ringing it. How could she exist without him?

He held her as she cried. "I know you love me. But you have to go."

"I can't do this. Who am I fooling? I'm just an amateur . . . and I can't bear to leave you!"

"You're not an amateur. Miss Winthrop never would have asked her friends to help you if she'd thought you were an amateur. Your teachers wouldn't have encouraged you if they hadn't believed in you. You have to go."

"Why? Why should I? It's too awful! I'll die!" she sobbed.

"I know it's awful, believe me," he whispered. "I feel like I'm going to crawl into a hole and die, too. But . . . we have things we need to do, right? Separate things. And I understand now, you need to go, to go to Paris.

"Last night, when you read that letter to me . . . even though I didn't understand what the words meant . . . I saw your face, Kit. Your eyes sparkled, you looked so happy and . . . fierce, in a way. You have to see what's out there—and find out for yourself if this dream you have now, of being an artist, is really what you want. I believe in you, and I love you too much to be the person who tries to stop you."

He was giving her the greatest gift she'd ever received. She tried to speak, but he kissed her again.

And then they spoke no further words, but held and touched each other, memorizing the smell and the taste and the feel of each other, and the sounds of each other's voices crying softly. And all there was to know.

Before the soft light of morning gave way to the imperatives of the new day and the future, she heard from a far corner of the lake the loons calling out to one another once again.

Part V

"If my true love will not come
I will never find another"

Chapter 50

"I made something for you both," Kit said to Lucy and Elliot. Her sister and brother had been sitting on her bed as she packed. Kit zipped her suitcase and double-checked that all her documents were in order: passport and work visa, traveler's checks, plane ticket, all neatly organized in her shoulder bag. She wore jeans, a blue cotton sweater over an embroidered peasant blouse, and sneakers. Clothes she'd be comfortable in for the long journey.

"This one's for you." Her hand trembled with emotion as she handed a rolled sheet of drawing paper, tied with woven grass and decorated with a daisy, to Lucy. The other sheet, rolled to fit inside a birch-bark sleeve, was for Elliot. They each undid the fastenings and unrolled the large sheets of paper.

Lucy looked serious.

"Do you like it?" Kit asked.

Her sister began to tear up. "I guess I didn't believe that you really were an artist. I thought you were just going to Paris to piss off Mother and Daddy."

The paper held a detailed pastel portrait of Lucy, as Kit imagined her a few years from now, with a knowing, confident smile and big, glamorous sunglasses atop her head. "What do you think?"

"It's beautiful! I think I look like a movie star!"

"And I look like that guy on *Wild Kingdom*! Not the old guy—but the one who wrestles with alligators!" Elliot proclaimed. The portrait of her brother featured a slightly more mature young man, with binoculars, a map, and a safari hat. He even had a small garter snake peeking out of one pocket.

She'd hoped she'd captured Lucy and Elliot as they might like to imagine themselves. "Saying goodbye makes me feel like crying, too. But I know you guys have so much to look forward to, and that makes me happy. I wanted you to know, I wanted to show you, how much I believe in you."

The colorful pictures brightened their otherwise sad goodbye. Then Elliot asked, looking toward her dresser, "What about the Bluebird of Happiness?"

"Where do you think you're going?" her mother asked coldly, confronting Kit as she carried her bag down the front hall. Of course, her parents both knew, now, that she was leaving today for Paris. Max had agreed to drive her to Logan Airport outside Boston for the international flight.

"Oh, Mother! Please be happy for me."

Now that she was about to go, her heart ached at saying goodbye to her parents, her family. At leaving Cedaredge and New Hampshire. "You and Daddy know that this is what I want. And it's all arranged with the DeLettres, Miss Winthrop's friends." She had hoped that the reference to this old friend of the family, Esther Winthrop, might assuage their anger and disappointment. Give them confidence in her choice.

"I'm just waiting for Max." She looked at her watch. She had planned with plenty of time.

"Max left for Connecticut an hour ago," her mother stated.

Kit looked at her mother, dumbstruck.

"Genia was desperate to get back home," she informed Kit.

"And given the circumstances, your father instructed Max to take Genia and your aunt and uncle back to Connecticut."

"*But—they knew!* They knew Max was supposed to take me to Logan Airport!"

"Well, maybe you should have planned better. Perhaps this will give you some time to reconsider this reckless project of yours."

Her father came out of the living room and joined them in the hallway. "Please, Kitty. There's no harm in giving this whole notion a little more thought. It all seems so sudden."

Panic drenched her like a cold sweat. How was she going to make her flight?

"Is there someone else who'll drive me?"

"I'm sorry, Kit," her father said, shaking his head. He and her mother both stood firm. Two immutable forces blocking her way.

She put down her bag. She didn't know what to do. And for a moment, the idea of what it would be like *to just stay* rose up in her imagination. It would be a let-down, the end of her dream of independence. But it would be so much easier . . .

Two things happened. The first was that Michael's words came back to her: *You have to see what's out there—and find out for yourself if this dream you have now, of being an artist, is really what you want. I believe in you . . .*

And the second was Lucy's pointed statement. Standing now beside her mother and father, her independent-minded and contrary sister announced, "There's a bus that goes to Boston from the Franconia Dairy Bar. A Trailways bus. Remember? You shouldn't miss your plane, Kitty."

Kit flew past her parents to the telephone in the hall near the pantry. Her trembling fingers paged through the phone book until she found the number for the bus company. She dialed the number.

"What time does the bus pick up from the Franconia Dairy Bar? I need to reserve a ticket to Boston—for today. Yes, I can be there in twenty minutes."

"I have to go!" she said to the four members of her family standing in front of her.

"Katherine Morgan! This is a ridiculous plan." Her mother raised her voice, understanding now that she had lost this battle with her daughter. Her father had his arm around her mother and Kit saw that he was crying. Suddenly, their power over her was diminished; from this day forward, she would be solely responsible for herself—for every success she might have, and for all the mistakes she would make, too. So be it.

She embraced her mother, and then her father, and Lucy and Elliot. "I love you all!"

She ran out of the house, down the front stairs, and over to the garage with her suitcase and shoulder bag banging against her side. She strapped her suitcase to the back of the sky-blue moped. Then, with less than twenty minutes to go, she drove out the driveway and down the hill. Away from Cedaredge Farm and toward Franconia. She'd be sorry to have to leave the moped at the Dairy Bar.

The bus would take her to Boston, and from there she'd catch a taxi to Logan Airport. She was on her way to Paris.

Chapter 51

He'd brought Kit home after their night together by the lake. They had tried to be gentle with each other as they let go and said good-bye: one last kiss, one last warm clasping of hands. And then, she was gone.

A week later, Michael was called back out to Cedaredge with Landsman. As he got out of his truck, he had to stop and steady himself. To be here now, with Kit gone, nearly brought him to his knees.

Landsman greeted Bob Morgan, offering his condolences. "Awful business, Bob. How are you and Bunny and the kids holding up?"

Morgan stood in the parking lot, hands in his pockets, with Banjo by his side. "We're managing. The boy's father and step-mother took his body home to Connecticut. Very difficult for them."

In a quieter voice, Kit's father continued, "Have to admit, John, I'd started to have mixed feelings about that boy marrying my niece. And what the hell was he doing out there with the cattle, in the rain, for Chrissake?"

A vivid memory of that crazy, twisted afternoon came back to Michael. Would a day come when any of Bob Morgan's children would answer that question? That would be for them to decide.

Morgan sighed. "Terrible, terrible thing," he said. "My sister and her husband have taken Genia to some friends on the Cape.

Try to put all of this behind them. Bunny and I will be taking the kids back to the city next week."

"And Kit . . ." Landsman said with sympathy. He must have heard the news through Charlie Overbee. Michael felt his throat close, the tears burn in his eyes.

"She's gone," said Morgan. "Nothing her mother or I could say would stop her." His eyes were rimmed with red. To Michael, Bob Morgan looked nearly as sorrowful as he felt.

"Yes, she's gone." Morgan now looked directly at him. "But I guess you knew that."

Michael held Bob Morgan's gaze. He felt as if some part of him had died. But also, despite the searing pain of loss—or perhaps because of it—he could now look Morgan in the eye as a man.

He'd had to grow up, to find the strength to set free the one person he loved the most. Knowing that the *goodbye* would cripple him. Yes, he did know she had gone. And he understood why.

Morgan cleared his throat, stood up straight then, and began walking toward the pasture. Michael followed with Landsman. "And the damn cattle are still gone, too, after Freddie scared the hell out of them and they ran off into the woods," he grumbled. The grass grew high, and purple asters bloomed in thick bunches along the path. Beside the stone foundation of the barn, the roses had faded and were almost gone.

The three men stood by the fence, looking out at the empty pasture. Banjo came and stood beside Michael, leaning against his leg. The dog's ears drooped—even he seemed sad. Beyond the field, the maples were mostly still green but beginning to turn, with scattered leaves on fire in red and orange. Gold shimmered in the branches of the pale, white birch trees. And in the distance, the great mass of the Presidential Mountain Range had shifted in color; now summer's greens blended with autumn's purples, reds, golds.

"Are the far fence rails still down?" Michael asked, breaking the silence at last.

"What do you mean, son?" asked Morgan.

"I mean, is there a way for the cattle to get *back into* the pasture, from the woods?"

"I see. Yes, there's still a huge gap back there in the fence, nothing's been mended yet. Haven't had the time. Or the energy, I suppose . . ."

Michael turned on his heel, walked back to his truck. He pulled his guitar out of the cab and returned to where Morgan and Landsman were standing. He was humming a soft tune now.

Bob Morgan looked at him like he was crazy.

John Landsman smiled.

"If those cattle have been gone for a week, this could take a little while," Michael said, tuning up the guitar. "I suggest everybody get comfortable."

Maybe time would cure all wounds; he doubted it. But what Michael did know was that for him, music was the only medicine that might begin to heal his shattered heart.

> "*My love is like a red, red rose*
> *That's newly sprung in June*
> *My love is like a melody*
> *That's sweetly played in tune.*"

His voice broke with grief. The tune, gently plucked on the steel strings, rang out across the pasture. He took a deep breath, and continued:

> "*So fair art thou, my bonnie lass*
> *So deep in love am I*
> *And I would love thee still, my dear*

'Til all the seas run dry.

"'Til all the seas run dry, my dear
And the rocks melt with the sun
I will love thee still, my dear
While the sands of life shall run.

"So fare thee well my only love
And fare thee well a while!
And I will come to you again
Though it were ten thousand miles."

Not one of them had anywhere to go that afternoon. And so they sat on the stone foundation, Banjo curled up at their feet, and Michael sang one lonesome tune after another. And once in a while, he thought he might have even heard Landsman or Morgan himself humming along. As if the music gave its own special comfort to each of them.

Sometime before the sun started to dip in the sky, the first cow appeared on the far side of the fence, followed by her sisters. The big, wary animals stepped with care over the broken posts. Once inside the pasture, they sniffed the evening breeze for any hint of danger or unwelcome surprises, snorted, and stamped their hooves. After a time, one, then two, then the rest began a gentle trot toward the barn.

Freddie, grazing on sweet alfalfa grasses, flicked his tail and lifted his head in a brief welcome. And before it was dark, the entire herd had been drawn back by the music. They approached Michael, Landsman, and Bob Morgan, looking as foolish and awkward as you could imagine, their eyes wide with curiosity, as they all reached their necks through the fence to gawk.

The cattle, at least, were content to be home.

Chapter 52

Fall arrived on a brisk, busy day in September.

Michael put in his final week at the veterinary clinic. On his last day, Lucy and Elliot paid him a surprise visit. "Kitty wanted you to have this," Elliot said, sniffing, and holding out to Michael the small Bluebird of Happiness sculpture.

"Oh . . ." He forced himself not to choke up in front of Lucy and Elliot. "Thank you," he whispered.

"We're on our way back to New York," Lucy said. "Mother and Daddy are waiting in the car." And then, suddenly, she wrapped her arms around him. "We are going to miss you so much!"

At the end of the day, he said goodbye to the Landsmans.

"You've done a great job, Michael, and you are always welcome here. You just let me know." His boss surprised him by giving him a big bear hug—and then compensated for being emotional by slapping him hard on the back.

"Thank you," Michael said. It came out like a croak. As he set off into the unknown, he didn't know if or when he would be returning. But he would always be grateful to John Landsman for hiring him that summer, for giving him a chance.

He met Tom for a farewell beer at Ollie's, and Jenny sat close beside Tom. There was no denying that Tom and Jenny made a great couple. He couldn't believe that his little sister would be a senior this year. Seeing her and Tom together, he realized that they both looked so much like . . . *adults*. Holy crap! Where had the time gone?

She and Tom had been looking for apartments to rent, Jenny said. "Don't mention it to Mom and Dad! We're not planning anything right away, but maybe after Christmas."

When Michael got up to head out, Tom stopped him. "You've got to check this out before you go," he insisted.

"What's that?"

"Ollie got one of the first models of this new game, for the bar. It's a video game! It's called *Pac-Man*."

"Tom's latest obsession," Jenny said with a smile.

"Do you really think people who come to Ollie's want to play a video game? I think they'd rather be listening to music and flirting with girls."

"You'll see—you're going to love it! Just one game, okay?"

And one day, Michael was filling up the truck at the gas station in Littleton when, from the opposite side of the gas pump island, he heard, "Hey, stranger!"

He looked up and saw Theresa, her dark hair as big and poufy as ever, getting out of a beat-up Dodge. The roof was strapped down with suitcases. "This is my fiancé, Brad," she said, pulling the shirtsleeve of a serious, older-looking guy who was filling up the car. Brad nodded a friendly but disinterested greeting. "We're moving to Concord. Brad just got a job there as manager of a Radio Shack. We're getting married next June." She flashed a sparkly ring. "It's an authentic diamond!"

"I didn't think it was a mood ring," he teased her.

"For your information, I'm a distributor of mood rings now, and other jewelry. I've got Dawn, Sherrie, and Jackie working for me. I'm an entrepreneur!"

He'd always known Theresa had . . . leadership potential. She certainly had a knack for taking charge. "You look really happy, Theresa." She did look happy—much happier than when she had been dating him. He came around and gave her a quick hug.

Theresa scrutinized him. "You look like shit, Mikey," she said, and then she laughed. He probably deserved that; how could he blame her for taking some satisfaction in his miserable state? But Theresa had a good heart, and she put her hand on his arm and said, "You take care of yourself, okay?"

In other circumstances, the trip to Dartmouth College from Franconia would have been nothing more than a lazy drive on a beautiful September afternoon. But for Michael, those hundred or so miles on backcountry roads through the small towns of Bath, Haverhill, and Lyme represented a much greater distance: the distance between the familiar world he had grown up in and a world that was largely unknown and undefined. Finding his way in this new territory was going to be complicated, challenging, what he had believed for so long that he wanted.

In the weeks that followed Kit's departure for France, Michael had existed in a kind of numb unreality. He had gone through the motions of the last days of work, packing for college, saying goodbye to his friends, his mom and dad.

But alone now on the Dartmouth Green, with all the eager, nervous freshmen striding past him or playing Frisbee on the thick, manicured lawn, he stood paralyzed with unhappiness. And he asked himself, again: How am I going to get up every day and go to class? How do I keep myself from throwing in the towel and crawling home with my tail between my legs? How do I not fail?

Kit was gone and his entire motivation for being here at college, for making something of his life, had vanished across the ocean, for good. *How was he going to do this?*

And then he heard her voice, and it gave him strength: *You're smart and ambitious and curious about the world—like I am! It's not enough to go through life playing the game according to the rules we grew up with. We want more! We want a life where we set the terms!*

In fact, even with a rocket-size hole blown through his heart, it turned out to be easier than he had imagined—or feared—to fit into this world and to do well. When he'd decided, after the summer he'd first met Kit, that he wanted to go to college, Michael had taught himself how to set goals and focus on the task at hand. He did those things automatically now, with very little effort.

He hadn't coasted into Dartmouth on money, family, or a college application padded with extracurricular activities like riding championships or pseudo-educational trips to the Virgin Islands. Instead, he was smart and he knew how to apply himself. And unlike so many of the other first-year students, he had no interest in—and so wasn't distracted by—the endless rounds of parties that dominated that first semester of freshman year.

The great social equalizer turned out to be sports.

With November came an early snow, and tryouts for the ski team. Michael dragged himself out of his comatose state and geared up. He had spent his entire life skiing on the icy and unpredictable New England terrain. Now, he launched himself off the most dangerous peaks and ridges without caution, recklessly ripping down the newly snow-covered verticals, over rocks and ice. He made the first cut, ahead of some of the upperclassmen. And that, more than anything else, established his place in the hierarchy of this world.

Chapter 53

Time passed. Before he knew it, he'd somehow made it through the entire semester, with only final exams to go. The campus began to empty out for the Christmas holidays; now, just a few students with late-scheduled finals still haunted the quiet dorms. The deserted grounds were fine with him. He liked walking across the barren Green, head down against the cold wind. Reveled, almost, in the lonely silence. It suited his state of mind.

One day before his last exam, Michael took a run up by Occom Pond. A frigid, gray desolation had settled across the campus on this quiet afternoon. He looped back, stopping by Hopkins Center to pick up any last pieces of mail before the break.

He peered into the dark square of his mailbox. Empty. No surprise there.

As he turned to leave, the postmaster called out from behind the mailboxes, where he stood inserting letters and packages. "'Scuse me? You wouldn't happen to be Michael Pearce, would you? I noticed you checking that post box."

"That's me."

"Can I see your ID? Just to be sure."

Michael flipped out his college meal card with the ID next to it. The postmaster slid a letter through the back of the box. "This one didn't have much of an address on it—just: Michael Pearce, Dartmouth College, Hanover, NH USA. Afraid it's been sitting back here for a week or two."

The postmark read "Paris."

Michael sprinted back to the dorm, holding the letter tight against his chest. His heart leapt into his throat, and he took the stairs up to his room two at a time. His roommate had gone home for the holidays and Michael had the tiny dorm room to himself. He closed the door, sat down on the bed, and opened the letter.

Kit, being Kit, had written the letter in French.

Cher Michael—

C'est dimanche après midi et je suis assise dans le Café de Flore où je fais le dessin d'un vieil homme et son chien. Ça ne le derange pas—c'est Paris, après tout! Tout le monde ici est écrivain ou artiste.

J'aime mon travail dans le galerie DeLettre, tout près du Pont des Arts. Pierre et Céline sont si gentils et c'est tellement fascinant d'être parmi de vrais artistes, même si tout ce que je fais c'est de répondre au téléphone et de faire des courses.

Le soir, je prends des cours de dessin et sculpture—j'espère que, l'année prochaine, je pourrais être admise à l'École des Beaux-Arts dans le Départment de Sculpture.

Autrement, je me promène partout dans Paris avec mon carnet à dessin. Je suis seule mais je ne me sens pas seule—il y a trop des choses à voir et à apprendre. Je suis contente.

Je veux que tu saches que c'était presque impossible de te quitter.

Et que je t'aimerai toujours. Toujours.

Kit

Out of the envelope fell a small woven braid of dried flowers: For-get-me-nots. Michael cradled them in the palm of his hand, staring at the tiny, faded blue blossoms. Then he laid the flowers on the bedside table.

He held the single sheet of paper in his hand and read out loud the mysterious, incomprehensible words, as if Kit were speaking to him.

Then he put on his jacket, with the letter tucked safe inside, and walked over to Baker Library. He settled into the Tower reading room. And that afternoon, with a French-English dictionary, he translated the letter, word by word. As if he were untangling a knot, fitting together pieces from a puzzle. Reading it to himself again and again, until it was dark outside and time for the library to close.

Dear Michael—

It is Sunday afternoon and I am sitting in the Café de Flore sketching an old man and his dog. They don't seem to mind at all—it's Paris after all! Here, everyone is a writer or an artist.

I love my job at the Galerie DeLettre, close to the Pont des Arts. Pierre and Céline are so kind and it is so exciting to be among real artists at last, even if my job is just to answer the phone and run errands.

At night I take classes in drawing and sculpture—I hope next year to be accepted at the École des Beaux-Arts in the Sculpture Department.

Otherwise, I stroll all over the city with my sketchpad. I am alone, but I am not lonely—there is too much to see and to learn! I am happy.

It was almost impossible for me to leave you, Michael. I want you to know that.

And that I will always love you. Always.

Kit

Outside the Tower window, the giant Christmas tree on the Green glowed with fairy-tale blue and white lights. He wondered what Kit was doing at this exact moment, and he imagined her gazing up at the Eiffel Tower as she had once described it to him, all decorated with lights.

The next day after his last exam, he walked across the Green in the pale winter afternoon to the registrar's office in McNutt Hall. He climbed up the stairs and knocked on the door.

"It's open. Come in."

"I'm wondering if there's still time to register for another class, for the spring semester."

"Might be. What were you thinking?"

Michael flipped through the spring course catalogue. There: "Introduction to Conversational French," he said, pointing at the course description.

He gave the registrar his name and she flipped through his records. "You're a science major, I see . . . ?"

"That's right."

"Hmmm . . . well . . . why not, I suppose." She looked through the class schedules and found an opening. After making a few notes on a form and handing it to him, she said, "There, you're all set. I guess you never know when being able to speak a foreign language might come in handy—even for a scientist."

He walked out into the wintery New Hampshire afternoon. Kit's voice, and the memory of a soft, warm summer breeze, whispered like a song he could just make out in his head. He decided to take the long way back to the dorm, along the path beside the Connecticut River. The pale December sun glistened and rippled on the water's surface, as the river flowed gently onward.

He thought of its passage, of how these waters would eventually flow into the sea. Would any of those millions of droplets one day wash up against the shores of France?

He pulled up the collar to his coat against the cold and hurried onward. The light shifted, faded into evening, and the snow began to fall.

Part VI

"Let us go, lassie, go"

Chapter 54

That December night in the gallery, after she'd recounted to Pierre the whole, long story—that night was the turning point. She'd decided to leave Paris, then and there.

To come home.

Her mind was made up by the time Pierre's wife, Céline, appeared on the doorstep to her studio the next afternoon with a confession that began: "*Je dois te dire quelque chose de terrible . . .* There is something I must tell you, something awful. I think this man, Michael Pearce, I think he came to the gallery once before. Many, many years ago."

"What are you saying, Céline? When was this?"

"You had just gotten married, Katherine. You were in Rome, on your honeymoon. I didn't think to tell you."

She'd been twenty-two.

A terrible grief descended upon her. And then, rage, a desire to smash things. But it had not been dear Céline's fault. And in the end, she'd had to ask herself: *What would I have done, at that time, if I'd had the chance to reunite with Michael?*

Probably screwed it all up.

It has taken her so long to understand anything about love.

Packing up a life—particularly one that included some large works in bronze—proved to be no simple matter. Pierre would continue to represent her in Europe. In the States, she'd have to see. Figuring out all the logistics granted her a last, precious gift of time with Pierre and Céline.

"We hadn't known what to expect, Pierre *et moi*, when you arrived to stay with us," Céline reminisced. "At first, *si timide*—so polite and quiet. And then, *tout d'un coup*, you found your wings."

Now it all seemed like a dream to her: gaining acceptance to *l'École des Beaux-Arts*; finding her tribe, a hodgepodge of eager, ambitious students, many of them from other countries and sharing traits similar to hers. All of them curious, oddball, fiercely committed to art and to reinventing themselves.

And she'd been gloriously anonymous. The way she looked, spoke, the family name "Morgan," all meant nothing to anyone. She was just some kid—maybe English, Canadian, or American—who spoke French with a funny accent. She'd felt as if she'd been reborn.

"But I could see from the start," said Pierre, "you were very ambitious."

Even in her last year at the *école* her work had begun to attract notice. Which only fueled her desire to be further recognized, to prove that indeed she could make a place for herself in the world as an artist. Yes, she'd always been clear about her ambition.

What Pierre and Céline didn't know about were all the times, over the years, when she'd sat in her room finishing a bottle of wine by herself, composing yet another letter to Michael—and then, waking in the morning with a crushing headache and despair, burning the letter in the sink. Burying the sodden ashes in the garden.

He must hate me, she'd decided at last, *for never writing more than the one letter, with no return address*. Or, *he's found another girlfriend, he's married. He's moved on.*

When she'd finally found a measure of self-confidence and stability in her life, she would try to look back at that summer and the love they'd shared. But remembering hurt so much. And eventually, she'd persuaded herself that it was *too* perfect, like the dream of a child. A dream that vanishes in daylight.

But the memories would not fade and in time became the source—she recognized this now, accepted it—for every beautiful or successful work she had ever made. The fire burned, and fueled a kind of relentless focus on creating.

"I've not been very lucky in love, though. Have I?" she mused sadly to Céline one day, while boxing up her tools, reference books.

"I will admit, Pierre and I felt you did make some . . . unfortunate choices . . . in husbands," Céline said, shaking her head.

Relationships never seemed to make sense. Or perhaps only one ever had, but there was no going back. In what she'd convinced herself was a decisive move toward maturity, in her early twenties she'd analyzed her options and concluded that an artistic partner would have a suitable temperament to hers. They'd understand each other, at least.

"Was I crazy, Céline?"

"I think maybe just young," her friend replied tactfully.

She'd flung herself into two ill-considered marriages, one after the next, both with flamboyant, narcissistic, and controlling artists. Divorce, in both cases, swiftly followed.

Despite all her logical analysis, it was as if she'd set out to fail.

How to distinguish love? To differentiate it from control and manipulation that hobbles the wild spirit, the soul? Now it seemed like she'd spent a lifetime wrestling with the difference between the two, and inevitably choosing the losing side.

After the second divorce, she'd left Paris and traveled to the Far East for a time, looking, she'd said, for peace of mind—but in truth just trying to escape the intractable sense of failure.

She'd studied the arts of mask making and the glazing of fine celadon pottery. A master of calligraphy had schooled her in this elaborate and meditative art, while another had taught her the delicate ritual of the tea ceremony. In the remote hills of Chiang Mai, she'd climbed the stairs of ancient temples following the orange-robed monks. In Hong Kong, she'd bowed at the feet of the great golden Buddha who rises from the sea on Lantau Island.

A fortune-teller studied her face and her palms; amid the smoke and incense he'd said: "In this life, for you, one great love." She asked for the wisdom to accept what could not be changed. And then, in the magic and clamor of these places, she'd lost herself.

One day in March, just before her final departure, she and Pierre were going over the paperwork required for having one of her pieces shipped directly to an old friend of her family's, the veterinarian John Landsman. It would be a gift from her father.

"Your family must be very pleased that you are returning," Pierre said.

"I hope so. My parents have moved to Palm Beach, you know. The farm was sold several years back. My brother Elliot keeps me up to date with all the family gossip."

Elliot now taught at MIT in Cambridge, where he'd received his undergraduate and graduate degrees in biology. He'd managed to assuage their father's wrath at his decision to turn down Princeton by quickly meeting and marrying a lovely woman from Wellesley. "At least your grandmother Morgan would have been pleased," their father grumbled, according to Elliot.

Lucy, a fashion editor and social mover and shaker, had recently decamped from New York City with her partner, Emma, to Palm Beach to look after their parents. Not surprisingly, their mother had balked at what she deemed a socially unacceptable relationship—until Lucy became editor of *The Shiny Sheet*, the Who's Who of Palm Beach.

Eventually striking it rich, Genia had married an oil and gas millionaire and moved to Texas. Brandon's demise had never been questioned.

Freddie, according to Elliot, had lived out his days in peace at Cedaredge.

She, Pierre, and Céline celebrated her last night in Paris with a dinner at Pierre and Céline's flat. "We are so proud of you, Katherine," Pierre said. "In these past years, since you came back from Hong Kong, you have become our most successful artist of the Galerie DeLettre. I would be wrong not to admit that you have made us all quite a lot of money—*merci*!" He and Céline raised their champagne glasses to her.

"Pierre is very crass," teased Céline. "More importantly, *chérie*, you stand on your own two feet, you are your own woman. Beautiful. Strong. An artist. Not the little girl who arrived like a waif on our doorstep many years ago. Now—go, and find that part of you *qui te manque*, that is still missing to you. *Nous t'aimons, tellement*. And our arms are open to you, always."

Chapter 55

"I added French to my major. Saved up every penny for the next four years. Then, the summer after my senior year at Dartmouth, I went to Paris. To find Kit."

His old friend John Landsman looks at him for what seems like a long time. Then turns back to stare at the fire. "I see," is all Landsman says.

John and his wife, Frances, still live in the farmhouse along the Gale River. Frances is pretty frail these days, and a nurse comes in every morning to help care for her. But John—he's amazingly spry. He's outlived most of his contemporaries, including both Michael's parents, who died three years ago now, and within months of each other.

It pleases him greatly to see that his old boss has become something of a local celebrity. He is a hero to the few old farmers who remain, whose animals he cared for during his decades-long career as a country vet. And he is a legend to the small crop of young people trying to make a go of it with modern, free-range, organic farms.

John officially retired in April. But he still gets out to the farms a few times a month, mostly riding shotgun in the clinic van with his younger partner, Stewart.

Michael gets up and drops another piece of wood onto the fire. It hisses, smokes a little, and then catches. Outside a light rain is falling on this early-June afternoon, and it's chilly. Typical New

Hampshire spring day. They're settled in comfortably in the living room of the farmhouse. In front of them, the crackling fire releases a sweet smell of apple wood.

"She'd written a letter to me, my freshman year, and mentioned the name of the gallery where she'd found a job. What was in my mind I can't even imagine, now—showing up in Paris four years later! I was delusional, I guess. Somehow, I just believed she'd be right there, waiting for me. Or if not, that I'd be able to track her down.

"Turned out she'd gotten married, had gone to Italy—that's what the woman running the gallery said to me. Let me tell you, John, I spent a pretty miserable ten days in Paris. And then I came home."

After all these years, he remembers how the loss had gutted him. Nearly destroyed him. And then, the years it took to orient his mind around this new reality: a life without Kit. Forever. It was like a death.

"Anyway, that was it. That's when I finally understood that I had to move on. And . . . you know how the rest turned out."

"You foolishly decided to give up on the noble pursuit of veterinary medicine!"

"Yeah—I was right on track to becoming a permanent ski bum in Colorado! Kit really understood one thing about the two of us: she and I, we were both determined to bust out, leave behind the lives we'd grown up in. We were not so different in that way."

"And then Walt read you the riot act, as I recall," John says with a chuckle.

"That's right! I'll never forget Dad showing up like that, out of the blue. Mom and Dad almost never came out West. He drove up from Denver, took me out for a cup of coffee and asked me point blank if I intended to waste my education and be *a bum* for the rest of my life. Then he drove back to the airport and flew home."

John laughs. "Your old man wasn't a big talker. But when he had something to say, he got right to the point."

"It sure did piss me off. But—I guess his strategy worked. I ended up applying to University of Colorado medical school the following year."

"Easier than getting into veterinary school," John points out.

They sit in companionable silence. Then, John shifts in his seat. "I wonder if you could make us a little more tea, Michael?"

"Sure thing." He goes to the kitchen with their mugs and turns on the flame under the kettle. Letters and some brightly colored flyers lay fanned out on the countertop. The nurse must have just brought in the mail. The water comes to a boil and he refills both their mugs, with the teabags in them. Even this second cup gives off a nice, spicy aroma.

In the living room, he hands John his mug. The old man thanks him, and remarks, "So, you're back home in Franconia for your niece's wedding, then?"

"Yes. It's very hard to believe that Tom and Jenny have been married for so long! And even harder to believe that I have a niece about to get married herself."

John takes a sip of his tea. "What about you, Michael? Never found time to get married?"

He's not expecting his friend to put him on the spot like this, and the immediate stiffening of his expression must betray his surprise. John smiles. "I'm old now, I can ask these impertinent questions, you know."

"Work has always kept me so busy, John. You know that. I've

dated, of course. Once—maybe twice—things might have gotten serious, but . . . in the end, it just never seemed fair to drag a woman into my life and make her compete with my job." It's an excuse he's honed over the years. "And now that I'm head of the cardiology department . . ." Michael says, as if he's committed himself to some religious order.

"You were such a passionate young man, Michael," John muses. "I remember."

"Weren't we all passionate at eighteen!" It seems like another lifetime, a different country from this solitary, monkish island he's become stranded on in middle age.

"And you were in love."

John is like a second father to him. They've never lost touch over the years and he's always been the connection to home. But at this particular moment, John is getting on his nerves. What happened to their usual conversations, about work? Why does he keep coming back to this old history?

Whoever Michael might have been back then, that person no longer exists. He surprises them both by blurting out too gruffly, "*I was in love with Kit.* A girl who you warned me away from, John. She was only going to break my country boy's heart, you said." John stays quiet for so long that finally he reaches over and pats the old guy on the back. "Just giving you a hard time, my friend."

"I suppose I didn't want you to get hurt. The way I had been."

Michael is suddenly on his feet. He walks over to the fireplace and stares into the flames. Fear, or apprehension at what John might be about to tell him, blocks his vision. And then he turns to face the old man. "What are you talking about?"

"I think you know that Bob Morgan and I were friends? We knew each other as young men."

"I remember that—you said you'd met on the ski lift at Cannon."

"That's right. After Bob's parents died, he asked for my help. Said he was coming up to Cedaredge for the summer to try to get a handle on the dairy business. I'd been working for a few years by then, had my own veterinary practice.

"Bob arrived at the farm with his fiancée, Barbara Karlsen. She was . . . very beautiful . . . I couldn't help being envious of Bob. And to my surprise, Barbara actually seemed interested in the farm—and me.

"That summer, Bob spent his days in town working out arrangements with financial people. While he was busy, I thought I would help out by teaching Barbara what I could about dairy farming." Landsman pauses. "Truth was, I just wanted to be around her. Before I knew it, I had fallen in love with Barbara myself. Things between us might have gone too far—she certainly seemed willing—if I hadn't decided it was time to ask Barbara to marry me."

"You *proposed* to Bunny Morgan?"

John's look gives him his answer. Finally, John continues. "Barbara laughed at me when I told her how I felt. 'Marry you? John, that's very sweet but you can't be serious. Move into some little flat over a shop in Franconia? I'm going to marry Robert, live in New York, on Fifth Avenue.'

"Her rejection crushed me. I'd convinced myself that she felt the same way I did. But she'd only spent time with me because she was bored. Wanted to make Bob a little jealous. Well, I was devastated."

He looks at John, trying to imagine him as a young man. And remembers the young man he himself once was, the target of a very similar flaying from Barbara Karlsen—by then, Bunny Morgan. "You know that you dodged a bullet, John."

"Of course! And thank goodness Frances came along.

"When I gave you that advice, years ago, I was afraid that pretty Katherine Morgan might be like her mother, Bunny. Just flirting with you until she eventually married a wealthy New York lawyer or banker. I didn't want you to get hurt, always hoped you'd meet someone nice, a country girl like my Frances."

"Kit didn't turn out like Bunny Morgan at all, you know," he says sharply. John looks surprised. He takes a deep breath, decides to be straight with his friend.

"Last winter, just before Christmas, I went to Paris for a conference. I might as well be honest, John, I never stopped thinking about Kit. I did an internet search for Katherine Morgan and found out that she was living in Paris again, that she's an artist—a well-regarded sculptor—and her work is represented by a prominent gallery. I went to the gallery.

"John—that afternoon, I finally found a sense of closure. It was as if Kit had taken all of our shared memories and transformed them into these beautiful works of art. Sculptures that will last forever. That's when I understood that what we'd had that summer had mattered to her, too.

"I know I'll never see Kit again, but it doesn't really matter anymore. I feel connected to her in some important way that will never change now. And—I don't know—it gives me a kind of peace. It really does."

What he leaves out of the story is this: DeLettre, the gallery owner, had implored him to stay. He wanted to call Katherine, to let her know that her old friend Dr. Michael Pearce was visiting the gallery. But that December afternoon, he'd said no. Seeing her work had overwhelmed him with memories and regrets—and an avalanche of pain. He'd used up all of his courage, and rushed out of the gallery in a hurry.

"Hey, don't go getting all emotional on me," he says to John. "It's okay. I've come to terms with it. It's fine. I'm fine."

John begins to struggle up from his seat.

"Here, let me help you," he says, taking the older man's arm.

"The rain has stopped. Let's go out into the garden," John says.

"Are you sure? It's still pretty cold out there."

"Yes, I'd like to get some air. And—there's something I need to show you, Michael."

John stands beside him, leaning on his cane, as Michael unlatches the French doors and pushes them open. They step out onto a deck that overlooks a flower garden where bunches of purple and white irises are glistening, still wet after the rain. The sun has come out and the Gale River sparkles in the late afternoon light.

The enchanting sculpture of two children frolicking with a calf throws a spell over the pretty backyard flower garden. The angle is perfect, and light pours across the surface of the life-size bronze piece, and catches the joyful expressions of the children.

Needless to say, he is speechless.

"Bob Morgan presented me with this sculpture this past April," John says, "when I retired. He and Bunny have moved to Palm Beach, but he flew up from Florida specially for my retirement party."

"I've seen this piece, in Paris, at the gallery. How—?"

"She's here. Katherine is here."

For some reason, he cannot understand what his friend is telling him. The words . . . they don't make sense. "What? What do you mean?"

"Bob was so happy. And Bunny—well—I suppose she was, too, though I'm not sure she ever forgave Katherine for leaving.

Still, suddenly, after living in Paris for all those years, Katherine decided to move back. She'd gotten divorced many years ago, so it wasn't because of that. Bob told me that all she'd say was, 'something happened, and she realized it was time to come home.' That was January, I'd say."

Which would have been not long after he'd visited Galerie DeLettre.

"Do you mean she moved back to New York? Or—Florida?" Like a person on the other end of a bad phone connection, he is still trying to comprehend his friend's words. Trying to wrap his mind around what John is telling him.

"No—I mean, here—Littleton. She bought one of those old warehouses, down by the Ammonoosuc River. Converted it into some kind of artist workspace."

He stares, dumbstruck, at Kit's sculpture in the garden. After a while, he hears John's voice, calling from the kitchen.

"There's a brochure somewhere with information about her place, the Bluebird Studio, in with all of this mail . . . here it is." He hands Michael the printed piece. "I think she teaches classes there, too."

His jacket is in his hand, and his car keys. "John, if it's all right with you, I think . . ."

"Yes, son. You should go."

Chapter 56

She hears the trees whispering, along the old farm roads, as she once did so many years before. The rough granite boulders beside the river greet her with their rumbling voices. After all these years, how easy it is to step back in time, to remember that girl with a bright blue moped who'd announced she was a pagan. That girl makes her smile.

Though much of New Hampshire has changed, the Presidential Mountain Range holds dominion over the landscape as it always has. There are still farms, and hidden places to swim that she's been delighted to discover. Water still reveals secrets to her, both in her dreams and waking.

This evening as the light fades, Kit stands in the upstairs window of the building she is renovating in Littleton, on the Ammonoosuc River, the location for The Bluebird Studio. She's attracted a few young students this spring, for classes, and they're just cleaning up their workspaces for the evening.

Installed in the center of the small plaza outside, between the studio and the river, stands her sculpture of the young man and his beloved, hands clasped, climbing a hillside strewn with flowers. Her deepest longing, she now understands, forged in bronze.

The piece is elevated on a stone platform, and draws the last remaining glow of the day to the faces of the two lovers they once were. She and Michael. *Peut-être*, maybe, this sculpture will send forth its enchantment into the universe and bring him back, from wherever he is on the planet, to find her.

She still believes in magic.

The kids head down the stairs while she walks around the studio, flicking off the overhead lights. She muses over how much she enjoys the sweet, silly banter of Josie and Sally, the serious focus of Martha, who reminds her of herself at that age, and the two boys, Tim and Frankie, who she suspects are here for the girls. It feels good and right to be the adult in their lives who cares about them getting their hands muddy, making art.

It's funny, she thinks, they seem more guileless and innocent, and yet so much happier than she was as a teenager. But maybe she perceives their lives too simply.

She heads down the narrow staircase in the dark, thinking she must remember to install a handrail in here. Outside, it's chilly, but looking up she sees the sky has cleared. With her back to the plaza, she locks up the door.

"Good night, Madame Morgan!" Josie calls out. "Thank you for the class. See you next week."

"*Bonne nuit!* Drive safely. And don't forget to *faire attention* to the world around you." She turns now, waving to her students. "Put your cell phones away. Keep your eyes open for the unexpected!"

Then, she sees him.

For a long moment she stands as if a statue herself. Maybe she stops breathing. He is seated on the stone pedestal at the foot of the sculpture. How in the world? Ah, but she would know that smile anywhere. He just looks at her, and doesn't make a move. Either he doesn't want to startle her—or he expects her to come to him!

Well, maybe after all, that's fair.

Before she realizes it, she is crying. She can't stop herself, as if these tears have been dammed up for too many years, and now the decades-old barrier has burst. Her students notice, too. They stop to look at this man who seems to be the instigator of their teacher's sudden emotional outburst.

There is nothing else to do but walk over and sit down beside him. Still sniffling a little, and trying to regain her dignity, she remarks, "I was wondering how long I would have to wait for you, Michael Pearce." He places his hand on top of hers. She is startled, foolishly, by how infinitely right this feels. And her heart says: Yes, I am still yours. And *je l'ai toujours été.*

One of the boys is watching, he's curious, and then he glances up at the sculpture of the two lovers. For a second, she dreamily imagines that something makes him stop and wonder. Some hunch, perhaps?

But then the girls say, "Come on, Tim! We're hungry. I think Ollie's is open. Let's go!"

Chapter 57

"What if we take a drive along the back roads?" Michael suggests. "It'll be cooler in the woods."

An old saying, she remembers from summers at the farm, is "If you don't like the weather, wait a few minutes." The temperatures have been chilly the past few days. Today, it's warm. And the heat has been building all afternoon. As soon as they'd departed the wedding reception of Michael's niece and her new husband, he'd peeled off his suit jacket. But it seems he is still hot.

Kit sits next to him in the car, feeling quite comfortable in her sundress. "Yes, why not!" She tilts her head to catch the breeze through the open window, lifting her hair so that it cools her neck. He's watching her. He smiles, as he did at the wedding, when he introduced her to his family.

What is it that he thinks? How does he see her? As a girl? A woman? A stranger, or a person he knows?

At first, they say very little. They drive along the dirt road, under a green roof made of leaves from the slender white birches and the old, wrinkled maples. The conversation starts and stops; she's aware of the sweet rumination of the tires rolling along the unpaved back road, the flickering of light and shadow among the trees. Their words to each other begin as tentative, race forward, becoming animated, then stumble awkwardly. Neither one of them really knows what to do, if they are ready for this.

He doesn't want to let his guard down, she guesses. And she

fears allowing herself to simply let go and savor the sweetness of being with him again.

There is so much regret, too—all those lost years! Would anyone really blame them if, instead, they each withdrew back into their safe, adult shells with polite apologies? So much of life has passed them by! The important accomplishments, the sorrows and losses. How do they begin again? Is it even possible?

"I wonder if you still have that little Bluebird of Happiness?" she asks gently. It feels risky to pose this question, to allude too quickly to the past and to their young love.

"I do."

She has to admit, she is a little surprised—and pleased.

He says, "Being a physician requires, well, I suppose I'd say it requires the ability to maintain a certain emotional distance, a detachment. It's critical, in life-or-death situations. Surgery, for example. But that distance comes at a price. I keep your bluebird on my desk, in my office. When I consult with a patient, it reminds me"—and here he pauses, clears his throat—"it reminds me of hope. And dreams. And that the patient sitting across from me is a living, breathing human being with hopes and dreams. Not just a problem to be fixed. I guess, as a doctor, I sometimes need to remember what those emotions feel like."

She has drawn on emotion all her life, for her work—but how many mistakes has she made, too, when emotion overtook her! Still, Michael's self-judgment seems so harsh; she instinctively wants to object.

But he starts to say something else, as if he is trying to explain. "You see, I've been alone my entire life, really, and you, well—"

Suddenly, looking out the window, she understands where he has been taking them in the car. "*Ah, mon Dieu!* I remember this place. *Incroyable! C'est toujours aussi beau.*" He pulls up beside a wide, open hillside and parks the car. The fields and the views of the mountains are unchanged. As beautiful as they are in her memory.

"—and you . . ."

"*Oui? Et moi?* And I . . . ?"

"And you . . . You've become, well, *French*, Kit!"

And suddenly they are both laughing. What does this have to do with anything? "Maybe that makes things more *intéréssantes, non?*" she suggests.

His shoulders relax and his body seems looser, somehow. He grins, as if he is thinking of something funny, concocting a plan maybe. Then he asks, "Do you remember the day we went hiking here, and had our picnic?"

"Of course! And there was that beautiful pond!"

"Yes, exactly!"

She senses his excitement now, and catches it from him.

"How do you feel about a hike up the hill," he suggests, "and then maybe a swim?"

"*I would love a swim!*"

They both take off their fancy dress shoes. It's been such a long time since she's felt the grass under her bare feet! "I have a bathing suit, too!" she says, pleased with her forethought.

"You know, when we were very little children," she continues happily, shoving her sandals into her bag, "those summers at Cedaredge, my parents would never let us go anywhere without bathing suits. Just in case we discovered a new place to swim. Now that I am back, I always carry one in my bag—like that little girl! Expecting some wonderful adventure."

"*Bathing suit?*" He stops her.

She looks at him, questioning. It's as if he's put aside the weight of self-importance that comes with being "Dr. Pearce," and has become once again the mischievous boy she remembers. Teasing her, giving her a hard time. *Alors*, that young man was not buried so deep as she had supposed . . .

"*Oooouuui* . . . ? Yes, bathing suit."

"Don't you remember the rules?"

"Oh! You and your rules. You always had to remind me about *rules*. What rules?"

"*No bathing suits.*"

She bursts out laughing at him. "That was never a rule!"

Then she turns and begins walking through the field toward the path that leads up to the pond. "*Tu es serieux?* No bathing suits? You are pretty confident—for an old guy!"

"Or—just counting on the fact of fading eyesight! You know, at our advanced age."

"Let's go! *Vas-y!* Let's see if you can keep up with me, *Monsieur* 'no-bathing-suit'!" Kit runs ahead, and then he is beside her, catching her, and pulling her into his arms. "Do you remember you sang to me, that day?" she asks, breathless.

"*Let us go, lassie, go,*" Michael sings softly. And then—he kisses her. And for a long time, they stand among all the flowers, the daisies, the black-eyed Susans, and the purple lupine. All the flowers of the mountain. When at last they look at each other again, it is not difficult at all to see beyond the years.

Michael embraces her once more, in a way that takes Kit's breath away. When he releases her, they both laugh and trip over each other as carefree as children. As if they have their whole lives ahead of them.

"Come on, let's go for a swim," Kit says, taking Michael's hand. And then she tosses her bathing suit out into the long grass as they climb the hillside together.

Notes on Traditional Folk Songs

All of the songs Michael sings come from the long tradition of Scottish, Irish, and early American folk music (all of which are intertwined with each other). Many of these songs began as poems several hundred years ago and have been continually adapted and reworked by individual singers on both sides of the Atlantic. In the case of this story, archaic language from old poems or songs has been changed to modern usage ("siller fountain" is changed to "silver fountain," for example). All of the lyrics are in the public domain.

Wild Rover: Historically, the song has been referred to in Irish and Scottish folklore since the late sixteenth century. According to T. M. Devine in his book *The Scottish Nation 1700–2000* (Penguin, 2001), the song was written as a temperance song. It is found in *The American Songster*, printed in the United States by W. A. Leary in 1845, and spread from Scotland to America through the temperance movement. An alternative history of the song is suggested by the fact that it appears in a collection of ballads, dated between 1813 and 1838, held in the Bodleian Library. The Greig-Duncan collection, compiled by Gavin Greig 1848–1917, contains no less than six versions of the song. The song Michael sings is a combination of several variants.

Old Blue: "Old Blue" (also known as "Old Dog Blue") is a folk song believed to have originated in the American south, possibly from the minstrel shows of the late nineteenth century.

Wild Mountain Thyme: This Irish-Scottish folk song is also known as "Purple Heather" and "Will Ye Go, Lassie, Go?" The lyrics and melody are a variant of the song "The Braes of Balquhither" by the Scottish poet Robert Tannahill (1774–1810) and the Scottish composer Robert Archibald Smith (1780–1829), but were adapted by the Belfast musician Francis McPeake (1885–1971) into "Wild Mountain Thyme" and first recorded by his family in the 1950s. While Francis McPeake holds the copyright to the most commonly heard modern version of the song, it is generally believed that rather than writing the song, he arranged an existing traveling folk version and popularized the song as his father's. When interviewed on the radio, Francis McPeake said it was based on a song he heard while traveling in Scotland, and he rewrote it later. Bob Dylan's recording of the song cited it as traditional, with the arranger unknown, though Dylan's copyright records indicate that the song is sometimes "attributed to" McPeake. Michael's version of this song is based on a rearrangement of verses from the original nineteenth-century Scottish poem by Robert Tannahill.

The Water Is Wide: "The Water Is Wide," also called "O Waly, Waly," or simply "Waly, Waly," is a folk song of Scottish origin from the seventeenth and eighteenth centuries with an Irish variation from the nineteenth century. It remains popular in the twenty-first century. Cecil Sharp published a version of the song in *Folk Songs from Somerset* (1906).

My Love Is Like a Red, Red Rose: "A Red, Red Rose," a poem written by Robert Burns, is based on traditional Scottish sources. Michael's song is based on the original poem from 1794.

Acknowledgments

I treasure the memories of the long, lazy childhood summers and the brilliant, snow-filled winter vacations spent in the White Mountains of New Hampshire; for these I have my parents, Dean and Tina Holbrook, to thank.

I owe a debt of gratitude to all of the friends and family members who read versions of this story over the past years and offered their insights and support. Among these were Jane Flynn, Phyllis Strong, Paul and Betsy Golden-Rosengren, Angela Knightly, Alan Braunholtz, Tina Holbrook, Amanda Sater, Elinor Dulit, Mira Perrizo, Dorothy Kindred Yewer, and Steve Brandt. My late friend Joel Reidenberg took pleasure in reviewing with me those scenes taking place at his alma mater Dartmouth College; his wife, Pascale gave invaluable translation help with the French text. Ezra Dulit-Greenberg gamely read aloud chapters of an early version of the book to help me "hear" Michael's voice.

This book would never have gotten off the ground without the tireless editorial help, professional encouragement, and emotional support of my friend Laura Ross. Laura edited the first version of this story, various versions in the middle, and the final manuscript completed in March of 2022.

Cheerleading came from The Gang of Five—writers that include myself, Kristen Baum DeBeasi, Vali Hawkins Mitchell, Rebecca Moore, and Julian Woodruff—as well as from the group Authors Publish and my insightful teacher Ella Peary. I also learned a lot from Rachel Weaver of the Denver Lighthouse Writers Workshop and Jeff Deck of the New Hampshire Writers Project.

In the spring of 2022, I suddenly and unexpectedly faced a serious illness. I'd spent so many years working on this manuscript, and now feared this story might never be published in time for me to see it. In this dark moment, Karen Wyatt, publisher at Sunroom Studios, swooped in and offered to publish the novel in record time. A posse of women organized by Laura Ross assisted her, including Katherine Griggs, Ashley Prine and Lisa Thornbloom. I humbly accept that I will never be able to thank you all enough.

To the Neurosurgery, Radiology and Neuro Oncology teams at UC Health Anschutz, University of Colorado Hospital, thank you for giving me more time. I am so grateful to you, and to Dr. Kathleen Cowie of Summit County, for your empathy and compassion and your desire to ensure that the life I have left is one worth living.

There is only one other person who has read this novel almost as many times as I have, and who cares about it as deeply as I do: my husband, Alan Michael Dulit. My dearest Alan, without you there would be no love story. These flowers of the mountain are for you.

About the Author

A native of New York and the White Mountains of New Hampshire, Christina Holbrook now lives in Colorado with her husband, Alan Dulit. She received a Bachelor of Arts degree in French and Political Theory from Wellesley College. Holbrook's column *Lark Ascending* ran in the *Summit Daily* in Frisco, Colorado from 2016 through 2020. More recently her short fiction and essays have appeared in numerous literary journals and anthologies. *All the Flowers of the Mountain* is her first novel.

For more background on the book and links to other works by the author, please visit www.christinaholbrook.com. Follow her on Instagram @christinaholbrookwrites.

CPSIA information can be obtained
at www.ICGtesting.com
Printed in the USA
LVHW041913120723
752179LV00002B/185